THE PERFECT MAN

Naeem Murr

THE PERFECT MAN

WILLIAM HEINEMANN • LONDON

Published in the United Kingdom in 2006 by William Heinemann

1 3 5 7 9 10 8 6 4 2

William Heinemann
The Random House Group Limited
20 Vauxhall Bridge Road, London SW1V 2SA

Random House Australia (Pty) Limited
20 Alfred Street, Milsons Point, Sydney
New South Wales 2061, Australia

Random House New Zealand Limited
18 Poland Road, Glenfield
Auckland 10, New Zealand

Random House (Pty) Limited
Isle of Houghton, Corner of Boundary Road & Carse O'Gowrie,
Houghton 2198, South Africa

The Random House Group Limited Reg. No. 954009

www.randomhouse.co.uk

A CIP catalogue record for this book
is available from the British Library

Papers used by Random House are natural, recyclable products made from
wood grown in sustainable forests. The manufacturing processes conform to the
environmental regulations of the country of origin

ISBN 0 434 01114 2

Typeset in Perpetua by Palimpsest Book Production Limited, Polmont, Stirlingshire
Printed and bound in Great Britain by Clays Ltd, St Ives plc

For Christian Wiman

LONDON, 1947

Gerard Travers lifted the little dark boy off the train and on to the platform at Victoria. It had been a hard journey from India for the child, who had cried constantly for his mother and had wet himself every night. Gerard heard a shout and turned to see his older brother, waving and pushing through the crowd.

'Raggy, Raggy-boy,' Haig called. He was a crude, mutton-chopped version of the tall and leonine Gerard.

After they embraced, Gerard raised the child in his arms, confronting Haig with a pair of large, mournful eyes. The boy was sucking and gnawing at the back of his hand. 'Here's the sprog, Eggy – as forewarned.'

Haig peered into the boy's plump face, smiling and patting his leg. 'Christ he's already got a permanent frown. How old is he?'

'Five . . . ish.' Gerard put the boy down.

'Ish?'

'He was born during the monsoon.'

'Well that's helpful. What are you going to do with him, Rags?'

'I have an honest proposal. Where's Brenna?'

'Oh, she had something she couldn't get out of today. Volunteers a lot, you know.'

'And how's . . . ? What is she, six now?'

'Cecilia. Seven. She's tip-top.'

As they walked toward the front of the train for the baggage, Gerard hesitated, put a hand on his brother's shoulder, and took a moment to examine him. 'I got a shock when I saw you coming through the crowd.'

'A shock?'

'Thought it was the old man.'

'Well, I'd never be able to deny I was his son, much as I'd want to.'

They pulled the luggage from the pile on the platform, and just as they were about to exit, Haig said, 'The boy!'

They rushed back to where Gerard had got off. The little Indian boy, crying, held the hand of a woman who was bent over him, talking gently.

'There's the little blighter,' Gerard said. 'Oh my lord.' He met the woman's scathing face. 'Lost him in the crowd.' He called down to the boy. 'You must stay with me, Raj.'

'This is *your* child?' the woman said.

'He's in my charge, madam. An orphan. I brought him here to treat his leprosy.'

The woman snatched her hand out of the boy's.

'Thank you for your kindness,' Gerard called as she hurried away.

He took the child's hand and they all left the station and got into a taxi.

'Heard from Olly?' Gerard asked as it pulled out.

'America. He's as all over the map as you are. He was in New York. Met some woman who runs a nightclub. Older than he, as usual.'

'Always lands on his feet, doesn't he? Women love him. It's that abandoned look. They start lactating the minute he walks into the room.'

'Raggy!'

'Does he still have his . . . problem?'

'With him for life, I should think.'

'I'm surprised he's lasted this long.'

Haig nodded.

'Did he come back for Father's funeral?'

Shaking his head, Haig said, 'I had to tell everyone you two were too grief-stricken. I couldn't tell them Olly had sent a note asking me to make sure they put a stake through his heart before they closed the coffin, and you sent a very expensive telegram – C stop A stop P stop I stop T stop A stop L stop. I can still hear the old bastard saying it.'

The two men smiled and sat in silence.

Finally Haig said, 'I think Brenna's worried you're coming for the rest of your share.'

'I wouldn't make you sell the house. God knows, though, it should have been burned with his body in it. I don't know how you could live there.'

'Only things are a bit tight. I lost a lot in that Italian—'

'It was the war. Would have made a fortune. I'll steer you right, though. Got my fingers in a prime opportunity.'

'Brenna would kill me.'

'What Brenna doesn't know won't hurt you.'

Gerard snatched the boy's hand out of his mouth. 'Stop that.' He had been sucking on it for days and the skin had become raw.

The boy pointed out of the window: '*Chirdiyao ka rang gharo jaisa hai.*'

'What's he say, Ger?'

'English,' Gerard said to the boy, who frowned and flapped his hands. 'He's speaking Hindi. I don't speak Hindi.'

'Good lord, Ger. Didn't you ever talk to his mother?'

Gerard didn't respond.

'I'm sorry.'

'No need. I've been a fool. You know I've often thought that when there's siblings they share everything out between them. Olly got all the luck with women.' Gerard pulled himself up and cleared his throat. 'Brenna's great. I don't mean . . .'

Haig nodded, raising a hand to show no offence had been taken.

'But my God, Eggy, you met a few of them: Heather, Chloë, Loretta – women to die for. All crazy about him and he broke their hearts.'

'You bravely stepped into the breach a few times as I recall.'

'We can't have people misusing beautiful things, Eggy. Anyway, on the whole I've had no luck in that department. Nina took me for pretty much everything I had.'

'You mean she didn't give you everything *she* had.'

Gerard ignored this. 'And that Argentinian woman almost got me killed.'

'As I recall she'd just finished tying you to her bed for a bit of kinky high jinks when her husband walked in.'

'I was damn well helpless.'

'I'm surprised he *didn't* kill you.'

Gerard smiled. 'You know why, don't you? Have I never told you?'

'No.'

Gerard leaned in. 'He was of the other persuasion. A patented palm-tickler. Ordered his wife out and had the time of his life.'

'No.'

'Tell you the truth, I was so relieved I still remember it fondly.'

'No!'

Gerard sat back again, laughing. 'Nothing's ever as bad as you think, Eggy-boy, long as you survive.'

Now Gerard nodded toward the child. 'His mother was the most beautiful creature you've ever seen in your life. Sprog's got her eyes – look at them, huge ruddy great things. Stunning. She was like every strange and beautiful thing in that country in one face. And her *expression* . . .' He shook his head. 'The wisdom of ten thousand years.'

He pulled the boy's hand out of his mouth again. 'I wish he didn't look so bloody Indian. Nothing of me in him. He's black as pitch.'

'He's not that dark. And he does look like you. Why didn't you leave him with his mother?'

'No clue where she is.' He hesitated. 'I am a fool. You know what I'm like when I get something in my head.'

'I know: *idée fixe.*'

'And an astonishing idea it was too, Eggy. I mean, I thought I was going to stay in India for ever. And this woman would be – well, like my wife.'

'Except that no one would know about her, of course.'

'Not at first, but I thought eventually yes. I'd teach her to speak English, educate her.'

'Oh my God.' With exhausted despair, Haig massaged his closed eyes. 'Oh my God.'

'Anyway, I won't go through everything. I bought her. Outright for twenty pounds.'

'You bought her?'

'I think from her parents, but I can't be sure. And I married her. I did marry her – in the native way. I didn't want her to get pregnant, tried to be careful. Only knew when she began to show. I asked her to get rid of it, but she didn't understand. I'd had no luck teaching her English.'

'Always the bloody same. Ever since you were old enough to speak. You'd get something in your head. You'd get obsessed and as soon as you got it you'd lose interest. This isn't a damn investment scheme.' Haig gestured toward the boy.

'I know that. I know that. I *tried* to teach her, but she didn't seem able to retain a single word. So finally I hired this Indian chap to work with her full time. And he spent about an hour with her on the first day, and he comes to me, and he's cringing as if he thinks I'm going to kill him. And he says, "Memsahib, your . . . your woman."'

'"My wife," I said.

'"She's . . ." Gerard acted like the Indian man, searching for the word, staring abjectly into Haig's face. '"She's simple – like a simple person."'

Haig stared open-mouthed for a moment. Then he began to laugh, doubled over – wheezing, body-racking laughs.

Moments later, the taxi stopped outside a three-storey Georgian house that had somehow survived the bombing. Haig went up the stone steps, still wiping tears of laughter from his face. Gerard, holding the boy's hand, remained on the pavement staring at the house.

After opening the door, Haig looked back and became serious. 'Is it still hard for you?'

'Seems like he'll still be in there.'

'Would have been better for you to see his body, see him buried.'.

'Better for *you*,' Gerard said. 'For Olly and me . . . I don't think we could give him the satisfaction of dying.'

'*Tati jana hai*,' the boy said, whimpering.

'English, Raj.' Gerard pulled him up the steps. 'And stop eating your hand.'

The second the door closed behind them all, a woman's voice summoned Haig sharply from the next landing.

'Coming, dear.' Grimacing, Haig pointed Gerard toward the sitting room, and hurried upstairs.

Gerard sat the boy next to him on the slightly worn green velvet couch, pulling his hand out of his mouth again.

'*Tati jana hai*.' The boy looked as if he were about to cry.

'You know English, Raj. Say, "My name is Rajiv." *My . . . name*—'

There was the sound of someone descending, and Gerard stood as a tiny, stiffly elegant woman entered, wielding the exquisite, intricate weapon of her face. She acted as if the boy weren't there, not even glancing at him, and without a word or gesture of greeting sat at the very edge of the armchair that faced the couch. It was as if she had come in to interview a servant and had decided the instant she had seen Gerard that he wasn't suitable.

'Brenna, you look—'

'How long do you intend to stay?'

'Five days. I'll be out of your hair on Tuesday.'

'Back to India?'

'Off to Australia. A lucrative opportunity.'

'Really? What's her name?'

'It's minerals. It's not interesting.'

'Are you here for money?'

'I'm here to visit my family – of which you are one.'

'That's a long trip. That's going to be hard on—' She stopped, her face a little stricken.

Taking a moment to gather herself, she began again. 'Is his mother going to join you there?'

'Haven't a notion where his mother is.'

'How careless of you. But then you've always been a little—' She flushed, seemed suddenly furious at herself. It was as if she had spent years composing and memorizing lines for this brief scene, which she was now massacring. She glanced at the boy, who was chewing on his hand. Then she frowned, noticing something. On the rug beneath him was a constellation of dark spots.

'Oh, oh, oh!' she shouted and jumped to her feet. Gerard flinched, as if afraid she were going to strike him. She picked the boy up by his waist. Brown streams braided his bare legs.

'Haig,' she shouted.

Haig, who must have been listening at the top of the stairs, thundered down.

'Take this. Put it in the bath.'

Haig received the boy gingerly, holding him at arm's length, and ran out.

'What kind of man are you?' she screamed at Gerard.

Hurrying out, she returned a few minutes later with a bucket of soapy water and a cloth. As she got on her knees, though, something seemed to occur to her. Looking furiously up at Gerard, who had sat on the couch again, she flung the wet cloth into his lap.

'He's your son. You clean it up!'

Helplessly, Gerard examined the cloth until Brenna, with a strangled squeal, snatched it back and began to scrub frantically at the rug.

The house's front door opened and a girl's voice called thanks to someone in the street. A clatter followed as she ran upstairs. A few seconds later, the sound of her sprinting down.

'Celia,' Gerard exclaimed warmly, standing as a girl in a grey and maroon school uniform entered.

'*Ce*-cilia,' she corrected, staring at him with unabashed curiosity and delight. She was as petite as her mother, but had Haig's broad, open face, her mousy hair tied back in a ponytail.

'Mummy, what are you doing?'

Brenna just continued to scrub furiously.

'We've had a bit of a spill, I'm afraid,' Gerard explained.

'You're my bad uncle.'

'Suppose I am.'

'Is that boy upstairs yours?'

'Yes.'

'Did you adopt him?'

'In a manner of speaking.'

Stepping closer, she took his hand. 'Can I show Uncle Gerard my room, Mummy?'

Still her mother didn't respond. Cecilia threw Gerard a glance that expressed both amusement and confusion. He shrugged as if equally perplexed as she led him out of the room, the two of them stepping carefully over Brenna.

LONDON, 1949

Rajiv, a rangy seven-year-old, entered the sitting room and pulled up with a guilty look as he saw Brenna, who was on the phone.

'I am most dreadfully sorry,' she was saying. 'I can't imagine how this happened. I can only think that the bank made a mistake or that my husband somehow forgot to transfer the funds. I quite understand, Mr Osgood. Yes. Yes. You will be paid tomorrow morning. First thing. Thank you.'

Putting down the receiver, Brenna covered her mouth with her left hand, and swiped imaginary strands of hair away from her face with her right – a recent compulsion.

Raj spoke: 'Mrs Whitman said she was in a rush, couldn't come in. Told me to give you these raffle tickets for Saturday.'

Brenna didn't acknowledge what he had said, or his presence. He put the roll of tickets on the telephone table beside her, went to the kitchen and drank a glass of milk. When he walked back past Brenna, hesitating again at the door, she still hadn't moved.

'I need to bring bus fare for the day trip tomorrow,' he said quietly.

The telephone rang and Brenna flinched. She didn't answer it or him. Raj went upstairs. After a few minutes he emerged from his room wrapped in an old tablecloth and wearing a towel turban. He sat on the stairs.

Cecilia bustled through the front door a little while later. 'I am in a foul mood,' said the nine-year-old imperiously. 'Just foul!'

'Yes, memsahib.' Raj helped her off with her coat, taking her bag and following her up to her room. She threw herself face down on to her bed and he sat beside her, rubbing her shoulders.

'I shall need a long massage today,' she said. 'Sister Jeffries told me

9

my handwriting was like a boy's. Snakes and snails and puppy-dog tails. And the whole class heard. I told her I was naturally left-handed. And she said no one is *naturally* left-handed. I *hate* Sister Jeffries. I need an extra long, extra long, *extra long* massage.'

'Yes, memsahib.'

When she had calmed a little, she said, 'How are your wives, Gupta?'

'They are well, memsahib. I married another one yesterday.'

'Good Lord, man. And how old is this one?'

'She is two, memsahib.'

'How uncivilized.' She rolled over. 'My feet,' she said, wiggling them.

He took off her shoes and socks, and began to massage her feet. 'I did get rid of one of my older ones, though. Sold her to the knacker's yard for glue.'

'Good gracious.'

They heard the front door open.

'That can't be Daddy, can it?' Cecilia said, closing her eyes with the pleasure of the massage.

A second later her eyes were wide open again, and she pulled herself up against the headboard. The two children sat hunched and rigid as Brenna's screaming voice echoed through the house. Finally, she went quiet.

A few minutes later, Haig entered the room.

'What's wrong with Mummy?' Cecilia said.

'It was just a misunderstanding, darling. I have explained. All is well, and she's perfectly fine now.' He went to leave, but struck by an afterthought turned back. 'Mummy . . . is sorry for raising her voice. She asked me to convey that. She got the wrong end of the stick. So, all is well.'

The children spent the next hour in Cecilia's room, continuing with their make-believe. Raj became a monkey for a while, tickling her and leaping all over the room. Then they played snakes and ladders. Whenever Raj was winning, he would, with expert sleight-of-hand, either undercount or overcount in order to make sure he landed on a snake.

At last he got off the bed, and said, 'Memsahib, I have to make water.' This was a new part of the game, which had begun just a week ago.

'Oh dear, how inconvenient.'

'Shall I go here?' He pointed at the floor.

'Don't be ridiculous. Come with me.'

She got up, took his hand, and led him out of the room. They both waited for a moment at the top of the stairs, listening. They could hear Haig's calming voice.

She led him into the bathroom.

'What is this place, memsahib?'

'This is called a toilet, Gupta. And this is what we use when we go to the bathroom in this country. Come along now, I haven't got all day.'

She knelt down beside the toilet and sat watching intently, giving stern encouragement as Raj peed: 'That's good. Now aim it properly.'

There was a loud knock at the door. 'Cici, who are you talking to?' It was Brenna. 'Who's in there? Open this door.'

Cecilia jumped to her feet, panicked, as Raj quickly zipped up his trousers and flushed the toilet. Cecilia unlocked the door.

Brenna peered in, horrified, brushing those imaginary hairs out of her face. 'What were you doing in here together?'

'We weren't doing anything, Mummy. Raj couldn't reach something on—'

'Don't you lie to me,' Brenna shouted.

Haig appeared, his exhausted, mutton-chopped face floating helplessly in the background.

Brenna's eyes fixed on Raj now. 'What were you doing in here you . . . *filthy* . . .'

She reached down to take hold of Raj, but Cecilia stepped in front of him. 'It was me, Mummy. I just wanted to look. I didn't do anything.' She was bright red.

Pushing forward, Haig intervened. 'Raj,' he said calmly, 'will you go to your room.'

Raj, still in his cape and headdress, quickly exited.

'Cecilia,' Haig said, 'you understand you mustn't do this again?'

She nodded.

'Please go to your room.'

Cecilia left.

Brenna's baneful eyes now fixed on Haig, her expression wild, her nostrils flaring. He reached to stop her swiping at her face, but she slapped his hand away. He put his finger to his lips, pointing toward the door to their daughter's room. Pushing past him, she ran downstairs.

In their separate rooms, the children listened to Brenna screaming again beneath them. Raj sat on the floor huddled in a corner, a toy Saracen on top of one knee facing a Crusader on top of the other. Cecilia lay on her bed, running her fingers back and forth over the flowers sewn into her coverlet as if something of her mother's compulsion had infected her.

The screaming subsided into terrible, moaning sobs, which seemed to go on for ever. At last they heard Haig's heavy steps ascending.

He went into Cecilia's room first. 'You should go down for your supper now,' he told her.

He entered Raj's room. 'Well, lad, you've got a treat tonight. I'm going to take you out to eat.'

'Yes, sir.'

'You need to get out of your . . . costume and we'll head off.'

That evening the children endured a silence they would not forget: Cecilia at the dining table, her mother's face like a dry gully; Raj eating chocolate cake in Lyons as Haig brooded over the uneaten mess of his own dinner. And both children read these faces with as much faith, hope and fear as the ancients read the night.

LONDON, 1954

Raj, who had just turned twelve, entered the school gates in the rain. In his right hand he held a heavy rubber ball, which he was squeezing rhythmically, echoing the anxious pulse of his heart. During playtime he would throw this against the outside wall of the gym, moving further and further away to catch it. He had done this in primary school also, and children would stop in their play to watch him, impressed by how hard and far he could throw.

Today everyone was inside because of the weather. It would be fifteen minutes before Greenberg, who taught history, turned up to take attendance and send them off to their classes: the bright Alphas, of which Raj was one, to study English literature with Big Boobs Bellamy; the slightly tarnished Betas to study physics with Freeman the Fondler; and the drooling, lurching Gammas to study mathematics with Peterson the Punisher.

Raj affected an absorbed frown as he entered the classroom. Angling forward, he made a prow of his lanky body and tried to steer as rapidly and unobtrusively as possible through the cruel shoals of boys to his desk. An apple core glanced off the side of his cheek and slammed against the blackboard just behind him.

'Shit wallah!' shouted Robbie Vincent, a fat boy who seemed to have been born with the poached eyes of an old alcoholic. He was flanked by his cronies: the lazily attractive Andy Halton, whose tongue played constantly through the gap where one of his front teeth had been; and Lee Monroe, a vicious-tempered, undersized boy, who looked like a wet rat.

''Ere, Gunga. Come 'ere. Come 'ere,' Robbie called.

Raj slipped the ball into his pocket and threw his satchel on his

13

desk. As he pulled up in front of these boys, he abruptly transformed into Mr Greenberg. Stooping, he widened his eyes crazily, pushed out his lower lip, and made a strange corkscrew motion with the extended forefinger of his right hand, as if trying to drill it through a wall. Imitating Greenberg's stammer and nasal whine, he launched into one of their teacher's most recent diatribes. 'Mr V-V-Vincent, am I to understand – to *understand* that you've not done your prep?' Another wild twist of the wrist. 'Wilful ignorance, Mr V-V-Vincent, is wilful murder. It means people can stuff your empty noggin with whatever they see fit. It means, Mr V-V-*Vincent*, that they can put a gun in your hand and tell you to put that gun to an innocent head. Those, Mr V-V-Vincent, who have the capacity to kill millions – kill *millions* – are among us, in this very classroom. And they – *they* are the ones who, who make such choices as not doing their prep. *They*—'

Snatching up the lapel of Raj's blazer, Robbie pulled him closer to show him a swastika he had just sketched in his notepad.

'Go and draw that on the board, Mowgli, nice and big. Go on.'

Raj stared at the swastika. Again he started to imitate Mr Greenberg, but Andy Halton pulled his tongue out of the gap in his teeth long enough to say: ''Ere, my mum says you're living with some posh white family down Whitehall. Where's your own mum and dad, then?'

Clearly this question had been rising through Andy for a little while, like a bubble of methane in dense mud.

Raj suddenly ran to the front of the class, picked up some chalk, and drew a thick swastika on the blackboard just as the bell rang for nine. On the way back to his desk he tried, as unobtrusively as he could, to push a big mobile world map a little way in front of it. As he got to his seat, Mr Greenberg entered and sat at his desk.

He took attendance, stammering and making that corkscrew gesture with his finger, which, after Raj's performance, caused a few of the boys to snicker. Becoming aware that there was something awry in the atmosphere of the room, Greenberg narrowed his eyes suspiciously. It was as he got up to sit at the edge of his desk and read through the day's announcements that he saw it. He pushed the mobile map out of the way and for a moment remained completely still. He looked back into the class then, the boys frozen and staring into the graffiti-scored lids of their desks. His face began to twitch oddly and he swallowed a few times as if something were caught in his throat.

'Do, do you know . . .' His ragged voice snapped and he began again. 'Do, do you know – *know* how dis*gusting* this is to me?' He was leaning over his desk, gripping its edges as if he could hardly hold himself upright, staring at the class with horror and anguish of an intensity none of the boys had never seen in an adult face. 'Do, do you *know*' – his voice rose to a scream now – 'what – *what* this is? Dis*gusting*. Obs*cene*. Who, who did this?' Coming around his desk, he looked as if he were ready to savage anyone who moved. 'Who did this?'

Plump Mr Freeman came in looking astonished. He had clearly heard Mr Greenberg shouting from his classroom across the corridor.

'Mr Greenberg?' he called timidly.

Greenberg turned to Freeman without any change in his expression, as if no one were beyond suspicion. Mr Freeman saw the swastika and addressed the class.

'Shame!' was all he could think to say.

Greenberg slammed his hand down on his desk. 'Who did this?'

Stinky Harris, the alternate whipping boy to Raj, looked up. Catching Greenberg's eye, he glanced at Raj. Greenberg strode over to Raj and snatched up his right hand. It was covered in chalk.

'Did, did you do this?'

Raj nodded.

Mr Greenberg, holding his chalky hand almost tenderly, examined Raj for a long moment. Calmly then, he turned back to Mr Freeman and said, 'Thank, thank you, Mr Freeman for your assistance.'

'Shame,' Freeman said again, throwing a reproachful glance at Raj before he left.

Mr Greenberg quietly told Raj to wipe the swastika off the board. Raj, rigid, his head tucked into his shoulders, did this as Mr Greenberg read out the rest of the notices. Without a word more, he sent them to their classes.

Big Boobs Bellamy was a beefy woman in her early forties with a thick Geordie accent. She cut her greying hair mannishly short and wore bright red lipstick. Though she looked formidable, she was a very sweet woman whose classes were a walkover. She loved poetry and would often cry as she read poems in class. Raj was her favourite student. A number of boys were looking at Raj, who was staring blankly out of the window. They had heard already about what had happened with Greenberg.

Mrs Bellamy addressed the class. 'Well, I'm looking forward to hearing your poems.'

'Do we have to read them out, miss?' said Larry Cottage, a nervous, harelipped boy.

'Of course. Poetry is as much about the art of delivery as it is about the act of creation. I'm sure your poem is just grand, Larry.'

'It's not, miss.'

Smothering him with a cloying crimson smile, she glanced around for her first volunteer. She stood very rigid, her hands coupled tightly at her belly. This gave the odd impression that she had her own breasts in a head-lock. The boys knew she was eager to get to Raj, who wrote poems they felt were just like the ones in the book.

'Mr Arden.' She settled on a heavy boy with a doomed expression. 'Why don't you read us yours?'

'Mine's about a shark, miss.'

'And how does that relate to the war, Michael?'

'Not sure, miss.'

'That'll be a question for the class, then.'

Arden raised his scrap of paper and read:

With your razor-sharp teeth you tear the flesh.
Glide, glide the silver bullet swiftly through the swirling mass.
You rip out the guts and crunch up the eyes.
Glide, glide the silver bullet swiftly through the swirling mass.

'That's all I've got, miss.'

'Well, Michael, that's very promising.' She turned to the class. 'What is the shark in Michael's poem? How is it working? What is the name of what Michael is doing?'

Her bright pursed lips sought the room and settled hopefully on Raj, who would usually answer her questions when no one else had, but he was still staring out of the window.

'Rajiv?'

He looked toward her, clearly having no idea what she had just asked.

Quickly she addressed the whole class again. 'What's it called?'

'The shark, miss?' Morton Seymore said.

'Yes.'

'Glide?'

Some of the boys tittered.

'I don't mean its name – and I don't think "glide" is the shark's name, Mr Seymore. I think "glide" is what it's doing. No, Michael's shark is a metaphor.' She wrote this on the board. 'Met-a-phor. We have gone over this a number of times, class. The shark is a metaphor for war. The war is being compared to a deadly shark.'

'Larry, how about you?'

'I don't really want to read mine, miss.'

'Come along.' She frowned slightly and tightened her bosom-lock.

'Mine's not a metaphor.'

'That's all right.'

Despite his seeming nervousness, Larry stood up and read with melodramatic gusto, almost shouting the poem:

Out of the trenches Nigel his men led.
'Take that, Jerry,' he said.
'You'll all soon be dead.
Filled with Blighty lead.'
'Achtung! Achtung!' replied the square head.
Nigel fell into a Panzer's tread,
Which smashed his head.
And his dog, who was called Old Red,
Sat on his grave and howled until he was dead.
But at least he still had his head.

He looked proudly at Mrs Bellamy.

'The dog had Nigel's head?' she said.

'The dog had its own head, miss. Which Nigel didn't. Told you it wasn't any good, miss.' Suddenly miserable, he sat down.

'It *is* good,' she said. 'Of course it's good. And some very, *very* vivid imagery, Larry. *Excellent* work.'

Larry flushed happily.

She turned again to Raj, who was still staring out of the window. 'Why don't you read yours out for us, Mr Travers?'

A general moan went up.

'Oh miss,' Martin Abby whined, 'he should read his out last. I don't want to read mine after his.'

But Raj had already stood up. For a moment he just stared blankly at the front of the class. Then he pulled off his sweater, shoved it up inside his shirt, and clamped his hands under the mound it made. Imitating Bellamy's Geordie accent, he said, 'Vivid imagery, Larry. What's this kind of poem called, class?'

'Rajiv,' Mrs Bellamy shouted. 'What are you doing?'

'A metaphor,' Raj said. 'This poem is a metaphor – met-a-phor. Which means it's being compared to something. And what can it be compared to, class? Not a pool of vomit, no, Larry, but that's very close. Yes, that's right, Michael: a pile of dog shit.'

'Sit down this instant,' she screamed.

Now Raj began to sway back and forth, cuddling his fake breasts and singing: 'Oh my little fishy with my little missy when the boat comes in. Oh little missy with my little fishy, oh little missy when the boat comes in.'

Mrs Bellamy, tears starting to her eyes, hurried out. She returned with Peterson the Punisher, the ex-sergeant-major, who looked gleeful with sadistic anticipation. Snatching up the collar of Raj's shirt, he dragged him from the classroom.

'I have *never* been so humiliated.' Brenna snatched her scarf off her head as they entered the house. 'What possessed you to behave so abominably?'

It was the first time either had spoken since she had picked him up from school and quick-marched him home. Raj, following her into the sitting room, didn't answer.

She telephoned her husband at his office. 'Listen, Haig, Rajiv has been suspended from school for just the most obscene and insulting behaviour. Yes. Suspended. Two weeks. It was this morning. I've been up at Mother's all day. He's been sitting on his hands outside the headmaster's office. Now, I want you to come home this instant and deal with this. I don't care. I'm not having anything more to do with him. I *don't* care. If you're not here in half an hour, Haig, I can't tell you what I'm going to do. You get here and you talk to this boy and call up Mr Reeves and explain that we simply *can't* have him skulking about this house for the next two weeks. Do you understand?' She slammed down the receiver.

Raj, who was standing in front of her, was now as tall as she. Her little weapon of a face glinted menacingly in front of him.

'You come here,' she said, 'live in our house, eat our food. Your father hasn't sent so much as a penny for your keep, and you repay us by doing this?'

She was brushing those imaginary hairs out of her face and Raj now began to imitate this.

'You are a *nasty* creature,' she said.

'You are a *nasty* creature.' He echoed her shrill voice.

'How dare you.'

'How dare you.' He was flaring his nostrils and furrowing his brow just as she did.

Reaching out, she took hold of his cheek between her thumb and forefinger. He didn't move or say anything, just continued to stare at her as she pinched harder and harder. A trickle of blood ran down his cheek and she pulled her fingers away. His face completely expressionless, he took a ballet dancer figurine down from the mantelpiece and flung it into the fireplace, shattering it.

'Go on,' she said, 'break whatever you want, you little . . .' She hesitated, but leaning in close whispered it through her gritted teeth: 'Black bastard.'

He picked up a small crystal vase and flung that into the grate, but it was too tough to break. He walked over to the display case and opened it. One by one he took out the beautiful china plates and dropped them on the floor. Brenna just stared at him, her hands holding the edge of the mantelpiece as if for support. As he took out the gravy boat, the front door opened. Brenna and Raj froze, staring toward the sitting room entrance as if they had been caught in some illicit intimacy as Cecilia walked in.

'What on earth's going on?' she said.

'He's been suspended from school for the most insulting behaviour and, as you can see, he's gone quite mad. He's smashing everything.'

'Raj' – Cecilia walked over to him – 'what are you doing?'

He didn't respond.

She took hold of his arms. 'Go up to your room this instant.'

'Go up to your room this instant,' he mocked.

'What happened to your cheek?'

'Go up to your room. Go up to your room this instant!' he repeated.

Again the sound of the front door. Haig entered. Putting down his briefcase, he examined the mess with an expression of profound exhaustion.

'Look what he's doing,' Brenna said. 'He's gone quite mad.'

'Rajiv, why are you doing this?' Haig asked.

'He won't answer you,' Brenna said.

'Rajiv, why are you doing this?'

'He won't—'

'*Rajiv*,' he said more firmly, 'why are you doing this?'

Raj remained silent and empty-faced in front of Cecilia, still holding the gravy boat.

Sighing, Haig turned to his wife. 'The boy is twelve years old.' Picking up his briefcase, he turned around and left the house.

When the front door slammed shut, Brenna began to cry. Cecilia hurried over to comfort her. Looking back at Raj, she screamed, 'This is *our* house. Why don't you just get out.'

2 May 1954

Dear Haig,

Gerard is as Gerard does, as we both know. A friend forwarded your letter. I've been in the Midwest for two years now – Missouri. I met a woman, Ruth, who is perfect for me. We are kind and intimate strangers, which suits us both, I think. She lives on a farm just outside a town called Pisgah, which consists of a half-dozen streets and a few stores – Celli's Groceries, Neef's Religious Bookstore and Gunsmiths, Suggs' Hardware, Snyder's Drug Sundries and Soda Fountain, The Gay Frock Shop, Novus Shoes, Pisgah Ice and Storage, and the Utz Mill and Grain Company. That's pretty much it. It's a beautiful place, though, surrounded by cornfields and woods full of deer, and populated, for the most part, by solid northern Europeans.

I am well. I work this tiny farm (imagine <u>me</u>, a farmer), growing hardly more than enough to keep ourselves, really. Ruth makes her living writing romance novels. We have a great time choosing people from this small town for her to transform into the heroes and heroines of these tawdry worlds. We select the most unlikely pairings of farmers, shopkeepers, schoolteachers, enhancing their

best physical features, filling them with fire, and flinging them together. When we pass any one of our transformed characters in town, Ruth will – and she has a marvellous memory – relate one of their breathless love scenes. The town thinks us touched. We are always falling about.

I'm amazed you can stay in that house, Eggy, though perhaps it is smarter to live in his cave than to run, like Rags and me. I once believed travelling would change me fundamentally, purify and rid me of him. I suppose I imagined I could just pluck him out, leave him on the peak of a mountain somewhere. Clearly I'm too weak, as Father always said. Or perhaps the truth is that no one can ever change: transformation is just a fantasy, like Ruth's romances, invented, as God and heaven were, to make life bearable.

I should tell you – in part because of your request – that my old demon is still with me. The farm is quite a difficult place because there are so many ways by which one can do oneself harm. So the voice is very active and opportunistic. What a canny demon it is, always transforming. Already it is taking on Ruth's voice – the voice of this woman telling me lovingly, reasonably to end myself. But there is something of the ghost about Ruth, too, so I can fool myself we are already gone, the two of us.

But to your request. I'm sorry about all this. It took me four days to muster the courage even to open your letter. Because of what you're asking, I thought it best to give you a sense of things.

What a mess Gerry has put you in. I've talked to Ruth. We can't possibly, of course, take the boy on any permanent basis. But to provide some relief, since it sounds as if Brenna is heading for a breakdown, we will take the boy – my nephew, I suppose – for the summer. St Louis is the closest city. Our old car won't make it that far, but this town has a train station – I enclose details – and I can pick you up there. Just let me know when.

Your loving brother,

Olly

PISGAH, MISSOURI, 1954

Sebastiana Celli – Annie – sat on the counter of her father's general store in a bright yellow house dress. She had a remarkable face, the archaic beauty of Greece and Rome which looked almost grotesque on her skinny, twelve-year-old body – those thick, dark eyebrows, that patrician nose, lips too sensual for a child, and a profusion of black curls cut raggedly, impatiently short.

No one had come into the store for hours. Annie wanted to go and look at the Missouri. One more week of rain like the last and it would be over its levees. Her papa was out with the volunteer fire service, helping to move people and cattle from the lowlands.

As she tried to throw another piece of dried macaroni into the shoe she had kicked off, the store door opened, ringing the bell. When she saw it was strangers – a Negro boy and a man with sideburns like an old Southern general – she jumped to the floor.

'Good afternoon,' the man said, speaking as if he weren't sure she could understand English. 'We're trying to get to Ruth Winters' farm.'

Annie saw now that apart from his skin the boy didn't look like a Negro. He seemed about her age, and almost as tall – and she was taller than any of the boys in school.

'Good afternoon,' she said, smiling as she imitated the man's accent. 'My papa's not here, but I'll get Frankie to take you. He's out back.'

'Oh, we don't want to be any trouble. Is there a taxi?'

'A taxi?' She laughed. 'Are you from England?'

'Yes,' the man said.

She turned to the boy – the real object of her question. 'Are you?'

The boy, who was staring at her discarded shoe, glanced up for a moment, but didn't say anything. He had big, expressive eyes, and looked very stern and sad.

The man laughed nervously. 'He's been a bit under the weather. Touch of laryngitis. His name's Rajiv and he's originally from India.'

She kept her eyes on the boy, trying to get him to look up at her again. 'My papa's from Italy – Atessa – and my mom's from Poland – Koscian.'

The boy didn't respond.

'I'll get Frankie.' Annie ran back through the kitchen into the yard, where her brother had, in the last couple of weeks, set up his auto repair shop.

He was working on an old Dodge sedan. While undeniably handsome, with his Elvis quiff and many of the features that made Annie so startling, Francesco had nothing of her form. His face was like a collection of rare, exquisite, delicious things, thrown willy-nilly on to an old china plate.

'Frankie,' she said, 'there are some strangers here from England and India and they need a ride up to Ruth's place.'

'Jeez-Louise, Annie, I've got to get this done.'

Reaching up, she rubbed the frown from her brother's forehead. Not yet sixteen, he was too young to be developing such deep lines, she thought. He always looked strained, as if he were having to work constantly to keep his face from collapsing into anger or despair.

'The boy's from India. He can't speak. I think he's been kidnapped.'

Frank nodded, pushing her hand gently away and wiping his own hands with a red shop rag. 'Annie, what the hell happened to your hair?'

'It was too long.'

'Look at your legs, running around in those damn woods all day. If you go out into the sun those scratches are going to turn to scars. Who's going to marry a girl with scars all over her legs?'

Annie didn't say anything. Four days ago she had been in Papa's truck making a delivery with Frank when it had begun. It had frightened her. She had no idea what it was and Frank almost pulled the truck into a ditch when he saw the blood on her fingers and smeared on the inside of her thighs. He was both fierce and fearful – fearful for her especially. Because this had happened in front of him, she sensed it was as if he now, reluctantly, had a part in it, in her not being a child any more.

Annie followed him back into the shop.

'I'd shake your hand,' Frank said to the Englishman, but pleaded his oily hands. 'Annie tells me you need a ride to Ruth's place.' He barely glanced at the boy, as if it were somehow rude to look at him for too long.

'I don't mean to put you to any trouble,' the man said.

'It's no trouble,' Annie insisted, nuzzling her head against her brother's arm. The man was smiling at her, which pleased Annie, but the kidnapped Indian boy was still staring at her shoe.

'I am *most* dreadfully sorry, Rajiv,' she said, imitating the man's accent again, 'but I must remain.' She saw the Indian boy smile just slightly before he followed the man and her brother out of the store.

Frank dropped them in front of a small white farmhouse a few miles out of town.

'Raj, listen,' Haig said as they climbed the five steps to the porch, 'you have to speak. You can't carry on like this. I wanted to say that I'm really—'

Haig's knocking set off the baying of an old hound, which came cantering from the back. The hound was white with brown patches. In red, on its flank, someone had painted the number 53. It barked self-consciously, glancing around and wagging its tail. At last it climbed on to the porch, sniffed at them, and trotted away

Haig tried the door and it opened. They entered the dark, wood-panelled interior, Haig calling softly as they moved through the house into the kitchen. A half-made cherry pie, now covered in flies, had been left out on the counter. The back door was wide open.

Haig made them sandwiches, using luncheon meat he found in the ice box, and they sat on the back porch for a couple of hours, watching the hens scratching about in their pen. The hound lay beside them,

making all kinds of revolting licking and snorting sounds. Near the
pale red barn, behind a fence, stood a cow, lowing mournfully.

As the sun set, they heard a car grinding up the front driveway
and hurried back through the house.

It was a police cruiser, out of which stepped an officer with a
boyish, sternly embarrassed face. He was ordinarily proportioned –
even quite slim – except for his belly, which was as big as a beach
ball.

'Mr Travers?' Casting a discreet glance at Raj, he shook Haig's
hand, then pulled a small towel from under his hat and wiped his
neck with it.

'Siggy Judd, County Sheriff. There's been an accident. Ruth's at the
. . . uh . . . with your . . . Difficult time. I'll take you down there.'

'Down where?' Haig said. 'Is it Oliver?'

The sheriff nodded. 'Took him down to Jackson.'

Haig and Raj got into the cruiser and were dropped off half an
hour later outside a hospital. The sheriff said he didn't know any
details and seemed anxious to leave. He told them to tell the receptionist that Ruth and 'the other fella' were downstairs.

Haig gave his brother's name to the receptionist.

'I just love your accent,' she said. 'My friend Nedra told me you
call a hood a bonnet and a trunk is a boot and a sweater is a jumper.
Is that right?'

'Yes. It's Oliver Travers,' Haig repeated anxiously.

'Can't see him here.'

He went to speak, but she lifted her finger as the phone rang. It
rang again as soon as she put it down and she seemed to know everyone personally, melting into sing-song conversations about their near
and distant relatives and whether they had heard about that case of
swine fever up in Cooke County, and how the flooding had already
begun upriver and they were saying this year was going to be worse
than '43. Finally Haig interrupted, telling her that the sheriff had told
him his brother was downstairs. She replaced the phone.

'Downstairs?' She looked confused. 'That's the morgue.'

'He's not dead,' Haig said. 'The sheriff would have told me if he were dead.'

'Oh lordy, well that's all that's down there, honey.'

She checked another list and then placed her hand very gently and protectively over her throat. 'Heavens,' she said. 'Oh heavens, I am sorry.'

Haig and Raj took the stairs. They pushed through some heavy swing doors into what looked like a railway station waiting room. A woman who was sitting on a long wooden bench filling out a form looked up at them, and then stood. She had a dab of flour on her cheek and was wearing a baby-blue apron. Slender, in her early forties, her long hair, which was the colour of tarnished brass, had been hastily bundled back and secured with two knitting needles. She had a fiercely intelligent face, its expression both sympathetic and defended – everything about her seeming at once to give and to hold back. She shook their hands and told Haig carefully and bravely that his brother had killed himself by drinking strychnine and was in the next room if he wished to see him.

Some hours later this woman drove them back to the farm past Dutch gabled barns and fields of corn in a lovingly preserved Model A, which shook their bones over the rough roads. She showed Haig to the spare bedroom. Raj was to sleep on the couch in the sitting room beside the stove. She told them to help themselves to food and went out to see to the cow, whose moans now sounded unbearable.

It was six in the morning a week to the day after Oliver's funeral. Ruth was sitting with a cup of coffee in the swinging bench out on the back porch, the sun just broaching the tree line. She wanted time to herself. Haig made her uncomfortable. He seemed to feel that Oliver's death had established a special intimacy between them, itself the vanguard for other feelings that might naturally arise between a man and a woman. It was clear that the thought of stepping right into his brother's life was taking hold of his imagination. He had begun to talk about how much he hated his job and the city, and that his wife was no longer the woman he had married. He had also started to compliment her gratuitously. Of all things he had asked, the previous evening, if he could feel her muscles. She had been brusque. No doubt he thought her a hard nut. And cold. She had not cried once. Then there was the question of that boy, who crept around like a mouse and still hadn't uttered a single word.

She just wanted to be alone. Oliver had been perfect, his past and all his unhappiness sealed; as she had sealed hers. He was like a dream-figure, endlessly approaching across vast distances. Haig was shocked by how little Ruth knew about his brother, but they had both preferred it like this, living in the present, as needful and mysterious to each other as parent to child and child to parent. Whatever was inside them, however terrible, was transforming, under the pressure of hard work, silence and tenderness, into something resembling love. The cost, though, was that they were never *in* love, since they existed for each other too obliquely. Love occupied the spaces between, worried the edges of their consciousness like a song neither could quite remember.

More confusing still, it was Haig's impending visit that had provided whatever killed Oliver with enough traction to get out of the pit in which he had kept it trapped all these years. He became increasingly restless as the date of his brother's arrival approached. He had suffered bad times before, like that night when he woke her up and asked her to hide the old carving knife, its blade lean with sharpening, which he couldn't stop thinking about. And just hours before he did it, Oliver revealed that there was a voice in him which told him to do terrible things, and that whenever he learned to fend it off, it would transform and re-emerge. It had become like her voice — *Your voice, Ruth*, he said, *but awful, cruel*. She wanted to tell him she knew whose voice this was, and realized for the first time how vulnerable their particular intimacy had made them: without the warding gestures of language, the prophylactic of confession, they had caught each other's secrets like a virus.

The back door opened, shocking her.

'Morning,' Haig said.

She tightened her shawl around her neck. 'I hope I didn't wake you.'

'It was the coffee. Smells wonderful.' He sat next to her on the swinging bench.

'Please help yourself.'

He raised a cup, which she hadn't seen.

They were quiet for a moment. Then Haig sighed, and said, 'Ruth, the boy . . . We have to . . .'

Ruth had noticed this about him. He would begin to say something, then falter, clearly hoping, pressured by his silence, that she would jump in to save him. But Ruth just waited.

'Things are bad at home, as I've explained, and I really can't . . . It really wouldn't be good for me – for him – to . . . for me to bring him back.'

'Look, I don't know this boy. I've never wanted children. And you have to understand that the circumstances have changed.'

Haig reached now and put his hand over hers. It was everything she could do not to snatch it away.

'He's a really . . . he's a nice boy and he could help you here on the farm and be company for you.'

'I don't need company.'

'Ruth, my wife won't have him. She just won't.'

'But that's hardly . . . You're asking me – a stranger, really, a *stranger* – to be responsible for your nephew. Oliver and I weren't even married.' While this was true, she felt the warm pressure of tears, as if she had betrayed him. She didn't want to cry in front of this man. He was staring at her lips now and had gently eased his fingers between hers. She was absurdly frightened that if she cried he would feel compelled to kiss her.

She freed her hand, acting as if she needed to adjust her shawl again. 'Just the rest of the summer,' she said. 'Then you have to come fetch him. Is that clear?'

He nodded. 'Thank you, Ruth.'

She was so furious at herself, at how ridiculously sensitive and feckless she was. She had agreed to look after this strange child for three months simply because she couldn't hold out against the pathetic threat of this man's pitying desire; because even the possibility that he might try to kiss her was, under these bizarre and emotional circumstances, just too much to bear.

Ruth returned from her Sunday morning walk to the swollen Missouri and back. She felt so lonely it had even occurred to her to go to church. But she was repelled by the thought of sitting through one of Reverend Hewitt's interminable sermons, watching that vain little man preening his silky brown hair and simpering with idiot delight at his own sophistry.

At least Haig was gone. She and the boy saw him off at the station yesterday. The boy spoke for the first time when the train pulled out, murmuring, as a freight car full of pigs rolled by, 'Bet those seats are cheap.'

Since it was the first time he had spoken, she wasn't sure what to make of it. It was as if someone had given her a dubious gift and it had now begun to do something strange.

He went on in a funny voice: 'First class, second class, third class, fourth class, or I can put you with the pigs, sir.'

'So you do speak then,' she said as they walked out to the car.

He nodded and retreated once more into his shyness, pretending to sleep for the whole drive back.

Approaching her house now, she saw him sitting on the porch steps scratching Fifty-Three's ears. At the sight of her, he snatched his hand away and stood, as if he weren't sure he had a right to touch anything of hers.

She cooked him a large breakfast of eggs, ham and biscuits. When he noticed she wasn't eating herself, he told her he could make his own breakfast.

'Weekdays it's oatmeal,' she said.

'Is that the same as porridge, miss?'

She nodded.

He put on a face of comic revulsion, crossing his eyes.

'You can put fruit in it.'

'But I like fruit, miss. Why would I put it in porridge?'

She smiled, which clearly pleased him. He was a nice-looking lad, not gormless like some of those meaty German kids, but alive with guarded looks, his slender body jerking and trembling with a twelve-year-old's misfiring energy. His dark skin was clear and smooth, his eyes arrestingly large, with long, thick lashes, and his hair was so dark it had a blue sheen to it.

All at once it struck her how astonishing it was that he was here. How did she get herself into these things? First the scandal of living out of wedlock with a man ten years her junior; now she had a little dark boy. She thought about the kind of rumours that were probably spreading: a stranger turns up in town leaving her with this child on the same day her lover kills himself. Worse still, this Indian boy now sat where Oliver had sat just two weeks ago. How utterly random: one life for another. All at once she felt tremendously alone, and into the vacuum of this rushed her grief for Oliver. She began to clear the food away, though the boy had just started to eat. As she picked up the plate of biscuits, she realized what she was doing. Returning it to the table, she saw that the boy was looking down at his breakfast and had placed his right hand above his eyes like a cap's brim, as if to give her privacy. His perceptiveness and sensitivity horrified her as she struggled to contain her anger: anger that would surface whenever she became aware of her inability to establish the life and self she wanted, of the immensity of her desire for *something*. Anger: at Oliver for what he had done, at herself for agreeing to take on this boy, at Haig for entering her life like a virulent and contagious weakness. Damn that damned family. She had never wanted a child, and now, as if from a prolonged incubation of this anger and isolation, out of those slow contractions of passionate sadness that had afflicted her ever since she had first been overwhelmed by her desire for a man, this strange, dark boy had emerged, blinded by his own hand.

She sat back down.

After a little while Raj glanced up and said, 'I'll help you around the farm.'

She still felt a little too emotional to respond.

After he had finished his breakfast, Raj said, 'Are there snakes round here? Someone at school told me there's snakes in America.'

'There are,' she said, 'but they're more afraid of you than you are of them.'

He shook his head wildly, his eyes widening. 'No they aren't. No they aren't.'

He looked so serious, she couldn't help but smile.

She sighed. 'I can't keep this farm going,' she said. 'It was Oliver's thing, really. This is my house, and I guess I can lease the land, but things are going to be a little . . . tight. I actually make some money writing books – romantic literature for ladies.'

The boy placed his hands over his heart, fluttering his eyes, and she laughed.

'I'll get a job,' he said. 'I'll clean the house. I very good cleaning wallah.'

She nodded. Now came the most difficult thing. 'Rajiv, I understand that you can't help it, but look, I have three sets of sheets and we can work out a kind of rotation. I'm going to clean and dry out your mattress today.' The boy had closed up his body and was staring down into the table. She felt awful. 'Anyway, we'll sort it out, but we just need to make sure you're not sleeping on wet sheets. Is that okay?'

The boy nodded, his eyes still averted.

'Okay, Rajiv, would you mind emptying your plate into that bucket there and then taking those scraps out and throwing them to the chickens.'

'Just throw them?'

'Yes, just throw them over the fence there.'

'On to the floor?'

She laughed. 'The ground. Yes, they'll eat them.'

Through the open back door, Ruth watched him throwing the

scraps over, and backing fearfully away as the chickens came running. Then he put down the bucket and stared into the trees beside the barn. He had spotted something. As she went to see what it was, she heard a knock at the front door.

Annie had told Lew to meet her at Ruth's. She wondered if he was stuck doing more flood preparation at his farm, though the waters had gone down.

Ruth opened the door and Annie handed her the pound cake. 'My mama made it, but I did help.'

'I'm going to get as fat as a house.'

'You'll never get fat, Miss Winters.' Annie felt a little guilty saying this. It had come to her because she had heard Mrs Glatz say to her mama that women like Ruth had to dedicate their lives to their figures so as to keep their men happy. Ruth fascinated Annie. She was drawn to her elegance and intelligence, provoked by her reserve.

'I'm sorry for your loss.'

'Yes. Thank you.'

'Is that boy staying here?'

'Rajiv? Yes. He's out back.'

Annie followed Ruth through the house. The boy was staring into the trees.

Turning to them, he pointed. 'There's a girl over there.'

Annie laughed and shouted, 'Lew.'

Lew emerged from the dense, swaying leaf shadow beneath the trees. Annie could see how the Indian boy could have thought he was a girl, his wheat-coloured hair down past his ears.

'How are you doing, Lewis?' Ruth called gently as he approached.

'I'm okay now, Miss Winters.'

'It's good to have you back.'

'I'm sorry for your loss.'

'Thank you.'

'Can we show Rajiv the branch?' Annie asked.

'Of course.'

'I can't go,' the Indian boy said. 'I've got to do some things.'

'What have you got to do?' Annie said.

He hesitated. 'I've got to help Miss Winters.'

'That's okay,' Ruth said.

'I really can't.' He was staring stubbornly into the ground, just like that first time Annie had seen him. She glanced up at Ruth, who gave a shrug.

'We're building a fort.' Annie really wanted him to come and couldn't understand why he wouldn't. She had been the first to meet him and felt that he, as yet unexplored, was hers. Besides that, Lew had changed after nearly two years in that terrible place. There were strange, new distances in him. He talked to himself, seemed to see things where there was nothing, and a few times his hand had strayed to the back of his neck again. When she had seen this Indian boy in her papa's store, it was as if she had been remembering it from a dream: he was here for them. Now they would be three.

'Okay, you don't have to come,' Annie said, 'but can I just show you something quickly.'

Before he could respond, she snatched up his hand and began to lead him toward the woods. 'Oh, hurry, hurry,' she cried out, as if she had seen something. 'We'll miss it.' She started to run, still holding his hand, Lew following, and she kept running until they were far enough into the woods she knew the boy wouldn't go back.

Walking on they passed Mrs Barnacle's old log cabin in a clearing. Mrs Barnacle was digging in her vegetable garden. Annie called a greeting and the old woman looked up as if furious, swivelling her head like a chicken.

'She's a Seventh Day Adventist,' Annie whispered. 'Thought the world was going to end a little while back, but it didn't and she's been miserable ever since.'

The dark boy smiled.

She led him and Lew to the lightning tree. Rajiv had no trouble climbing it, which pleased her. They all balanced themselves around the lip of the charred, hollow centre of the oak.

'Lightning did that,' she said.

'How come it still has leaves?' Raj asked.

She shrugged. 'Doesn't know it's dead yet, I guess.'

Lew leaned in. 'Some dinosaurs had two brains.'

Annie felt a twinge of anxiety whenever Lew spoke now: he had started to say some strange things.

''Cos they're so humungous,' he went on, 'they had one in their butts to work their back legs. So if you shot them in the head they'd keep moving, like cockroaches.'

Raj suddenly put on a strange, nasal voice. 'I'm terribly sorry, sir, I can't answer that question, but let me consult my butt.' Clearly nervous, he let out a high-pitched laugh.

Annie smiled at him. 'Do you have brothers and sisters?'

He nodded. 'In India.'

'Why are you here?'

'Oliver Travers was my uncle.'

'Who's that other man?'

'My uncle as well.'

'Where's your mom and dad?' Lew asked.

'My mum died and my dad's in Australia.'

'Mum.' Annie couldn't help imitating his accent. 'My mum.'

'In Australia,' Lew said, 'they have the top ten most poisonous snakes and insects in the world.'

'Oh yeah?' Raj said.

'They'd have the top twenty if it wasn't for the cobra – that's from India. They have a spider in Australia can jump right up from the ground into your face.'

'Goes for the eyes,' Annie said.

'That true?' Raj asked Lew, but Lew's attention had been taken by something in the trees.

'Yeah,' Annie took up. 'We read it in the *National Geographic*. They can dig your eye out with their fangs.' She demonstrated with two hooked fingers.

'No.'

'Honest. That's right, ain't it, Lew?'

But Lew, utterly absorbed, had begun to murmur something to himself.

'And the spiders,' Annie continued loudly to distract Raj, 'can use that eye to see. That's why they hardly ever go for people with glasses, 'cos it's really hard when they need to change their prescriptions.'

'Liar, pants on fire,' Raj cried out. Though laughing, Annie could see that he was slyly observing Lew, and after a moment Raj asked him, 'Have *you* got brothers and sisters?'

Lew didn't respond. Annie hated this. 'Lew,' she shouted.

Still he didn't respond, so she reached over and touched his knee. He reacted instantly, as if he had been shocked. 'What?'

'Do you have brothers or sisters?' Raj repeated.

Lew shook his head.

'You had a brother.' Annie wanted this done with.

'I had a brother,' Lew said, 'but I harmed him. I killed him.'

'You didn't do nothing,' Annie said. 'He just drowned.'

Lew was staring strangely at Annie. Raj clearly didn't know if they were joking or not.

'He drowned,' Annie said.

Raj nodded. 'My mum drowned. In the monsoon floods. She was trying to pull out a water buffalo that got stuck in the mud and she was swept away.'

A voice called up: 'Hey, guys.'

It was Nora. Annie leaned over the edge and didn't try too hard to hide her irritation. 'Howja know we were here?'

'I tried down the branch. Alv said you might be here.'

'Alv?'

Nora looked around. 'Don't know where he is now. He found part of a deer's head. Gross. Still had skin on it.'

Suddenly this half-rotted skull loomed over the edge of the tree. Lew screamed and Raj pushed himself back into Annie. Its appearance was closely followed by Alvin's plump round face, grinning stupidly. Worried for Lew, who was now covering the back of his neck with both hands, Annie snatched the skull from Alvin and flung it away.

'Hey,' Alvin shouted, 'what you do that for?'

Annie clambered over to Lew, prised his hands gently from his nape, and put her arms around him. Turning back to Alvin she said furiously, 'What are you doing here?'

Alvin was too absorbed with pulling himself up on to the rim of the tree to respond. When he had steadied himself, he stared at the Indian boy with his buggy eyes a moment, then his words gushed out in a nonsensical stream, punctuated by that odd little snort of his laugh. 'My dad says you're different from a Negro; says you come from a place where they don't believe in God or improving yourself; they got men there can move their internal organs around; you're blacker than some Negroes though. I seen Negroes look almost white. You do look like a white person a bit but you've got pale palms.'

'Oh, shut up, Alvin,' Annie said.

Alvin looked abashed. Annie knew he wasn't being cruel. It was just his nature. He began to pick at something in his nose.

'Guys,' Nora cried plaintively from the base of the tree.

Annie leaned over the edge again. 'Come on, Nor. Just climb up. It's easy.'

Nora looked up at the tree helplessly, which irritated Annie. Nora was a solid German girl, blonde and stocky, her breasts already sizeable, but though – or perhaps because – her body wasn't designed for grace, she was almost obsessively particular about the way she carried herself. At church picnics she would take a full ten minutes to arrange her limbs on the grass, smoothing every crease in her skirt, tucking her legs modestly to one side, laying her napkin square in her lap. It was as if the soul of a cat had found its way into the body of a cow. The second this formulation came to Annie, remorse flashed through her. There was a part of her, and she hated it, that was so impatient and critical.

'I'll help you up,' Annie said, but Raj had already leapt down.

'It's easier to get up the other side,' he told Nora.

Nora followed him round and he made a little cradle of his fingers to give her a leg up. Annie noticed Raj modestly averting his eyes as Nora rose above him, which made her smile. She and Lew pulled her the rest of the way, which was hard, since she was heavy – not fat but solid. Having to do this annoyed Annie again: Nora was strong, but clearly felt it just wasn't ladylike to haul herself up. Finally Nora settled herself primly at the rim, her face flushed. Raj quickly rejoined them and they all sat around the hollow, their legs dangling into the darkness.

After a moment, Annie said, 'That deer was killed by a shadow demon hiding out in the woods. It's murdered seven people so far.'

Interrupting, Nora said to Raj, 'Thanks for helping me up.'

'My pleasure, memsah—' He stopped.

'What?' Nora said.

'Nothing.'

'I know I'm a bit heavy.'

'No you're not.'

'He was looking up your skirt,' Alvin said, making his snort.

'Why are you always so disgusting?' Nora said. 'No one would know your dad was the minister.'

'Anyway,' Annie continued firmly, 'now we have to track him down.'

Nora gave a little sigh. Annie knew she would have preferred to go and have a malt in Snyder's. She thought they were all too old for this. The flush had finally drained from her face, and Annie noticed a cluster of inflamed pores in Nora's cheek, a yellow spot just below her lip. This was new. She had always had lovely skin, so pale that during the summer it would just redden and peel off over and over again.

'Yeah,' Alvin said, 'and he cuts his victims' guts out and leaves them on people's doorsteps.'

'Gross,' Nora said.

'No he doesn't, you muttonhead,' Annie said. 'He takes their souls, and he's trapped them in an underground lake, and he's making a

huge, ginormous monster out of the animals he traps – wolves and
deer and cougars and bears. And he's going to turn all those human
souls evil by keeping them out of sunlight, and he's going to put them
in the monster.'

'Is it worse than the ghost dog?' Alvin asked.

'There isn't any such thing,' Nora said.

'Lew and Annie have seen it,' Alvin protested. 'Lots of people have
seen it.'

'Annie just makes things up. Lew, Annie was just making it up,
wasn't she?'

Lew shook his head. 'No, we saw the dog,' he said. 'And we saw
the man turn into the dog.'

Annie tried to stop herself smiling at the shock in Nora's face. The
effect of Lew saying this was electrifying. Anyone who looked at Lew
knew he couldn't lie. It was in his eyes – his father's – so intensely
blue they seemed blind somehow, as if they had seen all there was to
see. Besides that, she really wasn't making this up. Annie remembered
so clearly when they saw the boogerman that day, and he had vanished
just as the dog had appeared right in front of them on the other side
of the branch.

'Ten times worse,' Annie said.

'What's this ghost dog?' Raj asked.

'The nigger boogerman's ghost dog,' Alvin explained. 'He's in the
woods somewhere. The boogerman turns into the dog when he wants
to eat children.'

'Anyway,' Annie said, 'we've got to find the shadow demon and
kill him before he gets any more souls. He was last seen at the sinkhole.' Annie stepped across the dark hollow and descended, followed
by Lew and Alvin. Raj helped Nora down the easy side. Annie then
led them all into the dangers of the forest.

PISGAH, 1952

Annie and Lewis, crawling along the trunk of a fallen tree, were cross-ing Bull Branch. Days of heavy rain followed by high winds had uprooted many trees, especially along the banks of the rivers and streams.

Annie stood up unsteadily, the water swift and swollen beneath them. 'This was a battle. The wind was trying to bring down the sky.' Squatting, she patted the tree and added a little incongruously, 'Poor darling.'

Lew had made a weapon from a fence stave, which was unbalan-cing him. 'We have to fight.' Trying to stand, he slipped and narrowly prevented himself falling into the water.

Annie lay flat, pressing her ear to the tree. 'Eagle-eyes, the tree says we have to go back to the fort and get ready.'

She glanced around. 'Where's Roh?'

'Darn, he's gone again.' Lew flung his weapon into the water. 'We'll just leave him.'

'We can't just leave him.'

'I'm going to lock him in the barn tomorrow. I am.'

'We could tie some string to him. He could be our prisoner.'

'We'll have to put something in his mouth to stop him screaming.' Lew had scrambled back to the bank and was looking around anxiously.

'Roh,' Annie called into the woods, joining him.

'Do you think he even knows that's his name?'

'He knows. Where would he be? Down by the mill?'

'Not now. It's too late.' Lew checked to see where the sun was. 'I bet he's by the sinkhole.'

They arrived out of breath. The roughly circular natural pool, about as big as a baseball diamond, had one half of its circumference open to a clearing in the woods, the other half closed off by a limestone rock face which rose as high as forty feet in places. On the other side of the pool, Rohan, Lew's seven-year-old brother, soaking wet, lay upon a small ridge.

'Roh,' Lew shouted, 'come back over here.'

His brother didn't respond, utterly captivated by the veins of light reflected up from the pool on to the rock face.

'He's gonna go crazy if I try to fetch him now.' Lew's cheeks and arms were covered in scratches and bruises from such battles with his brother.

'He'll come himself when the sun's too low,' Annie said. 'We can just wait here. It's nice here.'

They sat at the edge of the pool.

'I found a spicy book under my mom's mattress,' she said.

'Did you read it?'

'Bits of it, and there's this one bit where the man, well I don't rightly know what he did but the woman said it was like riding a bolt of lightning.'

Lew made a grimace.

After a moment Annie said, 'Lew, do you think we're going to get married?'

He shrugged.

'It means we could live in the same house,' she said. 'We could have our own farm.'

'Don't want a farm. I want to sell insurance.'

'Why?'

'This insurance man came round the other day. He had a new Pontiac with the head of Chief Pontiac on the front. And he said he went all over, went as far as Kennett. Showed me his cavalryman's pistol. I couldn't even lift it. He said it was for when other insurance salesmen tried to muscle in on his territory and it left a hole in them big as a silver dollar.'

'What's insurance?'

'Well, it's like if your house burns down they build you another one.'

'For nothing?'

'I think so. He said they'd pay us for all kinds of things, 'cept flooding. Said we should have had insurance for my mom.'

'What, they get you a new mom?'

'No, chowderhead, they give you money to bury 'em and stuff. Pop told him we didn't own the farm or nothing.'

'You could run my papa's store. Then we could eat anything in it we wanted.'

He flung a couple of stones into the water.

'So we're going to get married then?' she said.

He shrugged. 'Sure.'

'Then you have to kiss me on the mouth.'

Lew bunched his shoulders. 'Don't want to.'

Annie quickly grabbed his cheeks and threw her mouth against his. Screwing up his face, Lew pushed her away just as they heard a splash.

They stood as Roh doggy paddled toward the bank. The light had faded, the inside of the sinkhole turning dark. Roh was now on the shallow stone shelf that extended out a few feet into the pool, before the drop-off, and waded toward them. Once he was at the edge, Lew pulled him up out of the water and slapped his hand.

'Don't hit him, Lew.'

'He's always running off.' Glancing at her, Lew seemed to notice something. 'Annie, your mouth's bleeding.'

Feeling the blood trickle down her chin she wiped it off. 'I hit your teeth.'

Roh, shivering, but completely passive now, stared at the raw scalp of reddish light over the trees. He looked like a normal seven-year-old, not one who was touched in the head, who didn't speak, and seemed to respond to nothing but patterns of light. They didn't take his hand because he didn't like to be touched, so they marched Indian file, one in front of him, one behind.

*

Lew asked Annie if she wanted to stay to supper, but she told him she had to get home. She didn't like to stay at his place. The farm-house was dilapidated and damp, the roof covered with a patchwork of tar paper and tarp. The only traces of his mom were those funny-looking candlesticks on the sideboard and a pair of her tiny boots just inside the door – Annie's own feet were twice as long. There was still a square patch of less faded paint above the fireplace where a mirror had once hung. His dad, for some reason, had cleared out all the mirrors the day she had died, dumping them behind the barn.

She helped Lew peel the potatoes he brought up from the root cellar, most of which were rotten. She often fantasized about him being saved: sometimes that Roh, who was now rocking himself in the corner, would get better, but more often that he would die, gently, in his sleep. Then she would find someone for his dad. Miss Kelly maybe.

She heard footsteps on the porch and Lew's dad entered.

'Hi, Mr Tivot,' she said.

'Getting dark out there, Annie.' A blood-soaked rag was wrapped around his filthy right hand.

'What happened, Pop?' Lew said.

'Something's wrong with the choke on the Deere. Keeps cutting out.'

She could see Lew was frightened. He knew they were one bad injury away from being unable to support themselves. Picking up a bucket, Lew went out to get water.

Annie couldn't help staring at his dad, who made her think of those photographs of sharecroppers Mr Dawson had showed them in history class. Never anything but that same grim expression in his hollow face, with those shocking blue eyes. He never looked at you directly, as if he were ashamed. She wondered if he were a fugitive, like every-one said. From what, no one was sure. Mrs Yost said he had probably murdered his previous wives, and most likely did the same to Bella. But she was just mad at him because he was too proud to take the peach pie she brought round after his wife's death. Odd, though, that he wouldn't leave this place, get a job somewhere. It was as if he just couldn't imagine anything else.

'Annie,' he said, 'you don't want to be riding home in the dark.'

Lew came back in with a full bucket.

'Lew, where's my bike?'

'Where you left it, I guess.'

She widened her eyes and he understood.

'I'll show you.'

Outside, she pulled her bike off the ground and leaned it against what remained of a patched-together fence. She put her arms around his neck.

'So we'll get married,' she said. He nodded, but she could see his dad's shame had started to infect him and he glanced away. She pushed her lips against his, but it wasn't like it said in the book: no fire; no quenching. She felt as if her soil had gone soft in the rains, even old and deeply rooted things liable to be torn out with just a breath of wind – sadness – and there was nothing she could do. She kissed him again and cycled off.

Lew woke in the middle of the night, his heart pounding. Shannon Kitchens was in his dream. He put his hand between his legs. His thing was hard and warm. He pressed and rubbed it. A strange feeling, like things were heavy down there and he wanted to go to the toilet. He had seen Shannon today picking flowers from the hedgerows behind her house when he was coming home from school. She had to be twenty-five now, or thirty. Old anyways. She could sometimes look pretty like a fairy or something, with that long red hair of hers, in her green dress, and she would sing to herself all the time. Then she would look at you, and she would look strange like an animal, with those heavy eyes, and that grin with half her teeth missing on one side. Some said Otto had beaten her simple; or she had always been simple like Roh. Some said she had been like Otto's wife not his daughter ever since Mrs Kitchens left him, gone back to her folks in Montana. She wasn't his real daughter anyway, but off the orphan train, like his own mom. And some said she had just never been the same after the rape. And that man done it, the boogerman, gotten off by that smart city lawyer. And everyone knew what happened to her, with the sack tied round her head and all. And Seamus said last week she had let him look at her parts and touch her, but he was a fat liar.

Lew rubbed himself, churning it all together, the elf beauty and the beast face and what happened in the barn and showing Seamus her parts. Roh let out a loud sigh in his sleep. Lew didn't want to wake him and thought now about that magazine he had hidden in the barn, which had been in a pile that Annie's mom was going to throw away and had pictures in it of women in bathing costumes. He took the key to their bedroom door from under his mattress. They locked it because of his brother. The lock was a pain: you had to lift the door up from the bottom a little and jiggle the key. He finally got it unlocked. He gave up trying to lock it from the outside because there were some loose floorboards in the hall that whined like hell and he was afraid he would wake his dad.

He crept out of the house. He felt a little frightened of the dark, but it was a full moon, and he really wanted to look at those pictures. In the barn he passed the sow, which had just farrowed, and got the magazine from behind the feed bins. Turning to the page with the women in the bathing costumes, he began to rub himself again. Shannon came back into his head, then Lola Blickensderfer, who had slipped on the stairs in school and he had seen her yellow panties, and Annie's mom when she had bent over to pull that thread off her robe and he had actually seen the nipple of her breast. Abruptly then the memory of Annie when they had last gone swimming and it had struck him that there was nothing there between her legs. But this disturbed him. He didn't want to think about Annie in this way. Shannon re-emerged, like a creature, simple and mad, and he saw that great ornery old sow's teats right in front of him, and his body convulsed and there was the strangest, most wonderful feeling; and something else, warm and sticky, all over his hands. He sat back against the barn wall, a little frightened. This had never happened before. He put the magazine back, cleaned his hands off on some straw and left the barn.

His heart jumped as he saw that the front door was open. Maybe he hadn't latched it properly. But his bedroom door was also wide open and his brother's bed was empty. He couldn't wake his pop. How would he explain things?

He went out again and around to the rear of the barn. The one other time Roh had gotten out at night, they had found him looking into the moonlight glinting from the mirrors his pop had dumped back there. No luck, but far off in the woods he saw the glow of a campfire up near the bluffs over the river. He knew his brother might have headed that way, and thought instantly of the boogerman.

It was so frightening to be in the woods at night. He thought of the white dog, though it hadn't harmed him and Annie that time. As he got closer, he heard men's voices, and just as he got to the base of the ridge, a shot rang out. His whole body went numb and limp and he lay breathing hard against the dirt. He could hear the river rushing below. As quietly as he could, his heart thumping around his insides like a bumblebee in a jar, he crawled up toward the plateau. The voices were louder; in strife now. Someone cursed. He heard it then: his brother screaming like he screamed when you were trying to get him to do something he didn't want to. All at once Roh went quiet. Lew felt as if he were falling right off the earth. Terrible silence. A moan. Another curse from someone. More shouting. He clutched the dirt, shaking. A shadow flung itself across the trees above him. A moment later, he saw a man he knew very well, and that man was holding his brother by one ankle, like a slaughtered chicken, his brother's arms dangling down. He almost cried out as Sal – Sal Celli, Annie's dad – swung his brother back and then flung him out into the river eighty feet below. White spots floated in front of his eyes, the cry he hadn't made scalding his throat. All of a sudden he felt strangely heavy, warm and tired. He might even have fallen asleep. But he became aware at some stage that there were no more sounds. He rolled himself down the slope and it took him a while to get up and start moving back home through the woods, his limbs numb and trembling. He ran into his dad's room and shook him awake.

'What is it?'

Lew started to cry immediately and couldn't catch his breath. 'Roh.'

'What's wrong?' His dad got up now and ran into their bedroom, Lew following.

'Where's your brother?'

'Sal killed him. Sal killed him.'

'What?' Kneeling down, he took hold of Lew's elbows. 'Where's your brother?'

'Sal killed him. I went in the woods and there was a fire and Sal threw him in the river.'

'Sal? Were you having a nightmare? Where's Roh?'

'He got out and he was on the bluffs and there was men there and Sal threw him in the river.'

He followed as his dad took the shotgun from the wall rack. His dad then ran back into his bedroom. Through the open door Lew watched him step on to the window ledge and retrieve a key from above the curtain rail. With this he opened his lockbox and pulled out some shells.

Lew moved away from the door as his dad came back out loading the shotgun. When he had put on his boots and thrown a coat over his long-johns, he said, 'Take me to where you last saw him.'

They ran through the woods, his dad shouting Roh's name, which terrified Lew in case the men were still around. On the bluff were the ashes of a recently put-out fire. A shattered bottle and some cigarette butts lay around.

Lew, still crying, showed his dad where Sal had thrown Roh into the river. They scrambled down. His dad splashed out a little way, but the river was high and moving fast, and there was tree debris everywhere. Helplessly his dad shouted over the water, 'Roh, Roh.' Then he turned back towards the house and started to run, ignoring Lew, who called and couldn't keep up. When Lew got back, his dad wasn't home. He guessed he must have gone to Otto's. When he got there, his dad was on the phone. Shannon was sitting at the kitchen table. She seemed ordinary now, and not so simple, though her eyes were heavy and sad. She told them Otto was out coon-hunting with Bennet and the boys.

A half hour later Sheriff Siggy arrived, together with Bennet, Otto and Finn. Bennet, as ever, was in charge, and said that Lew should stay with Shannon while they all went out to look for Rohan.

Shannon made Lew some hot milk. He sat in her lap, still crying, and she combed her fingers through his hair. He told her what he had seen, but she remained quiet. Now there didn't seem anything strange about her at all, just a few teeth missing on one side, just her sad eyes. This nice lady had been raped, and Lew was ashamed for how he had been thinking about her, which he knew was sinful, and now, his body convulsing with the dregs of his tears, he felt himself falling back against her neck, sinking, with his brother, beneath the muddy waters of the Missouri.

Lew was woken by his dad the next morning. In a strange bed, he was confused for a moment; then his nightmare started.

Siggy dropped them back at the farm.

While Lew was frying eggs, his dad, sitting at the kitchen table, said, 'They told me Sal was with them coon-hunting up at Sharp Top.'

Lew turned to his dad. 'No, I saw him. I saw him do it. I—'

His father put his hand up. 'All right . . . all right.' He massaged his temples with his thumbs as if trying to work something through his mind. 'I told them I's going to take it to the state sheriff.'

At the sound of a car in the driveway, they both looked at the door. Bennet Burger appeared, taking off his hat as he entered.

'You find him, Mr B?' his dad said, standing up.

'Not yet, Clyde. Some boys are dragging the river down there.'

Mr Burger pulled the second chair out from the table. Settling his hulking body into it, he made a gesture for Lew's dad to sit, as if their home were now his. His pop slumped down. Mr B. awed Lew: those deep-set blue eyes beneath exploded grey eyebrows, that lantern jaw, and those crushed-together lips all warned that if you ever wronged him he would never forgive you. When he was around nothing existed but what he gave his attention to.

He looked at Lew. 'Son, I'd like to have a private word with your father.' He kept his eyes on him as Lew shifted the fry-pan off the stove and went out.

Lew waited on the porch steps until Burger left just twenty minutes or so later. When he ran back in, his pop, in the same chair, was staring into the floor and looked as if his bones had melted.

'They arrest him?' Lew thought of sitting on the chair in front of his pop, but couldn't bring himself to enter that space that had just been occupied – was still somehow occupied – by Bennet Burger.

'Mr B. just told me what he told me before: Sal was with them up at Sharp Top when you said you saw him.'

'No, Pop, I—'

'They think it was the same man, the man who done that thing to Shannon.'

'It was Mr Celli.'

'You saw another man. You confused him.'

'No I didn't, Pop. I saw him.'

'It was the middle of the night. You were lying in the bushes.'

'I saw him. He was no further than that stove from me.'

Reaching over, his pop took him by both wrists and pulled him closer. Trembling, he wouldn't look Lew in the eyes. 'Son, you listen to me. Sal is Annie's father and he didn't kill your brother, and I don't want you saying it to no one. You understand me?'

Lew felt as if his mind had sheared slightly out of his head, as if some tremendous force had borne down and twisted its weight upon the whole world, breaking things out of their shells. Snatching his wrists free, he ran. As he clattered down the porch steps he heard Annie shouting. She was cycling up the driveway. The sight of her filled him with fear and he started to run. Throwing her bike aside she chased him across the field. The thought of her catching him became the most terrifying thing he could imagine. As he got to the woods, he snatched up a rock and flung it. It hit her on the shoulder. He picked up another rock and entered the woods, running in a little way. After a moment he stopped to check if she were still following. She wasn't. Despite his sickening fear that she would, he felt almost grief-stricken that she hadn't. A cardinal fell and rose, fell and rose, as it flew by; little white wild flowers filled a sunny glade. His brother was dead. Nothing had changed.

Lew, hidden under the porch, waited until he saw his dad leave for the fields. Almost two weeks ago a snag boat found Roh's body caught in the branches of a tree that had collapsed into the river. Little clot, like an eagle's nest up high in a winter tree. Lew didn't go to the funeral. He snuck round to the grave afterwards, but couldn't believe it held his brother.

When his dad was out of sight, he slipped into the house. He needed clothes. He had already taken a blanket and was sleeping in the old summer kitchen, though he could hear critters and it frightened him to be out in the dark. A couple times, his pop had caught him sneaking in. He had taken hold of Lew, begging him to stay home, once shaking him with fury, but he just bore it until his dad released him and ran away again. During the day he wandered the woods, going to all the places his brother had been drawn to because of their light – the sinkhole, the ruins of the old mill, the cattail swamp near Miss Winters' place. He always expected to find Roh lying there, feeding on the light. He survived on potatoes out of the root cellar. Sometimes he hated his dad for not believing him, but he only had his dad, and he hated himself more for leaving the bedroom door open. All that day before Roh was killed he had been thinking about how neat it would be if it were just he and Annie. No fair he had to spend all his time looking after someone who wasn't right in the head. He didn't know what to do with his anger. When he got done hating his dad and himself, that feeling would keep swelling, and all at once he would think of Annie and be filled with the most wonderful anger toward her. Of all the people he could hurt, it was Annie he could hurt the most, and he needed there to be some hurt other than his in the world. Lying down, pressing his face into the earth, he would imagine Annie crying, begging him to talk to her. He would leave her crying sometimes, getting angrier and angrier, and sometimes he would forgive her, and Annie would come live with him and his pop. In that way they would get back at Mr Celli because he would have lost his daughter. His own daughter would know what he was.

Once he heard the Deere choke and rattle to life in the lower field, he snuck out from under the porch and into the house. On the table lay a letter from his dad. Annie must have written it for him, since his dad couldn't write. It begged him to be there at supper. It said he was worried sick and needed his son in this difficult time. At the bottom Annie had written, 'We love you, Lew.'

Confused tears, partly rage, started to his eyes. What they needed to write was that they were wrong, that his brother had been murdered. He got clothes and then went down to the root cellar to get more food. When he switched on the light, he saw that the shelves at the back were packed with sugar, coffee and flour. There were also a half-dozen oranges. Oranges, his dad knew, were his favourite thing in the world. For just a second he was thrilled to see them – he was so hungry. Then it struck him: these things had to have come from Celli's. Even if his dad could have afforded them, which he couldn't, it meant he had been in Celli's store, talking to him, giving him money. If not, he had accepted charity, which he never did, from the man who had killed Roh. He pulled everything off the shelves, smashing what he could, pulping the oranges. The only things he left intact were the vegetables his mom had canned, which they had never touched after her death.

He ran out of the cellar, straight to town through the fields, and approached Celli's Groceries through the alley between Novus and Snyder's. He couldn't bear the thought of anyone seeing him. Right outside his store Mr Celli was helping Tack Metzler load a couple of butane tanks on to the bed of his truck. Tack had a body like one of those blow-up clowns who came back up if you knocked them down. Mr Celli, a thin, nervous man, was at least a foot taller than Tack, but always did everything he could to make himself seem smaller than the person he was with, stooping and ducking his head. Tack looked like he was telling a funny story. Celli was listening with his mouth and eyes wide open, so eager he kept jumping the gun and laughing before Tack was done. And when Tack finally was, Celli squatted down on the sidewalk, howling and slapping the top of his head like Cheeta.

After Tack drove off, Celli remained outside. In his store apron, his arms akimbo, he now greeted the people who passed him as if he were the king of Main. Clear as anything Lew could see Mr Celli flinging his brother like a dead critter into the river. Now, here, two weeks later, he was laughing, shaking hands, as if Roh had never existed. Lew stepped out a little way from the garbage can he had been hiding behind and Celli saw him. His smile vanished and he drew back into the shadow of his awning and then into the store. Lew had seen it, the horror in Celli's face, his guilt. Again that terrible force seemed to twist down on everything in the world, wrenching rage out of his heart. He ran home and got the lockbox key from above the curtain rail. After he had filled his pockets with shells, he took his father's shotgun, which was almost as big as he was, and ran back into town. In that same alley, he loaded the shotgun. When Main was clear, he ran across and into the store, his heart pounding. Celli wasn't at the counter. Lew walked up the centre aisle and saw him on his knees, stocking shelves. The second he looked up, Celli fell backwards, hollering something in Italian. Lew aimed the gun over at some tins of molasses and fired. The kick knocked him off his feet. Mr Celli screamed, covered his head, and crawled like a lizard down the aisle. Frank appeared from the back.

'What the hell are you doing?' he shouted.

On his feet again, Lew fired into the ceiling, scattering plaster everywhere. Celli scrambled up behind Frank and ran out of the store.

Frank marched right down to him. He took the shotgun out of his hand, throwing it on to the floor, then flung Lew over his shoulder. Annie ran in, her dad screaming after her.

'Call Siggy,' Frank shouted.

She didn't move, staring at Lew, who was dangling helplessly over her brother's shoulder.

'Now, Annie!'

She ran into the back.

Lew felt he had no power in his limbs at all. Frank sat at the edge of the sidewalk, holding Lew firmly in his lap. He told people who were coming to the store that it was temporarily closed due to a burst pipe. Before they walked on, a number of them put their hands on Lew's head or his shoulder, telling him they were sorry for what happened to his brother.

Lewis entered the imposing office of Dr Walthrop, who was in charge of the Cedar Hills Sanatorium for Pediatric Mental Illness. He had arrived just this morning from juvenile detention. Three weeks had passed since he had shot up Sal's store.

The doctor sat writing in a large notebook at his desk. His broad shoulders made his head seem small. His eyes were very close-set beneath wild, greying hair that put Lewis in mind of an animal pelt.

Looking up, the doctor seemed not only surprised to see him but angry. 'Who told you to come in here?'

'The lady.'

'She did nothing of the sort, young man. This is my private office. You wait outside until I call you in.'

Lewis left. The lady didn't seem to think anything of him coming straight out. Before he could even sit down, the intercom buzzed. Just like the first time, with a smile, she told him to go right in.

Lewis entered tentatively and stood in front of the desk again.

The doctor was still writing, utterly absorbed. A full ten minutes passed before he looked up. It was as if he couldn't believe what he was seeing. Scowling so fiercely those close-set eyes seemed almost to merge into one, he shouted, 'What in God's name! Didn't I just tell you to wait outside?'

'But the lady—'

'Get out of my office!'

Lewis hurried out. He was shaking.

'Ma'am,' he said.

Smiling, the lady gestured toward the seats.

'But ma'am—'

'Just take a seat and I'll tell you when you can go in.'

Again, before he could sit down, the intercom buzzed, that noise now piercing him. With exactly the same smile and in exactly the same way, the woman asked him to go right in.

The doctor was examining a file. Lewis remained standing in front of his desk for what might have been another ten minutes before he looked up. This time he smiled and Lewis felt almost tearful with relief.

The doctor spoke very gently and kindly. 'Lewis, my name is Dr Walthrop and I'm here to help you get better. Do you understand?'

'Yes, sir.'

Anger flickered across the doctor's face again, as if there were something in this response he didn't like. He began to rap the end of his pen on the desk's green leather surface. Lewis's chest tightened, but a moment later Walthrop's smile returned. Getting up, he came around the desk, sat on the edge in front of him, and cleared his throat.

'Now, Lewis, according to your statements you believe that this man, Mr Salvatore Celli, killed your brother by throwing him into the river.'

'He did, sir. I saw him.'

'Forgive me for asking, but was your brother kicking, screaming?'

Lewis shook his head.

'So perhaps he was already dead?'

'I don't know, sir.'

'Well, in that case the first thing we can establish is that you didn't actually *see* this man kill your brother.'

Lewis didn't understand what he was getting at. 'I'm not lying, sir.'

'How did your brother get out of your bedroom? Your father said you kept it locked.'

'I went out, sir.'

'Why?'

Ashamed, Lewis looked down at the man's shoes. 'To go to the bathroom.'

'Why didn't you lock the door behind you?'

'Forgot.'

The doctor put his pen beneath Lewis's chin and eased his head back up. 'Lewis, one of the great truths about human beings is that none of us ever does anything we don't – at some level, for some reason – intend to do.'

'I didn't mean to leave it open. It wouldn't close.'

'I interviewed a number of your friends, including Sebastiana – the daughter of this Salvatore Celli – and gathered that you had actually struck your brother on the day before he died. Is this true?'

'He kept running off.'

Though nodding gravely, the doctor seemed deeply disappointed.

'She also revealed – in not so many words – that the two of you had had some contact of a sexual nature that day, and my impression was that your brother's behaviour had interrupted this, making you angry with him.'

'No.' Lewis shook his head.

'So you let him out of the house.'

'I didn't mean to.'

'You then claim that he went to some fire in the forest.'

'I saw the fire.'

'I'm a psychiatrist, Lewis. A good psychiatrist has an instinct for the truth. We're no different, in many ways, from the shamans and soothsayers of old. I am an *exceptional* psychiatrist. So let me tell you what really happened that night.'

'What really—'

The doctor tapped his pen hard against Lewis's forehead to stop him speaking.

'Bear with me. My sense is that during that earlier incident at the sinkhole, by interrupting your sex-play your brother became associated in what's known as your *subconscious* with Sebastiana's primary sexual protector – her father. So in replacing the truth of what happened—'

'I don't understand, sir.'

Lewis flinched as Walthrop rapped his forehead again. 'Then you'd best listen, young man. To replace the truth of what actually happened on the bluff, the image of Sebastiana's sexual protector – her father – activated earlier that day during the interrupted sex-play, appeared from your subconscious as his opposite – as his own destroyer.'

'I don't—'

'Lewis, how do you know I'm here in front of you?'

'What?' Lewis couldn't make sense of anything he was saying.

'You know because your mind' – another tap with the pen – 'interprets visual and other sensory data it receives and tells you I'm here. But when reality is something you don't want to see and can't accept, the mind either gets rid of it altogether or substitutes an image that both depends upon the reality and interprets events in a way that is acceptable to the psyche. It's a kind of short-circuiting. The image substituted for the truth is a metaphor, and though it seems absolutely real it is imagined, like the pictures you get in your head when you dream at night. The children in this institution, Lewis, are here because they are dreaming while they are awake or because they have dreamed while they were awake and believe those dreams to be true. Your memory of Mr Celli throwing your brother into the river is not real. It's a kind of dream image you substituted for the reality because the reality is unthinkable. Our work here is to have you accept and integrate that reality and move on. In short, Lewis, if you are to get better and go back home, you must come to accept the truth. And the truth . . .' He paused. 'The *truth*, Lewis, is that *you* killed your brother.'

Lewis couldn't respond for a moment, each word of this last statement, like the cars of a runaway freight train, shunting, one after another, into the dead end of his mind.

At last he found his voice. 'No. No, I didn't. I'm not lying. I didn't touch him.' His whole body was shaking again. He began to shout louder and louder. 'I didn't touch him. I'm *not* lying. Sal threw him in. I didn't touch him. I saw him. I *saw* him.'

Walthrop had already reached back to press something on his desk. Seconds later two nurses hurried in.

Four months had passed since Lewis had first arrived at Cedar Hills. He was sitting on the porch in the chair he liked. Under the seat was a little landscape of dried bubblegum. It comforted him to run his fingers over this familiar texture and pattern. Even after the years they had been down there, you could still smell the bubblegum on your fingers. It reminded him of the bubblegum stuck under the desks at school and made some part of his life seem surer. He had killed his brother. He accepted that now. There had been no fire in the forest. He had led Roh up to one of the bluffs above the river and had pushed him in. He could almost remember it.

That strange older boy with the rotten teeth appeared again from behind the big sycamore. Crab-like, he began to approach.

Staff notes. 9/5/52
Patient: Lewis Tivot
The patient has developed a number of obsessive behaviours, most prevalent just after he wakes in the morning. He rubs various things with his fingers and smells them. A pine cone, for example, which he keeps under his pillow, some caulking a workman left behind after he had fixed the broken window in the east wing, and, on Wednesday, he would smell Nurse Evans' hands as soon as she entered the ward, since she washed her hair every Wednesday morning and the smell of the shampoo lingered on her fingers. Nurse Evans has been instructed not to indulge this request. He also follows a fixed

route around the sanatorium and appears to be making sure that everything is the same. He was disturbed when they repainted the walls in the shower room because there was a mould mark there that he seemed to think looked like a human face. He did not appear to believe it was anything more than mould, however. There is also only one seat he likes to sit in on the porch and he will wait if another patient is in it. He always asks the duty nurse when he wakes up how long he's been here. Nurse Kolks one morning, in a joking manner, told him he had just arrived. This resulted in a nervous reaction and the patient had to be sedated (see action log). Nurse Kolks was given an official letter of reprimand. The patient has been waking most nights with nightmares. As requested by Dr Walthrop, the duty nurse encourages him to remember and relate these nightmares and we are recording them.

The boy frightened Lewis, with his furtive but determined approach. He had awful teeth, black and yellow. Lewis had noticed him in the dining hall wincing as he ate. The boy hesitated and seemed to be making a signal toward the sycamore tree. Lewis wondered if he might become like this. Digging out a piece of the dried gum with his nail, he smelled it. Was he himself mad? If he was, he wouldn't know. He didn't understand most of what Dr Walthrop said, but one time he did say it was a good thing he had made up that story about Mr Celli and believed it. It meant that some part of him was good and couldn't stand the part that had killed his brother. But this idea of dreaming while you were still awake frightened him. His nightmares were becoming increasingly real, as if some part of him didn't know which world to believe. Last night, Annie and Roh had been swimming in the sinkhole, the water all ablaze with sunlight. He was standing high above, on the rock face, and they were calling for him to join them. Roh could speak like a normal boy. He went to jump in, but something snagged his shoulder. It was the long, gnarled branch that came out of the stump of a tree beside him. He freed himself, but as he went to jump again, he saw darkness seeping up from the bottom of the pool, as if ink had been released. In a moment the glittering pool turned black. Annie and his brother began to scream and were drawn down into the dark waters. He turned around and the tree had become Mr Celli. Sal Celli had saved him. Sal was all gnarly like the tree, and his right arm – the arm that had held – *no*, hadn't hadn't *hadn't* held his brother – was huge and muscular. It fell all the way to the ground with veins like roots growing through it. But it seemed as if Sal couldn't move this arm, like the arm Linus got polio in.

That strange boy stood close now, though he was still facing the sycamore.

Dear Lew,

   I wanted to rite you sooner but I was upset. Papa said you was trying to shoot him but Frankie says you was just shooting the store up. A man who said he was going to make you beter talked to me he seemed to know what I was going to say before I said it. It felt bad like I said things I shouldn't have said but he said it would make you beter he ▮▮▮▮▮▮▮▮▮. I went to see your dad but he didn't seem to want to see me ▮▮▮▮▮▮▮. I did help him rite you that letter though. I miss you Lew. I saw a wolf yesterday but Frankie says it was a stray dog. I dreemed we lived in the trees and had children and they all lived in the trees ecsept for some who lived in the river and could breath underwater and people looked for us but we could go inside the trees. A skunk sprayed Melvin. His mom washed him with tomato juice so we call him tomato head. The Luxton boys took over our fort next to Medow Branch. I told them to get out but Marvin ▮▮▮▮▮▮ ▮▮▮. In Vernon a boy had a farm scale fall on him. I miss you and I want you beter and I will come see you when it is alowed. ▮▮▮▮▮▮▮▮ We can meet at the tree. I wish ▮▮▮▮▮▮ ▮▮▮. Get beter.

   Love,
   Annie

Turning around with ceremonial slowness, the boy with the bad teeth addressed Lewis. 'It's here, killed its own son on the bloody birch, tore him to the winds and cried out, "Hail the glorious golden city, I'm pressing, pressing on the upward way, new heights I'm gaining every day." Your name is?'

'Lewis.'

'Lewis. Lewis of the ville, the slugger. Have you hit them out of the park? Home run!' He smiled, mirthless, with those yellow-black teeth.

The boy's eyes frightened Lewis. They seemed evil. 'What's your name?'

'Kane. That's the two of us, carved from the bloody birch, his blood-gone-water still on us, salty. Licked off by dogs. You know those dogs with their tongues round their noses.' He laughed as if he were trying laughter out for the first time. 'We killed our brothers, the two of us.' He went for that laugh again but froze in the middle of it.

'Why did you say that?'

The boy had now sat on the edge of the porch. 'Listen, Lewis of the ville, the slugger. Have you hit them out of the park? Home run! It's at the back of your neck. Like an octopus. You can feel it in your throat. One of its legs is in your throat. It scratches around in there. It knows what you're thinking. It tells them. Wa-Kon-Te is trying to find you. Can you hear him? He's out there. He shall give you a sign. It is the no dark valley, the sunlight, sunlight in my soul today, the love divine all loves excelling, joy of heaven to earth come down. Wa-Kon-Te. Dying God's last breath. Breath of death to give life. Blood of *Jeeezus* Christ. You can hear him in the trees. He shall find you, Lewis of the ville, the slugger. Have you hit them out of the park? Home run!'

From the moment he appeared in my office, I knew the Tivot boy would be a fascinating subject. His nightmares are clearly sexual in nature. He talks about the 'sinkhole' being a place at once of attraction and danger. In one dream it's surrounded by what he calls 'pricker' bushes; in another by sharp stones. It is clearly the vagina dentata. It glitters and goes dark. It lures and then sucks those in it to the centre of the earth (earth womb). Salvatore has now become—? (I shall try to find a name for this.) His traits are multifold, sometimes frightening, sometimes comforting. Protean. Other salient traits: he is both powerful and wounded (Fisher King?); he seems to have become, somehow, the genius of the boy's dreams (Genius of Dreams. G.O.D. Interesting.) Is he the teeth around Sebastiana's vagina? Oh, come on, Walthrop, you can do better than that! In this most recent dream Salvatore's arm is clearly a phallus.

NB Tell night-duty nurse to wake Tivot up three times a night. Try to get down more dreams. Need catalogue of dreams. Make sure to get every detail. I will try to develop a schematic for his dreams, create an overarching narrative in which those dreams can be resolved to his psyche's satisfaction.

NB Ask Jane for an extra week with Danny this summer and remind her that my son should call *me* Daddy, not that dumb-ass dentist. The boy is getting confused.

Lewis watched Kane walk away, sidling along the edge of the institution and around the corner. How had that boy known he had killed his brother? What had he called it? Wa-Kon-Te. Last breath of the dying God. It lives in the trees. Had he said that? That it lived in the trees? Kane was mad. Lewis of the ville, slugger. Stupid dumkopf. Something seemed to scratch in his throat. He reached to his nape, but suddenly felt afraid to put his hand there. He could almost feel it, the pulpy flesh, sending its signals. Stupid. Forcing himself, he put his hand on the back of his neck. Nothing. He walked out into the grounds. The wind had built a little. He kept checking the back of his neck now, which felt raw and cold. He went to the big sycamore, alive with the wind. Suddenly something hit his face, fell to the ground. On the grass, its mouth pulsing open and shut, lay a hatchling, a blue jay perhaps. He lifted it, wet and helpless in his hand, and shuddered to see that one of its legs was a misshapen stump. All of a sudden he imagined the chick reaching up to him out of this semi-death, its head and beak becoming huge, and he dropped it. Power of helplessness, of death. Last breath of God. The sign. Kane said there would be a sign. Wa-Kon-Te. The last breath of God. The life of death.

Mr Tivot was taking Annie to visit Lew at Cedar Hills today. It had been near sixteen months since she had last seen him, though she had written every few days. Dressed and ready, she packed some things she thought he might like: a fossil she was pretty sure was a shark's tooth; a pile of funnies from the paper; a huge old liberty head penny, thick and brown as a Hershey Bar; and her mom had helped her bake a little apple pie.

She trod quietly around her papa, who was reading the *Jackson and Pisgah Herald* in the sitting room. He hadn't really responded when she told him she was going to see Lew. Other people thought it unnatural that she was in contact with the boy who, as far as the town was concerned, had tried to kill her father.

In the kitchen, her mom was wrapping the pie carelessly in grease-proof paper. Annie put her arms around her waist. Her mom was still in her white bathrobe, which smelled of cigarettes, and which she had taken to wearing all day sometimes. At the church social Annie had heard Mrs Metzler call her Marilyn Monroe. Aaron told her this was an actress. His brother had seen her in a film called *Love Nest* wearing only a towel. She squeezed her mom harder.

'Little cat, you have to let go of me.' She patted Annie's arm. 'I'm tired today.'

'Mom, Seamus said he's in a madhouse.'

'Is for disturbed children, this place.'

'Do you think he'll be better now?'

'I don't know, darling.'

She didn't let go. Her mom always seemed to Annie to be dreaming of escape, staring out of the kitchen window or standing at the back door with her cigarette. Her mom abruptly drew in a deep breath. Sometimes it seemed to Annie that her mom only smoked to help her remember to breathe. Like Papa, she was, as people would say with a whisper, a Cath-o-lik, though all that remained of this was the big silver crucifix around her neck, which was as disturbing to some of the women in town as a shrunken head might have been. She also had a painted wooden crucifix in her bedroom, blood leaking from Christ's head, side, hands and feet. Much better, Annie thought, than that statue of Jesus in church, which made him look (she crossed herself as she thought it) simple-minded. She loved His wonderful agony, His eyes looking up to heaven as His body, all bone and sinew, was drawn to the earth. Her mom said He was dead and alive at the same time, that of all the gods only Christ was ever dead and alive at the same time. She seemed personally proud of this, like Papa when he was talking about some Italian baseball player. This Christ seemed so much a part of her mom's sadness: she was here and not here, between this kitchen and whatever place she saw through the window. One day she simply wouldn't remember to take that breath. A part of her was already long gone, but most men and women in this town couldn't keep their eyes off the part that was still here.

'Do you think we'll be able to have him in the house?'

'I don't think so, darling.'

Gently her mom unhooked Annie's arms, lit a cigarette, and looked out of the open back door into the yard, which was littered with tools and car parts beneath the branches of that old horse chestnut. 'Heavens,' she clucked. 'We say only if he keeps tidy the yard he can use it.'

Her papa came in. 'Where's Frankie?'

'Darn, my crystal ball,' her mom said, 'I leave it upstairs.'

'He's in his room.' Annie hated it when her mom provoked him.

'Don't you get damn clever with me, woman. You say I know, you say I don't know. None of this damn funny garbage. You hear me?' His chin trembled with fury. 'Don't bother get out of your sleeping clothes. Look at you. *Sei una puttanaccia!* You never clean anything in this damn house. *Va al inferno!*'

Taking her papa's hand, Annie led him back to his armchair in the sitting room, and sat in his lap as she did at least three times a month when he woke her in the middle of the night to sit with him because he was having a nightmare. She let him spit out his last few curses at the kitchen doorway. It always pained her, the way he would act up. Around men, especially, he had a silly, exaggerated manner. Frank hated it, said papa acted like a dog, did everything but roll over and show his belly. Her dad seemed even to get sick of himself at times, and for a few days he would storm around in a foul mood, finding fault, calling all his friends *testa di merda* and *figlio di puttana*. Only Annie would listen to him as he raged, telling her about the people he had beaten up in the past for looking at him sideways, recalling all his perfect comebacks for some *sumaro* or *finocchio*, and when that wasn't enough he would have to beat them. Paff! Paff! He'd fling out his wiry arms, spit flying from his gritted teeth, his face going red. Finally he would calm, calling her his *bambina*, saying he was going to run away with her.

He softened now. 'When you leaving?'

She checked the clock over the mantle. 'Mr Tivot should have been here a while ago.'

'Are they gonna fix him so he don't try to kill me again?'

Annie didn't say anything.

'You bringing him that pie?'

She nodded.

'We have oranges in the store. The boy he likes oranges.'

Frank clattered down the stairs.

'Eh, Lone Ranger,' her papa shouted. 'Where you going?'

'Linus's. Helping his dad spray his trees.'

'You helping *his* dad? Why, you his son? Something I don't know with your mama?'

'He's paying me.'

'Paying you to be his son? I should pay you, eh? Good deal, uh. You gonna give me some of this money?'

Annie hated it when her papa said these stupid things, and the way Frank would just stare at him with tired disgust, waiting for it to be over.

'Anyone else need a son? Son for sale, no good for nothing. I put an ad out, uh.'

Annie could see that Frank was about to retaliate. Why couldn't anyone in her family just walk away? She leapt up from her papa's lap.

'Frankie, I have to show you something.' Taking his hand, she led him out of the house. It was like pulling a powerful dog on a leash.

'Why can't he damn well – just *once* – let me walk through the house?'

'Are you really spraying?'

'No. Me, Jude, and Linus are going to try out Linus's new rifle down the quarry. Tell Mom I'll clean up the stuff in the yard when I get back.'

Snatching Annie up into his arms, he smothered her face in baby kisses. Squealing, she pushed him away. As he put her down, Clyde appeared. He was walking.

Coming to a halt in front of them, he said quietly, 'I'm afraid my truck has . . . stopped working. We'll have to go see Lew another day.' Looking away, he placed his hand over his chin and half his mouth. Annie got the sense that he wished he could cover up his whole face.

'Use my truck,' Frank said. 'I can drive Tatmeyer's Buick. I'm fixing a dent for him.' He knew as well as Annie how difficult it was for Mr Tivot to accept anything, so he threw Annie the key and hurried off behind the store. Staring into the ground, Mr Tivot looked in real pain.

Annie put the truck key into his reluctant hand. She knew he hated to be in town where people might see him. 'I'm going to get some things. If you start the truck, I'll be out in a second.'

*

Mr Tivot hadn't brought anything and eyed Annie's gifts with concern. Annie had long ago given up trying to get him to speak and for the three hours of the drive looked out of the window or stole glances at his profile. She had noticed some small changes in him since what had happened with Roh: every now and then his face would concentrate, as if he knew he had forgotten something vital. As if you could forget your heart or your hands. And there was an added agony today because his desire to see his son had forced him to override the scrupulousness that prevented him from taking anything from anyone. He was in a borrowed truck and Annie had put money for gas, which she had taken from her savings, on the dashboard as soon as she had got in. He fascinated her: she couldn't understand how someone could survive without having anyone to talk to or touch. She had never seen him so much as jostle Lew's hair, and often wondered what his life with his wife must have been like.

When they arrived, they were told to wait on a bench in the gardens. Annie asked Mr Tivot to hold the bag of candies, so it would seem as if he had brought them, while she held the pie and the oranges on her lap. She felt slightly sick with anticipation. Lew soon appeared, escorted by a nurse. Putting her gifts on the bench, Annie ran to him. He looked as if he hadn't slept in weeks and barely returned her embrace. The nurse said she would come back for him in an hour and that the doctor would like to see Mr Tivot before he left.

Sitting between them on the bench, Lew didn't seem in the least interested in their gifts.

'What d'you do round here?' Annie asked.

'Nothing,' he said. 'They keep waking me up. I have to tell them my dreams.'

He touched the back of his own neck nervously a couple of times, for some reason, then bent forward and seemed to be feeling for something under the bench.

'Have you been having bad dreams?' she said.

He nodded.

Annie saw that his dad was leaning away from Lew, covering his own nose and mouth with one hand and staring at him intensely. Abruptly he got up, and without a word walked toward the main house.

'Pop,' Lew called, as shocked as Annie by his sudden departure. But he just kept walking and entered the main doors.

'I guess he's going to see that doctor,' Annie said.

Lew closed up again. He hadn't looked at her once.

'Heidi got chiggers,' she said. 'She showed 'em to me.'

He didn't respond to this either. After a moment he said quietly, 'I'm sorry I shot the store up. I want to say sorry to your pop.'

'I'll tell him.'

'I'm sorry I said those things about him. Dr Walthrop said it was because I did something I didn't want to do, so I blamed him because . . . I don't really know why. I don't understand him. But he said it wasn't lying because I believed myself and that's different. Weren't like I knew I was lying, I mean.'

Annie nodded. He was touching his nape again.

'Did you hurt your neck?'

He snatched his hand away. 'No.'

Annie's insides felt as if they had been scraped out. Why wouldn't he look at her?

Half turning to her now, he whispered: 'I feel them sometimes. But they're afraid of Wa-Kon-Te.'

'Of what?'

'Yesterday, out by those trees, I found a squirrel and the side that was up was okay, but the other side was all maggots. It's the last breath and it's death and life, like the old Hallelujah Jesus from the shadows.'

'What? What's Wa-Kon-Te?'

'Don't say it so loud.' He looked at her for the first time, and with fear. 'You seen a hawk eat a sparrow? I seen one do it under my window. And there's nothing left 'cept pin feathers. And that breath comes and blows on it and it's cottonwood. Like years ago out by the river when you said it was snow. Summer snow. 'Member?'

She nodded. He looked at her now and appeared to actually see her, to have come back into himself, jumping from image to image until he had arrived at what connected them. Annie had the dimmest sense that he had just done something heroic, struggling back to her through the world of this awful place.

'Where were the chiggers?' he said.

'All on her butt.'

He smiled. She thought he was reaching to his neck again, but he was just rubbing his nose.

She got off the bench and sat on the grass. 'The Luxtons are still in our camp.'

'We'll set traps for them.' He sat down next to her. 'We'll dig holes and cover them in leaves. I read how to make catapults, like the Romans. We could have one on the other side of the branch.'

'We could fire rotten eggs,' she said. 'And cow pies.'

They both laughed. Annie lay down on her back, idly ripping at the grass.

Lew pulled out a couple of liquorice twists from his goodie bag, gave one to her, and lay down as well. The twists jutting from their mouths, they flung grass into the air and watched it drift above them.

'We're going to build a fortress,' he said. 'Behind the pricker bushes, and the only way into it's going to be a secret tunnel.'

Annie didn't respond. She couldn't speak. She was too happy.

Clyde sat in the small chair in front of the doctor's desk, holding his hat in his lap.

'So Mr Tivot,' Walthrop said, 'how does your son seem to you?'

'Seems all right. I'm wondering when—'

Walthrop cut him off. 'Your son was the perfect case.' He looked out of the window, drumming his pen on the desk for a while before turning back. 'Creativity at its source: in wrongness; in the lie.'

Clyde nodded as if someone had put a gun to his head and told him to nod.

'Original sin and a great imagination, Mr Tivot. It's all you need.'

'Sir?'

'For everything – *everything*: art, culture, religion.'

'I know Lew done a bad thing, but—'

'My son calls me by my first name, Mr Tivot.'

'Sir?'

'What kind of man becomes a dentist?'

'I don't know, sir.'

'I understand your wife died.'

'Yes, sir.'

Walthrop nodded slowly, but seemed agitated, staring right through Clyde. He switched tracks. 'Must be nice to farm. Physical work. Tolstoy used to join the peasants sometimes, spend a day harvesting with a scythe. Said he was never happier. I understand that. I love the smell of farms. *Real* smells, not the damn carbolic of this place.'

'Doctor, when can my son come home?'

Again Walthrop went blank. After a moment he murmured, 'I feel close to Lewis. I have a son. I know it's a strange thing to say, but he's a very beautiful boy – Lewis, I mean. Perfectly beautiful. Doesn't seem possible sometimes when you look at him.'

Leaning forward, Clyde put his hands on the doctor's desk as if he were about to crawl across it to this man.

Walthrop remained blank, lost in thought. Abruptly then, and with a flicker of what seemed like anger, he snatched a file out of one of his desk drawers and threw it across to Clyde. 'Sign the bottom of the last three sheets. You can take him home today.'

Linus fired again, the sound echoing through the quarry, and another bottle shattered. He had the rifle propped on a sandbag. Securing it against his shoulder with his chin, he cleared and reloaded the chamber with his right hand. Polio had made his left arm useless. Frank and Jude sat behind him on the bed of Jude's truck, drinking beer.

'Yeski Martin,' Jude, who was getting as fat as his father, sighed out. 'She was in the bleachers yesterday with her legs wide open, and man-oh-man I could see clear to the Promised Land. She knew it, too.'

'Heard she's dating a marine from KC,' Frank said. 'Bet he don't know she's fifteen.'

Another rifle crack; another bottle shattered.

'It's me she wants,' Jude said. 'She was taxiing me in. No panties.' Opening his legs, he made elaborate gestures toward his crotch. Suddenly he farted loudly and began to rock his enormous body back and forth, shouting, 'Abort, abort entry, abort. No, Captain, I'm going in. I'm going to land this baby.' He farted raucously again. 'You've been hit. Abort, I tell you. Never, I'm going in, Captain.'

Linus, who had finished another perfect round, sat up, laughing at Jude's performance.

'How is it' – Frank was leaning away, covering his nose – 'that you can fart at will?'

Jude took hold of his own stomach. 'Plenty of storage.'

'That's another six,' Linus said.

'You've won.' Frank got himself another beer. 'You always win. What did I get, five, five and four? Jude?'

'I nipped one, I'm sure.'

'Zilch,' Linus corrected.

'Yeski,' Jude said, 'is the most racked and stacked, but Helga is the cutest.'

Frank disagreed. 'Esta's the cutest.'

Linus looked dubious. 'She's got a nose on her, that girl.'

'You know what she does with that nose?' Jude wiggled his eyebrows. 'Let's just say she's very flexible.'

'Shut up.' Frank flicked at his cheek.

'Esta wants to teach English like Miss Kelly,' Jude said.

Linus got up, brushing himself off. 'Do you think she's a virgin?'

'Esta?' Frank said.

'No, Miss Kelly. How old is she?'

Frank shrugged. 'Don't know. Thirty-something.'

'There's no way' – Jude raised a finger – 'any man has journeyed to her dark places.'

70

The boys laughed. They were reading *Heart of Darkness* in Miss Kelly's class.

'Bet she's a tiger in the sack, though,' Jude went on. 'Looks the type.'

Jude gestured for the rifle. 'Set up them bottles. Last round. Winner takes all.'

Linus ran off to set up six more bottles, his useless arm flapping at his side. Frank finished his Schiltz and reached for another.

'Whoa, easy on the beer, Tonto. Is that six?'

When Linus got back, Jude, without getting off the truck bed, fired the rifle with one hand, holding his beer with the other and saying 'damn' between each shot.

Linus tapped his fist against Frank's arm. 'I'll tell you who's going to be the cutest girl in town in a few years.'

Frank frowned slightly and didn't meet his friend's shy glance. 'She's gone to see the Tivot boy.'

'At the nut house?' Jude said.

'Yeah, gone with his dad.'

'Don't your dad mind?'

'Bellyached like he always does.'

Jude missed his last bottle. 'Well, the boy did try to take his *cojones* off with a twelve-gauge.'

'You need something a damn sight bigger than a twelve-gauge to hit my dad's *cojones*.'

His friends didn't respond to this and Frank could feel his face burning.

'I've got to go.' Releasing a long-held breath, just like his mom, he jumped down off the truck.

Walking away from the quarry, Frank looked back at his two closest friends. He felt disconnected from them. He had drunk too much and not enough: he wasn't yet free of his mind, as he could be sometimes, like a ghost, with his life behind him. What Linus just said about Annie troubled him. She had such a grown-up face, but was so innocent. She loved to sit in the laps of the old men who played cards on the porch of the Franklin. He would see an old hand resting on her shoulder or knee, and it would knot his stomach. He was so mad at his mom. It wasn't his job to be telling Annie her body could get her into a world of trouble and to stop throwing herself around like an old rag doll. All he wanted was for her to be safe. Safe. He wanted her to stay away from the Tivot boy and that unlucky family; to meet some nice guy in college and have kids. He had already told her that if she didn't start acting like a lady she would end up like Miss Kelly. *There's no way any man has journeyed to her dark places.* He smiled. Arriving at the river, he headed west to Maud and Magnus's place. Miss Kelly had taught English at Hickman for over fifteen years, nervous and bone-thin in her bobby socks and squeaky Oxfords, with that crazy frizzy hair and those ridiculous glasses. Not ugly, though, just buried somehow, in nerves, hair and glasses, flying around town on her bike, singing hymns. But how many married women were any happier? Not his mom.

He cut across what had once been Heavenly Haven's crazy golf course, now overgrown, and began to get excited about bringing Esta here. She had spent the first ten years of her life in Boston, but her parents, who were teachers, had come here seven years ago with a crazy notion about returning to the land. She had changed so much in this last year, had filled out, grown her hair a little longer. Sometimes she joined the group he hung out with, but was so different from those other girls, quiet, with that odd, bony, slightly skew face of hers. One night she turned up at the Kar-a-Nova, and he had laughed at how badly she danced. She came to the flood plain also, where a dozen of them built a fire, drank, and horsed around, but she went completely quiet, clutching her knees. He wondered if she were judging them a waste of time. But she joined in their makeshift game of foxes and hares, dodging him with impressive athleticism, missing the point, until he cheated, running directly to her. She didn't let him kiss her, though; said he hadn't caught her and that was that. Afterwards, walking back to the cars with her, he asked why she had been so quiet. She said it was as if the bottom had fallen out of her personality: she had been seized with shyness. He had never heard anyone speak like that. *Seized.* Who used the word *seized*, except to describe an engine? And he noticed her lovely but bitten-down fingers and the green of her eyes, and all in all she appeared before him complete and astonishing, only as someone you have known for years can. He felt seized. Yes, exactly right. Seized.

They met a couple of times at Snyder's for malts, and she agreed to go out with him this Friday. He was going to bring her here and get her to climb with him on to the roof of the cabin the Garrisons used for storage. He, Jude and Linus used to climb on it all the time. A maple gave shade above it and there was a view of the lake. That's where he planned to kiss her. Annie said it was a neat idea. Then again, climbing a tree and swinging down on to a roof was pretty normal behaviour for Annie. He sensed Esta would be game, though, and was here to check the tree wasn't too difficult to climb.

As he got closer to the cabins, which were spread out through the woods, he became more cautious. Maud – Dragon Lady – who everyone said was a drunk and beat her husband, had once caught the three of them, when they were kids, on that roof. She marched them into her house, where they were sure she was going to call their parents. Instead, she brought them cookies and milk, and told them how naughty she had been as a little girl. It was strange to see her soften, to realize that the raw-red in her face wasn't drink or anger: she was just high-coloured.

Now he could see that one of the cabins, closer to the main house, was occupied, a sweet little convertible Buick out front. Climbing the maple was easy, but just as he was about to swing down on to the roof, his heart clenched: Magnus was standing, smoking his pipe, just behind the occupied cabin. Frank kept very still. Strange to see Magnus in overalls. Usually he wore a moth-eaten tweed jacket and a little hunting hat with a quail-feather in the band. Tall, frail, genteel, he spoke with an accent some said was English. He had changed the name of this place from Heavenly Haven to The Lodge, and wandered around it like a lord surveying his estate. He would kiss women's hands and could quote poems from memory. He also spent a lot of time with Bennet and his cronies. His dad said it was just so he could get free booze, and if you blinked your beer was down his throat. Frank lowered himself very gently on to the roof, and when he glanced again, just a second later, Magnus was gone. But where? He had disappeared. Frank waited for twenty minutes before climbing down.

When he got home, Annie was in the kitchen eating a sugar sandwich.

'They released Lew,' she said immediately. 'We brought him home. Just like that.'

'Just like that? He's been there over a year.'

'Mr Tivot ran out of that doctor's office with a piece of paper in his hand. It was like we was escaping. We even left Lew's clothes and stuff behind.'

'So is he going to try to shoot Dad again?'

Annie didn't say anything for a moment, just stared at two squirrels warring in the horse chestnut.

'I don't think so,' she said.

He laughed. 'You don't think so?'

She kept her eyes on the squirrels. 'I don't think so.'

Maud was cooking split pea soup. She was a little round woman, her small features marooned on a brick-red, bloated, scowling face. Magnus entered the kitchen with the slow, brittle grace of some exotic insect. Close to six and a half feet tall, he had a mottled, skull-like head.

'Did you fix that leaky roof in twelve?' she asked.

'Oh, my dear' – he removed his hat – 'I did try. Unfortunately, I became rather dizzy. My head's far enough off the ground, you wouldn't think heights—'

'Did you damn well do it or not?'

'I really was afraid I would fall. I haven't, truthfully, been feeling myself lately.'

'So you didn't do it?'

'Madam, tomorrow I shall wear blinkers and endeavour—'

'Then what *did* you do today?'

'Oh, maintenance of a general order – prophylactic maintenance.'

She took hold of the pan, lifted it slightly and slammed it down. He jerked back a little.

'I could have been a rich woman,' she said, almost to herself, 'living in a decent place, married to a decent man.' She turned to him. 'I swear I hate you so much.'

He seemed to have become fascinated by the counter top, rubbing it with his elegant hand.

She tried to calm down, staring back into the green, bubbling liquid, but couldn't stop herself. Turning to him again, she shouted: 'What in God's name do you ever do? I bought this place. I run this place. I do the books. I clean the rooms. I fix the cabins. I buy the groceries. I do the cooking. Jesus, *what* do you do?'

'My dear, I do wish you wouldn't take the Lord's name in vain.'

He ducked quickly as the wooden spoon, with which she had been stirring the soup, ricocheted off the wall beside him.

'God damn you,' she screamed.

He quickly escaped the house. Outside, he took a deep breath and a moment later his face looked as serene as ever, as if what had just happened were no more than a sharp smell on a passing breeze. He had a leisurely smoke of his pipe and then went to cabin seven, which he had commandeered as his own, since The Lodge was never full. It contained everything he owned. A large picture of the Holy Virgin hung on one wall. On a shelf beside the bed, on which he now laid himself, stood a half-dozen books: *The Complete Works of Longfellow, The Poems of John Donne, The Birth of Tragedy, L'Immoralist*, and *The Decline of the West, Volume 2*. On an old wood and iron travelling trunk beside the bed, two frames each held a yellowing picture: one of a woman in a fur coat and flapper hat, standing in front of a fountain; the other of a British officer smoking a pipe, his arm curled affectionately around the barrel of a cannon.

Reaching up, Magnus pulled the hefty Spengler off the shelf. Propping himself against the headboard, he slotted on a pair of reading glasses and opened it at a page where a playing card had been inserted. Now he licked a finger and turned an onion-leaf page, letting his eyes play over the text, a canny smile surfacing periodically, as if he were thinking, 'Oh, Spengler, you old dog.' Or he would look briefly dubious and then indulgent, as if he had spotted some specious reasoning, but had decided to let his old friend get away with it – *this* time. Finally, after no more than five minutes, with a sigh of pleasure, he replaced the playing card and closed the book, leaving it on his chest. For the next three hours, he lay as still as a medieval effigy, staring out of the small window at the trees until the room grew dark. After lighting a kerosene lamp, he ate a few crackers with cheese, and took a moment to decide between his three records: 'Muskrat Ramble', 'Chinatown', or 'Fidgety Feet'. Deciding on the last, he put the player on repeat mode and returned to his bed. On it, as the same song played over and over and over again, he writhed like a man being electrocuted.

PISGAH, 1954

Annie was sitting high up on the steep bank of the stream, looking down on Raj, Nora, and Lew, who were paddling in the water, turning over stones and looking for fossils. Alvin hung upside down, sloth-like, from a tree limb above them.

'When exactly do you go back?' Annie called.

'Couple weeks,' Raj said.

Lew looked up. 'Why do you have to go back there?'

'I was only here for the summer.'

'Do you want to leave?' Annie said.

Raj shook his head. 'I hate it there.'

Alvin let himself go, landing with a splash in the stream.

'You've soaked my dress, you stupid dumkopf,' Nora shouted.

Alvin grinned devilishly, full of his manic energy. 'We can hide him; keep him in Lew's barn with the pigs.'

'I wish you could live with us,' Nora said.

'You could live with me,' Lew suggested. 'Don't guess my pop would mind.'

'Why can't you stay with Miss Winters?' Annie asked.

'She's not my family.'

'Water moccasin!' Alvin shouted, pointing at Nora's legs. Nora screamed, but there wasn't anything. She chased Alvin, but he was too quick, climbing that same tree.

'I wish we could all live in a house together,' Annie said.

Nora waded out of the stream and sat on the pale shale of the far bank, her body in a clear pool of sun, her blonde head in leaf shade. She had turned her skirt up, tucking the hem into the elastic around her waist, and with most of her strong, pale and wet thighs exposed was sorting carefully through her collection of promising stones, gathered in her lap. Annie, from her high vantage, became aware that Raj and Lew, as well as Alvin, hanging once more from his branch, were also staring at Nora. It was a captivating sight: Nora's childish attention to those stones in her lap contrasting strangely with that new, womanly body. In the bright sun on her soaked, cream dress, Annie could see her bra clearly, and that her nipples were erect. It was motherly, childish, sexual, and Annie felt strangely excited and disturbed, could almost feel that weight of warm stones between her own legs. Wrapping her arms around her chest, she felt like a silly girl: how childish her make-believe games and notions were. An intense loathing for herself spread – a scum of skin upon the small and stagnant pond of her.

Abruptly then, Alvin freed them all, singing, 'I can see your panties; I can see your panties.'

'Shut up you.' Sitting up, Nora pushed her dress between her legs.

The spell broke. Annie's self-loathing sank back into her, and the boys returned to their search.

Annie had never felt quite this vulnerable. She was heartbroken that Raj was leaving. He and Lew were hers, though she felt a little jealous of them sometimes. Miss Winters' house was close to Lew's, so Raj and Lew were often together without her, sharing the mysterious life of boys. She would find them in the fields with stick rifles, or playing basketball at that hoop nailed to a tree in the field behind Harper's place, or at the sinkhole. She wanted the three of them to be always together, imagined them like the Lost Boys, or the Pied Piper's children, never found, just the sound of laughter in the rocks. Raj was completely comfortable with Lew, but shy around her when Lew wasn't with them. And her relationship with Lew was strange. They kissed sometimes, and things had gone a little further than that. It was awkward, though, and for some reason, as if it were an unspoken pact, they never touched each other in front of Raj.

*

After a little while longer at the branch, Annie led them through the woods to Mrs Barnacle's house. Annie had money to give her. For years she had been a part of this masquerade, pretending she was paying Mrs Barnacle for the sale of her knitted goods and eggs in her papa's store. In fact it was the money Mrs Barnacle had given to Mr B for rent, which he always returned to her, as well as some extra put in from the church collection. They all knew she couldn't bear to be a charity case.

Mrs Barnacle both fascinated and horrified Annie a little. She had been on the wagon trains all the way from East to West as a girl. Her family had settled in Washington State until they had been ruined by a cattle-killing winter, from which she remembered only that they had to suckle her younger brother on a rag soaked in cow's blood. The man she married moved her halfway back across the country, settling her in the house she lived in now. She had a number of miscarriages, and the two children she did birth died in infancy. Her husband was always away, looking for places to homestead, he said, or gold-mining, though she was never really sure what he did. His absences stretched into years, though he would write letters. She got a job as the first female mail carrier in the state. Finally his letters stopped. She heard nothing more from him for thirty years until a young man, his image, appeared at her door. Refusing her invitation to come in, he handed her three hundred dollars, said only that he was deeply ashamed, and hoped she would find it in her heart to forgive his father. As he rode off, something struck her about the way he had said this. She rode after him and demanded, 'How many?' He held out five fingers of his right hand, and one of his left. Annie would imagine Mrs Barnacle thrashing that old roan pony she had used for the mail until she caught up with him, but thought more about that young man and his decision not to send the money anonymously, but to travel the whole country, meeting face-to-face each of the six abandoned wives and families listed in his father's will. A number of times Annie had tried to get old Mrs Barnacle, born in the last century, to talk about her life. But she seemed to remember nothing. Just a few details here and there: eating a rattlesnake once, seeing Colonel Custer, the strong smell of the bodies of the natives, and a man hanged. It seemed amazing to Annie that her whole life – a century of change, of wars and plagues, of the death of her own children, of abandonment and betrayal – had shrunk essentially to nothing, to concerns about her chickens and catching good yeast for her bread. Annie hadn't lost hope, though. It was just the right question she needed, one that would hit a rich and pressured seam.

They all followed Annie into the yard and up to the front door of the little cabin, wary of the fierce red rooster. They wanted to see Mrs Barnacle's new puppy hound, which Goldwin had brought round for her a few days ago, after the death of her old dog, Betty. The hungry chickens surrounded them immediately. Annie knocked, but there was no reply. The rooster began to get threateningly close. Cracking the door, she called for Mrs Barnacle.

'Phew, this place stinks,' Alvin said.

'Shut up,' Annie said, though she covered her mouth as they all entered.

'Mrs Barnacle,' she called gently as Nora shut the door behind them. The place was so dim and close, the odour of kerosene from the old Red Star stove veining through a smell like that which comes out of the back of a butcher's on a hot day. Annie heard the puppy whining weakly and scratching at the bedroom door, but as she hurried across the room, she saw it – the hand reaching over the edge of the armchair. Mrs Barnacle lay on the floor, her eyes still wide open.

Annie was flooded with horror. 'She's dead. She's died.'

'She's gone stiff and blue,' Alvin shouted, strangely excited. 'She's poisoned herself.'

Nora moved toward the body.

Alvin ran past Raj and Lew to the front door and began to rattle the handle as if he couldn't open it. 'It's a trap,' he shouted.

Lew screamed like a young child. Raj, hunched into himself as if someone were about to hit him, looked bewildered and terrified.

'We're all going to die,' Alvin shouted, still rattling the door

Annie couldn't help herself. Overwhelmed with fear, she screamed. Only Nora remained calm. She went to Alvin and shoved him out of the way so hard he fell on to the floor. Then she opened the door. Lew immediately ran out as Nora returned to the body and put her hand against the old woman's neck.

'What you do that for?' Alvin shouted, getting up and brushing himself off.

'She's completely cold,' Nora said calmly, turning to Annie, who then glanced at Raj. He looked as ashamed of his cowardice as she was of her own.

'You didn't have to push me, you . . . *bitch*.'

'Shut up, Alvin,' Annie shouted.

Alvin left.

'We need to get people here,' Nora said. 'I'll take the road back to my house, case a car comes and I can stop them. You guys go to Tatmeyer's place. He's closest.'

The three of them ran back through the gauntlet of hungry chickens, Nora heading off toward the road, Annie and Raj through the woods. There was no sign of Alvin or Lew. After a couple of minutes, Annie remembered the whining hound and realized it might have been in that back room for days.

'Oh God, the puppy,' she said to Raj. 'Tatmeyer's probably working the field by the swamp. You go find him. I'll be back in a second.'

As she closed on the house again, she wished she had asked Raj to come with her. She was frightened to go back in, and the mindless, living hunger of those chickens seemed to embody her fear. But thinking of how brave Nora was, she forced herself back through the chickens, and into the house. The body was moving. She screamed, and Alvin quickly stood up.

'What are you doing?'

'Nothing,' Alvin said. 'I just wanted to make sure she was okay.'

Annie saw that some of the buttons of Mrs Barnacle's blouse had been undone and it had been pulled down to expose her old breast. She stared at Alvin with horror.

He began to cry. 'I wasn't doing nothing. I just wanted to have a look.' Quickly he covered the breast, buttoning up her blouse.

Annie ran into the bedroom, which stank. The puppy lay on the floor, panting. She picked it up and took it out with her. Alvin was now standing by the kitchen table. She ignored him, sprinting to the door, but he called desperately, 'Annie. Annie, please don't tell anyone. Please don't tell. Please.'

She was out of the house now, and running.

When Alvin got home, he felt sure that everyone would know by now what had happened. Annie's *What are you doing?* was like something his nerves were swarming, trying to devour, like the moths he threw into his fire ant farm.

He could hear his parents in the kitchen and entered. His dad was pacing in front of the stove.

'Why?' his dad was saying to his mom. 'Why is this a strange request?'

'I'll clean things thoroughly,' she said. She was sitting at the table.

'But you touch your face without thinking. Look. Your hand just went up to your mouth right then. All I'm asking—'

She saw Alvin. 'Where have you been? We had a dentist appointment at four.'

His dad glanced over, but seemed too irritated with his mom to fully register him and went on. 'I don't understand why you're being so pig-headed. I'm not going to risk facing my congregation with one of those on my lips. It's filthy.'

Alvin realized he was talking about his mom's cold sore, which had appeared a few days ago. She had never had one before.

'Can we stop this, please?' she said.

'We can stop when you understand that what I'm saying is completely reasonable. You can use a bucket of disinfected water for your cup and your plate and anything else you touch.' He walked out and returned a moment later with a pink towel. 'This is your towel. You'll wash the rest of those towels in boiling water. When they're ready to come out of the water, call me. Do *not* touch them. Do you understand?'

She turned away, staring through the door into the sitting room. She could do this, his mom, suddenly look as if she were in an unseemly place, a busy bus station being accosted by beggars, and would armour herself in severe dignity.

Alvin's dad, understanding that he wasn't going to get any further with her, turned to Alvin. 'Where have you been?'

Alvin wanted to say that Mrs Barnacle was dead, which would explain why he had not returned in time, but any mention of her seemed somehow an admission of what he had done.

'Just hanging out with friends.'

'For the last time this month, buddy. You're grounded. Do you understand me?'

Alvin nodded.

'Are you all right, Alvin?' His mom was clearly surprised he hadn't protested. Alvin glanced at that cold sore, and she reflexively lifted her hand to cover it.

'*Don't* touch it,' his dad shouted.

'I wasn't going to. Alvin, I'll get your supper.'

'He'll get his own supper.'

His mom banged her hand down on the table. 'I will get his supper.' She and his dad stared hatefully at each other.

At last his dad said, more quietly, 'Wash your hands before you touch anything you give to him.' And he walked out.

After she had made him some hot dogs, his mom went into the yard to collect the washing off the line. From the kitchen, very faintly, Alvin could hear his dad rehearsing his sermon. He wondered if his dad would take him on a home visit this weekend. Mrs Allison was very ill. He loved these visits. He would never forget that amazing shriek from Mrs Klotzburger when her mother died, that feeling of knowing you were in a house where someone had just breathed her last breath; or sneaking into the room where Mrs Snyder's husband, Moose, who had served him a malt just a few weeks before, lay paralysed by a massive stroke. He had stared down into that man's horrified, helpless eyes. Often his dad would have him wait in another room, especially if someone were ill or had something private to talk about. He would take his chance, then, to sneak around. He had stolen all kinds of things: a long prayer to overcome the craving for alcohol that had been pinned to the inside of Bill Heider's closet; a little bag of nail clippings and hair from the Bancrofts' place, which had to be from their youngest daughter who had died of MS; the gold wedding ring of Mrs Yost's dead husband; a baking soda can full of kidney stones; a hidden photograph of a young man in the uniform of a Nazi stormtrooper; an antique christening gown from the Andersons that had dozens of names sewn into it; old letters in German; women's underwear, which he took out of wash baskets. He had so much now that it was outgrowing the space beneath the loose boards at the back of his closet.

His mom returned, her arms full of clothes, and began to iron.

'What have you been up to?' she asked.

'Nothing.'

'Were you seeing Laura?'

'Told you I broke up with her.'

'Are you seeing anyone else?'

'Sort of.'

'Who is it?'

'Nora, sort of.'

'She's big-boned, that girl: she'll spread.'

'So what?'

'Why did you break up with Laura?'

'She's getting too serious.'

She nodded. 'You've got to be careful with these girls. They trap you.'

She continued ironing in silence. He could still faintly hear his dad, and said softly, 'Annie's telling lies about me.'

She put the iron up. 'What lies?'

'She doesn't like me. She's telling people horrible things about me.'

'Why would she do that?'

'She's jealous, I think. Because of Nora.'

'Does she like you?'

He shrugged. 'She's been acting funny.'

'What's she saying?'

He was trying to hold back the panic in his chest. 'We found Mrs Barnacle today. She was dead.'

'What? Why didn't you say something?' She came over and sat next to him at the table.

'We found her because Annie wanted to give her some money and we wanted to see her new puppy. And she'd died. And we all ran to get help. And I went too. And then Annie said I'd gone back and touched Mrs Barnacle.'

His mom's eyes went blank. She looked all at once like a stranger in those old photographs where the people never smiled. He had taken a few of these for his collection until he realized that after a while the photographs, unlike the objects, emptied out somehow, and came to mean even less than nothing.

At last she murmured, 'What a terrible thing to say about you.'

He wished she would look at him directly.

She put her hands flat on the table, as if she were going to get up, but then seemed to change her mind. 'Try to get through this.'

'Through what?'

'Just a few more years. Then we'll go.'

'What do you mean, we'll go?'

'I mean you'll be able to go. Go to college or get a job. Go anywhere. Start again. Just a few more years.'

He felt a terrible, deep pain. He realized not only that his mom didn't believe he hadn't touched Mrs Barnacle, but that she had never believed anything. What had she said? That he could forget her, his dad, his home, his friends. But his dad and friends had never looked at him like his mom looked at him now, as if there were nothing to salvage from him or his life, that he should throw it all away and start again. Her too. Throw her away. It made him so angry; glancing at her cold sore, he was almost overwhelmed by a deep revulsion for her.

'Yeah,' he said. 'I'll go somewhere.'

Now, with that empty, two-dimensional face, she went to kiss his forehead. He pulled away.

'Oh, I'm sorry.' She reached to her mouth.

He got up from the table and headed to his room.

'I shouldn't have shared that glass,' she called after him. 'I could see Mrs Hanratty had something on her lip. I just didn't want to be rude.'

Angela was comforting Joanne, the receptionist, whose boyfriend had left her the night before.

Dr Weaver's voice came from the other side of the reception desk. 'Nurse Gordiano, is it usual for the staff to use this area as a lounge?'

'Sir,' Joanne tried to explain, wiping her tears, 'Angela was just—'

'Well, I'm sure she was. But Nurse Gordiano has been off duty for an hour. I cannot have the reception area cluttered with extraneous people.'

Angela met the doctor's gaze, a dangerous flare in the dark, incendiary liquid of her eyes. 'Dr Weaver is right, Joanne, as he invariably is.'

Angela put on her coat. As she used an elastic band to bring some semblance of order to the chaotic black curls of her hair, she noticed Dr Weaver glancing at her neck. She then strode past him and down the hall. Just as she was about to exit, he called her name. She stopped, looking back. Clearly he expected her to return up the hallway to him, but she remained where she was. Finally he came to her.

The dying daylight lanced through the glass doors of the entrance and into his eyes. In them she saw the sun on the Mediterranean and thought of her young girl's body, naked and nubile, swimming far out from the shore of the Italian fishing village in which she had grown up. But there also, in his eyes, the shadow of the shark that had once passed beneath her, filling her with fear and a strange ecstasy.

'I just wanted to remind you,' he said, 'that Mr Vandorn only gets half his usual dose tomorrow morning.'

'Is that not written on his medication schedule?'

'It is,' he said, 'but—'

'Dr Weaver, I'm not in the habit of dispensing medicine in a cavalier fashion. Nor are any of the other nurses here. We are women, which appears to irritate you, but in case you haven't noticed we are not devoid of will or volition. Have no fear, Dr Weaver, in my non-extraneous capacities I will not be too busy filing my nails to read the medicine charts of those under my care.'

'Angela,' he called as she made to walk out.

She turned back. 'It's Nurse Weaver . . .' She faltered, flushing under his covert smile. 'Nurse Gordiano, I mean, Dr Weaver, and I was under the impression you wished me to vacate the building.'

'Your skirt,' he said gently.

She saw now that her skirt was unzipped. As she tugged the zipper, the rubber band in her hair broke, releasing a deluge of thick black curls around her face and shoulders.

'Dio mio,' she murmured.

They both bent down for the broken rubber band, but he managed to snatch it up first. The setting sun bathed them in roseate light.

'There's a garbage can outside,' she said. 'I'll throw it away.'

'I'll keep it,' he said. 'I know just how it feels.'

'Did you want anything else?' she asked firmly.

'No, Nurse Gordiano.'

And she hurried out into the melting sun.

Ruth glanced at the letter again. She hadn't read it because she needed to finish this chapter today. She felt nervous: Haig hadn't sent so much as a note all summer, despite her numerous enquiries regarding his plans to collect the boy. She got up from her desk, sat on her bed, and opened it.

12 August 1954

Dear Ruth,

I realize I have been somewhat remiss regarding communication. And you have every right to be, as you gently put it in your last note, 'disappointed'. Nor could I argue that I haven't, in some way, abandoned the boy. I have to say, though, that he would be better off almost anywhere other than here. My wife refuses to have him back in the house. She and the boy have never got along and her ire has been piqued by our rather straitened financial circumstances. This is the result of a failed speculation advised and administered by the boy's father, from whom we have not heard since news of the share collapse. Needless to say, since I speculated without her knowledge, she and I are not on the best of terms. We have had to withdraw our daughter from her public school, and move from our house to a rather incommodious flat in Knightsbridge.

Ruth, I'm not sure what to say. The boy is just a few years from an age when he can work and begin to support himself. He is a good boy, and I'm sure provides company for you, and some comfort following Oliver's death. Certainly you should feel no compunction in getting him to do his fair share of work around your home and the farm.

If you need to put him into a government institution of any kind and require my signature, please send the relevant documents to me at the following post office box:

PO Box 229

17 Charecroft Way

Shepherd's Bush

London, W12

I wish I could convey how devastated the writing of this letter leaves me, what an injury this is to my integrity as a man, a gentleman, and the head of my family.

With gratitude and deep regard,
Haig Travers

Ruth felt as if her chest had been cleft in, soft as clay. Reading the letter again, its embedded insults began their acid etching. He had not given her his new address, but some post office box, as if his communications with her were somehow sordid. *Company for you, and some comfort*, as if this boy were some kind of consolation for a pathetic widow. Not only consolation but compensation: *no compunction in getting him to do his fair share*. As if Haig were doing *her* a favour. She gripped the letter so hard her fingers almost tore through it. An injury to his integrity. *His* integrity. This man who, she was sure, would have left his wife and child if she had given him the slightest reason to hope he could. She had said yes to the boy just to get Haig away from her. Was there a single good man in the world? A single good, *feeling* man in the world? She had respected Oliver, even loved him in some way, but he wasn't a man, just the semblance of one.

Flinging the letter down on to her bed, she went to her desk. Shoving her manuscript aside, she pulled a notebook out from one of the drawers and began to write frantically.

Even over the corpse of his own brother his eyes slipped to my breasts. Mrs Travers, have you no self-respect? I imagine you and your daughter flaring flaccidly against his monstrousness, his lies, but you're the kind of woman I bet who so needs a man she ignores the adulterous stench of him. You have a pretty daughter no doubt who dangles about her papa's neck. He pets her, teases her, as he once teased you while you performed your bitch's shimmy to win your man. What has he made of you now? Disembodied head, shrivelled with reproach, jealously watching your rival, your sweet daughter. Papa, here are the clean whites of my eyes, my white neck and my white shining ass! He has a PO box for his mistresses and for the matter of dealing with his bastards – little parasites eating out women's

*hearts. This one he left here, little nigger child creeping about
my house with his white goggle eyes. Your husband came here
to wipe the shit from his hooves and is now concerned for his
masculine integrity. Unable to have me, he humiliates me with
a half-caste who has already found the little whores of this
town. A little black greasy boy to keep me company. I see
Haig's face worming up in him, the puerile and single-minded
dream of his blood waits and watches, this creature, this nigger
not nigger child from worlds away, this monkey boy you'd carry
in a cage, this abandoned beast who at the cost of a kiss is
here with me in all his grotesque need. I should keep him in the
basement, throw scraps. I should file his teeth into points and
make him a monster, charge a dime a head to watch him eat
rats. Vile little parasite. Why wasn't he killed at birth? So many
who should have been strangled. So many who shouldn't be
given the chance to breed. So ma*

'I knocked, Miss Winters.'

Ruth almost fell off her chair.

'Judy, you gave me a shock.'

She got up and walked quickly towards the door to make sure Judy
didn't come in. She had a jay's eyes, always ready to snatch something up.

'I thought you were going to call me to arrange a trip to St Louis,'
Judy said.

'I'm sorry, I've been so busy.'

Judy was peering over at her notebook.

'Would you like some iced tea?'

Judy checked her watch. 'I suppose I have some time, yes.'

Showing Judy to the couch, Ruth went into the kitchen to put the
kettle on. Damn, this was the last person she wanted to see. The
minister's wife, for some reason, seemed to be trying to make friends
with her. She had turned up out of the blue last month. Such a strange
visit: Judy seemed incapable of making conversation and had sat in

silence, answering Ruth's questions monosyllabically and as if they were slightly irritating. Agony for Ruth — and Judy too, she thought — but the woman returned the next day, and after another prickly session suggested the two of them go to see the ballet in St Louis one Saturday. Ruth said yes just to get her out of the house. Then Judy phoned a week later to pin her down, and got irritated with Ruth's equivocations, saying she couldn't be that busy since she had no husband and no social commitments.

Ruth brought out a tray. After putting the tea on the table, she offered Judy some cookies.

'No thank you.'

'Are you sure?'

'When I say no I mean no.'

Ruth put down the cookies. 'Is everything okay?'

'What do you mean, *everything*?'

'I don't know. I just mean how are things going?'

'Fine.' She frowned as if this were an odd question.

Another painful silence, but Ruth noticed that Judy seemed a little more nervous than usual, worrying her faux pearl necklace.

'Were you writing one of your books in there?'

'Yes.'

A rare question, which Judy didn't follow up.

'They're not hard. The stories and characters are always more or less the same.'

'I don't read books,' Judy said. 'If I have spare time I'd rather be doing something useful.'

'You've never read a book?'

'I've read some of the classics, but I certainly wouldn't read any of those books. Anyway, Redmond says the Bible leaves all other books in the dust.'

'What's your favourite part of the Bible?' She felt a cruel urge to upend this rude and difficult woman.

'I don't make judgements like that about the Lord's word.'

'There must be some passage, some psalm?'

'They're all equally good to me.'

'I love the last passage in Bubbaronomy spoken by the eponymous disciple: And yeah they shall come and the women shall lament in the passing of Urea when the cries of the offal-bearers despoil the righteous and shall be drawn through the bowels of the earth for judgement.'

'Yes, yes, they're all equally good. It's the Lord's word.'

Ruth nodded. It hadn't made her feel any better.

Judy suddenly reached up to touch her lip just beside what looked like a cold sore. 'I was round at Mrs Hanratty's and I think by mistake I picked up her glass. My lips were very dry. I'd forgotten to put Vaseline on them. It was very windy over to her place. It's the first time I've ever had anything like this.'

'Oh . . . oh, yes. They're a pain. Sometimes it helps, when you feel one coming up, to put ice on it.'

Judy had bent forward a little, hugging herself as if she were cold and staring at the rug. There was something helpless and pathetic about this posture and Ruth felt guilty. Still, this woman was like something caught in her throat. She decided to let the silence linger.

At last Judy said, 'Why did you stop dating Goldwin?'

'I didn't want to be more than friends.'

'You were here for five years alone.'

'I had Fifty-Three.'

'Why didn't you marry that English man?'

'He didn't ask me.'

'So why did you let him live here if he wouldn't marry you?'

'He was very hygienic.'

Judy stared at her with astonishment. 'You let him stay with you because he was hygienic?'

'I'm joking, Judy. He stayed because I liked him and he liked me.'

'Not enough to give you a ring.' She seemed almost angry. 'I couldn't live like this.'

'Like what?' Ruth felt herself hardening against this woman.

'Like this,' she said, a little heated. 'Like this.' She was looking around the room as if it were spattered with excrement.

Ruth had had enough and stood up. 'I need to get on with my work.'

Judy didn't move, and seemed even to be tightening up her body as if preparing to struggle against being thrown out.

'I need to finish my book,' Ruth said. All at once Olivia, the character she had based on Judy, came back to her: the deeply shy secretary with her fierce façade who had finally won the heart of the handsome and arrogant Mr Simmons, whom she had based on Bennet. Ruth had inhabited Olivia for months, creating a life for her, had grown to like her. But this woman was impossible.

'My husband' – Judy looked up at Ruth – 'hasn't touched me since the day I told him I was pregnant with Alvin.'

Ruth didn't know what to do now and sat down.

Judy gave her an odd, unpleasant smile. 'I'm joking.'

Ruth nodded.

There was a thudding of feet on the porch. The kitchen door shuddered open, and Raj hurried in, supporting Annie, who was hopping.

'Ruth,' he said, 'Annie stepped on some glass.'

Getting up, Ruth motioned for Annie to take her seat and told Raj to get the first aid box out of the bathroom.

'I'm bleeding on your floor,' Annie said apologetically.

'Don't worry. Hon, you're a little old to be running around barefoot.' Ruth noticed that Judy was staring strangely at Annie.

Raj returned with the box and as he put it down said, 'We found Mrs Barnacle dead.'

'What?'

He turned to Judy. 'Alv was there too.'

'He didn't say anything to me,' Judy shot back, as if suggesting the whole thing were a lie.

'She'd had a heart attack,' Annie said. 'They took her in the ambulance.'

'Oh, that poor woman,' Ruth said. 'How did you find her?'

Annie winced as Ruth dabbed iodine on the cut. 'We wanted to see the puppy and I had some money to give her.'

Ruth was now trying to cut the bandage, but the scissors in the first aid kit were too blunt. Raj got up and disappeared down the hall. Judy was still staring strangely at Annie.

'She was just lying on the floor,' Annie said.

'Does she have any family?'

Annie shook her head and all at once Ruth remembered what she had heard about Mrs Barnacle, the image everyone in Pisgah had of her chasing down that young man and demanding to know how many. That was thirty years ago. Now her life was over.

Raj finally reappeared, holding the scissors from her sewing box. When she took them, Raj, without a word, walked out of the back door.

'I'll drive you home, hon,' Ruth said.

'What happened to Raj?' Annie looked through the kitchen.

'Oh, I don't know. Judy, would you like a ride home?'

It took a second for Judy to uproot her gaze from Annie. She checked her watch. As she did with every gesture of kindness, she made it seem like an imposition. 'You're going to make me feel like Mrs Porter: she drives the twenty yards to her mailbox.'

Ruth couldn't suppress her irritation. 'If you want to come, come. If you don't, don't. Let's go, hon.' She helped Annie, who looked embarrassed and confused now, to her feet.

Judy didn't respond, but followed them out and got into the back of the Model A.

Ruth stopped at Judy's first. Judy didn't make a move to leave the car for a moment. Finally she said, 'You two aren't going to sit in here gossiping, are you?'

'Gossiping about what?' Ruth said, unable to hide the impatience in her voice.

'People's private matters – what else do people gossip about? Things they should keep to themselves.' With this she got out of the car.

As Ruth drove on, Annie said: 'Miss Winters, is Raj going back to England?'

'That's where his family is,' Ruth replied a little sharply.

Annie toyed with the hem of her dress. Ruth glanced over at her. It was almost bizarre how lovely she was — that strong, strange face slightly absurd upon those scruffy limbs, her beautiful thick hair, black and curly. She wanted to tell her to sit up straight, not to be ashamed of her height and long limbs. She wished she could teach her how to hold herself. What was so captivating was the contrast of the wild young life of her with the *thingness* of her face — yes, a thing, a beautiful object, to be coveted. And it was easy to covet Annie, because no one seemed to have any real claim on her. She was neither like her father, that ridiculous marionette, or her mother, that big, morose blonde. Sorry she had snapped at her, Ruth wanted to tell Annie what a relief it was when she and Raj had come in, breaking the suffocating grip of that woman. It was as if her home had suddenly drawn breath. Released it, rather — with the shout of their heedless youth.

'Was it frightening finding her dead?'

'It was awful.' Annie looked at her. 'It was awful that she was alone. Not that there's anything wrong with being alone,' she added quickly. 'Nora was so good. Raj, Lew and me were just useless.'

'What about Alvin?'

After a moment Annie said, 'I don't remember where he was.'

They pulled up outside the store. Frank was smoking on the stoop. Ruth got out. 'Your sister cut her foot. She might need stitches.'

He got up immediately flicking away his cigarette. Ruth opened Annie's door and Frank lifted her out.

'*Principe mio.*' Wrapping her arms around her brother's neck, Annie kissed his cheek.

'Where are your shoes?' he said.

'Lost them somewhere?'

He asked Ruth to come in, but she shook her head.

'Thanks, Miss Winters,' Annie called back.

As Ruth pulled out, she thought of Judy, of what happens to supple youth, of how calloused we become under the constant worrying of our senses, how most of us are condemned to grow into ridiculous, fixed characters, the masks of *commedia dell'arte*. We defend ourselves so desperately, but defend what? What is there to defend? She tried to shake herself free of that woman, who felt like the beginning of a fever. Why was she, herself, so sensitive to people? Why did she find them so difficult? How was it that they got so easily through to her? Tonight she would lie awake, thinking of what Judy had said and the wounded crouch of her body. Of the relief of the children coming in, and of Annie's beautiful face. Of Raj . . . Raj. Why had Raj walked out like that? All at once her scalp tightened and she shuddered: her sewing box was right beside her desk in her bedroom. Her notebook was open. She let out a little cry and pulled over, afraid she would lose control of the car: *bastard, half-caste, little black greasy boy, nigger, parasite*. She felt physically sick for a moment and opened the door. Then she realized she had to explain as soon as she could. Her heart lurched like the engine of that old car as she pulled back on to the road and headed home as quickly as she could.

Annie sat at the kitchen table with her mom, who was flicking absently through catalogues. Frank had raced her up to Jackson and she now had twelve stitches in the bottom of her foot.

'She has no family?' her mom asked.

'There aren't any pictures or anything in the house.'

Her mom clucked. 'Shame.'

She was still in the white robe and rabbit-fur mules she had been wearing this morning – and for the last four days now.

'Have you been out, Mom?'

'Out where?'

'Just out. You should visit Miss Winters.'

'Oh, she's a brain-box – too brainy for me.'

Annie realized that if her mom died like Mrs Barnacle, she would know only that she had been born in Koscian and had spent her girlhood and teenage years in Chicago. She had one friend, Caroline, in Baxter, whom she visited every Thursday. Caroline had endless trouble with a husband who had a chronic illness, and a mother-in-law who would fling herself down the stairs if she wasn't given enough attention. The only things her mom ever talked about were Caroline's latest woes and what looked good in the catalogue.

'All her things, who is getting them?' her mom asked.

'Didn't have anything except those chickens, really. Can we keep the puppy?'

'No, I got enough to do.'

Her papa came into the kitchen holding a package, which he put down on to the table.

'Another package,' he said. 'What's this package?'

'Towels.' Her mom continued to thumb through the catalogue.

'Towels? We need more towels? Towels for the whole town. Maybe is flood? If flood we have towels. Come to our house, we have towels for everyone.'

'Papa,' Annie said.

'Your mama she sits here all day ordering towels and plates and little porcelain hobos. Where are the hobos?'

'In the picture, they don't look like this,' her mom said.

'Sebastiana, do we need more towels?'

Annie didn't answer. She didn't like to be pitted against her mom. She had taken to hiding the things her mom ordered, piling them into a corner of the basement – boxes full of towels, sheets, exercise equipment, and figurines.

'Why we need towels when we have our daughter?' Taking Annie's hair in both hands, he made as if he were drying his body with it, wiping it over his chest and under his arms.

'Papa!' She laughed.

He pinched her cheek. Wrapping his arms around her shoulders he shook her, almost pulling her off the stool.

'Watch her foot, Sal,' her mom said.

He bit her earlobe and rubbed his coarse cheek against hers. 'Look our daughter,' he declared, finally letting go and stepping back. 'Most beautiful girl in the world.' He opened his arms out proudly. 'From the catalogue of my loins. Special delivery.' He gestured toward Annie. '*Basta!*'

The back door opened and Frank came in. It hurt Annie to see him wince at the sight of his father. Why was he always so serious? Even in baby pictures he seemed anxious. But now that anxiety had mixed in with anger, and had begun to distort his face. She couldn't remember the last time she had seen him smile. He had never been able to hide what he was feeling, which was almost always anger and outrage. No difference for him between big injustices and little ones: everything met with equal fury.

'And here is special offer, half off, no warranty, damaged goods – spends all time with girlfriends instead of helping his papa in the store. Where you been, uh?'

'Had to bring Mrs Bingham's Buick back to her.'

'What, you bring it one piece at a time?'

'Sal, just leave him alone,' her mom said.

'Just leave him alone, uh? And leave you alone, uh? *Mondo boia!*' He snatched the catalogue, spilling her coffee.

'What you looking for in here, more towels?'

'Another husband.' She met his eyes directly now. He made as if he were going to hit her but she wasn't afraid and didn't flinch.

Cupping both hands over his crotch he shouted, '*Sei la regina puttana della merda!*'

Frank went to leave the kitchen, but their father took hold of his shoulder. Frank shoved his hand off and walked out. Their father followed.

'Get your damn hands off me,' Annie heard Frank shout. Her mom got up and hurried into the sitting room. Annie listened to the sharp strife of their voices. Lifting her bandaged foot just a little, she stretched the arch as much as she could and then hit it against the floor. After a few seconds she felt it – as if something had touched her bone. The blood quickly soaked through the bandage. She hopped into the other room, where the three of them were screaming, took her father's hand and said quietly:

'Papa, can you take me back to the hospital?'

They all went quiet as she raised her foot a little. Blood was dripping now on to the floor.

'Oh baby, what happened?' Her mom stepped away. She had a horror of blood or illness of any kind.

'I'll take her,' Frank said.

'Papa will take me.' Annie met her brother's eyes and he looked away, ashamed. The telephone rang.

'Keep your foot up,' her father told her, getting his coat on.

Her mom answered the phone and Annie heard her say, 'She can't speak now. Yes. No . . . she . . . okay.' She called to Annie. 'Annie, it's Alvin's mom. It's important. One minute.'

'She has to go, uh,' her father said angrily as Annie took the phone. 'Hello?'

'Annie,' Alvin's mom said, 'I know you have your family with you.' There was a pause. 'Alvin told me about you finding Mrs Barnacle.' Silence again. 'Annie, Alvin is very . . . upset.'

'I haven't said anything,' Annie said. 'I won't say anything to anyone.'

She could hear Alvin's mom making strange sounds, stifled breaths.

Her father snatched the receiver out of her hand. 'She got to go now, Mrs Hewitt. Sorry.' He put down the phone.

'What you not tell anyone?' he asked her.

'Sal, the blood's dripping from her foot, look,' her mom said.

When Ruth got home, Raj was still not back. She looked over what she had written, appalled, imagining what he must have felt. Her filthy little habit; her mother's voice. She unlocked the attic door, climbed up, made her way through a hazard of old furniture and boxes, and placed the notebook in a pile with a few dozen others. She knew she should burn them, but couldn't. It was her art, in some way; and an emotional counterweight to the empathy she had felt afflicted by almost all her life.

Just as she was locking the attic door, the phone rang, shocking her. Her first thought was that it was something to do with Raj.

She ran into the kitchen and snatched up the receiver. 'Hello?'

After a moment: 'Ruth, it's Judy.'

As ever, Judy now left an indeterminate silence.

'Yes.' Ruth's body clenched with a visceral dislike of this woman. 'Did you get Annie back okay?'

'Yes. Yes, I did.'

Another silence ensued. Ruth was so worried about Raj she didn't have the patience for this. 'Judy, what do you want?'

'What I said today.' She hesitated. 'What I said to you. I was joking.'

'Yes, you told me.'

'You see, the thing is, you made a joke earlier about that English man—'

'His name was Oliver. He lived with me for two years. You met him on numerous occasions.'

'Yes. Him. You'd made a joke that you stayed with him because he was hygienic.'

'Yes. Is that all then, Judy?'

'But that's why I made that joke then.'

'Judy, you told me at the time you were joking.'

'Thank you.'

This hoarsely whispered *thank you* seemed to express genuine suffering and gratitude. All at once Ruth felt – as if she needed to feel this any more intensely right now – as impatient and cruel as her own mother. She became aware of her posture, the way she was holding the phone, looking up at the ceiling, her tongue running over the edges of her teeth, her other hand canted impatiently against her hip. When she was a child, her mother, in this exact posture, would then roll her eyes as if she were on the phone with all the stupidity in the world. And Ruth would feel special, protected inside her mother's impatience and contempt because it was never directed at her. Indeed, it was a way for her mother, obliquely, to express love in the implicit comparison of this venial, idiotic, ugly world with her beautiful, clever daughter: it was a thicket of thorns around them, protective and isolating.

'Don't worry, Judy,' she said more softly.

'What would I have to worry about?' The defensive harshness was back. 'It was a joke.' A sound then, like a sob, and the phone was hung up.

Ruth took a seat on the back porch. How long should she wait before she called Siggy? The sun had almost set. Fifty-Three lay at her feet and began a loud liquid licking of his body.

What was wrong with her? Why couldn't she open herself up to others? She thought of poor Goldwin, who had courted her briefly before she met Oliver. Goldwin was the first man she had dated in almost four years. She knew immediately that it was absurd – a forty-six-year-old lifelong bachelor. She wasn't in the least attracted to him, with his fleshy, hangdog features, and his obsessive fussing with those thin strands of dyed black hair, greased and swept so carefully over his bald crown. It was as if he considered his scalp something so obscene that the possibility of its exposure were the stuff of nightmare, his thick blind fingers constantly reaching up to make sure he was decent. (She tried to resist that snaky cruelty uncoiling itself inside her.) He was sweet, really, bought her flowers and chocolates. On their fourth date, he gave her a polished granite brooch that had belonged to his mother, which she politely refused. Why hadn't she told him then that it wasn't going to work out? She was lonely, that was part of it, frightened of becoming nothing. And curious to have herself mirrored in a man again as something desirable, to try to catch glimpses in his surface of a woman who had once been able to give and receive pleasure. What was she now, spending so much time here on this porch, taking in the sky, the barn against the sky, the sky behind the trees? Little more than a crude receptor – a coarsely articulated spine – to conduct, vaguely, the soft trembling of a deeper life. The alternative – ingestion, excretion, sex, reproduction, age, sickness, dying – she found horrifying, absurd; summed up in the sound of Fifty-Three licking his genitals. But she loved Fifty-Three. And for all her ascetic posturing, it required so little – Haig's letter – for her to produce that foul language, the squid-shot of ink.

The one mirror she had in her home had become a reproach. A personal ghost, created from all she had improperly felt, haunted her reflection. And did so more and more as age made her face increasingly tenable. At one time she had no face, nothing to haunt, because she had been, if not beautiful exactly, flawlessly attractive. One former boyfriend, whenever she entered a room of people, would exclaim, 'Ah, the main course has arrived.' And her face would be devoured, one of the few consistently emptied plates in the great pot luck of society. What was she now? Ruth smiled. No longer the fried chicken; she was the raw broccoli and mayonnaise salad, the mysterious fish dip. She could bring her face home untouched each time, and freeze it for the next gathering.

But Goldwin seemed very happy with the fish dip. On their last date, he took her to a fancy restaurant in St Louis. He had memorized dozens of the 'Did you know?' sections from *The Jackson and Pisgah Herald*. Why were there so many who knew nothing about how to converse, how to listen, how to tell the simplest of stories, to remember and reflect? How was it that so many people, born sensitive and intelligent, turned into Calibans, becoming increasingly eccentric and isolated? After his 'Did you knows?' ran dry, things became awkward until she mentioned Fifty-Three. On the subject of his own hunting hounds, he came to life, telling wonderful and hilarious stories, impressing her with his arcane knowledge of breeding, training and canine physiology. When the bill came, he paid with all the crumpled small notes from his barber business. It made her feel almost tearful, the way he cleared his throat and frowned as he counted them out, as if this were important, though slightly unpleasant, male business he was sorry she had to witness. When they got back into town, he asked if she wanted to see his hounds. Agreeing, she experienced him in his medium. Those hounds were his body, his senses, his history and mythology. Firm but benevolent, he was the apotheosis of anus and olfaction, the true north of all those whining, whipping bodies. (Her cruel snake uncoiling.) Needing to use his bathroom, she entered his little cabin: stacks of *The Jackson and Pisgah*

Herald funnies; socks drying over the footboard of his bed; piles of pennies and bottle caps; two enormous freezers, filled, no doubt, with butchered meat; and a bathroom so unimaginably filthy it was as if she had walked straight into his bowels. But it was a life no less singular and contracted than her own, which set off that old and echoing shudder in the place of her emptiness. When he dropped her off, he got out of his truck. She knew he would try to kiss her now, this shy man. Before he even shut his door behind him, she broke it off, said she was done with relationships, a hopeless case, and apologized. As she watched his tail lights recede on the blacktop, she felt deeply for him: things might have worked fine if he had always been driving away.

That night she had dreamed he was butchering her with an almost crazed intensity and tenderness, conducting her out of her skin before an audience of hounds.

The next day she had taken the train to New York City for no reason but to cleanse herself of herself. She never expected a handsome young Englishman to begin a conversation with her about one of the Vermeers in the Met. Wasn't prepared for the way he touched her, with exquisite propriety, his manner that of a skilled physician. Four days later Oliver returned with her. Two weeks after that, Goldwin's letter arrived. The thought of it made her wince to this day.

Now her gentle physician, her ever-approaching Oliver, was gone. He had brought his death with him: mistress, compulsion and final infidelity.

And she had been left with this boy. An intelligent child, watchful, but not defended. He was nice to look at, with those strong features and long eyelashes, which shone bronze in the sun. He seemed happy, despite everything, had a gift for joy. He would hum and rock his body as he ate, seemed intensely – if a little indiscriminately – alive to the pleasures of this world. He was sensitive also, especially to her need for solitude, moved stealthily around the house, trying to make himself invisible, and kept mostly to his room. One time, when she complained of a sore shoulder, he began to massage her, but she asked him to stop, sensing he would have behaved like a servant if she had let him. In forgetful moments he would take on her gestures and use her expressions. She would often notice that he was mirroring her posture. In the same way, when he was with Lewis, he took on Lewis's otherworldliness, the two boys like sylvan creatures, with their long bodies and soft, fragmentary language. With Annie, his eyes devoured every gesture. Ruth had laughed out loud one time when Annie was telling one of her animated stories and she noticed Raj opening and rounding his lips, as if his eyes and ears weren't enough and he were trying, like an infant, to get Annie – the whole of her – into his mouth. She understood this: she kept Oliver's work gloves in the cabinet beside her bed and still put them on each night to have her hands in his, and to look at his hands, which had shaped the old leather. Raj was a good boy. God, why had she written those things?

Fifty-Three raised his head, his ears pricked, and got up. A moment later she saw Raj approaching the house, out of the darkness. Fifty-Three escorted him in, Raj scratching the old hound's neck. Without really looking at her he climbed into the light and sat on the porch steps.

'Saw a family of raccoons,' he said.

She sat beside him. 'Raj, you have to understand that I don't mean those things. I just wrote them in my journal because writing like that reminds me of someone I miss and it makes me feel a little better. I know that sounds like a lie, but it isn't.'

He glanced up at her and seemed confused. 'The journal on your desk? I wouldn't look at that. When I went to get the scissors from the sewing box, I saw the letter from my uncle on the bed. I shouldn't have read it, I know.'

Overwhelmed by an almost narcotic relief, Ruth couldn't respond.

'What I could do,' he said, 'is that I could live anywhere. I could live in the barn even, and I could work this farm like my uncle used to. I've seen what to do on Lew's farm, and he said he'd help me.

I'm too old to go into a kids' home or something. I could just get a job right now. I don't want to go back to London.'

Ruth tentatively put her arm around him. 'Listen, Haig is—' She stopped herself. 'I'm not going to send you anywhere. We've both been abandoned by that family, so we'll make the best of it. And if things don't work out I'll chop you up and feed you to Fifty-Three.'

'Fifty-Three would never eat me,' he said, rubbing the old hound's head. 'I secretly feed him those biscuits you make.'

'What's wrong with my biscuits?'

'Nothing. Fifty-Three loves them.'

'Fifty-Three eats cow pats.'

'No, they're nice,' Raj assured her as they both got up and headed into the house. 'They're just a bit . . . heavy sometimes.'

'Heavy?'

'Chewy – in a nice way.'

The screen door squealed shut behind them.

Miss Kelly entered the classroom. She welcomed them back and said she hoped they hadn't turned into wild creatures over the summer. This tickled her and she indulged in laugher in just the way she indulged in that single square of Hershey's chocolate she ate after her peanut butter and jelly sandwich every day at lunch. Annie liked Miss Kelly, who was sweet and hopeless. She was in her mid-thirties and might have been quite attractive except that she had never mastered her frizzy brown hair, which attacked her head like some nightmare animal. Then there were those ugly thick glasses, always slipping from her little nose, and that carelessly applied lipstick, ghoulishly staining her teeth, and how thin she was, her pale freckled skin sealed to her bones.

After taking roll she said, 'Well now, the first thing is that we have a new member of our home room, Rajiv, who comes to us by way of India and England.'

Annie felt nervous for Raj, whom she could see was shrinking a little under this attention.

'Did I pronounce that right, Rajiv?'

'Oh, you can call me Roger, miss,' he said.

'Why?' she said. 'Rajiv is a simply beautiful name, which probably has a significant meaning in India. Do you know what it means, Rajiv?'

'It means Roger, miss.'

A couple of the children giggled.

Miss Kelly pulled down the roll-up world map above the board and pointed. 'This is India. Columbus was trying to find India when he came here. That's why Indians are called Indians. Indians from India were originally a mixture of Arians — white, blond people from the north — and Dravidians, who were . . .' she hesitated, 'indigenous.'

'You mean they were Negroes, miss?' This had come from Aaron Fitzhammer, a big, lumpish boy in a YFA cap. He wasn't being cruel, but was genuinely confused. Annie wished Miss Kelly would stop this and move on. Raj had crumpled into himself.

'Can anyone tell me what "indigenous" means?' Miss Kelly asked.

Annie put up her hand. 'It means they were there first, Miss Kelly.'

'Right. Like the Osage were here in Missouri first.'

'The Negroes weren't here first,' Eileen Metzler declared sharply. She had a strawberry birthmark in the shape of a mitten over her left cheek; her father was the secretary of the Missouri chapter of the KKK.

'We're not talking about them right now,' Miss Kelly said.

'I thought Negroes came from the jungle.' Aaron's utterly perplexed expression set off a general titter of laugher.

'They do have a jungle in India.' Miss Kelly was getting flustered. 'In fact they have elephants like they have in Africa, but the elephants have larger — or is it smaller? — ears.'

'Why would they have different-sized ears?' Aaron was almost crying with the strain of all this.

Miss Kelly was in quicksand and Aaron had become a weight around her neck.

'Anyway,' she stammered, 'what I was saying is that Indians are a mixing together of the Dravidians and Arians.'

'How did they mix together, Miss Kelly?' asked Seamus Haliday, a sly, sharp-witted boy with pure red hair, his naked eyes like two blue marbles pushed into white clay.

Miss Kelly ignored him. 'So what I'm saying is that America is now like what India was all those thousands of years ago. Lots of different people from all different places mixing together on this continent.'

'White folks shouldn't mix with Negroes,' Eileen Metzler shouted furiously

Miss Kelly didn't know what to do now. This was clearly not how she had intended things to turn out. Acting, as ever, from kindness and empathy, she had foolishly thought that if she could introduce Raj with some sort of historical and geographical background it would help him fit in a little better.

Seamus, sensing the kill, said, 'So you're saying that in like a thousand years we're all going to end up looking like Roger?'

'Better than looking like you, carrot top,' Annie said.

'Well, you're already halfway there, dago girl.'

'Seamus, that's enough,' Miss Kelly said.

'Better than being an albino mushroom dumkopf like you.' Annie was so mad she went to stand up, but Nora, who was sitting next to her, took hold of her hand and pulled her back down.

'Annie, you're going to stay behind after school if you say another word.' Miss Kelly, brightly flushed, looked as if she had been canning all day.

Lew entered the classroom, far away as ever.

'Lewis.' Miss Kelly vented a little of her frustration. 'Late on your first day. That's not a good sign, is it?'

'Sorry, Miss Kelly.' He didn't give an excuse and sat down next to Raj.

His presence changed the atmosphere of the room. It was as if a leopard had just sauntered in. Everyone, including Miss Kelly, was in awe of him. Annie felt a little heart-clutch of proud possession as he glanced toward her and smiled.

At lunch, Annie, Raj and Nora sat together in the cafeteria. Lew had left. He said his dad needed him for something this afternoon, but Annie wondered if he was just ashamed he had no lunch with him. Annie liked to watch Nora eat because she did it so primly, which she certainly hadn't learned from her family. She had started to use an astringent for her acne, which would cause her whole face to go red and peel, and was thinking about getting the new radiation treatment.

Seamus, Aaron and a couple of other boys brought their lunch to the next table. It was clear they were curious about Raj. For a while they whispered and laughed over their lunches. Finally Walter Novus, whose dad owned the shoe store, called over, 'Hey, Roger, we're kicking your ass in Korea.'

'He's from India, not Korea, you muttonhead,' Annie said.

'I'm from England.' Raj was clearly tired of all this.

Seamus spoke. 'Roger, which one's black then, your dad or your mom?'

'He's——' Annie began, but Raj cut her off.

'My mum.'

'Where is she, then?' Seamus asked.

'She's dead.'

'How'd she die?'

Raj didn't answer for a moment. Finally he turned to the boys, his face full of sad gravity, and said quietly, 'We lived in a small tribe near the Pungabini Mountains in the north of India. She was the youngest daughter of the chief, and was sacrificed to Kali the Destroyer because we'd had two years of bad harvest and they blamed it on her marrying an outsider.'

All the boys looked at him astonished.

'Sacrificed?' Seamus said.

For a second Raj appeared close to tears. 'They staked her to the ground and stampeded a herd of elephants. My dad – he was a mercenary and hunter – hid out and tried to shoot the elephants as they came close, but there were too many.'

Staring off into space, he took a sad bite of his sandwich. The boys had gone completely quiet. Annie couldn't stop herself smiling, though. Seamus spotted it and realized that Raj had pulled one over on them. Furious, he said, 'Your mom was a nigger, nigger boy.'

'Why don't you just leave us alone, you knucklehead,' Annie shouted, turning herself around.

'Drop dead, garlic breath.'

Annie was just wild now and gave Seamus a glancing slap that caught his cheek. He reacted by throwing a hard punch right beneath her eye. She tried to get up to hit him, but her sweater snagged on one of the bolts holding the bench together. Taking his chance he punched her again, hitting the side of her mouth. Nora got up and Seamus ran, Nora chasing after.

Annie freed her sweater and covered her face. She hated it that she was crying, but couldn't stop herself. All the boys who had been having lunch with Seamus stood awkwardly around calling him a knucklehead and a no-ball man. Everybody liked Annie. Raj nervously touched her shoulder and said he was sorry. Nora returned, flushed and out of breath. She pushed in next to Annie. As efficient as she had been with the death, she eased Annie's hands away and examined her face. Her eye was already swelling, and blood leaked from her lip.

Frank pulled up outside the store, but remained in his truck, not wanting to go in and have his dad make jokes about what he had been doing with his girlfriend. Esta had asked him to come for a walk with her this morning out by the flood plain and had broken up with him. Almost two years from the day of their first date. In a week, he had planned to ask for her hand.

How quickly she had outgrown him. In the beginning she kept asking why he of all people, the most handsome man in the world, was interested in her. Perhaps that was why she never let him do any more than kiss her: she didn't trust him. One of the reasons he dropped out of school was to earn money so he could drive her around, take her places. In the last couple of months, though, something went a little cold in her. He just wouldn't let himself see it. Yesterday, walking with her down Main, they bumped into Rudy Kruger, who worked with her on the school newsletter. Esta came alive, she and Rudy debating Korea, joking around, the two of them throwing him, every now and then, the scraps of their smiles. God, it burned him. Of all people, Rudy Kruger, who called every foul in pick-up basketball, who had an ugly, lumbering style at every sport, but could still score, which seemed to go against some natural law. He had no grace, no feel for the game, was concerned only with the rules and what you could do more or less inside them to win. Rudy had to win. And he made a big song and dance about every bump he took. If you backed him too hard to the hoop or your pitch hit him, suddenly he was rolling on the ground, screaming *sonofabitch*. And like all those type guys, his sweat smelled strange – sweet. If you played him too close you could smell it on you for days. With five older sisters, it figured: either he would be a fruit or what he was. His whole life surrounded by adoring women, there was nothing special about them to him. He had dated since sixth grade, and would always act as if his girlfriend barely existed. You wanted to shake the silly, mooning girl, ask her if she had ever seen him shoot the damn basketball.

On their walk at the flood plain this morning, Esta told him she had been accepted to the School of Journalism at Mizzou. He knew this was where Rudy was going also. He asked if she was seeing him. She said no, but admitted that she and Rudy were becoming more than friends. For a second he had wanted to find Rudy and beat him senseless. Frank had never lost a fight. He only fought when he felt he was right; then he would rather die than lose. Now he pressed his forehead hard against the steering wheel. He would lose to Rudy: Esta had chosen him. And even if he were in the right, he had a sense that this shitwad with his sugary sweat would be the one person who could beat him. And Rudy would claim Esta's virginity just in the way he scored his hoops or got on base, with a scowl, as if you were just being bloody-minded to try to defend against his right to win.

But she had made the smart choice, going for a man who had never suffered a moment's doubt or defeat over a small-town mechanic in his oily overalls. Frank felt rage now – at her a little, but mostly at himself: celibacy for these two years. He listened to his friends, their crude stories about how far they got with this or that girl; what they had done. Most of it was lies, he knew, but Esta meant so much to him he couldn't even bear to mention her when such things were being talked about. Wasted years. So many girls who liked him. Kiefer's sister threw herself at him that night after they had seen the Hep Cats at the Kar-a-Nova. He thought of the evening he had driven Linus's girl-friend, Hattie, home from a game because it had started to rain. He was happy she and Linus had got together. She wasn't that pretty, but she was a sweet, friendly, funny girl. She seemed to adore Linus, and Linus adored her. But when he pulled up outside her house, she didn't leave his truck, just kept talking nonsense, staring at his lips, playing with her hair. She laughed so hard at a couple of dumb things he said that she fell into him. He felt it then, gouging its furrow through him – lust, which that visiting preacher had said was a kind of self-hatred, like all the deadly sins. As the rain sealed them in, adding to the pressure, he tried to hold out by thinking about Esta, who had just started to allow him to kiss her neck, and of Linus, his oldest friend. In this way he resisted long enough that she was forced to say something she might never have said: she liked Linus, but was really only seeing him because she felt kind of sorry for him. Remembering the horror, guilt and deep hurt he had felt as a kid when Linus had finally come out of the hospital with that useless arm, he told Hattie coldly that he had to get home. Flushing with shame, she asked him not to tell Linus what she had said. After getting out of his truck, she walked to her door as if she had forgotten how to walk properly. How strange and diminished she looked, but his lust still clung to her, and he watched her as one might watch an ember, as she entered her house, going out.

Now he felt he should have taken every chance – Kiefer's sister, Hattie, every girl who ever caught his eye. If he had, he wouldn't hurt like this.

At last he got out of his truck and entered the store. Bennet stood at the counter with all his cronies: tall Magnus, who tipped his hat; Otto, Bennet's foreman, a bitter, raw-skinned knuckle of a man; Goldwin the barber, ever fussing with the fragile strands of hair he kept swept over his bald crown; Irish Finn, his mournful, deeply creviced face suspended between jug-ears; and pregnant Sheriff Siggy, whose expression was that of a tough guy forced to walk his wife's chihuahua.

Of course, his father, boneless monkeyman, was with them, and called out: 'Here he comes – James Dean. "You're-a tearing me apart!"' He made as if he were trying to rip off his white apron in imitation of the movie scene. Then he took hold of Frank by the back of his neck with exaggerated affection. 'Where you been, movie star? Seeing your girl?'

'Who's this girl?' Bennet asked.

'There's no girl,' Frank said, unable to meet Bennet's unkindly judging eyes. A big man, six-two, with hair that looked like a helmet made from the cool metals of copper and tin, Bennet's jaw was a graveyard shovel, his mouth a lipless slit. How could all those mistresses he was rumoured to have, Frank wondered, bear to kiss him?

'Esta. You know Esta?' his dad said.

Even though Frank felt uncomfortable, it relieved him a little to be here among these men who seemed outside time. Creatures more or less of the same kind. No women here.

'That's the daughter them city-slickers come out here.' Otto scratched the razor-burn on his neck. 'Loaned him some traps last week and when he brings 'em back he's pale as the Pope's pecker and he says: Otto, them raccoons and groundhogs sure don't want to die.' Otto laughed. 'Told him: Ain't nothing wants to die.'

'How old are you now, Frank?' Bennet asked.

'Eighteen.'

Siggy, who was resting a Coke on his belly, said, 'You worried about getting called up?'

'Might just join up.'

'You joining nothing,' his dad said.

Siggy sighed. 'One them twins got a star by his name couple days ago. See it? Wasisname – Ronald. What's the other one?'

'Donald,' Goldwin said.

'Nice boys,' Siggy said. 'They should send Donald home. No one should have to give up two sons.'

Otto tugged Bennet's shirtsleeve. 'Ain't you glad you got no sons, Mr B?'

Bennet frowned and didn't respond.

It had always struck Frank as fitting that Bennet, who was so male and spent near all his time with men, had fathered four daughters.

'Sure, war's not all bad,' Finn cut in brightly, his Irish accent undiminished despite the twenty-five years he had spent in America. 'Went to a lovely town one time. Over in your part of the world, Sal. Name escapes me, but the waiter there he brought me a dish – fish, it was. Nice too. And I say, How'd you cook this? And you know what he says? He says it's not cooked. Raw fish, it was. What's the name of this place, now? Had a big tower in it with a bell. Met a fine girl there called Diletta. That's Italian for "delight". Imagine that now, you call someone Delight. Sure, Diletta sounds better. Everything does in that language. Shit is *merda* – "Give me a double scoop of that *merda* with a cherry on top."' Finn stopped. This was often the way with him, a great disconnected rush, then he would look around like a dog that had farted in the house. He knew it was wrong, but didn't know why.

'Goddamn,' Siggy said. 'I'd have given my left nut to have been on the push through France.'

Goldy fixed his always slightly dismayed gaze on the sheriff. 'Failed the medical, didn't you?'

'Chronic problems of a gastrointestinal order,' Siggy explained, ruefully rubbing his belly.

Otto snorted. 'Means he got the shits every time a gun went off.' Leaning in, he added, 'Had a buddy liberated them French towns told me any officer couldn't get laid ten times a day was a sissy.'

'That true?' Goldy searched Otto's face with pathetic curiosity.

'Told me those girls was so desperate——'

'Once *officer*,' Magnus interjected grandly, 'was synonymous with gentleman. My father fought in the Great War. I can hardly imagine him in the trenches. Scrupulous man. Didn't like to mix things. When he bathed he used different towels to dry different parts of his body. Had to have his potatoes and meat and vegetables on separate plates. Didn't like to converse. He would have you say everything you needed to say, would provide a response if one was merited, and that was the end of it. My mother *adored* him. She wouldn't let anyone cut his hair but her, and treated it like the hair of a Nazarene, kept every strand. After he was killed, she stuffed a pillow with it, which she slept on until the day she passed. She worshipped the very ground he walked on.'

'That why she got hitched to the first Yank she met?' Otto said.

'*Maman* did that for me, to get us out of France. Married that damn expectorator. What is it with you Americans and spit? I recall he spat even while my mother walked down the aisle to him. Spat into a handkerchief, which he then put back into the pocket of his tux.'

The men's heads all turned now as Frank's mom emerged from the back. It relieved Frank to see she wasn't in her robe. She wore a bright shirtwaist dress, white with a pattern of red cabbage roses. Her presence set off a kind of restlessness in the men.

'Well, the world it won't end, will it,' she said. 'Not while you all in here gabbing.'

'Sweetheart, darling,' his dad simpered, 'tomorrow, me and the boys, we——'

She raised a hand to cut him off. 'You not going nowhere tomorrow.'

Frank noticed now that she hadn't done her blouse up correctly. Toward the top the buttons were in the wrong holes. Where the button had been missed, the blouse had opened a little and he caught a glimpse of her bra. How could she have been so careless? He wanted to say something, but didn't want to embarrass her by drawing attention to it.

'Oh, darling, *tesora mia*.' Hamming it up as ever, his dad got on his knees. The men needed his dad along because he was their jester, their whipping boy, and because he allowed them to buy beer at cost for the trip.

Magnus took hold of her hand. 'Madam, we *all* fall to our knees before you.'

She snatched it back. 'Maud, I'm thinking, is happier for you to be at The Lodge tomorrow, working, Magnus. Sal, get up.' She slapped his dad's shoulder and he stood.

'I intend,' Magnus declared, 'to employ some help for her.'

'Who?' Bennet said.

'Ruth's . . . I wanted to talk to Miss Winters, see if the boy might be willing.'

'That little nigger boy?' Otto said.

'He's not a Negro,' Magnus corrected, 'he's Indian – from the Empire.'

Otto wrung out his ugly smile. 'Whatever he is he's black as sin.'

'His father was an Englishman,' Magnus insisted, as if this trumped the influence of all other blood.

'Jesus,' Otto declared, 'that must have been a cold, dark night—'

'That was a hell of a thing for Ruth,' Siggy interrupted before Otto could say anything too obscene in front of Frank's mom. 'That Englishman up and dying like that.'

'And leaving her with another fella's mistake,' Otto said. 'Might be it's his.'

Putting a heavy arm around Goldwin's shoulder, Bennet said, 'She should've stuck with Goldy here.' Goldwin shrank a little at this, reflexively reaching up to dab at his fragile strands of hair as if they were a fresh wound. 'Now there was a thing,' Bennet continued. 'Ruth takes a weekend trip to New York, comes back with a complete stranger.'

Frank had noticed that Bennet seemed to enjoy making people uneasy. Otto did too, but for Otto it was just meanness. For Bennet it was a random tug at the leashes of these men. Ever since he was little, Frank had felt both profoundly drawn to and repelled by Bennet. It was difficult to get a sense of him. He supported many of the poorest in town; had even bought up mortgages during the Depression to prevent people losing their farms, asking for no repayment. He could have lived anywhere, but chose to be the big man in Pisgah, spending his time hunting and drinking with his childhood buddies – in whom he always looked so disappointed. But it seemed to Frank that a person isn't disappointed unless he has hope that others can be better than they seem. While Bennet's impulse was to dominate, while he seemed to have an almost obsessive desire, from what Frank had seen and heard, to push people to their limits, Frank suspected that Bennet *wanted* to be wrong and never lost hope that someone would prove him so. Frank sensed that somewhere in him Bennet believed that even the lowest might behave against expectations, might ascend to unexpected heights of courage and decency.

'Been to see her lately?' Bennet asked.

Goldwin frowned. 'Why would I?'

'Women need a man's attention.'

Goldy looked miserable.

'Bennet,' Frank's mother chastised softly. Her tone struck Frank as too personal.

As Bennet released Goldy, Finn jumped in with his bright, melodious voice. 'Talking of black fellas. During the war in France, I met one. Working on the railroad, he was. I ask him directions to the place where they have the dancing girls. And this fella, he answers me in French. Sure, he didn't have a word of English. A black man, can you imagine it? Looked like he should have been working a snag boat down the Missouri. Speaking French! The world is an amazing place.'

'Ruth's a real nice lady,' Siggy put in softly. 'Shouldn't keep to herself so much.'

'Some people they like to keep to themselves,' Frank's mom said. 'Looking after a husband and kids isn't every woman's idea of heaven on a June day.'

'Lucky for Sal it's yours, then,' Otto said.

Frank's mom didn't respond. Frank noticed that the men seemed uncomfortable.

'Was she married to that English fella?' Otto was peering into the mouth of his empty Coke bottle.

'You know it very well she wasn't,' Frank's mom said. 'Why you want to chew on that? You like an old woman.'

Otto looked up at her curiously now. 'So you don't think marriage is a sacred institution then?'

Frank couldn't believe how red his mom went, and so suddenly. His dad, staring into the floor, was poking and pinching at his own ear, as if he wanted to tear it off.

Turning quickly to his dad, her voice faltering, his mom said, 'Sal, the spoiled stock in the back, did you get rid of it? I not having there no longer.'

Frank caught Otto staring at the gap in his mom's blouse. Why didn't she just leave? He began to feel angry. The store bell rang. Annie and that Indian boy came in. For some reason Annie was holding her hair angled across her face like a veil. She pulled up, clearly surprised to see all these people.

'Where you been, Annie?' her mom called.

'Just down by the branch. We found some arrowheads.' She pulled a couple from her pocket with her free hand, her other still holding her hair across her face. 'Raj found a neat trilobite fossil.'

Everyone looked at the dark boy, who held out the calcified creature and said, 'This varmint won't be troubling you folks no more.'

'Boy's a regular cut-up,' Otto said. 'Weren't you going back to England, boy?'

'He's going to stay here,' Annie said.

Bennet smiled at her. 'Like all the other boys: following you around with his tongue in the dust.'

'No one's following me around.'

'Who, little ol' me,' Siggy cut in playfully, with his hand on his chest. 'Why them boys are merely bein' helpful.'

This was making Frank uncomfortable, all these men staring at Annie, their eyes lingering on his sister's bare legs.

'I don't know what you're talking about,' Annie said.

Tapping the Indian boy on the shoulder, Siggy pointed at Magnus. 'That fella there, he's from England.'

'Can't you tell he's a bit light in the balls?' Otto said.

'Eh!' Sal cut in angrily. 'Two ladies here.'

'Better than being light in the cranial cavity. Of French and English extraction, my good fellow.' Magnus introduced himself. 'An exile among barbarians like your good self, brought here by a Yank GI whose epitaph read: Spectacular Expectorator.'

'Come on, Raj.' Annie took hold of the boy's hand to lead him through the crowd.

All at once Frank's anger overwhelmed him. 'Look at you,' he said. 'You're filthy. You're not a kid any more. Haven't I told you to stay out of the sun? You're getting to be a regular tar baby.'

When he said this a couple of the men glanced at the boy.

Annie's childish coyness was fuelling Frank's anger. 'Why are you doing that with your hair?'

'Leave me alone,' she said. 'Come on, Raj.'

'He's not going anywhere.' Frank put his arm across the boy's chest. 'You go home now.'

'We've got a math test tomorrow,' Annie protested. 'He's helping me.'

Frank suddenly snatched away the hand with which she was holding her hair.

'Stop,' she cried, but they all saw it now, the swelling at her lip and beneath her eye.

Siggy cleared his throat to introduce his official sheriff's voice. 'Who did this to you?'

'No one. I just fell over,' Annie said. 'Let go.'

Still holding her wrist, Frank turned to the Indian boy. 'Who did this?'

'I just fell over,' Annie shouted. 'Let go of me.'

With his other hand, Frank took hold of the Indian boy's shirt and pulled him closer. 'You tell me who did this. Was it Lewis?'

The boy just stared at him helplessly.

'Let go of him!' Punching her free hand down against Frank's arm, Annie tried to pull loose.

'Francesco.' His dad attempted to calm him. 'Francesco, come on.'

'Who was it?'

The Indian boy just closed up his body and Frank finally released him. He was still holding on to Annie's wrist. Struggling furiously, she slapped him against the side of his neck.

'Frank,' his mom called. '*Please.*'

He let his sister go. She ran through the back of the store into the house. The Indian boy left out the front. Frank's heart was racing. He looked at his dad, who was almost cringing beside him. He felt his mom's hand then on his shoulder and she appeared before him.

'Frankie,' she whispered, 'why you do that to Annie in front of these men?'

Still furious, he hooked his finger into the loop of cloth made by her missed buttonhole.

'It's been so long,' he said, loud enough for everyone to hear, 'I guess you've forgotten how to put on anything but your robe.'

She reached to the gap with a look of shock, and he left her there to do up her blouse in front of those men.

Frank went straight into the kitchen and phoned Jude's place. Jude's mom answered and he could hear her calling meekly for her son. She was the kind of person you forgot was in the room. She was like the bad reception of her own life, at the point of breaking up into nothing but static.

Jude got on the phone. 'Hey, buddy.'

'D'you hear from your sister if something happened at school today?'

'Yeah. Nor said Annie would have got him but she got caught up.'

'Got who?'

'That Haliday runt – what's his name?'

'Okay, thanks.'

'Whoa, Tonto, what you going to do to him?'

'Not going to do nothing to *him*.'

'Oh come on, Buddy, Cal's all right. Not his fault his brother's—'

'You think he's up at Woody's?'

Jude hesitated. 'Does a bear wipe its ass on a bunny? You want me to come with you?'

'No, I just want to have a word with him.'

'Might that word be *Banzaii*!'

'Get back to your *National Geographics*.'

'Theys for edicasional purposes, massa.'

Frank put down the phone. As he went to leave, he hesitated. He knew Annie was crying in her room and could still feel her small wrist in his hand. His lungs felt somehow sore and brittle, as if he had inhaled heat. She was what he had; all he had. He wanted to go up there now, say sorry, stop her crying. He wanted to tell her Esta had dumped him. But there was a sound – Mom or Dad coming back into the house – and he left.

It was too early for most to be in Woody's, but Cal was playing pool at the back, a gawky-looking kid with no chin and a buzz cut. He had dropped out of high school years ago to work at Bennet's meat packing plant, and wanted to be a pool shark. He and Cal had got into a bad fight a few years back when Cal had called Linus a cripple. Frank had knocked out one of his teeth and still felt bad about it, but he couldn't stand the thought of someone hitting Annie, and couldn't very well beat up a thirteen-year-old kid.

Usually Cal practised on his own, but today he was with Mary Vanburg, who waitressed down at Fat Jack's. She was a thick-set girl with a face like a gathering storm, her eyebrows dense and dark.

Frank walked around the table. Mary was shooting. She missed the cue ball entirely and giggled.

'Come on now,' Cal said, 'look down the shaft, nice and smooth.'

Glancing up at Frank, Cal nodded a greeting. He seemed a little nervous.

'Hey, Frankie,' Mary said in a playful sing-song, 'heard you're a free man.'

'Who'd you hear that from?'

'Little birdie.'

He turned back to Cal. 'You hear about what your brother did today?'

Chalking his cue, Cal stood up without saying anything. He missed an easy shot and went to take another.

'Ain't it my turn?' Mary said.

Scratching his ear, Cal sat down.

'I want you to tell your brother—'

'I ain't telling him nothing,' Cal cut him off. 'What he does he does. I don't mind 'im.' His eyes were still empty and he wouldn't look at Frank.

'You're going to mind him and you're going to tell him I'm going to kick his gutless, pantywaist tail if he touches my sister again.'

Cal just sniffed and rubbed at where his chin should have been.

'Oh big man,' Mary jeered, 'popping off to hear yourself roar because Rudy's banging your girl.'

Frank turned to her. 'Ain't got nothing to do with that and it ain't got nothing to do with the fact that every man in this town, his hound, and near anything else with a tool's been banging you since you were out of diapers either, you sow.'

Cal went to stand up, but Frank shoved him back down.

The storm in Mary's face darkened. 'If anyone's getting banged,' she said with quiet, vicious satisfaction, 'it's your mom, every Thursday up at The Lodge, regular as clockwork.'

She stared at him with pure hatred. Frank snatched the cue out of Cal's hands. She screamed and flinched as he smashed the light above the pool table.

Bearded and bow-legged, Woody came running from behind the bar, shouting, 'Hey, hey, hey, hey.'

Frank put the cue on the table, his whole body shaking.

'If I busted your cue,' he said to Cal, 'I'll pay for it.'

Cal just stared into the floor.

Frank turned to Woody. 'I'll pay you for this,' he said. 'I'm sorry.'

Woody, who had known Frank all his life, shook his head and stroked his beard as Frank walked out.

Annie lay on her bed in her nightgown listening to 'Unforgettable' over and over. Saturated with the most wonderful self-pity, she had been crying, on and off, for almost two hours – especially when she took bites of the pear her mom had brought her. The fact of eating seemed full of pity. If she needed any more provocation, she would examine the thick bruise, like a bangle, around her wrist.

The door opened. Her brother stood at the entrance looking both guilty and confused. Finally he came over and sat heavily on the bed, his beer breath almost overwhelming.

'Esta left me.' All at once he seemed to notice her black eye and cut lip again. An exaggerated look of sympathy overcame him. He stroked her hair as if she were a cat.

'Look what you did.' Sitting up, she showed him her wrist.

She had never seen him this drunk; it both frightened and fascinated her. He didn't seem like anyone she had ever known. He kissed her hand and held it against his cheek.

He went to get up, but she took hold of his belt and tugged him back down. 'What happened – with Esta?'

'Don't let no one ever touch you.' He wrapped his arms around her knees and kissed them through her nightdress. 'It doesn't matter,' he mumbled. 'In the end it doesn't matter.'

'What doesn't matter, Frankie?' She rubbed the back of his neck.

'Nobody matters.' He spoke in a slow, rambling way, as if he couldn't manage both breathing and speaking at the same time. 'We all live and we all die and nobody matters. That's it. What is it, people just animals, that's all. Be a sucker, that's it. You go here, go there, that's it. Opportunity's there, take it. Take it if you want it. Why not?'

Releasing her knees, he placed his hands on her shoulders, gently pinning her to the pillow, a pathetic, pleading expression in his face. 'Don't let no one do nothing to you,' he said. 'Don't let no one touch you.'

'I don't.'

He lifted his hands from her shoulders, but kept them hovering above her. He looked desperate, as if she wouldn't stop moving and all he wanted was for her to stay still.

'I love you,' he said, 'and that's it. I love you and that's it. That's all.'

'I love you too, Frankie.' She tried to touch his face, which looked so sad, but he pushed her hand against her tummy and held it down a moment; patted it then as if he wanted her to keep it still.

'No,' he said. 'I don't want that.' He seemed even a little angry at her. 'I don't want that.'

Raj had taken a seat next to Ruth on the porch. He had asked to read one of her romances and she had given him *The Summer Cottage*.

She wished she hadn't. She always thought of these novels as meaningless, but it felt uncomfortably intimate to have this clever, perceptive boy looking into that book. The sound of each page turning was as unpleasantly penetrating as an unexpected physiological intimacy, like listening to someone swallow coffee or moan in his sleep. This was further exacerbated because Raj seemed different today, sad. It wasn't the fact of his sadness that put her on edge so much as that she had known he was sad even before she saw him today, as if she had dreamed it. The sound of the ill-fitting drawer in his dresser crashing to the floor this morning had merely confirmed it, and the second he walked into the kitchen, despite all his efforts to be his antic self, she felt a sudden change of pressure in her chest. This unbalanced and frightened her a little. From the moment he had sat down beside her here on the porch, his body had slowly angled itself toward her. She recalled the dozen little tomato plants she once forgot on her desk when she left for a month-long trip. When she got back all of them, of course, were dead and dried up, stretched straight in ranks of pathetic supplication toward the window. When had this boy last been touched? He never presumed to touch her. She thought for a second about touching his hair, almost blue in the sun, or his elegant hands, which she now noticed were gently caressing the edges of her book. But there was no natural thing to do, and all at once she felt raw, irritated. This was becoming one of her mother days, her fingers itching to write.

She was trying to be good, though. Her notebooks were locked in the attic, up there together with her mother's failures – her *enthusiasms* as her dad called them. Her mother would suddenly get the idea that she was going to be a poet, a painter, a weaver of exquisite tapestries. She would spend hundreds of dollars on materials, including the kind of clothes, hairstyles and jewellery such a person might wear. Sitting with Ruth, energized and happy, she would extrapolate the kind of life she would have when she had learned those seven languages and was translating all over the world for diplomats. She developed extended fantasies that Ruth lost herself to equally: world leaders were on the verge of war, but her mother would step in and make a magnificent speech for peace, slipping effortlessly from one language to another, her passion and resolve itself becoming a kind of universal argot. When she decided to be a painter, she and Ruth had talked for weeks about what she would paint, and how Ruth would have to keep her sane, since artists tended to go mad and cut off their extremities. Together they relished her glorious insanity, the one paint-spattered dress made from curtain material that her mother would never take off, how her mother's eyes would become a world of colour and light in which they could both find refuge as they traded inconsolable grief, briefly, for visionary beauty. And it never struck Ruth as strange – she was too young, perhaps – that there was always a particular man in these fantasies, one of the diplomats, an aficionado of art, who would have a name like Matteus or Demetrius, her mother touching the back of her hand gently to her cheek. Then the materials her mom had ordered would arrive and Ruth would help her set everything up. A month later her father would carry it all, unused, into the attic. The attic groaned with them, straining like a brain. The windows of the house, with her defeated mother looking out of them, became the eyes of a senile genius, searching the fields for what was sealed and mouldering in her skull. Over the years her father, who had fashioned himself into a drag-anchor for her mother's flighty craft, would slowly smother these enthusiasms, his condescension and contempt never overt, but as subtle and deadly as a gas that robs the blood of oxygen. Finally she ceased even to fantasize, became a failed, cruel agoraphobe endlessly cleaning her immaculate house. I am hell. Which way I fly is hell.

Ruth had educated herself in that attic, reading the books her mother had bought.

Now that girl was a woman in her mid-forties, alone, back in this same Missouri farmhouse after a dozen failed relationships, right up to Oliver the Ever-Approaching.

'What does aphrodisial mean?' Raj glanced up from the book.

'An aphrodisiac is something that provokes desire.'

'Like what?'

'Like oysters.'

'Are you talking about a desire to vomit, miss?'

'Oh, Raj, I can't really . . . be having this conversation.' She had snapped at him, and felt bad.

'Sorry, miss.'

All at once a sense of unreality and grief washed through her. Where was Oliver? Who was this person, sitting here? 'Don't call me miss. You've been here four months. Call me Ruth.'

'Ruth. Is that short for something?'

'It's short for Ruth Winters. Rajiv, you are a natterer, aren't you?'

She got up and checked the meatloaf. It was ready and she served dinner.

The boy sat quietly.

'How was your day today?' She was trying to regain her composure. He rested his eyes upon her, such intelligent, complicated eyes for one still so young.

'Annie got into a fight because someone called me a name. She got a black eye.'

'Well I'm sure Frank will have something to say about that. Who was it?'

'Some ginger-haired kid.'

'What did he say?'

'Called me some names, that's all.'

'Did you feel bad about Annie getting hit?'

He nodded. 'I wish she hadn't done anything.'

He picked at his food.

'Don't you like meatloaf?'

He thought about it. 'It doesn't provoke my desire, miss.'

'Ruth,' she said harshly. 'Stop calling me miss; it makes me feel a hundred years old.'

He went quiet, staring down into his untouched food.

She snatched away his plate. 'I'll get you some apple pie.'

He continued to stare down into the place where his plate had been, hunched over as if he were praying. She felt almost dizzy: angry, helpless, guilty, grief-stricken, unable to deal with this, with him. She clattered the whole apple pie down on the table.

'Take it to your room. Have as much as you want,' she said. 'Just eat as much as you want.'

His body hunched a little more, as if he were bracing himself. She could see his long eyelashes, the very fact of which seemed a reproach. She felt monstrous. Suddenly he pushed away from the table and hurried to his room. She remained in the kitchen for a moment and thought about going to him. She wanted to. She did want to, but she was sure she would break down, and couldn't have him see her cry like that. Snatching up her coat, she left, walking the two miles to the cattail swamp. She sat against a tree, listening to the drowning trill of the redwing blackbirds, watching the midges and dragonflies, the cattails catching fire in the last sun, blazing unconsumed, memory, nostalgia, the last light of each day drawn deep into the earth.

When she returned, she saw that the boy had eaten a piece of the pie and had cleaned up the kitchen. It was spotless.

*

Annie walked between Lew and Raj. They were on their way to the county fair. Clouds faint as steam dissolved into the blue sky. In the air, a chill edge; Annie couldn't wait for the trees to turn. Raj had been here only five months, but it seemed to both her and Lew that he had been with them always.

'Where were you boys yesterday?' she asked.

Lew smiled. 'I was teaching Raj how to play basketball.'

'It was raining.'

The boys laughed, glancing at each other.

Annie felt a pang of jealousy. 'Why are you laughing?'

'We started diving into puddles,' Raj said, 'spreading cowpats all over ourselves.'

'I did the mud,' Lew protested. 'I didn't do no cowpats.'

'Liar. He was first in: couldn't wait to get his gnashers round a good cow pie.'

'What about you,' Lew retorted, 'wiggling around like a sow in heat. Good thing there weren't no hogs on the loose. Might've gotten ugly.'

'Love's never ugly,' Raj declared. He and Lew laughed hard. This was clearly part of some long-running joke between them.

'Stop it.' Hooking her arms around their waists, Annie reined them in just as they walked into the scent of skunk. Dozens of sparrows, like a gust of dry leaves, scattered across the path. Just ahead a crow limped guiltily away from the skunk's corpse. It had been run over by a tractor, its lower half imprinted with the tyre tread.

Pulling free, Lew put his hand against the back of his neck. 'I'll meet you guys there.'

'What's wrong?' Raj said.

Lew examined her and Raj anxiously for a moment before speaking. 'The sparrows.' He made a chopping gesture with his hand in the direction the sparrows had gone. 'Death cry. Can only go at the angle of the tyre tracks. See it. I have to go that way, just a little. Then I can cut back.'

Annie peeled his hand from his nape, and held it, forcing him to look at her directly. 'No. You're coming with us.'

He raised his other hand toward his neck, but she snatched it out of the air. 'No!' She hated that she was treating him like a disobedient dog, but she didn't know what else to do. 'Got run over by a tractor, that's all. Those sparrows got nothing to do with it.'

She looked to Raj for support, but he just seemed confused.

Lew also appealed to him. 'Can't you see the angle's the same?'

'I suppose,' Raj murmured. 'I mean—'

She slapped him on the arm. 'No you *don't*,' she shouted. 'It's just a stupid skunk. A stupid skunk got hit by a stupid tractor.'

Lew seemed to have calmed a little. More reasonably he said, 'Listen, I just don't want to go through town.'

'We don't have to,' she said.

'It ain't nothing. It's just like Raj said. I mean he saw it. I'm okay, Annie. I ain't going back there. I'll meet you. I promise.'

She glanced at Raj. Understanding, he hurried on, leaving them alone.

'I'm okay,' Lew assured her. 'It ain't what you think. Things get in my head and I have to get them out, that's all.'

Annie didn't say anything. He was meeting her gaze openly, and she felt her body unclench a little. Maybe it really was just that he didn't want to go through town. She released him and he headed quickly across the field.

She ran until she caught up with Raj. 'I'm sorry I hit you. I get so frightened when he says those things.'

'What did he mean, he wasn't going back there?'

She hesitated, wary of betraying Lew, but decided that Raj should know so he didn't encourage Lew's strange ideas. 'After his brother drowned he got sick and went to a hospital, a mental hospital. I'm sorry I got so upset, but he does this thing when he touches the back of his neck, and I remember some of the things he said when he was there and I don't want him to get sick again.'

Raj nodded. After a little while he said, 'Are things okay with your brother now?'

'Oh, yes. He was just upset. He'd broken up with his girlfriend.'

'You ever broken up with anyone?'

She shook her head. 'Never really dated anyone. How about you?'

He widened his eyes as if this were an absurd question. 'Oh yes. Lots of girls.'

'Lots?' She smiled. 'Is it hard to break up with them?'

'No. I just take them to a cemetery. Then I hand them a bunch of dead flowers and sing them a requiem.'

'What's a requiem?'

'A song for the dead.'

'You're the weirdest person I know.'

'Why thank you.'

'Do you miss England?'

Biting the edge of his lip, he took a moment to answer. 'Don't miss London. I do miss my sister, though.'

'Your sister?'

'My cousin, I mean. Cici.'

'Is she going to come visit?'

He seemed almost to flinch at this, a stone dropped into the well of his mind. A second later, though, the surface of his privacy stilled again, sealing his face.

'What's she like?'

She didn't think he was going to answer, his face grave, imperturbable, but abruptly he turned to her and winked. 'Nice as pie,' he said in a strange accent. Then in a Negro voice: 'Sweet as sorghum mo-lassis.' And finally in a voice she knew well: 'Lovely as heaven on a June day.'

Annie frowned. His silly grin vanished as he realized he had imitated her mom. The flicker of an indigo bunting gave reason for him to turn away. She didn't know what to make of him, at once so private and so goofy. He seemed happy all the time, though she suspected it was a happiness riding like a rodeo cowboy upon a huge bull of unhappiness. It never threw him. He rode it whooping, spinning and grinning, the strain of it only rarely coming through. In this he was heroic.

She admired him. She loved how energetic he always was, his silly laugh, his long-fingered, almost feminine hands, like weak-winged birds, fluttering out and drawing back. She loved his lean face, its sharp lines avid and deeply curious, though his eyes were a little foggy – distant and dreamy. This, she felt, was as much to protect you as to protect him: on those rare occasions they cleared, they took you right to the heart of his privacy, which was as painful for you as it was for him. But he hardly ever looked her in the eyes. Shyness perhaps, but she also sensed he didn't completely trust her. It drove her mad that she couldn't quite figure out what he thought of her.

'Would you keep me in a cage?' he said.

'What?'

'Would you file my teeth and charge people to watch me eat rats in your basement?'

She didn't like this – Lew was getting weird enough – and didn't respond.

More seriously he said, 'I don't think Ruth really wants me in her house.'

'Why do you think that?'

He shrugged. 'Would you love your parents no matter what?'

Annie wondered if someone had said something to him about her dad.

'I guess.'

'Do you always have to forgive your family and friends everything no matter what they do?'

'Why are you saying this?'

He hesitated, his attention caught by a dragonfly, making its signature, flourishing away. 'Because I've done really bad things.'

'What bad things?'

'Will you still be my friend after I tell you?'

'Yeah.'

He smiled, glancing slyly at her. 'You're just saying that because you want to know what I did.'

'No, then.'

'Then I can't tell you.'

'I know what you're doing,' she said. 'I'm not going to beg you.'

He shucked the seeds from a stem of wild grass.

'What did you do?' she said. 'You can tell me. I'll still be your friend, I swear.'

'On the lives of your unborn children?'

'Yes – no. I can't do that.'

'Then I can't tell you.'

Pushing into his path, she put her hands around his neck and made as if she were strangling him. 'Tell me. Tell me. Tell me.'

Scrunching his eyes up, he let out his silly high-pitched laugh, and raised his hands as if to remove hers, but didn't touch her. Wouldn't touch her. Earlier she had taken his hand to help him up a steep path and had kept hold of it – an impulse that was slightly cruel because she could feel how uncomfortable he was. She wondered if he had ever held a girl's hand.

She let him go, and as they walked on she said, 'Well, I did things too.'

'Not like the things I did.'

'Worse,' she insisted. 'Ten times worse.'

'The things you did,' he said. 'I did those things just to warm up to the things I did.'

'I did every bad thing in the world,' she said.

'I know that,' he said, sighing. 'I knew you would when I made you.' He couldn't stop himself smiling.

She hit his arm. 'Oh, you're so pleased with yourself, aren't you?'

They entered town. As they passed the Franklin Hotel, Annie asked Raj to wait and ran up to see the five old men playing cards on the porch. As a little girl she had often sat in the laps of one or other of these men, helping them play their hands: Malachy, with tobacco stains streaking his long white beard; Vernon who had a metal pincer for a left hand and part of his right missing also; huge Lester, who looked as if he had been cut from a block of pink granite; Mo, all the veins broken in his cheek, his nose like a piece of coral; and poor Zippy, whose mind was slipping away. He used to tell outrageous hunting stories in his thick back-hills accent. Now, like a human geyser, the pressure would build, and after a while he would shoot to his feet, his whole body trembling, as if he were being filled with the Word of God. Sometimes he would explode into rambling nonsense. Other times nothing would come and all the old hands would reach up and gently draw him back down. She loved these men, these exposed roots, the smell of them, the dead flesh of their hands. It gave her a feeling of enormous comfort that they were always here. Rounding them like bases, she gave each one a quick kiss on the cheek, and returned to Raj.

They cut down Lincoln. Annie tried to hurry Raj past the old sisters' dilapidated Victorian at the corner, and she thought they had made it until a shrill voice called, 'Sebastiana.'

'Oh no,' Annie said to Raj under her breath as Pela appeared before them, a tiny old woman in a babushka who looked, as she approached, as if she were trying to figure out which one of their eyes she was going to pluck out first.

She fixed on Raj. 'Look at you!' Then she shouted back toward the house, 'Olenka! Olenka, is Indian boy. From India.'

She snatched up Annie's hand.

Annie protested. 'We've got to meet some people at the county fair.'

Ignoring this, Pela dragged Annie through the front gate. 'We have scratch. We think it Sashenka. Vladi too fat to get this high.' She called back to Raj. 'Young man, take shoes off. We going into parlour.'

Catching Raj's eye, Annie made a comic grimace as they all removed their shoes.

Olenka, who rarely left the house, peered at Raj from the doorway. 'Is a big one, Pela.'

She was just as short as her sister, but heavier-set, her expression infantile, her face so thickly and inaccurately made up it looked as if a three-year-old had been allowed to go at it with a set of bright crayons.

Inside, Pela retrieved a key from under a vase of dried flowers and opened a door at the end of a dark hallway. They entered the parlour, which the sisters cleaned every day and used only on special occasions. Between two windows, on the wall opposite the door, stood a display cabinet. None of the objects in it could be seen because they were wrapped in rags. Pela dragged Annie over to an antique mahogany bureau.

'Sashenka,' Pela said, pointing at the sloping lid of the bureau.

'Sashenka,' echoed Olenka, peering suspiciously at Raj.

'One of their cats,' Annie explained.

'Cats are very cunning,' Raj said.

'When I come clean,' Pela explained, 'in here he sneaks – Sashenka.'

Olenka was now staring at Raj with astonishment. 'Cunning?'

Pela tugged Annie closer to the bureau. '*There*,' she insisted. 'Look.'

'I can't see a scratch,' Annie said.

Pela put her face right up to the wood.

'Could have been a hair,' Raj suggested. 'If a hair gets on the surface it can look like a scratch.'

Olenka was still staring at Raj with amazement. 'Take him out for run. I love the way they move his rumps.' She opened out and seesawed her little hands. 'Is like ocean. Ocean used belong us.'

'Not ocean, lake,' Pela corrected.

'Lake belong us and we has servants belong us.'

'Olenka,' Pela cried out, as if something wonderful had just occurred to her, 'why don't we have tea?'

'We have to get going,' Annie softly protested, but Olenka hurried out and Pela dragged Annie over to the davenport and almost pushed her down. Pela gestured for Raj, who also sat. A second later Olenka re-entered with a tray of tea things that had clearly been at the ready.

Pela opened the display cabinet. Carefully she unwrapped and stood up each of the objects, which were figurines – a half-broken Humpty-Dumpty, a King Charles spaniel, and a little black boy in a turban. On the top shelf she unwrapped and stood up a large horse.

'Has you seen our horse?' Olenka said.

'Very nice,' Raj said.

Olenka smiled, tipping her head like a bashful little girl.

Annie was trying to stop herself laughing.

'How is Lew?' Pela asked with concern. 'How our grandson?'

'Good,' Annie said.

'Tell him come visit. His mama, we have picture. We show him.'

Annie nodded. This made her a little sad.

The tea was cold and milky, the assortment of cookies utterly stale – the same plate of cookies they had kept at the ready for years.

After just a couple of minutes Pela said, 'We need show this boy something.' Snatching up his hand, Pela led him out. Annie followed with Olenka as Pela pulled Raj through the crowded and filthy kitchen, in which the two old women essentially lived, into the garden. In a pile, just a few yards from the back door, were dozens of granite rocks, the smallest the size of a bowling ball.

Pela took him right up to the pile, still holding his hand. Olenka hurried to secure his other.

'You see,' Pela explained. 'Rocks here from old wall. Man he going throw them. We want rocks out at pond.' She pointed toward the back of the long garden.

'Has you seen our horse?' Olenka said.

'I saw it. Beautiful horse,' Raj replied.

'So how you think' – Pela stared intensely at Raj – 'we get rocks from here to pond?'

'Well . . .' Raj said.

'Sashenka!' Annie pointed through the open back door. 'He was going toward the parlour.'

With a Russian curse, Pela hurried back into the house. Olenka, who looked like a child at a maypole, kept hold of Raj.

'I got to take him now.' Annie gently prised him from Olenka's grip.

'A run before he feeds?' Olenka said.

'Quick.' Annie tugged Raj's shirt. They sprinted the length of the garden and out through the gate.

When they got back on to the road she said, 'Now I'm glad Lew wasn't with us.'

'They're his grandparents?'

'Kind of, I guess. Lew's mom came on one of the orphan trains. The sisters adopted her.'

'Orphan trains?'

'Trains full of orphans from New York, because of the influenza and stuff like that. They'd just stop at towns and people would adopt one.'

'Why doesn't Lew want to see them?'

'They were mean to his mom. Used to be three sisters. The one who died was the meanest. They're refugees from Russia or somewhere like that. They were rich over there.'

'So how they end up in Pisgah?'

'Used to live in KC with their brother, but they got scared of the city, so he bought them this house out here. Every time you go near them, they want you to do something. Sucked in pretty much everyone in town, one time or another. Can't do anything for themselves and they can't stop thinking of people as servants.'

'Why don't they hire someone?'

'Too cheap. And the more you do, the worse they treat you. I helped them a couple times when I was little, and one time they walked right into the back of our house and dragged me out of my bedroom in my nightie to help them get a stain out of a linen table-cloth. They made me stand on a stool and pour boiling water from this really heavy kettle on to the stain from as high as I could get. Jeez, I burned myself so badly. My mom went round there – I guess she speaks a little Russian – and told them if they ever came near me again she'd smash their precious horse.'

Raj hurried a little way ahead of her and wiggled his butt. 'You like it the way my rumps move?'

'Makes me think of ocean,' she called.

Ten minutes later they joined the long line at the entrance to the county fairground, which wasn't due to open for another half-hour.

They were right behind Aaron, Walter and Seamus. The Olsens, who were with Widow Snyder, were just behind them, Mrs Olsen hugely pregnant with her sixth child. The others stood beside her, from oldest to youngest, like Russian dolls, one a slightly smaller replica of the other, two boys and three girls, with white-blond hair and eerily sad blue eyes. At the far end of the field Tad Messinger was hitting fly balls for his own three sons. He once played Triple A and wanted his boys to make it to the majors.

Annie glanced toward Seamus, who kicked at the dirt. He had never really apologized for hitting her. Aaron and Walter looked sheepish also.

Finally Raj broke the silence, pointing toward the Messingers. 'So what do you have to do in that game, then? Just hit the ball?'

'Ain't you never seen baseball?' Seamus said.

'We have cricket in England. Bigger bat. Games take years sometimes.'

'Years?' Aaron said.

Raj nodded. 'And it's always a draw.'

The three boys looked confused. 'Sounds dumb,' Seamus said.

Annie wished Raj would stop saying things like this. The boys were trying to figure out how he was different and how he was the same, and he wasn't really giving them much to hold on to.

'Annie's brother was really good at sports,' Seamus said. He was clearly trying to make friends again. Annie had heard about what had happened with Cal in the pool hall and felt awful.

Suddenly someone shouted, 'Incoming.'

Tad Messinger, showing off to his sons, had hit a huge line drive. It was flying towards Mrs Olsen, who shrieked, closing her eyes and covering her belly. The ball would have hit her, but Raj casually put out his hand, which the ball struck with a loud smack. The little bomb crater of ducking people filled in again as Raj held the ball out curiously in front of him.

After a thoughtful moment he said, 'Ouch.'

'Jeezle-peezle,' Walter said, 'he caught it bare-handed.'

Jimmy Messinger, the seven-year-old, was running out as a cut-off. Raj took one step, and with an effortless, fluid motion flung the ball. It sailed so high and fast over Jimmy's head, he fell backwards with surprise. Tad, who wasn't expecting the ball, had to dive off the plate as the ball clanged into the fencing behind him.

A bunch of people in the line laughed. Everyone was staring at Raj.

'Whoops,' Raj said

'Man alive.' Aaron gaped at him. 'You threw that ball three hundred yards.'

'How'd you learn to throw like that, Raj?' It was the first time Seamus, or any of the boys, had called him anything but Roger

Raj shrugged. 'Used to throw a ball a lot in England – just against a wall.'

Seamus whistled, shaking his head. 'You should play for us.'

Aaron was getting excited. 'Yeah, we should tell Coach M.'

'He can't play for us,' Walter cut in quietly.

'What?' It took a moment for Aaron to understand. His gaze sliding off Raj, he murmured, 'Well, man, bet he can spank that ball too.'

Raj looked like he wanted to crawl out of his skin. What an odd mix of privacy and showmanship he was, Annie thought. Happy to ham it up until the attention got too direct. Overwhelmed by a rush of pride and affection, she put her arms around his neck. Instantly her head was jerked back by a sharp, painful tug at her hair. She glanced around, furious, to be met by the livid, horrified face of Widow Snyder. She noticed a number of other people staring at her also, and realized how what she was doing might look. She let go of Raj. A moment later Lew joined them in the line. Annie felt those eyes all around her. Here she was, with a dark foreign boy and the mad boy who had tried to kill her father.

PISGAH, 1952

The men were crowded into Goldwin's barbershop. They had intended to go coon-hunting, but the wind had picked up, clouds had smothered the moon, and a sense of malevolent purpose had filled the woods. At one point both Otto and Siggy swore they saw the white dog.

They had all been drinking for hours, their expressions dulling as their faces gave in to gravity. The only light came from a couple of coal-oil lamps, inexpertly prepared, their sputtering wicks giving a shifting, shadowy life to the room. Four of them sat at a little fold-up picnic table playing poker: Bennet, nursing his cards like a brutal matron; Goldwin, his skein of hair as unravelled as he; Otto, simmering in his own bitterness; and Sal, who sat on an upturned bucket, his head so much lower than those of the other men he might have been mistaken for a child. Siggy lay slumped in the barber chair, his hands tender upon his swollen stomach. Just behind him, on the counter beside the sink, sat Finn, like a sad, sweet gargoyle. Magnus, who had a bad back, stood, leaning against the dark-panelled wall, his eyes on the crate of beer beside Siggy.

'What kind of dog is it?' Goldwin asked.

'What dog?' Otto said.

'The boogerman's dog.'

'White dog.'

'What do you mean, white?'

Siggy leaned up. 'White as a miner's fanny.'

'I know dogs.' Goldwin pointed at himself with pride.

'Get off this.' Bennet was getting impatient. 'Who gives a rat's ass what kind of dog?'

'I want to know.' Goldwin tapped his finger on the table as if this were a matter of honour. 'What kind of dog?'

'Big dog,' Otto said.

'What kind of big dog.'

'Fucking' – Otto emphasized each word – 'big, white dog.'

'What was it doing there?'

Otto reached over and slapped Siggy's knee with his cards. 'What was it doing there, Sig?'

'Singing "Big Rock Candy Mountain" with Harry McClintock,' Siggy said.

'Had a dog once,' Finn cut in. 'Wasn't a dog to be honest, it was a cat – kitten actually. And it wasn't mine. Not white either. Black as coal. Died because it got a tin can stuck on its head. I found it. Poor little fella. Cat in the iron mask. Sure, isn't that what you get when you're poor and you want something bad? Blinds you, kills you, and there's damn all in it anyway.' Puffing out his cheeks, Finn tipped his head up as if he were suddenly fascinated with the ceiling.

'You're priceless, Finn.' Magnus slapped his hand against the wall in genuine appreciation, since the Irishman's little outburst had given him the opportunity to pilfer another bottle of beer from Siggy's stash. 'How did Ireland ever let you go?'

'Left for love,' Bennet said. With Bennet's attention now on him, Finn became the focus – if a little bleary – of all the men. 'Tell 'em that story, Finn.'

Finn resisted. 'Oh, they don't want to—'

'Tell 'em.' Bennet spoke peremptorily. 'What was her name? Katy?'

'Catherine. Catherine Mulroney.' Pressing his hands as if in prayer to his lips, he sighed out, 'Finest girl you've ever seen – in the Irish way. She was older – twenty. I was fifteen. We kissed just once before she left for New York. We wrote. Love letters – sure they got spicy, I'll tell you. I'd send them to a friend of hers, Sharon, who had a proper address. Soon's I could, three years later, went to find her. And I did. In this filthy rooming house. Two kids, she had. Sure, it was a desperate place – rats everywhere, people coughing their lungs out in every room. There she was: woman of my dreams. In all those letters, she never told me she was married, kids. Told me she worked in a hat shop; said she'd wait for ever. Fantasy for her, I s'pose. For me it was everything. Before we can say two words to each other, the husband turns up – first time home in a week. Sure she tells him I'm her little brother, and he takes me drinking. Doesn't take long to get the measure of him, one minute warning me against marriage – man's curse, he says – the next crying about how much he loves his babbies and what a saint she is, while winking at me and saying, sure he could make a hole in another pint. Top it off he meets some woman he knows in the pub – and there was only one kind of woman in that place – and he slaps my shoulder and he winks at me again and says he understands I want to spend time with my sister, but if he's to stay away for the night he needs some of the readies and it was his wife after all. So I give him something and I go back. I wanted to help her out a little. She asks where he is, and I say I don't know. And I give her almost everything I have, tell her it's from her family. And I turn to go and she takes hold of my arm. And I remember the breath off her was horrible, and she says, Finn, take me away from here. I say all right. Two kids, she has, but I say all right. She's what I'd come for, waited all these years for. So she gets herself ready in five minutes flat and she takes my arm – got a little bag with her. And I say, What about the kids? And she says, They're his damn kids as well, he can look after them, see how he likes it. And we go to the Grand Central. I get two tickets out to Walton, Pennsylvania, where I had a cousin. And I'm sitting on the bench next to this woman who's holding tight to my arm, prettiest girl in Anegassin, the girl everyone wanted. Here she was. And her two kids lying in that place alone. And from somewhere a baby starts crying, and she begins to curse like a sailor, and she covers her chest – her milk has soaked her chest. I give her some of my smalls, which she shoves in there to soak it up a little, and I tell her I have to use the little room, and we kiss, and I remember how she was trying to cover up her soaking breasts. They'd let down, I remember her saying that: *Jasus, Finn, they've gone and let down.* And

I run out the back of the station without my coat or suitcase, without a penny.'

'This why you never get married, Finn, eh?' Sal peered up at the Irishman.

Finn settled his head into his large hands, which made him look even more like a regretful gargoyle. 'Never married,' he said simply.

Bennet flung down a card and took one. 'Never seen you with a woman, Finn. You ever done more than kiss a woman?'

Finn was still lost in thought. 'The breath off her was so foul.'

'That's Catholics for you,' Bennet said: 'either they're breeding like rabbits or they're virgins. The Virgin Finn.'

'Eh' – Sal raised a contradictory finger – 'I'm Catholic.'

'I sink the black,' Bennet said. 'Here's another one *sin cojones*.'

Magnus protested. 'Finn is a Galahad. I salute a fellow seeker of the grail. 'Tis the maiden that leads us.'

Otto snorted. 'Had a good look at your wife lately? I've thrown up better faces.'

'How dare you.' Magnus tried to draw himself up indignantly, but a surprise belch weakened him and he slumped back against the wall.

'Get off it,' Otto said. 'You're telling me Finn should have kept it in his pants for that Irish whore?'

'Least Maggy's got a wife,' Siggy put in. 'How long's it been since Erma left for her *vacation*, eh?'

'She went to look after her sick mother in Montana,' Otto said.

Bennet smiled. 'That why she cleaned out her savings and took everything she owned?'

Otto turned fiercely to him, that simmering bitterness coming back to a boil in his face. Bennet, implacable, stared him down.

Looking for something easier to savage, Otto quickly settled on Goldwin. 'What about Ruth then,' he said, 'getting back from New York two nights ago with an Englishman half her age?'

'No!' Siggy raised his sluggish head. 'Ruth?'

Goldwin turtled into his hunched body as Otto probed with his gaze. 'What was it she told you, Goldy?' He put on a high-pitched woman's voice: 'Sorry, Goldy. It's not you. I just can't see myself being with *any* man. Guess I been alone for too long.' He returned to his own voice, triumphant now. 'Week later she's teaching some Brit bastard how to start fires the old way.'

Incredulous, Siggy cried out, 'Not Ruth!'

'Sure that is one *handsome* woman,' Finn declared, as if this were enough to defend her.

'And a fine lady,' Magnus seconded, with valiant if slightly fragile ferocity.

Goldwin looked up at last, his moist, pathetic eyes appealing to each man in turn. 'Took her to Peterson's in St Louis. Five goddamned dollars for a lousy steak.'

'Yeah, but this guy's young,' Otto said. '*Stamina*.' He pumped his right forefinger in and out of his fisted left hand. 'She's making up for lost time.'

Goldwin stared bewildered at his tormentor. 'She didn't even eat hers. Four hours there and back in the truck.'

'Imagine that.' Otto smiled around at the other men. 'And she didn't have the decency to corral your stallion.'

Goldwin shouted, 'I've been taking her out for months.'

'Showing her a real good time,' Otto said. 'What was that last thing you did? Took her to the Kansas City cattle auctions, didn't you?'

'She liked it. She told me she liked it.'

'Yeah,' Otto said, 'nothing like the sight of a few thousand shitty cow rumps to get the juices flowing.'

Magnus stepped out from the wall. 'She loved me.' He had finally built up enough steam to respond to Otto's earlier insult to his wife. 'She gave up everything for me. She was married to some troglodyte who just wanted her father's money. She had wealth, she had position. I just worked in her father's factory. But do you know what I had?'

'A ten-inch tallywhacker?' Siggy ventured.

'Donne, John Donne. I'd suffered such men as her husband. Cursed expectorators. I had seen *ma pauvre maman* reduced to ashes in the grate of her youth. So when Maud, walking through her father's factory, got a steel splinter in her hand, I removed it, kissed her bloody palm, took that sacrament and I said,

> Take me to You, imprison me, for I,
> Except you enthral me, never shall be free,
> Nor ever chaste, except You ravish me.'

Otto snorted. 'She spread her yams for *that?*'

'She spread nothing. She divorced, we married, which, as you know, was at the cost of most of her fortune: cut off, cast out into the world. I did not lay a hand upon her before that.'

'And not since, from what I hear,' Otto muttered.

Exhausted by his outburst, Magnus fell back once more against the wall.

Sal had been scraping at something on the table during this exchange and now looked up at Siggy. 'Eh, why you never marry again?'

'Once was enough. Gave me no peace, that woman. Said I had no ambition. Told her, I'm the sheriff, damn it. Always had a stick up her ass. But it was that minister what done it. Remember that visiting minister up from Texas? Spoke like a nigger. What a voice on him. Talk about spooking the horses. Every woman in town. Women are like that: a voice can turn 'em.'

'Trudy she cleans the house,' Sal said.

'What?'

'What she did after this minister. Cleans the house like a crazy woman. This *my* wife, uh – cleaning the house. *Dio boia,* I think the world it's gonna end.'

'That son-of-a-bitch, I'll tell you,' Siggy went on. 'Bess said I was a millstone round her neck; said a man with no ambition has no right to live. I got drunk that night, thought I'd give her a fright. Figured it all out; unloaded my gun. And when I walk in she's sitting there on the sofa, and I put the gun to my head and I pull back the hammer, and she screams "Sigmund!" Then she points at the floor. "Not on the new rug," she says.'

Bennet leaned back as if to get a different perspective on his cousin. 'You didn't tell me this.'

'And you no found another woman?' Sal said.

'Got to find his dick first,' Otto put in. 'Hasn't seen anything below that gut for ten years.'

Siggy sighed dreamily. 'Now Ruth. I mean, I wouldn't have stepped in there or nothing' – he glanced at Goldwin – 'but she is one fine-looking woman. Shouldn't be on her own.'

'She ain't on her own.' Bennet was suddenly angry. 'Goddamn, look at the two of you. Not one fucking ball between you. That broad's getting herself nailed right now. Could have been either one of you doing it if you'd had the guts. Jesus wept. A woman wants what you tell her she wants.'

'Why haven't you gone for her, then?' Otto said.

'I'm a married man.'

Otto snorted.

'You got something to say?' Bennet stared at him in a way that made all the men nervous.

Otto kept still, looking down and strumming the edge of his cards. He seemed completely cowed, but suddenly he looked up again, glancing around at the other men, and said, 'Tell you what, I could sure go for a dog right now. Nice Polish. Good bit of fat on that. Sauerkraut, mustard. Nothing better than a good Polish, eh?'

No one reacted in any way, except for Sal, who stared at him like a man who has just been shocked out of a deep sleep.

The moment was swallowed painfully in silence. The men continued playing. Otto was soon four months' wages in the hole. Then Bennet let him have $600 credit, with his truck as collateral.

After a while, laying down another set of winning cards, Bennet said, 'Half the men in this room are virgins. Finn. Siggy's good as a virgin – ten years and you're a virgin. Magnus. Look at him, he's got John Donne, whatever that is. He could schtup every woman this side of the Mason-Dickson he'd still be a virgin. And poor Goldilocks here.'

'I'm not a virgin,' Goldwin said.

'Oh yeah,' Otto cut in, 'then tell us which one's the lucky redbone bitch?'

'Fuck you!' Goldwin was shaking. 'Five dollars for a goddamn steak.'

Sal, who had clearly been working himself up for the last ten minutes, suddenly turned furiously to Otto. 'Eh? What's this, uh? What's this Polish dog business, uh? Sauerkraut, uh? *Vaffanculo! Figlio di puttana!*' His face went puce and he slammed his hand against the table. 'Least my kids mine. Didn't pick up some scraps off a train, uh.'

Otto stood abruptly. Flinching, Sal almost fell off his bucket. He had raised his hands to protect his face, and as an afterthought clenched them in a pathetic display.

'You in or out?' Bennet said to Otto.

'In,' Otto said, 'but I've got to piss.'

'Guardian of beauty,' Magnus called to Sal, who was slowly lowering his hands as Otto walked out. 'Salvatore, your wife is beautiful, your daughter exquisite. Beauty is the burden borne by men brave enough to love it.' He gave Sal a limp salute.

Outside, the wind picked up as Otto urinated. Something seemed to move in the cluster of ailanthus behind the store. As he glanced back at those men in the safety of that lighted and sealed room, the night opened its mouth, breathed upon his neck. Terror rose in him. Buttoning himself quickly, he hurried inside.

As he went to return to his seat, Bennet said, 'Finn's coming in for you?'

'What?'

'You're wiped out.'

'Wiped out?' Otto looked confused.

'I'm going to send Sherman round for the truck tomorrow.'

'I just got that truck.'

Swivelling his head like a turret, Bennet levelled a look of cold disgust at Otto. 'You said some things you shouldn't have said tonight.'

'I'm drunk. I'm sorry,' he said. 'Sorry, Sal.'

Sal looked away with angry pride.

'I'm calling in what you owe me,' Bennet said. 'All of it. And I want you out of that house in a month. That's the foreman's house.'

'You're firing me?' He was incredulous. 'I'm drunk. I was kidding around. How could I get a job? What job could I get?'

'Whatever it is, it better pay well. You owe me a shitload.'

'But I thought we was just playing for the hell of it.' Otto looked around for support, but none of the men would meet his eyes.

'Ah look, Mr B.,' Finn said, 'he was just joking around.'

'Mr B., he's just drunk, that's all,' Goldwin put in.

Bennet seemed to consider these two appeals. Finally he said, 'I'm a sporting man. You owe me near four grand and your truck. You've insulted Sal, Goldy, Magnus. That's on this side.' He tapped the table with his left hand. 'What have you got to balance things up?' He tapped it with his right.

'What do you mean?'

'What have you got that I want?'

'Got an uncle in Colorado might leave me some money. I could sign it over to you.'

''Less you're going to go out there and kill him, you've got jack,' Bennet said.

'But I thought we was just, you know . . .'

Bennet pointed a pistol-like finger at him. 'If I haven't called in your bets before this, that was my choice. Tonight you opened your goddamn mouth one time too many.' Withdrawing his hand and leaning back, Bennet took a thoughtful moment, pinching the wings of his nose. 'Now the only things you got left is a wife who'd be in hog heaven to see you in the shit, lives a thousand miles away, and is uglier than you. And you got that girl.'

'Shannon?' He peered into Bennet as if trying to discern something in a fog.

'That simple girl,' Bennet said, as if refusing to acknowledge that she had a name.

'I don't understand.'

'You understand.'

'She's seventeen.'

'She's no kin of yours. What would she know anyway? Talks to the fucking fairies.'

'For you?' he said.

Bennet laughed. 'For pretty boy here,' he nodded towards Goldwin, 'and for Finn and my cousin.'

'Three?' Again he looked around at the turned-away faces of the men.

'Jesus,' Bennet said, 'it's them or some fucking farmhand, if it hasn't happened already. What are women worth in the end? Look at Finn; look at Magnus; look at my damn cousin. Look at yourself. Men and women been at war since day one. That's the best lesson any man can learn.'

Otto looked cornered and confused.

'Tell you what,' Bennet said. 'Turn of a card.' He spread the cards out. 'You get the highest, you get everything back no strings. I get the highest, you get everything back except . . .'

'How?' he said.

'We'll figure something out. You can bring her somewhere. We won't hurt her. I'll get something from Snyder's to knock her out. Won't be rough and I can guarantee with these peckerwoods it's going to be quick. Anyway, what's she going to do, go to the sheriff?'

Otto swallowed hard. He reached out, his hand hovering above the cards. Finally he slid one out. Bennet did the same.

'Oh Jesus, Mary and Joseph.' Finn came over to the table and laid a dollar down in front of Bennet.

'Goddammit all, I should have known you would've done it.' Goldwin threw a crumpled dollar down as well.

'My good man,' Magnus said, 'you shall have to take my word as my bond.'

Sal, staring at Otto with ecstatic triumph, slapped down a dollar. 'A nice Polish, uh?'

Otto was still confused. 'What's this?' he said. 'What's going on?'

'What's it look like?' Siggy said, sliding a dollar out of his wallet. 'When you were out there playing your pipe, Mr B. bet us he could get you to give up your daughter on one turn of a card.'

The men were laughing now.

'What do you think we are?' Siggy added. 'Goddamn animals?'

'I knew he do it,' Sal said.

'You knew shit,' Bennet said.

Otto was still bewildered, looking around at the laughing men. 'What about my truck?' he said. 'I've got a high card.'

PISGAH, 1956

Lew waited on Miss Winters' porch for Annie and Raj to get back from school. He was so glad to be away from his own house. The roof rats were everywhere now in the walls. Their squealing kept him up all night. He and his dad set traps this morning.

The leaves were turning. Soon his dad would put on his winter clothes and stop washing himself all over more than once a week. He could hardly bear the thought of another winter, which they would wait out like a siege, having to bring the young animals in, the outhouse toilet solid with ice, chilblains itching and burning on his hands and feet, the thickening stench of his dad's body, and the silence becoming sharper, as pain does, in the cold. Every night he would have to read to his dad from the Bible. His dad said the type was too small for his bad eyes. Never once had he admitted he couldn't read. It was a fancy Bible, *Charles Wood Jr* embossed in gold on the leather binding, and inscribed, *To my son from your loving mother. May you be washed ever in the blood of the lamb.*

Once he had asked his dad who this Charles Wood Jr was.

'Some fella.'

'Why do you have his Bible?'

'Must've give it me.'

'Why?'

'Had his reasons, I reckon.'

'His mom give it him.'

'What she got to do with it?'

'Nothing.'

'She weren't Christian. Had them candles.'

'I'm talking about *his* mom.'

'Whose mom?'

This was the way every conversation with his dad went, and lately he seemed increasingly confused, as if he were losing hold entirely on language and logic. It wasn't sickness: his dad could focus if he had to; if Lew took hold of his hands and said, 'Listen, Pop, *listen*,' he could respond just fine. It was just all that silence. His attention had come loose from the world. What made Lew saddest was when his dad would try to hide it by saying general things like 'I reckon' or 'Sounds all right to me.'

His mom was a scattering of mirrors behind the barn; his brother's bed lay untouched since that terrible night; his dad had no past and only ever told one story. It was about how he once severed the head of a rattlesnake with the edge of a spade, and when he lifted the head up on to the blade, it kept hissing, trying to strike, the headless body still rattling somewhere in the grass. He wondered who told his dad this story. His dad would never use the word 'severed'. In general his dad didn't tell stories, and didn't seem interested in listening to them. So why had this one got stuck in him?

He was beginning to understand that his dad wasn't normal; their life wasn't normal; and that they were poor, shamefully poor. He couldn't imagine what his life would be like without Annie. Or Raj. It was as if he had always known Raj, and over these last two and a half years had begun, in some ways, to feel closer to him even than to Annie.

It was getting strange with Annie. They had started to touch, but didn't know how far they wanted to go. It felt wrong somehow, as if they were brother and sister. They kissed with their eyes open, questioning. Strange to kiss when they had known each other so long. She said she wished she could be inside him. He knew, though, that inside was the awful heart, the blood. Two days ago in the old tobacco barn they went further than they had ever gone. He hadn't wanted to kiss *her*, only her lips; not even her mouth, salty, oily with the popcorn they had shared. He laid her down in slats of shadow and sun: shadow across her neck, sun across her mouth, shadow across her eyes. High above them, an empty hornet hive, once a heart. He wanted her to be still, but she struggled. Trying, gently, to hold her away, he felt it then at his nape, its tentacle in his throat. After wrestling herself on top of him, she took her dress off: light across her neck, darkness across her mouth, light across her eyes. He was sitting on the floor, his back against the barn wall. She touched her nipple to his mouth. He wanted this and didn't, the nub hardening against the tip of his tongue, the skin of her small breast so smooth. He had never felt anything smoother. Its exact heft, filling the palm of his hand, unlocked his limbs – ankles, knees, shoulders, elbows, their chambers turning. She stretched up above him, her throat in darkness, her open lips in light, and he could see the ribbed roof of her mouth. She had been clasping her hair above her head with one hand, and released it so it tumbled around his face. He tried again to hold her away, his limbs loosed, but between his legs the clench of it, aching. Reaching down, she pressed her hand there, causing that coarse knot to slip, only to snarl even more tightly. It was the most wonderful pain he had ever felt. But again the tentacle scratching in his throat, and the images came: Alvin's deer skull; the torn-off coyote leg in the trap; the rabbit in Tatmeyer's bean field, which had been skinned and left, covered in flies; and the jay chick that had fallen into his face in Cedar Hills. He slipped into the place between life and death, murderous Annie in her bands of light and shade, her mouth open, her breast so soft, the barbed hook of her nipple in his mouth, those strange sounds she made. She was all loss. She was everything: he felt no love for his father, himself or his life. But she was the inside, the innards, the place where the butcher sank his hands to warm them in winter. He didn't want to broach, just to hold her, fragile and terrible. That's when he had lifted her, carrying her to the barn entrance, holding her against the jamb, trapping her body as she trapped his life. Her left half was in shadow, her right half in light, one breast taut, the other slack and blind.

But she became upset: he was holding her too hard, not letting her move. She asked him if he didn't like her. He told her the truth: he couldn't imagine his life without her. What he didn't tell her was the fear and pity he felt in the blood and bones of her. What he couldn't explain was that he mustn't smell her, touch her, hear her, taste her, but had to cling to her surface like a water strider. The signs were everywhere. He had seen the pool of shadow in the deer skull, the gums rotted back from the teeth, as if that deer had learned to snarl. He had seen the flies like living jewels on the naked gel of the rabbit; soon would come the maggots, which would make it the light of the waters, worming upon the limestone places, layered with the bones of the dead, Roh's bones. He knew he had to learn to live by light alone, teach his nose, his tongue, his skin to see; to know not the depths, the organs, the innards; be not the living wound; know not the suck of mud; gave up all senses but sight. What other end? God made man from mud. Man now must lead these limbs to light. For the creatures of the earth have snouts and see dimly; our gods are light, blinding; our eyes fill us, steep our cells. But he could still feel her nipple against his tongue, could still see the band of shadow over her eyes, the open, empty socket of her mouth.

After they had made up, they lay at the entrance to the barn in the sun, the full sun. She was still naked, which frightened him in case someone came, but she didn't care. Annie never cared. He lay with his cheek against her belly, could still feel her nipple, like a soft coin in his mouth, and he kissed her below her navel, touched his lips to the margins of the thin, harsh hair between her legs. Had smelled her then, scent of ash, of dead leaves, of soil, truffle scent up through layers of earth; snouting, rooting at the mortal scent. Like her breast in his hand, it made him feel helpless, loose in his limbs, knotted at his core. He needed to see this scent in something, to get it out of him, out of him, out of him. But he remained, as she combed her hand through his hair, and he listened to the liquid sounds of her stomach and smelled her, and felt that, surely, if she were with him, his Annie, he could survive.

Lew could see them on the road now, two figures, Raj and Annie, and as they turned up the drive he could hear their animated voices, vivid and senseless, the sound of a world he was ceasing to be a part of, like birdsong in the morning.

*

Annie felt oddly shy to see Lew sitting there on Ruth's porch after what happened in the barn yesterday. She was glad he hadn't let it go too far.

She and Raj joined him on the porch. She sat beside the sleeping Fifty-Three, lifting his head gently into her lap and rubbing his soft, loose throat. After they had told Lew about their day in school the three of them lay quiet, listening to Fifty-Three snoring.

Finally Annie said, 'How old you reckon Miss Kelly is, then?'

'Old,' Lew said, 'like thirty-five maybe.'

'But she's a pretty woman, ain't she?'

Lew shrugged.

'Ain't she, Raj?'

Raj had lifted one of Fifty-Three's ears into his hand and was examining it as one might a fallen leaf. 'She's all right.'

'Wonder why she never married?' Annie said.

'Maybe no one ever asked her,' Raj said.

'Why, though?'

The boys seemed tired of this subject and neither answered.

'I couldn't live like her.'

'You mean without a manly man?' Hiking the sleeve of his T shirt over his shoulder, Raj tensed the small bicep of his thin arm.

'Alone like that,' she said. 'I want to have children. Lots of children.'

'She seems happy enough,' Lew said.

'She's going to teach school in Pisgah until she's an old lady,' Annie said. 'Puts her whole life into it. I helped her decorate the classroom last Christmas. Jeez, she was so excited. It was just like she was a little kid. She went all red. I wanted to ask her if she'd ever had a boyfriend, just . . . what she ever thought about.'

Jumping up, Raj grabbed the bird's nest he had pulled out of the gutter a few days ago, put it on his head, and began to imitate Miss Kelly. 'Lewis, tardy *again*. Now, class, let's take Annie. Annie's dad is Italian, which is European. Her mom is Polish, which is also European. But the Polish are lighter than the Italians. Oh, I don't mean that, Aaron. I mean, well, think of Europe as a chicken:

chicken's legs, Italy, dark meat, and very tasty they are too; chicken's breast – I'm talking metaphorically, of course – white meat, mom. Well, I'm glad you prefer breasts, Seamus, but that's not really the point. Personally I like a good leg . . . I mean I like my meat dark . . . Oh . . . Oh, my' – he fluttered his hands against his face – 'oh my!'

Lew was laughing and Annie was trying to stop herself.

'Will you ever forgive her?' she said. 'That was more than two years ago.'

'I was scarred.' Raj took off the nest and sat back down.

After a moment Lew ventured quietly, 'What about Ruth, then?'

'She was with someone,' Raj said.

'Not for years, though,' Lew said.

'Ruth's different,' Annie said. 'I could live like Ruth. I couldn't live like Miss Kelly. She kissed me.'

'On the lips?' Raj said.

'No, she was just excited about the decorations. She put her arms around me and kissed me on the cheek, and she wouldn't let go for a while. Made me wonder how long she'd gone without anyone touching her. And when I left it was dark, and I could see her in the classroom on her own, and do you know what she was doing? *Singing*. With her hands like this in front of her like she does in church' – Annie locked hands together at her chest, her elbows akimbo – 'and she was giving it everything she had, singing to the decorations. Made me feel . . . I don't know . . . And—'

A loud bang and a scream caused them all to flinch. Fifty-Three lurched to his feet, vomiting those gouts of sound that were his bark.

At the far end of the porch, Alvin's over-large head appeared, grinning triumphantly.

'What the heck's wrong with you?' Annie shouted.

'Got ya!' He began a mocking imitation of Annie. 'Miss Kelly kissed me, like I was her boyfriend.' Mincing around, he made kisses into the air.

'That's private,' Annie shouted, standing up.

He looked instantly abashed and even a little frightened. 'I was only joshing.'

'Why are you always sneaking around?' Lew said.

'Not sneaking. Got something to show you all. Found something.'

'What is it?' Raj said.

'Surprise. Found it in the woods. It's awesome. Come on, I'll show you.'

Annie felt wary. 'It's not gross, is it?'

'No, it's awesome.'

They followed Alvin as he jumped off the porch and picked up a canvas rifle bag. He led them through the maple woods behind Beecher's place, the trees tapped, the scent of boiling sap in the air. Then across the Jackson road and down into a gully. Lew had stopped at the top to get a stone out of his shoe while Annie and Raj slid down the scree with Alvin. A little way in front of them, Alvin pointed, his face fevered with excitement. At the bottom lay a thick tangle of telegraph wires. Trapped in these wires, probably drawn by the remains of a critter just a little way from it, was a large brown hawk. The bird's wings were spread, its left severed at the shoulder by a tightened loop of wire and separated just a few inches from its body. Worst of all, it was still alive, its head rotating, its eyes fierce.

Annie glanced at Raj, who looked horrified.

'Ain't that something?' Alvin shouted.

Stones clattered down behind them as Lew descended. Annie ran up as fast as she could, slipping a couple of times, and managed to get to him before he could see it.

'Don't come down,' she said.

Alvin had followed. 'He should see.'

'You're disgusting,' she shouted. 'Why d'you show us that?'

'What is it?' Lew said.

'It's a golden eagle,' Alvin said.

'It's just a dumb old brown hawk,' Annie said.

'It's an eagle.'

She turned back to Lew. 'It's just horrible. It's dead. Please don't look at it.'

'It ain't dead,' Alvin shouted.

Lew moved past her and down. She followed. It was late evening and the steeply angled sunlight shone right on to the bird. Raj's long shadow lay alongside it.

Excited, Alvin pulled his .22 from its bag. 'I'm going to kill it.'

'No you're not,' Annie said.

'I'm going to put it out of its misery,' he said, as if she hadn't understood him and he had to speak in her language.

'I'm not going to let you do this.' She stepped closer to him.

'Do what?'

'*This.*' He flinched as she put her hands on his shoulders. She stared into his desperate and innocent and cunning face, trying hard to understand what was going on in him. 'Why d'you do this? Why d'you bring us here?'

Alvin looked genuinely confused and hurt. 'It's . . . an eagle. It's . . .'

She took the rifle from him. The bird maintained its vigilance, even at the heart of this nightmare, as if its head and body were now part of two different worlds. Trembling, she felt tearful, and was angry at her weakness.

Gently, Raj eased the rifle out of her hands. 'I'll do it,' he said.

'You can't let him do it,' Alvin shouted. 'That's my rifle.'

Raj stood close to the bird, setting the end of the barrel just inches from the soft feathers.

Lew's voice came from behind them. 'Not yet.' Standing at the base of the scree slope, he indicated for Raj to shift over a little. Then he raised his open hand, adjusting its position until its distinct shadow lay across the bird's chest.

'Okay,' he said, and Raj fired.

'No one could have saved that woman's life,' Angela insisted, following Dr Weaver out of the emergency room. He didn't respond. The

patient's death had been horrible, her life devoured by those moni-
toring machines, which seemed now to beep and pulse with sinis-
ter satisfaction.

Turgid with suffering, a vein in Dr Weaver's strong neck
throbbed, its rhythm in mournful counterpoint to that of her own
heart. ~~They traded ragged, improvised, atonal solos of silence.~~ *She*
wanted to touch that vein, know the message of his blood, trans-
late the thrashing death-throes of that patient into throes of quite
another kind. She was not used to these feelings. Her body had
been dead to her since she had lost all her family in the space of
one year: her mother to cancer, her father to a blood clot~~, her~~
~~brother gunned down by police who mistook his lucky rubber~~
~~chicken for a pistol~~. *All those years she had spent in the convent*
following this, she had been pure spirit. But now her body had
come to life as if through the birth of this death. Resurrected, she
had re-entered the flesh.

'Dio,' she whispered to herself, touching her crucifix to her lips.
Still turned away, Dr Weaver was a beached fish, flung out of his
element – which was perfection. Such things did not happen to Dr
Weaver. But as she turned to walk away, his hand snatched hers up.
It was like electricity. ~~Her breasts swelled to the size of zeppelins.~~
Their eyes met, like strangers in a desolate plane, and spoke the
language of longing.

'Why did you follow me out here?' he said.

'You seemed—'

'I'm perfectly fine.'

His strong hand, which had completed the circuit of her limbs,
~~bridging the once cold cleft between her loins with a fiery arc of~~
~~static,~~ *fell away from hers as something caught his eye just behind*
her.

'Nurse Gordiano!' It was Nurse Fontaine. 'Get in there and clean
up that mess,' she said fiercely.

Nurse Fontaine followed her into the emergency room. 'Look at
your hair.'

Rebellious strands of Angela's thick curly black hair had come loose from her cap. ~~They were firing rifles into the air and scream-~~ ~~ing, 'Viva Zapata!'~~

'I'm writing you up for this – your second warning. And if you don't get your hair cut to a decent length by tomorrow, you can look for another job.'

'Tomorrow? But it's almost eight—'

Nurse Fontaine snatched a piece of paper from her smock and wrote a number on it. 'This woman does my hair in her home. I was going to have my hair done tonight, but you can take my appointment – eight thirty sharp.'

'Thank—'

'And let me tell you another thing. If I see you so much as glance at Dr Weaver again in anything other than an entirely professional fashion, ~~I'll suck these big brown eyes right out of your head, blend~~ ~~them with horseradish, and serve them up with your ripped out and~~ ~~still beating heart~~ *I will make your life a living hell.'*

She stormed out. Angela tur

Ruth heard the kitchen door open and voices. It was a relief to be distracted. Before Oliver died these asinine romances never took her more than a month to complete. She had started this one almost two years ago. Her despairing publisher was throwing copy-editing work her way, but she could earn four times as much if she could get back into her old routine. What was wrong with her? She used to be able to imaginatively enter these romances while also keeping them at a certain ironic distance, but Dr Weaver's masterful jawline and Angela's yearning loins were getting through to her, so she was defending herself in the only way she knew how. She went into the kitchen where Raj was pouring Lewis a glass of lemonade. Lewis's beautiful face, his eerily blue eyes, shocked her. She hadn't seen him in a while. There was something deeply wrong in this boy, and yet it was absolutely compelling, as if he were the hopeless guardian of some occult purity, which irradiated his features, giving his face an unearthly aspect.

Raj looked guilty. 'Is it all right to have this?'

'Of course,' she said. 'Finish it.'

The boys – God, they were nearly fifteen now – gulped the lemonade down their thickening adolescent throats. A long day of writing
had left her a little unguarded, not yet completely inhabiting herself,
and these boys in her house suddenly appalled her – their physical-
ity, the strong smell of their sweat, their big hands and feet. The world
swallowed boys and regurgitated men in a painful, heaving articulation of bodies.

'I thought maybe Lew could stay for dinner,' Raj said.

It took her a second to respond. 'Yes, of course.'

Lewis was fingering the lip of his glass. 'I'd better get back.'

'Stay,' Ruth said.

The boys glanced at each other, shocking her with the substance
of that communication: they had sensed that she wasn't quite here in
the world, her presence a kind of quiet annihilation. In that glance
she felt both violated and absolutely excluded – not just from their
lives, but from human life.

Lewis repeated that he needed to go and Raj followed him out.

She went to the back door and saw them by the barn, whispering,
Raj's arm loose over Lewis's shoulder. She couldn't imagine what they
might be saying; couldn't remember being – perhaps had never been
– that intimate or that young. If she ever brought home a friend, her
mother would be rude, would later deride the girl, imitating and
formulating her. It was their world. The only other indigenous creature was her father, ponderous, thick-skinned, who fed upon the
thorns. There the boys whispered in their forgotten bodies, her imagination gnawing upon them like a teething child.

Raj returned to her, smiling. How brave he was: she was one of
those figures in doorways, with a comely form but no face, everyone's face, who beckons and is doom. And yet he entered.

'Why didn't he stay?'

Raj shrugged. 'Are you hungry? I'll make scrambled eggs.'

She shook her head. Still, after more than two years, it astonished her how much he could eat: six eggs and half a loaf of bread. She sat at the table as he cooked.

'Where did you all go today?'

'Alvin came and wanted to show us something,' he said, adding, 'I feel bad.'

'Why?'

'After Annie went home, Lew and I ran away from Alvin. I felt guilty because . . . I don't know, I suppose I was the one everyone ran away from in England.'

'Why d'you do it, then?'

'He's strange,' he said. 'Took us to see a dead bird. Then he says these . . . things. Today, after Annie had gone, he started asking me about my dad. Told him I didn't know much, but he just kept going on and on, asking if my mum was his slave, things like that.'

'That's awful,' Ruth said. 'His mom's a strange bird too.' She pulled up. 'Don't tell anyone I said that.'

'I won't.'

'Oh, I almost forgot. Nora came by looking for you, said something about you doing a project together.'

He looked puzzled. 'That's not due for a couple of weeks.'

'She was all dressed up. Seemed *very* disappointed.' Ruth smiled at him.

He shrugged.

'So . . . ?' she said.

'So what?'

'She sweet on you?'

'I's a nigger, massa.'

'Don't say that word.'

He busied himself buttering his mountain of toast.

'Do you like her?' she asked.

'She's all right.'

'What do you think of Annie?'

He took a moment to scrape his eggs on to a plate. 'I like Annie.'

'You have to be careful. She seems really nice, but—'

He cut her off. 'She *is* nice.'

'I know she is.' Ruth was surprised she had said anything. It occurred to her that she was trying to protect him, but she was too used to self-examination to fall for that. She knew this feeling, though she hadn't been subject to it for many years. It quite shocked her. She was jealous. Not of Nora, but of Annie. She admired Annie, but Annie required something absolute in the feelings of others for her.

'Hey,' sitting down with his food, he changed the subject, 'Pela and Olenka got hold of me again yesterday. They lie in wait for me when I'm coming back from school. Olenka thinks I'm a horse. So they get hold of me in the street, tell me they just want me to help them carry their groceries. I end up cleaning their whole kitchen. And Pela keeps telling me what a bad job I'm doing and Olenka keeps whinnying and shaking her head.'

'No!'

He nodded with a mouthful of eggs. 'And when I'm done Pela brings in these big cans of paint and tells me to wash and paint the walls. I'd been there almost three hours.'

'God, they'll never change.'

'Anyway, just a warning. I told them I'd do it this weekend, so they'll probably come round here looking for me.'

'Hope they do,' Ruth said. 'I'll give them a flea in their ear.'

'Lew won't talk about them. Is it true they adopted his mom?'

'Yes, poor Bella. The sisters – used to be three of them – went out shopping one day and saw a big crowd of people at the train station and all these kids lined up under a big banner from the Children's Aid Society of New York. They picked out little Bella like she was a watermelon.'

'Annie told me once they treated her bad?'

'Badly,' she corrected, and for a moment tiny, ardent Bella appeared before her, as she had appeared that day at her door, just married and looking for a friend. She had experienced who knows what deprivations, but had that remarkable expression: intense, grasping, remembering, as if the world were reminding her of a wonderful dream she just had, looking at you as if you had been, last night, a tree heavy with peaches in the desert. But that poor girl had married the desert. Worse than a nightmare, Clyde was like a void in hope. Raj, she saw now, had something of Bella's look, though it was neither hopeful nor hopeless. You might be a peach tree in the desert, but he was prepared for those peaches to be ashen: that could not hurt him.

'The sisters made her life hell,' she began.

Raj looked at her surprised, clearly having thought by her sharp correction of his English and subsequent silence that this subject was taboo. And all at once – a little comically because his mouth was so full – he took on a look of absolute receptivity, a transformation that was as striking as watching a contortionist abruptly turn himself inside out. Ruth loved it that he had not yet lost the young child's capacity for almost self-obliterating curiosity.

'The sisters wouldn't teach her English – Bella was originally from Hungary. I went round there with a couple of other women from town one time to try to explain that she was their daughter, not their servant. She dressed them, emptied their chamber pots, trimmed their corns. Only time she was ever let out alone was when the weather was bad and they needed something from the store. Then they gave her a strict time limit – you'd see her running through town, usually in the rain. And in the few minutes it took Sal to fill her order, he'd try to teach her a word or two of English.'

'Is it true that they were once really rich?'

'I guess in the old days in Russia. Something happened. They became refugees. Their brother bought them that house about forty years ago. He's dead now, I think. They were so bizarre. One Sunday they turned up at church, all three of them – which they never did. They must have heard that we sometimes took up collections for people in need. They sat right at the front and halfway through the sermon, the older sister – the one who died – gets impatient, stands up, interrupts old Reverend Gordon, and tells the congregation she and her sisters need money, food and help fixing up their house. Then they march out. This was before people were wise to them. So sweet seventy-year-old Mr Reece offers to help. He puts up shelves, refinishes their floors, paints their walls, rewires most of the house, washes their windows, mends their siding. Not once do they bring him anything to eat or drink. They complained constantly about the quality of his work. He was a wreck: all the skin peeled off his hands. If he didn't turn up, you'd see the three of them marching down the street to get him, and if he didn't answer the door right away, they'd spread out around his house and bang on the windows with coins, shouting his name. Then one day their old ladder breaks while he's cleaning out their gutters and he damages two discs in his back. Next day the older one comes round to his house. He's lying in bed, delirious with pain, and she hands him a bill for the ladder.'

'Delicious,' Raj said, laughing.

'Oh, that's not the half of it. When the older one died, about ten years ago now, money was wired for the funeral expenses from a bank in Cincinnati. And one of the sisters must have made a mistake. Instead of a hundred dollars, ten *thousand* dollars was wired to their account in the Jackson Savings and Loan. Deirdre's son is a teller, and he said it was a month before the sisters even realized a mistake had been made, so there must be a fortune in whatever account it came from.'

'So they are rich.'

'Must be. Just too afraid or too damn tight-fisted to spend it.'

He pondered this a moment. 'So how did Bella meet Lew's dad?'

'Ah, the mysterious Clyde Tivot. He'd turned up in town a few years before Bella and had rented that place they still live in now.'

'Where'd he come from?'

'That was the problem. No one knew. Wasn't related to anyone and kept completely to himself. When he first arrived and people went to visit, he kept them at the door and refused any gifts – even pies and things – point blank. So a rumour starts spreading that he's a fugitive. Thing is, we already had our boogerman.'

'The man who turns into a dog.'

'So they say. It was just some poor hobo, lived in the woods. Anyway, since that role was filled, I think the town became quite enamoured with the idea of having its very own fugitive. Which was lucky for him because otherwise people would have insisted on know-ing who his people were and where he'd come from.'

'Do you think he is a fugitive?'

'I think he's just a very private man.'

'Do you feel like you're a part of this town?'

She smiled. He was going to try to get as much out of her as he could. 'An essential part: I'm a warning to all rebellious daughters.'

'So why did you stay here?'

'You're changing the subject.'

'Sorry.'

'So one day Clyde clearly decides he needs a wife. He appears at church one morning, all cleaned up, and he sits there staring at all the women, like he's at a cattle market. Over the next few months, while the women he'd selected were doing their chores, or walking around town or through the fields, he'd suddenly appear, in his Sunday best, and ask if they wouldn't mind walking a ways with him. Did it to me one time. I was just out the back here. I yammered on nervously. He didn't say one word, just stared right into my womb with those amaz-ing blue eyes of his. Ten minutes later, he clearly makes up his mind about me and walks off, just like that, without even saying goodbye. Did this to near every young woman in town – which left a lot of outraged women. I've no idea what he was looking for exactly, but he seemed to narrow his choice down to about a half-dozen and goes to stage two, which is to show up at their homes uninvited on a Sunday afternoon with some kind of bizarre gift, like pickled pig's trotters, or a bunch of every kind of flowering thing he'd managed to pull up – most of them weeds. Then he'd sit completely silent in their houses in front of them and their families. Some of the women had beaus or fiancés, and in a couple of cases they were also visiting. But Clyde seemed oblivious.'

'Were these women interested?'

'He was a good-looking man, and he wasn't what they were used to, and there was certainly something about being one of the chosen few. Anyway, you could just imagine it: him sitting there holding his hat between his legs in front of those outraged fiancés, and the fathers scratching their heads, and disdainful mothers crashing the dishes around and saying, "Well now!" every five minutes. But he never went back a second time to any one of them. So this strange man managed to reject pretty much every woman in this whole town.

'Then one day he comes across Bella, who'd escaped the three sisters and was wandering in the woods.'

'How do you know this?'

'She told me. She used to come round here. She seemed to like me. She told me she was crying, and then she saw him. He was just staring at her. She said she decided in that instant that she had to marry this man and get away from the sisters. So she literally *made* herself into a mature woman. Said it was like taking everything she had inside her and forcing it to her surface – into her skin. She was trying to sell herself again, as she had in dozens of train stations years before. He was mute as ever. She tried to explain that she didn't speak English very well. Eventually, she begins to point around her and say the names of the things she knows: bird, squirrel, tree. And each time she does this, he politely agrees with her, which makes her laugh. Then she points at the river. "River," she says. That's when he speaks for the first time. "Missouri," he says. And, canny little thing that she is, she repeats this, but deliberately wrong, "Massari." "Missouri," he says again, coming closer. "Mozoui." "Missouri." And by the time she says it right, she's reeled him in. She'd engaged him, as no one else had managed to, in the simplest of conversations, in which he could feel a little pity for her and a little superior, and that she needed him but was capable of learning. I remember her winking at me, saying: "This how you catch yourself a man, uh." I wish she'd lived. I think we would have been good friends. She was a very funny, smart woman.'

'You should tell Lew that.'

'I should. Anyway, within weeks he went round to the old ladies to ask for her hand. They agreed, which was a shock to everyone. Why would they give up their slave? They said they'd lost her papers, but signed an affidavit she was of marriageable age. What she and Clyde realized, as soon as they married, was that the three sisters now expected both of them to serve and provide for them. They'd launch themselves on little raiding parties down on his farm, pulling vegetables out of the kitchen garden, taking eggs, clearing out the root cellar. Bella and Clyde tried to put up with it as best they could, but one day Bella, who was pregnant with Lewis, hears frantic squealing, runs out and finds these three little viragos trying to kill one of their piglets with implements they'd found in the barn.'

'Viragos?'

'It means fierce women. Anyway, she fetched Clyde and he told them to leave and not come back. When he did, they threatened to reveal the truth, which was that Bella had only just turned thirteen when they married. He called their bluff, though, said they'd signed the affidavit and he'd take them to court, regardless of the fees. This was canny, since the one thing the old women couldn't bear even to think about was spending money, so they finally left them alone.'

'What happened to her?'

'Died when Lewis was five. Haemophilia, I think. Dr Henemen said he'd never seen anyone fight so hard to live. Little Lew would sit on the bed all day holding her hand. They hadn't figured out what was wrong with Rohan, but he would spend hours just staring into the fire. Poor Clyde. God, his life is like a Greek tragedy: His wife dies and one son ends up killing the other and going mad. And no one has any clue what that man did to deserve it.'

'Lew's better now, though,' Raj said.

She nodded. 'You like Lewis, don't you?'

'He's my best friend – he and Annie.' He picked up his dishes and brought them to the sink.

'I shot that bird today,' he said, without looking at her. 'With Alvin's gun. To put it out of its misery. Probably right to do it, but it felt wrong and that's why I did it.'

'What do you mean?'

'Still can't believe I'm here – in Pisgah. I'm still surprised when I wake up in the morning. Today I wanted to be here. That's why I shot the bird.'

She wasn't sure how to respond. He was such an intelligent boy, too young to be thinking and saying such things. Washing the dishes, he still hadn't looked at her. What he just said made sense. Two ways to tie yourself to a place: fall in love or commit a crime; assimilate or violate. At least it might seem that way to someone young.

She realized she had let the silence go on too long. 'I know what it's like to feel outside of things.' She stopped herself. She was about to tell him what she had experienced just a little while ago, watching him and Lewis whispering on the porch, but felt uncomfortable suddenly with this boy who wasn't her son and was almost a man, this stranger at the sink who had just disclosed this intimate – too intimate – thing, and yet remained somehow impenetrable and watchful. The possibility of some real and adult intimacy frightened her: the suggestion in what he had revealed that he and she might try to do something other than sluice what took place between them into the sea of their dreams. Did she trust him? For her, intimacy was an externalized and collaborative creation, a single object that would express, in the end, the absence of the two people who had made it. For Annie it was about the impossible – being inside someone at the same time they were inside you. For him? She had a suspicion about him: that like most men he wished to bring her into conjunction with his inner life, to settle her struggle – that fixed but eccentric cam, disordered as a baby's limbs. To have her feel, instead, as the planets feel, according to mass, proximity, trajectory and immutable law.

'I've never used a gun before.' He turned to her. 'I was afraid I was going to miss.'

'I have a rifle,' she said. 'It was my father's. It's in the attic.' She stood up, but hesitated. Did she trust him? She wasn't sure, but reached anyway into the old sugar bowl on the shelf above the sink, removed the key to the attic padlock and handed it to him. 'When you get up there, there's a flashlight just to your left. Make sure to step on the crossbeams or you'll come through the ceiling. The rifle's in a long wooden box, leaning up against the wall near the window, right in front of you. There's a bunch of other neat stuff up there you might like also. But you must promise me something. I have some personal things up there, and I want you to promise – *promise* – you will never go up there without asking me first, and that you will respect my privacy.'

She met his dark eyes, which were curiously evaluating her, evaluating the peach tree in the desert – and maybe there was a little unwonted hope there.

'Okay?' she said.

He nodded.

'Okay. Go and fetch the rifle. I'll show you how to clean it and I'll teach you to shoot. You can kill some of those damn rabbits that are besieging my cauliflowers.'

He started to laugh.

'What?'

'You're going to give me a real rifle?'

'Yes.'

'And you're going to teach me to shoot?'

'Yes.'

He looked up into the ceiling, raised his clenched hands above his head, made a whoop, and cried out in his best Midwestern accent: 'God bless America!'

When Nora got back from her trip to Miss Winters' place, her dad and brother were arm-wrestling at the dining table, which was shaking under the pressure. Her father had gotten so heavy now he was probably close to three hundred pounds, and had taken to driving around his Chevy dealership in a converted go-kart. Her brother was not far behind. Her mom stood in the kitchen doorway, looking on anxiously, a pink cardigan hanging from her narrow shoulders. Nora couldn't help but think of something timid and bat-like.

'You're going to break the table,' her mom called. Glancing at Nora, she smiled as if sorry for something – anything – sorry even to be smiling.

'Hey, Nor, see this boy,' her dad said. 'Thinks he's got his old man.'

'You keep lifting your damn elbow,' Jude complained.

'Jude, don't cuss,' her mom said.

Grinning, her dad slowly forced Jude's arm down. As he did so he released an extended fart, which got louder as he ground Jude's hand into the oak surface. 'Jackpot,' he shouted. 'Howja like 'em apples, Kemosabe?'

Jude jumped away from the table, covering his nose. 'Oh Christ, Dad, your insides must be rotten.'

Her mom had vanished into the kitchen. Nora headed to her room.

'Stop, stop, hon,' her dad called. 'I want a word with you. Where you been?'

'Nowhere.'

'Look kind of dressed up for nowhere. You got lipstick on?'

'Bit.'

'What you wearing?'

'Just normal. Just a twinset. What's wrong with it?'

'Nothing wrong with it.' Winking at her brother, who was now on the couch, her dad lifted his leg like a peeing dog. Crossing his eyes, he shook his leg to release a couple more sputtering farts.

'Oh Dad, that's so disgusting,' she said.

'And yours smell like the ashes of roses,' he said.

Jude had pulled his T-shirt up over his enormous stomach and was digging out the fluffy down caught in his hairy belly button.

Her dad put on a more serious face. 'I'm just saying you're not ten years old any more.'

'What's wrong with what I'm wearing?'

Her mom had fluttered into the kitchen doorway again.

'Do you think she really don't notice?' he called to Jude.

Her brother shrugged. 'I didn't get no brains. If she didn't get none we're shit out of luck.'

'Jude!' her mom squealed.

'Honey,' her dad went on, 'what I'm saying is any bigger and people are going to think you're smuggling communists.'

'What?'

'You're my daughter and I love you, but there's no denying that what you got there, hon, are some high-calibre hooters.'

Nora couldn't believe what her dad was saying.

'Karl!' her mom said.

'Almost as big as sunny Jim's here.'

Obliging his father, Jude hiked his T-shirt up over his chest and cupped the copious loose flesh around his nipples with both hands.

'You don't want to be feeding every hog in town for free,' her dad said. 'What you're wearing's too tight. You need to do what your mom does' – he pressed his fingers to his nipples – 'use Band Aids.'

'Karl!' her mom called again.

'What?' He reacted with self-righteous anger. 'She's your daughter, you should have told her. You tell her about the other thing?'

'I took them out,' her mom said.

Her dad turned back to her. 'There were cockroaches in the bathroom. Do you know why?'

'What's he talking about?' Nora turned to her mom, who hunched her little wings.

Jude spoke up. 'Dad, leave her alone.'

'Did you just grow an extra set of balls, Kochise?'

Cowed, her brother became abruptly and inordinately fascinated with the little clot of fuzz he had retrieved, rolling it in his fingers.

'Dad, why are you being such a jerk?' she said.

'It's blood.' He stabbed his finger into the tabletop. 'I know you wrap it up but it's blood. It's blood. It's like rotting meat. You got to put it in the garbage outside.'

She felt a rush of heat to her face. 'Mom told me to put it in there,' she shouted.

'It's my fault,' her mom said. 'I just forgot to empty the trash out of there.'

Nora didn't want her dad to see her cry. She had the strangest feeling that this was somehow about what had happened a few weeks ago with her cousin. She went quickly to her room and sat on her bed, pressing against her eyelids as if this might force the liquid back. A moment later she heard a knock so faint it could only have been her mom.

'Yes.'

The door opened and her mom peered in. 'Honey. Honey, are you all right?'

She wondered if her mom would be brave enough to take flight, flutter across the room to her. But she remained in the doorway almost wringing her hands.

'You'd tell me if I didn't look okay, wouldn't you, Mom?'

'Of course, honey. Your dad was just joking around. And that last thing, that was my fault. I should have taken the trash out.'

Nora wished she had got her mom's body, thin and angular, but nothing of her mom had gotten through, her dad's side, just as in real life, elbowing out her mom's. She was her dad's daughter, solid blonde like *Grosmutter*, who had given birth to him between shifts at a candle factory in Frankfurt. When Nora worked in the garden in summer, her muscles would swell noticeably in just days. She glanced up at herself in the vanity mirror. As quick as the rat-snake she had glimpsed at the bottom of the well, sliding into the water, loathing flexed down the full length of her body. Gently she touched her face, raw with acne.

'Do you think the radiation's working?' her mom said.

Nora glanced back at her. For a second she had forgotten she was there. 'It's working to line someone's pockets.'

'It'll pass.'

She wanted to be alone. 'I'm going to have a shower.'

'Let me give the tub a little scrub. Karl was cleaning fish in there, of all things.'

'I'll do it.'

'It'll just take me a minute.' Her mom shut the door.

Nora remained where she was. She wished Raj had been home. She hardly ever got him on his own. It wasn't fair: Annie already had Lew. She loved Raj's accent, loved to hear him say her name. He did such funny impressions of people and was the smartest boy in school. She fantasized about going back to England with him. Elegant England: Regent's Park, Piccadilly Circus, the hats at Ascot, *How do you do?* When they were out with Annie, Lew and Alv, he always helped her if they had to climb anything. He wasn't a Negro, he was English. Or like a maharaja, with elephants and a jewel in his turban. She had never seen a single blemish on his lovely skin. She had already imagined their children on one of her many free-falls into fantasy. But she would always be pulled up, tied as she was by a stiff, short rope to her dad, jarring her limbs. He called Raj a nigger.

'I'm done in there,' her mom called from the hall.

Nora took off her cardigan and blouse. Just as she reached back to undo her bra, the door flew open and her dad walked in.

'Get out,' she shouted, throwing her arms over her chest.

'Your mom seems to think you're upset with what I said?'

'Get out!'

He made a show of covering his eyes, clownishly sticking his tongue out and squinting through his spread fingers – like the peek-a-boo games he used to play with her when she was a kid.

'Dad,' she screamed, 'get out.'

'I've wiped your poopy ass,' he said, heading to the door. 'Ain't nothing there I ain't seen before.'

When you died something crept into me. It made a web and fed on my poor heart that throbbed and flapped like an old grey moth. It made me very sane – sanity as hard and necessary as the iron lung you were in. I won't forget that.

I imagine I'll come back again. Not as a person – I have failed as a person – but as some quality – sunlight caught in the shell of a cicada. Do you remember how you collected those cicada shells and glued and painted them – all on your little desk like jewels Mitzi – and I smashed them – why I don't know. Maybe because you had such patience to make and finish things. I was just a little boy but I will die regretting this –

*smashing the painted shells of insects with Mother's music box.
Its lid fell off so it kept playing Beethoven's Für Elise – doesn't
that prove we're alive.*

*So Mitzi leibshen I'll make it out as you did. You used to
laugh as if laughing hurt you. Sometimes I couldn't tell if you
were laughing or crying. I can still feel you holding my hand
Schwester – saying 'Ein weiterer Laut und Gott ist heir.' I held
my breath – afraid – until you tickled me.*

*For some life seems too short. For me it seems to stretch on
forever – I never quite got into the world. I feel I had enough
in me to be – perfectly – some glimmer or shadow. Not a man
– not this man.*

The Jackson and Pisgah Herald

DEATH BY MISADVENTURE

John Hoffmeyer was pronounced dead by misadventure by
the Jackson County Coroner, Dr Lehman, on Saturday 13
September.

Jack Perry and Norman Hellman, who were driving by
the Hoffmeyer residence, 4750 Old Dutch Road, on Saturday
gave a statement to the police that they saw Mr Hoffmeyer
sitting on the running board of his Chevy truck at approx-
imately one thirty with his rifle in his hands. They called a
greeting, but he did not respond.

Some hours later, returning from their fishing trip, they
saw that he was lying in an unusual way in the yard with
the rifle beneath him.

'We thought he'd had a heart attack,' commented Jack
Perry, who is a volunteer fireman and administered aid at
the scene.

'We just got him up into the back of my car and took him to Jackson quick as we could,' added Norman.

'He died immediately and without pain,' Dr Lehman said.

'There is still one question mark,' said Sheriff Judd. 'The rifle, which was on the scene when Peewee (Jack Perry) and Norm arrived, has since gone astray. We fear it may be a "trophy hunter".' He has made an appeal for this, since it is important material evidence. If it is returned to him by the end of the week, no questions will be asked.

The funeral will be held on the 20th of this month, and he will be buried beside his sister, Margaret, who died of complications arising from polio when she was fifteen.

John Hoffmeyer will be remembered for winning the slow-bicycle race three years in a row at the county fair as a child. 'He was like a bird on a wire,' commented Mrs Freeman, who has judged the competition for the last forty years. 'He could just balance on that bicycle of his all day.' He is survived by his mother, Mila Hoffmeyer.

Alvin was almost home, all of Hoffmeyer's things now safely hidden. The last had been his old Winchester hunting rifle, and he still felt light-headed with the fear and excitement of sneaking through the fields and across the main road with that thing.

He had found the rifle less than an hour after Hoffmeyer had used it. Incredible luck: he and his dad arriving at Mrs Hoffmeyer's just as Mrs Gephardt dropped her off after a trip to the very same hospital her son was at that moment being rushed to by Peewee and Norm. Just as they sat down for the usual thirty minutes of Mrs Hoffmeyer, who had emphysema, pushing out a word or two at a time between each fought-for breath, the phone rang. After answering it, she started to make a sound like an injured dog, and his dad took the receiver. When he put it down, he told Alvin he would have to walk home, since John had mistakenly shot himself and he was going to take Mrs Hoffmeyer to see him in the hospital. Alvin knew right off what crazy

John had done. Though he made as if he were heading across the field toward home, as soon as he saw his dad's car leave the driveway, he returned, slipping around the back to see if he could get into the garage Hoffmeyer had made into his home.

The big sliding door was wide open. He saw a dark patch in the mud right in front of that broken-down Chevy. As he went around the truck he bumped into the rifle, which was propped against its bed. He wondered why Jack and Norm hadn't just left it on the ground, where it must have fallen. He didn't touch the rifle right away but went into the garage, in which was a cot surrounded by piles of books and newspapers. All over the floor lay dozens of clocks, radios and small engines, their workings scattered. On a desk made out of pine planks between sawhorses sat an old Gourland typewriter with a sheet still in it. On it was typed the same crazy stuff that filled a huge box-file on the desk. The unlatched rifle case lay on the floor beside a roughly torn-open box of bullets. It struck him then, like a sudden cold spray against his spine: the suicide was right there in front of him, like a footprint in sand. The desk chair was pulled out and angled towards the rifle case. Alvin went through the sequence. After typing the note, Hoffmeyer retrieved the box of bullets from somewhere and tore it open. He got his rifle, loaded it, and walked out into that little pool of sun in the yard. How could you kill yourself in the sunlight? How could you get so lonely and crazy? He wanted to stay there, read this file, figure out everything this man had been thinking, feeling, every move he had made from typing this page to pulling the trigger. Once, accompanying his dad on a home visit to see old Mrs Hammon, who had broken her pelvis, he snuck upstairs and saw the old lady's daughter, Beth, through the hinge crack of a slightly ajar door. She had her back to him, sitting on the bed, feeding her newborn baby. He hadn't seen anything, really, but her dress was pulled down over her shoulder, and he remembered the way she was holding the baby's head against her body. Strangely, he imagined Hoffmeyer in exactly the same posture, cradling the rifle against his chest, as if he were feeding the barrel with the blood of his heart.

Imagining this, he got a vivid echo of that same little chill of excitement he had felt looking at that woman's unguarded back, her one naked shoulder, her hand cupping that small feeding head. What was the last thing Hoffmeyer – John – had thought about? That all these little machines would never work again? Or something personal – his mom, his sister, the stuff in that note? *Ein weiterer Laut und Gott ist hier*. What did that mean?

A car sped by on the road, shocking him out of his thoughts. Running, he fetched the rifle, and shut it in the case. He emptied out an army kit bag full of camping gear. In it he put the bullets, the box-file, the typewriter with the note still in it, and an ammunition box full of photographs and letters in German. He hid the kit bag and rifle in the overgrown field behind the Hoffmeyer house.

Today he had retrieved them and snuck the kit bag and rifle into his new hiding place – a derelict house which stood on their land just a couple of miles down the road from his own house. A fire, probably set by a hobo, had destroyed most of it. It was surrounded by warning notices and a half-hearted chicken-wire fence. He had broken into the unfinished cellar, and now everything he had ever taken was down there. The rifle was the last thing.

As Alvin turned on to the driveway of his house, he saw his mom standing on the porch, smoking. This frightened him. She hadn't smoked for years: his dad hated it. She held the cigarette up at her face, her other arm wrapped around herself in the gathering chill.

'Hey, stranger.' She was peering at him with an exaggeratedly sly smile as he came up the porch steps, and he knew immediately she had been drinking. 'Have you been gallivanting with one of your glorious girlfriends?'

'I was with Raj and Lew.' He wondered where she had got the alcohol.

'Ah, boys on the prowl, Raj and Lew, and my poor Alvi, sweet little peachy pie.' She plucked a burr from his T-shirt.

'He thinks I have two beers and I'm out of control.' She waved her cigarette hand above her head to indicate out of control. 'Don't know what he's so afraid of. Maybe he thinks I'll viciously muss up his hair. Said I swore at him. "Heavens" is not swearing. "Heavens." Is that swearing? Is it, Alvi?'

'Don't know, Mom.'

'Alvi' – her face became mock-lascivious – 'were you out there breaking hearts?' She laughed.

'Told you, I was with Raj and Lew. We found an eagle that was hurt and I had to put it out of its misery because it was upsetting Annie.'

'Annie? Is she still jealous?'

'Don't know.'

'That's what happens in this country. Sebastiana is turned into Annie; mean little jealous Annie, jealous of my boy, spreading lies.'

'She's all right now.'

'"Heavens" is sweet.' She pressed her palm to her chest. 'I mean, what does he want me to do? Not say anything?'

'I don't mind it.'

'Oh, Mommy's little man. If you were any sweeter, I'd eat you.'

'I thought I could have Raj and Lew over for dinner sometime.'

'Of course.'

'They could stay over maybe?'

'Of course of course of course of course of course of course of course.' She sucked on her cigarette.

'I shot the eagle. It was going to die anyway. I shot it in the heart with my .22.'

Making another sly smile, she winked at him. Then she seemed to deflate a little, looking out over the garden. 'I broke someone's heart once. Told me himself. Said he'd never be the same. When we parted ways, he wrote me just the most romantic letter saying that bits of him were falling off – something like that. And he signed it with his whole name – including his middle one. That was heartbreaking, like it was an official document. Anyway, I heard this morning from an old friend – wrote me a letter. Told me this fellow's now running a farm supply business in Kansas – thank God I didn't marry him – and he's married and has a son and a daughter, and guess what his daughter's name is? Judy. He named his daughter after me. Can you believe that? It's creepy. Don't you think it's creepy? Saying that name all the time. And his wife not knowing. Don't you think it's creepy?'

'Don't know. I'm going inside.'

'Yes, and when your dad gets back from ministering to the benighted, for heaven's sake don't say "heavens". It might put lines on his face. He'd have to double the cucumbers and cold-cream.'

Alvin went inside and made himself a baloney sandwich for supper. He returned with it to the sitting room window and watched his mom. She had wandered into the garden and seemed to be inspecting the plants, here and there plucking off a dead blossom – just as she had pulled that burr from his T-shirt. He was no more to her, right now, than a plant. Finishing his sandwich, he went to wash his hands and saw that the lock to the basement door, which was opposite the bathroom, had been broken. The thick old padlock was still intact, but the bracket had been jimmied out of that rotten old door. For a second he wondered if his dad had lost the padlock key, but then remembered that his dad kept beer down there: once a week he washed his hair in a mixture of beer and raw eggs, which he seemed to believe staved off baldness. It made Alvin feel hollow and a little sick to imagine the argument they must have had, his dad hiding the key and his mom being so reckless. He pushed the bracket screws back into the holes so his dad wouldn't find out right away.

Needing a stapler for his homework project, he went into his dad's room. Open on his dad's desk lay the sermon he was working on for Sunday. Titled 'What is God's Love?' it was a list, each line beginning, 'God's love isn't . . .'

> God's love isn't resentful of that last bad batch of government
>   seed corn.
> God's love isn't jealous of Mr Albertson's new Mercury Coupe
>   – even if he does drive it up and down Main for no good
>   reason.

> God's love isn't ordering corn hash and expecting the blue
> plate special.
> God's love isn't a Cardinals fan only in the post season — and
> will never be a Yankees fan.

The list went on for over forty pages. The final line was 'God's love *is!*' Seamus and Walter told him their parents thought his dad was the most boring minister they had ever been to. But his dad worked so hard, rehearsing for hours in front of the big triptych mirror he had set up in the bay window.

He looked around, feeling weird suddenly, as if he didn't know his dad. The room was a mess, which was funny for someone so obsessive about his appearance. For the first time it struck him as strange that his dad slept alone in here on this little trestle bed. The far side of the room was cluttered with his dad's exercise equipment: a bench press, dumb-bells, an ab-wheel, and a pull-up bar fixed in the door of his closet. There was also a steeply inclined bench so that he could hang upside down for a half-hour every day to get blood to his scalp. His dad was terrified of losing his hair, as his own dad had done, very young. The whole back of the closet was packed with cures for baldness, such as Dr Hephaestus's Homeopathic Hair Tonic, which was made with 'extract of real human hair' and 'a potent cocktail of oriental folic stimulants, as well as secret scientific ingredient, Polysodium Melixol 4'. He also had a Vann-Graff generator, because he had read somewhere that static electricity stimulated the scalp. His dad had thick brown hair — nicer than his mom's. If he had been a little taller, he would have looked like a movie star, but he was only five three, even with those things he put in his shoes.

He heard his dad's car grinding into the driveway and hurried back to his own room. He listened then to his dad coming in and drawing a bath. After his dad had been soaking for a while, Alvin returned to the sitting-room window. His mom was still outside, the sun setting. Squatting down, she was being assailed by Mrs Freidman's friendly tabby, which was pushing its whiskers against her knees.

Absently, she plucked at its ear, tugged the tip of its tail, and tapped at its nose, but as soon as the cat tried to get up into her lap, she pushed it down and stood. Wrapped in her own tight arms she stared at the reddish sun tangled in the trees as the cat eddied frantically around her ankles.

'Pick it up. Pick it up,' Alvin whispered softly, but she didn't even glance at the cat again.

He heard his dad come out of the bathroom. After a few moments, he knocked on the door to his dad's room. Still pink from his bath, his dad was sitting at his dresser in his white robe, craning toward the mirror, trimming his eyebrows.

'Where d'you go?' Alvin asked.

His dad was too intent to respond for a moment. Finally he said, 'Mrs Braxton's. I'll be surprised if she lives another month. Sweet old lady. Told her it wouldn't be too long before the good Lord called her home, and she said, "Reverend, when you're here it can't be soon enough." I only do God's work, but a little bit of appreciation goes a long way. Last time I was there she told me she'd be forever grateful to me, since there could be no better preparation for eternity than my sermons. Isn't that nice?'

'Yes, Dad. Mom—'

'Your mom's in a funny mood today. Women get like that. There's no real reason. I read somewhere that women have exactly the same physical make-up as the earth – three-quarters saline or something. It makes them susceptible to gravitational, tectonic and barometric fluctuations.' His father suddenly turned to him. 'Alvin, does my nose seem skew to you?'

'No, Dad. Looks fine.'

'Hit it the other day against a cupboard door your mother left open in the kitchen, and it's clicking now. Listen.' His dad leaned into his ear, squeezing his nose.

'I don't hear clicking.'

'There's a lump here, look. I swear if it swells any more I'm going to look like a Jew.'

'Me, Lew and Raj found an eagle today, Dad. It was trapped in some wire.'

'I think my eczema's coming back.'

'Do you want me to do your elbows?'

'You are a darling.'

His dad opened his robe and pulled his arms from the sleeves. Though lean, he was very muscular with a well-defined chest and a ribbed stomach. While his dad stared into the mirror, Alvin rubbed lotion first into his elbows, then into the sole of his left foot, which was afflicted with persistent psoriasis. After washing his hands, he then tied his dad's hair up with numerous clips to expose as much of the scalp as possible and gently massaged in the hair tonic.

'I liked your sermon.' He met his dad's eyes in the mirror.

His dad gave him a little frown and Alvin realized he shouldn't have read it without permission. But he quickly brightened up, speaking eagerly. 'I can't wait to deliver it. It's the *via negativa*, and it uses anaphora – that's a rhetorical term.' His dad got up and went to the inclined bench, hooking in his feet and lying inverted. 'Don't you think it works beautifully? People might say it's a little long, but that's the point. One lulls them with the rhythm, then that line strikes like a thief in the night. Oh, I like that – *like a thief in the night*. I should give them a little talk about the sermon afterwards perhaps. I'm just concerned about the delivery of that final line. Are you sure you can't hear it clicking?'

Alvin had hunkered down beside the inclined plane and now bent close to his dad's face. 'I can't hear anything.'

'"God's love is." I'm wondering if it mightn't be better to say it three times, slowing it down a little more each time.'

Alvin wasn't really listening, mesmerized by his dad's reddening, inverted face, the eyeless chin, the upside-down lips mouthing, 'God's love is. God's love . . . is. God's . . . love . . . is. I'm also thinking about toying with emphasis: *God's* love is. God's *love* is. God's love *is*. I could combine them. *God's* love is.'

Alvin's mom called for him.

'I'll be back in a minute, Dad.'

'God's *love* . . . is.'

His dad's face was puce, his hair caught up revealing a crazy scalp pattern; his naked, muscular torso hung shucked from his robe. He was still squeezing the bridge of his nose.

'God's . . . love . . . *is*.'

Gently Alvin closed the door behind him.

Raj, Lew, Annie, and Nora came out of school together. After getting sodas and snacks from her dad's store, Annie suggested they head off to the sinkhole.

Raj and Lew wandered on in front. Annie always felt a little insubstantial beside Nora, who walked with a kind of ponderous and precarious grace, as if she were balancing a very heavy book on her head.

'Annie,' Nora said, 'what are you going to do after you graduate?'

'Don't know.'

'Are you going to stay in town?'

'Might go to Mizzou, study literature or something. What about you?'

'I'm applying to nursing school in Jackson.'

'You'd be a great nurse.'

'I wanted to be an air stewardess, but they said I don't fit the profile.'

'Why not?'

'Not really pretty enough. They'd want someone like you. Tall and slim.'

'You're pretty,' Annie protested. 'And you're slim.'

Nora smiled. 'As my aunt always says, All you need's pretty enough for a one-way ticket to marriageville.'

'You thinking about getting married?'

'Ain't you?'

Annie shook her head.

Lowering her voice, Nora said, 'How many boys have you kissed?'

'How many have you?'

Nora seemed distracted, suddenly, her expression almost stern. After a moment she said, 'Do you remember my cousin Götz?'

Annie did remember him vaguely, coming into the store early in the summer, a sour, shifty boy. 'He was older.'

'Almost eighteen. They'd sent him because he wasn't getting on with his dad.'

'Did you like him?'

'I guess. We kissed a bit, but then I couldn't get him to leave me alone. And one night he snuck into my room. I did like him all right. We petted some, then I told him I had to get to sleep. And he acted like he was just joking around and caught my wrists up above my head in one of his hands, and he pulled my underthings off with the other.'

'What?' Annie was horrified.

'I told him to stop, but he just kept acting like it was some big joke.'

'Why didn't you scream?'

Nora shook her head, the skin between her eyebrows deeply puckered. 'Didn't want to get him in trouble, I guess. I really thought he'd stop.'

'What did he do?'

'My dad came in before anything could happen; must've heard something. Dragged him out of the house by his hair. I felt sick for my dad, him having to see me like that.'

'Like what?'

'Like that. He'd taken my clothes off and I hadn't made a sound and I didn't know how to explain that to him.'

'Wasn't your fault.' Annie put her arm around Nora. 'Did you talk to your mom?'

'My mom?' Nora rolled her eyes. 'Anyway, my dad didn't look at me or say a single word to me for a week.'

'Why didn't you say something to him?'

'I couldn't. It was like I was still trapped on the bed, like I couldn't move and couldn't make a sound. I hated it that Götz could trap both my wrists in one hand.' She put her wrists together as if they were shackled. 'Still makes me so mad sometimes.'

Annie kept her arm around Nora. She could hardly imagine the Nora she knew trapped and unable to cry out.

A short while later, Nora glanced up at her and said, 'Are you dating Lew?'

Annie felt ambushed by this. She shrugged.

'I won't tell no one,' Nora said.

'I guess. Kind of.'

Nora nodded and they walked on in silence. Glancing ahead at Lew, Annie felt a deep dislike of herself. Nora had been honest with her, but she didn't want to be honest with Nora. Some hateful part of her felt that the truth was different for her and Nora. Nora had already worked out who she was and what that might allow her to achieve. Annie felt at times that she could do anything, make anyone love her. And yet an averted glance, a smile going cold, a stifled yawn was enough to fling her instantly into self-loathing and despair. Apart from Lew, she had kissed one boy. It was last summer, on vacation with her family in a cabin by Cherokee Lake. Exploring the woods, she came upon a fat, freckly boy sitting on a stump, reading a comic book, a gallon of chocolate milk between his feet. He seemed ashamed, as if she had caught him on the toilet. Something predatory arose in her, set off perhaps by his discomfort and the strangeness of coming upon him in the woods. She got him to talk about his family. After a while he confided that he had worked out that his mom had been pregnant with him for almost a month before she got married. This delighted him, since his military dad had a 'flagpole up his ass' and his mom was so proper she washed his mouth out even if he said 'ain't'. Annie flattered and stoked him. Desperate to please her, he began to lie. He told her that a bunch of boys used to bully him until one day he had gone blind with rage and when he had come to they were all lying on the ground in a bloody mess. His face was flushed; he was breathless. Having split him to the quick of his loneliness, she actually felt a kind of love for him – or for that split quick, perhaps, into which she wanted to touch her tongue. Abruptly she stretched up and kissed him. He suckled awkwardly at her mouth, his eyes shut, his whole body trembling. At last she stood to go. He remained on the stump, bent forward. He couldn't stand, she knew, because he was excited, and stared up at her like someone who had stupidly wounded himself. The next day, when she came out of her family's cabin in the morning, she saw him standing at the margin of the woods. There he was, the fat, heavy-breathing, unpopular boy in his miserable life. He tried to catch her attention. She went cold, felt horrified, disgusted. She hated herself for feeling it, but that is what she felt. It wasn't just him, it was loneliness, desperation, bad luck, unfulfilled longing. It was all her fears and the horror of life, there, in the woods, a beast, waving at her. The thought of touching him, even of speaking to him again, revolted her so profoundly she had felt momentarily faint. Glancing at him without any acknowledgement, she re-entered the cabin and shut the door.

'I like Raj,' Nora said.

'Does he like you?'

'He does. Just doesn't know it yet.'

They arrived finally at the sinkhole. Just as they put down their things and settled on the rocks a little way from the water, a nearby ailanthus began to shake and there was a scream. A second later Alvin leapt out, grinning.

'I followed you guys here all the way from town. Could have picked you off one by one.'

'Why don't you just grow up, Alvin,' Nora shouted.

Joining them, Alvin said, 'We should go to the flood plains, build a fire.'

'Why, is there some kind of dead animal out there you want us to see?' Annie said.

He pursed his lips and wiggled his body, as if Annie were being a priss. 'I saw a dead cow washed up once. All bloated and—'

Nora flung a twig at him. 'Shut up.'

Alvin turned to Lew and Raj. 'Where'd you guys go yesterday?'

Raj looked sheepish. 'We was just playing around.'

'Yeah, I was going to track you' – Alvin picked up a long branch – 'but I had to go home.'

Lew was rubbing his own lips gently, staring off into the woods.

'Shot a stag with my rifle after you left.'

'With your .22?' Annie said doubtfully.

'Got a new rifle. I was up in a tree. Shot through its hip so it couldn't run. It was trying to drag itself—'

'Why do you say these things?' Nora screamed at him, her face bright red. 'They're *lies*. Why do you lie like that? Why are you always thinking about hurting things and killing things? Why are you always so disgusting?'

Alvin frowned, recalcitrant, scratching the back of his hand, where a poison ivy rash was developing, and poking his stick into the ground. Annie looked at Lew and Raj, who were now both glancing a little helplessly at each other.

'I did shoot it.' As Alvin began to walk away, both Annie and Raj called his name.

He turned back.

'Do you want a soda?' Annie asked.

He shrugged, glancing at Nora, whose face was still red. She said nothing more, and he joined them.

'Truth or dare,' Annie announced, tearing strips of paper out of her notebook and passing them around.

'Long as I don't have to do anything with Alv,' Nora said.

Alvin rubbed his long stick suggestively between his two palms. 'You never know.'

Raj picked up a tiny broken twig and held it out in front of him. 'Yeah, you never know.'

They all broke into laughter. Annie noticed Lew reaching up toward his nape, but he was just scratching his shoulder. His eyes caught hers for a moment and he smiled. Together with an abrupt rush of love for him, she felt guilt at how dismissively she had talked about him earlier.

'I'll start with the questions,' Alvin said, once they had put their dares into the middle. He turned to Nora: 'Have you ever had any impure thoughts about anyone sitting here. If so who, and what were you thinking?'

'Yes I have.'

'Who and what?'

'You only get one question,' she said with a prim little moue of triumph.

She turned to Annie. 'If you had to spend the rest of your life with one person here, who would it be?'

'Oh, that's not a fair question.'

'Yes it is.' Alvin was getting excited, his voice shrill, his whole body jiggling.

Raj began to imitate him, waving around his little broken stick. 'Yes, who? And what would you do with them? And how would you do it?'

Annie took a dare. She recognized Alvin's writing. 'If you're a girl, you must balance a potato chip on the naked nipple of the boy nearest you and eat it. If you're a boy, you must balance a potato chip on the lower lip of the girl nearest you and eat it.'

'Oh, that's disgusting,' Nora said.

Annie got a potato chip and Raj pulled up his shirt. She took a moment to balance it on his dark nipple, distracted by Alvin screaming, 'Yes, yes, yes! Oh, Momma!'

As she bent forward to take it into her mouth, Raj made the sign of the cross, mumbling dryly: 'Nominus patrus y spiritus sanctum.'

When it was done, he said, 'Your tongue touched my nipple. Does that mean we have to get married?'

Annie wiggled her tongue at Raj.

'Your question for Raj,' Nora said a little sharply.

'Okay,' Annie said. 'Who was the last person you kissed on the lips?'

Lew cut in. 'Does it have to be human?'

'Suzybelle is more than human.' Raj snatched up a consequence. 'I just wish she'd stop chewing her cud.'

Annie wondered if he had ever kissed anyone.

'You must change clothes with the person opposite you.' Raj stared at Nora.

'We'll never fit into each other's clothes,' Nora complained, though she looked pleased.

'You have to do it,' Alvin squealed, ecstatic.

'I'm not going to do it in front of you,' Nora said.

'We've got to see it,' Alvin insisted.

'We'll go up the side path.' Nora spoke decisively. 'And we'll come back when we're changed.'

As Raj followed Nora up the path and out of sight, Alvin, who was hopping around with strange, agitated excitement, was shouting, 'All your clothes, everything, *everything*.'

A minute later, Raj gave a loud whoop and one of Nora's shoes came flying into the clearing. Annie went over and sat with Lew.

He smiled at her. 'Not for the rest of your life, then?'

'It's more fun to take the dare,' she said. 'That's the point.'

'I would have said you. I wouldn't even have thought about it.'

She pushed his long hair away from his face. How different he was from the fat boy in the woods: that powerful neck of his, the heartless innocence of his blue eyes. Even after everything that had happened to him, he knew how to feel cleanly, purely, heroically. Not her. She couldn't work out the proper way to be or to feel. She loved Lew, but he was a part of her already, which meant that she could disregard him as she disregarded herself, for whatever needed to be explored, seduced, drawn in. She loved him, but the thought of Raj out there exchanging clothes with Nora was filling her with restless jealousy, even though she loved Nora too.

'Naked! Naked! Naked!' Alvin was running up and down the path. 'Naked! Naked! Naked!'

She looked back into Lew's face: heartbreaking, like the face of a lame horse, a doomed and powerful innocence, a thing only lesser things could destroy. It was a little like her brother's face, which could make her cry simply because he could be so purely hurt, so purely outraged, so purely happy – though Frank hadn't been happy for a long, long time. Had Lew? It was so difficult to tell. He seemed beyond joy or grief, beyond the normal range of human feeling.

Lew put his hand to her cheek. 'Why are you crying?'

'I will be with you for the rest of your life,' she said. 'I will.' They kissed, a long, passionate kiss, but she pulled away suddenly because she became aware that Alvin had gone quiet. Glancing around, she saw him then, a little way back, at the margins of the woods. He was flushed and breathing hard, staring at them seriously. Moments later, Raj and Nora emerged in each other's clothes. He had stuffed her bra with something.

'It just doesn't seem right that I look this good in women's clothes,' Raj declared.

Nora's voluptuous body was breaking out of Raj's shirt and pants. She had crossed her arms over her breasts. 'Where's Alv?' she said.

Annie glanced over to where she had last seen him, but he was gone.

Alvin added Nora's shoe to his stash in the cellar of the burnt-out house, and took Hoffmeyer's rifle out of its case. He felt so strange: agitated, exhilarated and exhausted, as if he were hollow, but a swarm of hornets were inside him, trying to get out. It was like happiness and misery all wrapped up together. He had snuck up to peek at Nora and Raj swapping clothes, Raj acting the fool, Nora playfully hitting him. Then he had hurried back to Annie and Lew, and it was as if he had run into something that had impaled him, seeing them kissing like that. All at once he felt as if he weren't there, or what was there was so disgusting he wanted to leave it behind: a squealing, stupid, ugly kid.

He loaded the rifle and took it with him back into the woods. He had to be very careful not to be seen with it. He aimed it at a few things: cow, car, cardinal, crow. After a little while he found himself at Miss Winters' house. She was kneeling in her kitchen garden, covering the faces of her cauliflowers. Very quietly he got into position and aimed the rifle at her. Clicking the safety off, he touched his finger to the trigger. Astonishing: how easy. The crack of the rifle and she would crumple like a badly pitched tent, face-first into the dirt. All the consequences then, rippling out, Pisgah filled with horror, fear, grief. He would have his secret then. Though he would never tell anyone, people would feel it in him. They would know he wasn't a child. Grazing the edge of the trigger again, he saw her push a strand of loose hair behind her ear, and felt her life in his arms, in the arms that cradled the gun. A woman's life. In his arms. He could survive in the woods, hide in the margins. No one would ever see him. He would hold them in his arms. Heart-shot, they would fall into his arms. His hands were trembling now, his whole body, and he had to put the rifle down as that ecstatic unhappiness swarmed up inside him again. After hiding the rifle, he snuck to the front of Ruth's house and slipped in. If she caught him, he could say he was looking for Raj. But it was her room he went to. He wanted something of hers. He still felt a little sweaty and shaky, as if she were lying dead outside. Looking around her closet, he noticed that part of the cedar-plank ceiling had been replaced by a piece of pine about the size of the top of a school desk. Shutting the closet door behind him, he climbed the sturdy shelves, and gently pushed on this area, which lifted. The piece of pine had been used to fill in a hole – perhaps a rotted-out section of the ceiling or an old flue. Excited and scared, he pulled himself up into the attic. After replacing the piece of pine, he took off his shoes. The attic was packed: perfect. From the dormer window he could see Ruth still in the garden. He imagined a life of stealing into attics, barns, and cellars, taking what food and clothes he needed. He looked around the attic. He couldn't be long, but was sure he would find something here worth having.

Late that night, after his mom had gone to bed, Alvin lay on the floor of the dark hallway in his home, looking through the gap under the door to his dad's room. He had discovered this years ago, and had watched his dad on many nights. Tonight his dad was exercising in his underwear, doing push-ups and working with the bar bells. Alvin had taken a small pile of Ruth's journals, adding them to his stash in the cellar. He couldn't believe what Ruth had written about everyone in Pisgah – about his own mom and dad even. His dad now stood in front of the three-panelled mirror, flexing his chest muscles, then the thigh muscles of his small, perfect body. Why didn't his mom and dad sleep in the same room? He couldn't remember them ever kissing or touching each other, and couldn't imagine them kissing like Annie and Lew had been doing. He would be a hunter. In many years he would return to Raj, Annie, Lew and Nora altered beyond all recognition – tall, powerful, bearded, silent. His dad now gave himself a wedgie. Turning around, he looked back over his shoulder into the mirror, flexing one butt cheek, then the other. After a few moments of this, he began to take up strange poses, using the furniture as props, always looking at himself in the mirror. Some were like dancer's poses. In others he pouted, or stretched out on the floor, snarling like a tiger, or tangled himself up in the bed sheet. At one stage, he performed an odd little dance, almost like a hoola girl. Finally he got tired, pulled a comic book from under his mattress, and began to read.

Hungover, Frank joined his dad and Annie at the breakfast table. His mom was frying eggs.

'You look like shit,' his dad said. 'What time you get back last night?'

Frank didn't answer. His mom brought him coffee and a plate of eggs.

'Damn shit.' His dad flapped his newspaper to straighten it and turned the page. 'You gonna work in my back yard all your life?'

'Dad' – Annie tried to distract her father – 'did you know that one beaver can fell fifteen trees in a week?'

His dad pointed at him with the tines of his fork. 'This one don't fell no trees. Sits around on his beaver ass all day scratching his beaver balls.'

His mom had her back to them, pretending to wipe down the counter with a filthy rag while staring out of the window. Thursday. Even through his thickened, throbbing brain, Frank felt the unease of this day. Dad was always in a bad mood on Thursdays. Every Thursday his mom went to see her school friend, Caroline, in Baxter. He had never been able to get what Mary had said out of his head. He met Annie's eyes. She was watching him as if she knew what he was thinking.

Reaching over, he combed his fingers gently through her curls. 'Don't you ever brush your hair?'

Annie smiled at him. He glanced back at his mom. It was almost too intimate to look at her, as if he were watching her while she were alone and unaware. Every now and then she took in and released a deep, sighing breath.

'Going to see your friend today?' he asked.

She wasn't paying attention and didn't respond.

'Mom,' he called louder, 'you going to see Caroline today?'

Glancing back, she nodded.

'Why don't she ever come here?'

'Her husband, he's ill.'

'What's wrong with him?'

'I need to get away sometimes. I like to get away.'

'So is he ill or not?'

Annie came to her mom's rescue. 'Do we all have to suffer because you have a hangover?'

'Mom visits some woman every week for the past twenty years and we've never even seen her?'

'Well now, Mr I Wanna Know,' his mom said, 'I didn't know you so interested in my friends.'

'Do you have a picture of her?'

'What's the big deal?' Annie said.

'Today' – his dad cut in, letting go of one half of his paper and stabbing his finger into the table – '*today* you stay here. Help me in the store.'

'She's expecting me.'

'That's it,' his dad shouted, slamming his hand down. 'You stay here. No more. *Basta!*'

Annie got up and took her plate to the sink. When she returned, she sat in their dad's lap and rubbed his forehead. 'You're getting lines,' she said. 'You're going to end up looking like Mr Schull.'

His mom walked out of the kitchen and came back with her year book, which she opened beside Frank's plate. 'This, Caroline.' She pointed at a cheerleader standing next to her young self. He glanced briefly at this girl, but immediately looked back at his mom, Annie's age, caught mid-leap. Happy.

'Joint disease he have, her husband. Also she have to look after her old mother-in-law.'

Frank met her eyes, which were full of furious hurt at being questioned. He thought of the wooden Christ in church, his slightly pleading, sad eyes – *Would I lie to you?* He couldn't see any trace of a lie in her face, but doubt scratched and scurried deep within him. He had to be sure.

'Okay,' Frank said.

As soon as his mom left to catch the noon train to Baxter, Frank drove straight to The Lodge. He hid his car up a logging road, made his way through the old miniature golf course to cabin four, and climbed on to the roof. He had kissed Esta here on their first date. In their two years together how many times had she said, looking him right in the eyes, that she loved him? They had been broken up now for as long as they had been together, but he still thought about her every day. The sound of a car drew his attention. He recognized Bennet's green Belair winding its way up to lodge nine, the most secluded. Suddenly light-headed, he scrambled down and sprinted through the woods. He got to the cabin too late, the Belair parked out front. The curtains were pulled. Should he wait until they came out? But how would he stop them from seeing him? Maybe he wanted them to see him.

He made his way down one side of the cabin, which was really just a trailer with fake log siding. As he got halfway along, he saw, propped in the crook of a stunted tree, Magnus's pipe and a padlock. Quickly he glanced around. He noticed the hinged entrance to the skirted crawlspace right in front of him. This was where the padlock had been. The latch was open. As quietly as he could, he raised the flap and looked under the cabin. The soles of a pair of shoes caught his eyes first. It was Magnus, lying on an old quilt, an upended flashlight beside him. As Frank crawled under, Magnus stared at him like a treed coon, holding one hand out to urge him back and pressing a finger to his lips. As Frank's eyes got used to the dim light, he could see what looked like a steel duct coming out of the cabin floor between a series of pipes. Making a fierce gesture for Magnus to get out, he took his place on the quilt as Magnus crawled past him. The duct was one of those simple periscopes made to look over the top of trenches. There was batting around the edges, so you could press your eyes to it, which he did. He could see the latticework of a vent and through that the bedroom clearly. There they were. They didn't kiss. Like one of those shells used to milk bulls, his mom laboured to coax the impassive Bennet into arousal. She worked on him exactly like she worked to refinish the oak banister, in her lazy, indifferent way, just trying to get him good enough, then presenting herself. She failed a couple of times and had to go back to work – so strange, the same in this as in everything else, her laziness ending up making more work than was necessary. Finally she got him through, Bennet's bored, truculent and ever-disappointed expression never changing. It was sickening. Not like porno, but absolutely real. As soon as it was over, which took just minutes, Bennet went immediately into the bathroom as his mom snatched up a bunch of tissues, jamming them between her legs so she wouldn't stain the sheets. Right above him then, he heard Bennet urinating. Obscene; a horselike thundering. The toilet flushed, draining loudly through the pipes around him. His mom then, she too urinating, small spatters, a gush, small spatters, and then a longer gush. Frank pressed his face into the quilt, his body shaking, the images rioting in his head. After a little while, he heard the Belair pull out. What now? Perhaps Bennet drove her to Baxter, where she would either see her friend or just catch the train back.

He crawled out.

Magnus was waiting behind the cabin. 'You shouldn't have seen that.'

Frank kept walking through the woods, Magnus hovering at his shoulder.

'Are you going to tell anyone?'

It occurred to him that Magnus had been watching this for years and he stopped to face this pathetic man. 'You've got to destroy that thing under there. If I come here any time after today and find that here I'm going to beat you until you cry piss and shit tears; you got me?'

Flinching, as if Frank were about to hit him, Magnus nodded. Frank wished he had the strength to hit him, but it was all he could do to keep walking. He didn't feel human, but like something forged in what he had seen, those images, which were senseless and made all the sense in the world. It was as if he had dreamed them a thousand times before. Now they had broken the surface, a wreckage in his head. And the worst thing was that he hadn't known – had managed to forget somehow – until now, how deeply he loved his mother.

Annie stood at the edge of the field watching Lew trying to uproot a stump. The old Deere's engine kept cutting out. How similar he was, in some ways, to his father: solitude finished in his long body.

At last he jumped down from the tractor and came to her out of this defeat, his walk like no walk, but as if he imitated walking in order to move. An almost female face, its beauty at once assertive and blank, with that smooth forehead, those otherwordly eyes, the oval of his pink, soft mouth. And yet his muscular legs and torso, his vein-vined arms, broad shoulders, and powerful neck gave the impression that masculinity had infected him from the ground up: soon it would take his face too, and the lovely girl beneath would be consumed entirely. It was the girl's face she loved, the man's body she desired.

'Can you fix it?' she said.

'That old rust bucket ain't never going to shift those stumps. And the ground couldn't be any wetter.' Leaning back against the fence in front of her he sighed.

She put her hand on his damp neck. 'I'm on my way to Ruth's. I'm interviewing her for the school paper. Thought I'd come by.'

Smiling, he removed her hand and kissed it.

'Things don't seem to fit,' she said.

He frowned curiously.

Her heart was pounding. She didn't know how to say it: that she wished they hadn't become physical, hadn't got older; that she knew her love, desire and all these years between them weren't enough. And at the same time he was hers. Twice now she had dreamed he was dead. Strange dreams, with Raj holding Roh's hand, Lew lying on the forest floor. She knew that some part of her wanted him dead. She had come to watch him work because she wanted to make him a stranger, to unlearn him, as you unlearn a word by saying it over and over again.

'Why aren't you going to school any more?' she asked.

'Can't.' He shook his head. 'Too much . . . noise. Don't teach you nothing.'

'What do you mean?'

He seemed pained. Looking back over the field, he raised his hand a couple of times toward his neck, but managed to control himself.

He spoke falteringly, without looking at her. 'Doing what I done . . . to Wa-Kon-Te's son I have to hide. Crow is in the tree I am. Makes the tree an eye by being a speck in the eye. And as long as Crow don't know he makes me the eye of Wa-Kon-Te, who's trying to find me, I'm safe. Safe from being forgiven. If he forgives me I don't know any of this. He can't see me, because Crow is in my branches. Crow makes me the eye that looks for me. I have to—'

Annie reached up to his face. He flinched, but she drew him close and kissed him.

'I'm sorry,' he said.

'I've got to do my interview. I'll meet you out by Tanner's farrowing shed tomorrow at seven.' Annie walked quickly away. She felt as if something had struck her chest, that blow spreading insidiously inside her, like a blood drop in a glass of water.

Lew called her name softly, so softly she might have pretended she hadn't heard him, which she wanted to do. But couldn't, and turned around.

'I shouldn't have said anything. It's hard not to tell you. It's hard to know so much and not say anything.'

She nodded and watched him return across the field to the Deere, walking in that way that was like a chant or ritual or mime of motion. 'Lew,' she whispered, too softly for him to hear. 'Lew, Lew, Lew,' over and over, until it was like the last snubs of sobbing, when the child has long since forgotten the source of her tears.

Ruth and Raj were listening to *Ricky Harris's Laugh-in*. Annie joined them in that strange atmosphere of being absorbed in listening and imagining. Made stranger because she couldn't stop thinking about Lew, how close she had just been to the edge of his aloneness, which had filled her with vertigo. She tried to laugh with them, but felt like a baby, with a heavy, loose head, making random expressions. In what kind of world do you go from the worst secret you could imagine – madness – to this puppet laughter?

When the show was over, Ruth went into the kitchen.

'I'm going to see *Casablanca* tonight with Evy,' Annie said to Raj. 'Do you want to come?'

'Can't tonight. Going over to Nora's. Got our presentation tomorrow.'

'I never see you any more.'

'Saw you yesterday.'

'Since then, I mean.'

'Well, that's true.' He checked his watch. 'In fact we're thirty-five minutes from our twenty-four-hour reunion.'

'I think Lew's going mad. I think he's going mad again.' She broke off, feeling tearful.

Raj looked uncomfortable, exposed and unable to find refuge in the null of humour.

'He was saying crazy things today about being a crow or an eye or something.'

Raj plucked at his chin, staring into the floor as if searching for something. 'He's said some strange things to me too. I just make a joke of it and he seems all right.'

'He has? Why didn't you tell me?'

He shrugged and sat up as Ruth returned with a tray of tea and cookies.

Taking a handful of cookies, Raj said, 'I'll leave you to your interview, ladies.'

'When are you heading off to Nora's?' Annie asked.

'About an hour or so.'

She said she would walk back to town with him.

The interview was brief, focusing on what it took to make a living writing romance novels. Slipping her pad and pencil back into her bag, Annie said, 'Can I ask you a personal question?'

'Off the record?'

Annie nodded. 'Is this how you wanted things to be in your life? I mean if Mr Travers hadn't died.'

'Oliver was almost fifteen years younger. I doubt he would have stayed.'

'But you're beautiful.'

'You're sweet, Annie. I look okay for my age, but I found that with Oliver I was becoming a vampire. I avoided any direct sunlight. I was wearing my hair down all the time so I didn't look like an old lady, though it drove me crazy. I developed a deep hatred for my neck, which has never done anything to me except support my head, poor thing.'

'But it's all right for you to live . . . like this? I mean, not to . . . not to have someone?'

'I have Fifty-Three. He adores me and eats leftovers . . . I don't know. I mean I sometimes see myself in ten or twenty years as this old woman with a stout walking stick, taking long hikes in the country. God, Annie, you look as if I just told you I was going to bury myself alive. I also think of retiring to St Louis, teaching new immigrants to read and write.' She laughed at herself. 'I fantasize about having this extended family of little, happy, grateful immigrants, like dancing midgets.'

Annie remembered to smile, but was feeling desperate. 'What kind of man do you think you could be with for all your life?'

'I don't know. They all seemed temporary, somehow – even Oliver.'

'What if you met a married man and you loved him and he loved you and he didn't love his wife, or his wife was sick or something?'

'That's an odd question.'

'What would you do?'

'You haven't met a married man, have you?'

'No. I just . . . What would you do?'

'Don't know. Try to stay away from him, I guess.'

'But you can't.'

'Annie, it seems like you're answering your own question here.'

Annie hesitated. 'You won't be alone, you've got Raj.'

'Talk of the devil.'

Raj came in with his school bag and immediately began to imitate the thick German accent of Dr Schneider, their history teacher. 'Are you laties talking about me? You should haft tolt me. Ont me I am the most foremost expert. I vould haft prepared topics for discussion, *meine liebe Frauen*. Topic one: in vhat vays in Rajiv a clear example of the *übermensch*?'

Annie walked slowly with Raj through the fields. He was now almost a head taller than she.

'Do you remember when we first met?' she said.

'Are you bringing this up because it's our twenty-four-hour reunion?'

'Do you ever think about your mom and dad?'

He considered this. 'Sometimes.'

'Do you remember them?'

'I remember my dad – used to let me swing from his horns.'

'Stop being stupid.'

'Don't know. Sometimes I think I remember India – but I might just have made it up.'

'What do you remember?'

'I remember someone giving me water,' he said. 'In a clay bowl.'

'Do you think of Ruth as your mom?'

He shook his head. 'Tell you the truth, I'm not even sure she likes me. Gives me the strangest looks sometimes, like she still can't believe I'm here. It's as if I'm not inside her house, I'm inside her. And she can be a bit short sometimes.'

'I love Ruth.' Annie hadn't intended to sound quite so defensive.

'I don't mean—'

'I know. I'm just saying. I see myself like her sometimes, ending up on my own.'

He tried to stifle a smile.

'What?'

'You on your own?'

'You don't think I can be on my own?'

'Annie, have you noticed that you're still zipping up your dress when you come out of the bathroom?'

'What does—'

'I mean you don't even like being in the bathroom on your own. I'm sure you'd keep the door open if you didn't think it would offend people.'

'You don't know me at all.'

'I know you won't be on your own.'

It irritated her that Raj didn't think she could be alone and she went quiet, which she knew he couldn't stand.

After a moment he said, 'I wouldn't let you.'

Appeased, she met his smile. Then she said, 'What are we going to do about Lew?'

Raj looked confused. Annie suddenly wondered if Lew had told him about some of the physical things that had happened between them. Did boys talk like that?

'He's someone who should never be on his own,' she said. 'I didn't see him for a few days last week, and when I did it was as if he'd been away for a year, the look in his eyes. So much seems to be going on in him, and it all seems so important. I feel stupid and irrelevant.'

'Oh, Annie.' Raj threw his hand over his nose. 'Couldn't you wait?'

'That's not me.'

A skunk waddled out of the margins of the cattail swamp.

'Oh yeah, blame the wildlife why don't you.'

Annie took hold of Raj's arm. 'Let's sit here for a while.'

'I've got—'

'Just a minute. You won't be late.'

'The mosquitoes are eating me alive. They don't bite you. You're the mosquito queen.'

'Just one minute.'

They sat, looking out over the cattails and the water, the whole place humming with life: enormous dragonflies, both particular and clumsy, like drunken conductors; red-winged blackbirds trilling and teetering on the cattails.

'We'll all have to live in a big house together,' Raj said, his attention drawn by a heron rising from the water.

'You, me, and Lew?'

He nodded, watching the ungainly grace of that bird.

'What about Nora?'

'If she wants to.'

'She likes you.'

Raj shrugged. 'She also likes Randy Gangle and his Brassy Boxcar Band.'

'Are you not interested in her?'

'Haven't thought about it.'

'Liar.'

'She's nice.'

Annie noticed a large mosquito on his nape. She watched it for a few seconds before catching it between her thumb and forefinger, crushing it. Rubbing his neck, he turned to her. She showed him her thumb, on which lay the mosquito's remains and a bloody smear. She raised it toward her mouth, putting out her tongue. Raj quickly grabbed her wrist.

'You *are* the mosquito queen.' He tried to stop her, but she dipped her head and got her tongue to her thumb.

'That's disgusting!' He was still holding her wrist and staring at her incredulously. 'You drank my blood. Give it back.'

She wiggled her tongue at him before drawing it in.

He rubbed the rest of the blood off her finger, his voice becoming high-pitched in imitation of Miss Kelly. 'Out damn spot. Ah Shakespeare, Shakespeare, a hand there was that chucked his cheeks and called him her silly-Billy.'

Going quiet, he seemed abruptly captivated by the metallic sheen on the water. The hand with which he held her wrist loosened, but before it could fall away completely, she gently closed her fingers around his thumb.

'We should arrange to do something with Lew tomorrow,' he said, still not looking at her, his expression serious and absorbed. 'We should see him as much as we can.'

Turning to her after a little while, he said, 'I thought you and Lew . . . ?'

She didn't respond for a moment, looking at his dark fingers lying over hers. An image, then, of Lew during that truth or dare game, the deep reproach of his innocence and love. All at once she hated herself and let go of his hand.

Nora was getting herself ready for Raj. Fresh from the shower, she examined her face in the bathroom mirror. Her acne was as bad as ever. She went to work with a pin and witch hazel, dipping the pin in hydrogen peroxide to sterilize it. She had started to have dreams about zits and blackheads so huge she had to prise them out of her skin with a teaspoon, until they covered the surface of her vanity like little black and white coins.

When she was done, she stared at the burning mask of her face. She would wear her hair down and put on her pink turtleneck, which flattered her, and that pretty pleated cream skirt. She wanted something to happen tonight. Wrapping the bath towel tight around her, she wished she had remembered her robe, and listened at the bathroom door. The last couple of times she had come out after a shower, her dad had been in the hallway. The first time he just walked by her, winking. The second, he did that old trick, pointing at her chest curiously, then flicking her nose when she looked down. Hearing nothing, she hurried across the hallway to her bedroom. After drying her hair and rubbing lotion on her legs, she went to her closet. When she opened the door, she almost fell backwards as her dad's stupidly grinning face popped out from between her clothes.

'Jesus,' she screamed. 'What are you doing?'

'Boo,' he said.

'What are you doing?' She had flung her hands around her body, afraid the towel might slip.

He looked hurt. 'Can't you take a joke?'

'Don't you ever come in here again.'

'Well, that's funny,' he said, stepping out of her closet. 'Last I checked, name on the mortgage was mine.'

'You're acting weird.'

'What's wrong with you, Puggy? We always used to horse around.'

'Dad, please get out. I've got to get ready.'

All at once his face went very still and something, a shadow, seemed to pass beneath its surface. It brought back to her the look on his face when he had saved her from her cousin. That hadn't been her fault, though. Götz had trapped her arms. Her wrists would go black and blue in the next couple of days. Götz had hurt them so much that after her dad had dragged him off, she was hardly able to pull her nightdress back down over her naked body, her mom watching her from the doorway like someone peeking from behind a curtain at a fight in the street. But why hadn't she made a sound? Why hadn't she called out? A molten shame rolled down through the hollows of her body, making a solid and shapeless clot of her – revolting. She couldn't meet her dad's eyes.

'Your face,' he said. She looked up to see him pointing at his own nose. 'It's bleeding.'

'Daddy, please get out of my room. Please.'

He left. She slumped herself at her vanity, staring into the mirror. On her nose a bead of blood had swelled out from a stubborn zit she hadn't been able to leave alone. She dealt with this and got dressed. As she applied her make-up, she wondered what it would be like to live in England. Even India. Somewhere – *anywhere* – else.

Half an hour later, the doorbell rang. As she hurried to answer it, her mom emerged from the kitchen.

'Who is it?'

'Raj. I told you. We're practising our presentation.'

The sight of Raj's sweet, curious, smiling face filled her with a leavening joy. He was so tall now he had developed a bit of a stoop. Holding his hands clasped behind his back, he entered her house like an ambassador.

'*Aloha*, Mrs Kroger,' Raj said as they passed through the dining room.

Wincing out a smile, her mom quickly withdrew into the kitchen. Nora took him to her room. She had propped two large pillows against the side of her bed. As Raj sat against one of these, she asked if he minded listening to music while they worked, and put on 'Love Me Tender'.

As she sat, Raj said, 'I thought that what I could do is give the historical background while you—'

'You have amazing eyelashes,' she said.

He fluttered his eyes. 'Of course.' Now his face became crazily intense, with one eye squinted. 'Just look at this soil.' He pinched his own cheek. 'Prime bottomland. Put a dead stick in there, next day it'll be sprouting.' He was imitating Cleever, who was notorious for selling the most frequently flooded land to city folks for their summer cottages.

'You don't like being serious, do you?'

'Interrupts my breathing.' He pointed to his throat.

His leg was shaking with nervous energy and he was glancing around her room. On the back of his neck she noticed the swelling of a mosquito bite and touched her finger to it.

'You've been bitten?'

'Savaged. Got so much of my blood we're now officially related.' She laughed.

The door opened and her dad entered. She snatched her hand away.

'What's going on?'

'We're doing a presentation on Samuel Adams tomorrow.'

'Well, there's a table out in the dining room.'

'We're fine here,' she said.

'Is this homework music?'

'Dad.'

'What have you got on your face? We're spending a fortune on treatment for your zits and you're covering your face with that junk?'

'Dad, get out of my room.'

He squatted down in front of them. Keeping his eyes on her, he put out his clenched hand.

'All I ask of you is two things.' He uncurled his forefinger. 'That you're not related to the bastard.' Now his second finger. 'And that his mother isn't a damn monkey.'

'We can go into the other room,' Raj said, pulling himself up.

'Well that's really big of you.' Her dad stood also. 'You know what, sonny, I have a special room for you.'

He put his arm around Raj and almost lifted him off the floor as he frog-marched him through the house and out of the front door. Nora followed, screaming at her dad to stop.

'There you go.' Her dad shoved Raj towards the porch steps. 'Enjoy.' Preventing Nora from following, he stepped back into the house and held the door closed behind him.

'I hate you,' Nora said.

Her dad wasn't looking at her face. 'I told you to use Band Aids,' he said.

Crossing her arms over her chest, Nora ran back to her room.

Annie was sitting on Evy's four-poster bed, waiting for her to get back from the bathroom. Frank should have picked her up an hour ago. Where was he? She had enjoyed the movie, but found Evy exhausting. Evy used to have such an amazing imagination when they were younger, but seemed interested now in nothing but boys and clothes. Annie loved Mr B.'s house, though – a plantation-style mansion ten miles out of town on forty acres. Downstairs, Evy's sisters, Lucy, Clare and Greta, were smoking and playing cards with their mom. While Mrs B. was an averagely attractive and petite woman, nothing of her had made it through to her first three daughters. All had inherited her husband's lifeless eyes, lipless mouth and lantern jaw. They were graceless girls with burly bodies and deep, harsh voices. Annie thought they almost looked like men dressed as women. They were much older than Evy – in their late twenties – and never seemed to leave home except to go shopping or to visit relatives in Kansas City.

But Evy had been lucky. For one thing she was petite, like her mom, and though she did have most of her dad's facial features – except his mouth – none of them dominated. By some biological sleight-of-hand, resized and repositioned, they all worked attractively together.

Hurrying back in, Evy jumped on the bed.

'So come on, what happened?' Annie said. Evy had started to tell her about a recent date before she had run off to the bathroom.

'Don't know why I liked him,' Evy resumed. 'Anyway, he started holding my hand in the movie. Just like that. I didn't really want him to, but I didn't know what to do. His hand was so sweaty. It was gross.'

'Did you kiss him?'

'He wanted to play pediddle when we were driving back. Told him I was feeling car sick.'

'Why d'you go out with him in the first place?'

'Well, he kinda looks like Marlon Brando.'

'How old is he?'

'I thought he was eighteen, but he's really old. He's like twenty-three.'

'Jeez. Your dad would kill you.'

'Kill him more like.'

Annie could hardly imagine Evy on a date, and wasn't sure if she believed her. Though Evy was a few months from turning fifteen, she looked no older than twelve.

'So' – putting her hand on Annie's, Evy widened her eyes in an exaggerated manner – 'when are you and Lew going to get hitched?'

Annie shrugged.

Evy frowned, annoyed. 'I tell you everything, Annie. You never tell me anything.'

She pulled her hand away, but Annie snatched it back. 'I adore Lew,' she said, 'but I don't know if I could marry him, really. I don't know if I could marry anyone.'

'You've got to marry *someone*,' Evy said. 'If you could marry anyone in town, who would it be?'

'Who would *you* marry?'

Evy smiled. 'You won't be mad?'

'Mad?' Annie suddenly realized who Evy was talking about. 'Oh, no, I'd love you to marry him.'

'Your brother is such a dreamboat. So what about you?'

'If it was anyone apart from Lew . . . Raj.'

Evy let out a shriek and made a grimace, squirming her body as if something disgusting were clinging to it. 'God, could you imagine what your parents would do? Seriously, though, Annie, who?'

The door opened and Mrs B. walked in. 'Annie, honey, Greta's going to take you back. Your mom just called. Your dad's truck has blown a piston or something, and she doesn't know where Frank is.'

Annie jumped up off the bed.

'She told you not to worry, honey. She's sure Frank just forgot.'

*

When Annie got home, her mom and dad were in the hallway, standing at the bottom of the stairs.

'Where's Frankie?'

Her mom pointed upwards. She was holding her hand over her mouth.

'Why didn't he—'

'Some drinks he have,' she said, without removing her hand.

Her dad looked frightened and confused. Annie saw now that a couple of the banisters were broken, and realized that her parents were afraid to go upstairs.

'Is Frankie all right?'

'He has lots of drinks.' With her free hand, her mom drew together the collar of her robe, clutching it tightly at her neck. 'We try to help him up but . . . he's not himself.'

'He pushed your mama,' her dad whispered.

'He didn't mean to—'

'In your face. What you say he didn't mean? In your face!' Her dad demonstrated, shoving out the palm of his own hand. In that same motion, he pulled her mom's hand away from her mouth to reveal a slightly swollen cut on her lip. Then he pointed at the broken banisters. 'Look. He kicked them in. Kicked them.' He made kicking motions. '*Lui e pazzo.*'

Annie climbed the stairs. At the top, she glanced back down. Her mom and dad were staring up at her helplessly. He wasn't in his own room, so she went to hers.

It took her a moment to take in what she saw. Standing at the foot of her bed with his back to her, Frank was wearing her favourite lavender silk blouse, which had split down the spine. He had on a pair of her panties, and was struggling to pull up a skirt, which he couldn't get much past his knees. Annie felt as if her heart had dissolved and surfaced in her skin, setting up a faint, enveloping throb.

'Frankie. What are you doing?'

Glancing back at her, he almost fell. His face looked as if it were about to slide right off his head, all the muscles deadened and drooping, his eyes bloodshot. Without saying anything, he continued tugging at the skirt.

As she moved toward him, he shouted something incoherent, though it was clear he wanted her to stay away. Losing his balance, he pitched forward on to her bed. He tried to get up, but the skirt had trapped his legs, so he pulled it off. He stood, attempting to keep his back to her. As she went round to help him, he let out another cry, flinging his hand down to cover his penis, which was hanging out of the side of her tiny panties. So odd, that remembered shame in the midst of this. Annie had never seen her brother completely naked.

'I'm going to take you to bed, Frankie.' She spoke into his face as if it were the entrance of a deep well into which her brother had fallen.

Her dad was at the door, peering in, horrified. She made a gesture for him to go away, but he remained.

Luckily Frank didn't notice. It seemed all he could do to remain conscious. Trying to support her brother as best she could, she led him, one step at a time, to the door. Almost there, he suddenly pulled away, throwing his hands against the top of her dresser to brace himself in an unsteady spread-eagle. He seemed in agony, unable to catch his breath.

'Frankie,' she gently encouraged, taking hold of his waist. But she jumped back as a stream of urine splashed over her shins. Her dad let out a soft, frightened curse. Still urinating, her brother sank to his knees and began to heave.

'Dad, we need to get him to a hospital,' she shouted. Kneeling down beside Frank, she rubbed his back as he began to vomit pure liquid like an old sump pump, convulsing what he had drunk on to the dresser and the floor.

'Dad,' she screamed. 'Get in here.'

Her dad came in, staring in helpless horror as Frank finally collapsed completely, curling up, breathing hard.

She pulled off the blouse Frank was wearing and used it to wipe the vomit off his face and neck. Then she dressed him and got her dad to help her carry him downstairs. Her mom, who had remained in the hall, ran up to help. Annie and her dad then drove Frankie to the hospital in Jackson.

Her dad woke Annie in the middle of the night. It had been a few months since he had done this.

'You're having a bad dream,' he said. 'Are you okay?'

This was always his excuse. Taking her hand, he led her downstairs. He sat in the sitting room armchair, pulling Annie up side-saddle into his lap. For a while they were silent in the darkness, listening to a tom cat moaning outside, to the stammering starting-up and shutting-off of the refrigerator. Her dad's pyjamas, damp with his sweat, gave off a slightly rancid odour.

'That boy,' he said at last. 'The black boy.'

'Raj?'

'*Si.* He was living in the house and he was wearing your mama's dressing gown. And I say to him, What you doing in my house? And he say, You is my papa. And I say no, and I say, Where's my wife? and he show me his feet and he's wearing her shoes and I go upstairs to find her, but then I hear the door downstairs. It's you and I know he's going to kill you. And I go to run downstairs, but your mama she comes out of the bedroom. The blood it's all over her legs and she look pregnant and she's in her wedding dress and she says she put Frank back inside her and she . . . she open her dress up . . .'

He was snatching at his breath, trembling. Annie pulled his head into her neck, kissing his temple.

'Why I come here?' he said. 'In Atessa, my papa he own four bakeries. We almost killed that boy. We waited for him and my papa he said, "*Devi stare calmo, devi avere il primo colpo pulito.*"' Her dad was getting louder now. 'I pounded him. *Figlio d'una puttana mafiosa! Nessuno me lo ficca in culo!*' Annie just held on, gently stroking her dad's cheek, his body going rigid and jerking around as he stared off almost crazily into the darkness, reliving whatever this was. 'My papa he held him. I said I don't need it. After, they beat my papa so bad he couldn't walk and he couldn't speak and he lost one eye. And he just sit all day, that's all he can do. And my mama, that *puttana*, she left him, and my nonna she come and she feeds and change him like a baby. Whenever he see me his eyes go like this' – he widened his eyes – 'and he make sounds like he's choking, trying to speak to me. And I wouldn't go near him. My papa he told me to hold the boy down. He was already knocked out, but he kept kicking his head, like it's a football, kicking it and kicking it. And I keep telling him, it's over. Over.'

'What did he do to you?' Annie said. 'This boy, what did he do?' This was the first time she had ever been able to get even the vaguest sense of what her dad was talking about when he had his nightmares. Usually he would break down into Italian immediately and all she knew was that he was talking about fighting because he was always making fists, gritting his teeth and kicking out. She had seen a picture of her Italian grandfather in a wheelchair, but her mom told her he had suffered a stroke.

'I was paddling in the stream and the boy – Marco Cantoni – he take my new shoes and he throw them on the roof of the church. He was a bully.'

'So then you and your dad—'

'That Otto. Fuckin' . . .' Her dad's body tensed again, the sinews in his neck taut as he almost lifted Annie out of the armchair. Otto always provoked his default fury and hatred. 'He's gonna get it. *Bastardo lurido*. He's going to shit his own face when I've done, uh. *Ruffiano leccacazzi. Una merda fra merda. Tutto che tocca finisce in merda.*' Her dad was getting angrier and angrier, flecks of spit flying from his mouth as he spoke. Annie pressed her hands hard against either side of his face, shushing, trying to calm him.

'You look at my son.' He gestured as if Frank were lying in front of them. '*This* my son? Fucking piss his pants. My wife? *Una puttanaccia*. That's it. Finish. I take you with me and we run off,' he said. '*Basta!*'

With this he broke down completely, sobbing. This was how it always ended. Like Raj in his own life, she had ridden this little emotional rodeo ever since she could remember. Bucking upon her dad's wrenching sobs, Annie was afflicted once more by that strange emptiness, all her feeling throbbing in her skin and nerves, pushed as far as possible away from her numb core. This had gone on, would go on, for ever.

*How dare Bennet come to visit me, as if he owned me, telling
me I had no right to break Goldwin's heart? What is Bennet?
Goat's scrotum; flaccid snapped head of a plucked rooster;
calf's tongue hanging from a butcher's hook. His salute is the
erect tail and wink of the naked anus. His brain is a damp
cave, ceilinged with bats, out of the clustered, hairy bodies of
which droop obscenely phallic stalagmites. In the town of the
impotent, Bennet is king. He rules us sitting on an upturned
chamber pot, his three bestial daughters leashed at his heels.
He flings them, now and then, a bull's pizzle to gnaw. He has a
will of blind rut. All around him yipping, gibbering, snorting,
crouch his loyal retainers: sapless Magnus who laps his wife's
blood from small incisions at night, who hangs from his ceiling
memorizing poems to trap another fool; Goldwin the bibulous
barber, who lets his bloodhound bitches litter on his bed, who
visibly struggles with the instinct to shove his snout into your
crotch; Otto the bitter with a face to make a Neanderthal
weep, his heart a hazelnut, ash its meat, who bought himself a
concubine neither flesh nor fish, neither Caliban nor Ophelia,
who opens her rotted mouth to curse the flowers, and lays her
shadow to bed in the waters; Siggy, the human haemorrhoid,
prised from Bennet's ass, where he lived snug for years; blank
Finn the mindless, his ejaculations a muddy slope down which
he careens, dragging us all.*

PISGAH, 1952

The firelight in the dark forest flung the men's writhing shadows against the trees. A dead raccoon hung from a nearby branch. Far off, the hounds bayed. Huddled to that sow of fire, the men had been drinking for hours.

'Where I lived in Ireland,' Finn spoke up suddenly, apropos of nothing in particular, 'bunch these English fellas used to hunt foxes. Sure, it wasn't fancy. No horses or nothing. Pelt across the fields, they would, chasing the hounds, tooting their little horns. Funny, isn't it? Wherever you go, it's the same.' He was hunkered close to the fire, roasting a hotdog.

To Finn's right, Otto continued to absently throw his hunting knife at the ground, trying, without success, to get it to stick in blade first. Sal shifted away a little, since Otto was throwing it perilously close to his foot, and settled into the place Goldwin had just vacated. The barber had wandered to the margins of the clearing to listen to his hounds. His favourite, Mina, a pure redbone, too old and sick to keep up with the pack, dragged herself after him, crumpling at his heels whenever he stopped. Magnus was standing also, leaning on his staff and staring gravely into the fire like some old soothsayer. Siggy, cutting himself some chaw, lay slumped in a folding chair beside Bennet, who sat on a cooler, grim potentate with his Easter Island head, holding his rifle like a sceptre across his lap.

It was Bennet who finally broached the silence, addressing Finn. 'You were in the war. Weren't that like hunting?'

Inspecting his hotdog, Finn answered quietly, 'No.'

'You ever kill a man?' Otto asked, now scraping the blade of his knife tenderly over his own stubble.

'Must've done, I guess.'

'You don't know?' Goldwin rejoined them at the fire, Mina slumping down behind him.

'Sure I didn't write them after to find out, you know.'

'You ever kill anyone up close?' Bennet said.

Finn took a moment to answer, that rueful, gargoyle face turning, indeed, to stone. 'One time. We were in a town called Beauville. Only I remember it 'cos one of the fellas tells me it means lovely town. Funny, isn't it? Call a place lovely town. Where you from, then? Lovely town, sure. Tempting fate, isn't it? Like calling a girl Chastity. Krauts had bombed the behind out of the place. Had a mate of mine in Ireland had cystic fibrosis. Name of Fergal. Know what Fergal means? Man of strength. Couldn't swallow his own spit in the end.'

'So what you do in this town?' Bennet said.

'Well my point is that Lovely Town was bombed to shite. There was house-to-house fighting. No one knew where anyone was or where the hell we were meant to be going. So I turn into this alley, and right at the end of it is this Kraut. Has his back to me. Doesn't have a notion I'm there. Looks relaxed, you know, having a sly fag, leaning up against the wall.'

'How far away was he?' Goldwin asked.

Finn pointed. 'About where Magnus is from me.'

All the men looked at Magnus, who meekly put up both hands in surrender.

'So you shot him in the back.' Otto, softly stropping the knife's blade over his lips, smiled.

'I did.'

Bennet leaned in. 'What you shoot him with?'

'American M1 carbine, piece of shite.'

'One shot?' Bennet asked.

Finn blew out his cheeks, shaking his head. 'I just pointed the thing and let loose.'

'Was he a young fella?' Siggy spat a brown stream into the fire.

'Never saw his face. What I remember is he tensed up. You know like you do if you think someone's going to hit you.' Finn scrunched his head into his shoulders to demonstrate. 'Like this, you know.'

'He had time to do that?' Siggy said.

'Sure he had time to write his last will and testament. Didn't hit him until the fourth or fifth shot.'

Sal cut in. 'You still think about it, Finn?'

Finn nodded. 'Had to stop going to the swimming hole of a summer. You know when the kids come out of the water and they're cold and their mum puts a towel around them, and they do that.' Trembling, he turtled his head into his shoulders. 'Always puts me in mind of it.'

'There we go,' Bennet declared conclusively, leaning back. 'He may never have sheaved his shiv, but he's the only one of you here got the stones to kill anyone.'

Otto pointed at Magnus. 'What about this fella? Near peed his pants when we give him the rifle to kill that coon.'

Siggy laughed. 'Man alive, that coon was all but wearing that barrel.'

'It moved,' Magnus protested. 'Cunning creature.'

'You was panting like a hound in heat,' Otto said. 'Never seen anyone shake that much.'

Smiling sheepishly, Magnus leaned in a little, as if to reveal a secret. 'I wanted to tear it apart with my bare hands.' He seemed amazed at himself. 'Quite a feeling. I actually imagined biting it.' He glanced hopefully at Siggy. 'It's astonishing what a powerful thirst such vigorous activity provokes.'

Siggy threw Magnus another beer. Magnus, for all his seeming frailty, snatched it out of the air quick as a bat, sucked down the beer with one tip of his head, and dropped the can with a small pile of others at his feet.

Sal put up his hand as if he were a child in school. 'I almost kill someone. Beat him.' He raised his fist, and then shook it as if it contained dice. 'In Atessa, a boy he threw my new shoes on the roof of the church.' The men waited for the rest of the story, but Sal suddenly changed it, his voice becoming theatrically loud. 'In Chicago, some bastard he says something to my wife. I beat his brains to shit.'

'Yessir,' Otto murmured, digging between his feet with the knife, 'no one's going to touch Sal's wife when Sal's around.'

'Whassat mean? Uh?' Sal retorted. 'You can't even keep your wife.'

'My wife's looking after her sick mom.'

'That's what she tells you, uh? *Cafone.*'

'Anyone interested in my wife's goddamn welcome to her. Anyone interested in your wife's—'

'Shut the fuck up,' Bennet said.

They all went quiet for a little while until Otto raised his gnarled, grinning face again. 'Okay, so a man pulls in this prostitute. It's a dark night. He don't realize till they get back to her place that she's eighty years old. She takes off her wig, takes out her teeth, pulls off her false eyelashes, unscrews her wooden leg. He runs out. She shouts from the window, "Hey, don't you want it?" He shouts back, "Throw it down here, I'll do it myself."'

Only Magnus reacted, his slender, hunched body convulsing with silent laughter.

Bennet called over to Goldwin. 'That English bastard's still here – six weeks now.'

Mesmerized by the fire, swaying with drunkenness, Goldwin mumbled, 'I took her out for near four months.'

'Okay,' Otto said. 'So this man and his daughter are driving along in a truck with all their possessions in the bed and they're stopped by robbers. The robbers take the lot, leave the two of them buck naked. The man he says, "We've lost everything." "Not everything," the daughter says and pulls a diamond ring out her vagina. "Pity your ma wasn't here," the man says. "We could have saved the damn truck."'

Now Siggy couldn't help himself and laughed, glancing guiltily at Bennet as he did so.

But Bennet was intent on Goldwin. 'I heard you cut his hair the other day. Cut his fucking hair.'

'It's my job. I cut hair. What do you want me to do?'

'Grow yourself a fresh fucking pair of balls.'

'So a fisherman has a wife,' Otto raised his voice. 'And he's with his buddy and they're both fishing. And he says, "You know, my wife has gonorrhoea, diarrhoea, and pyorrhoea." "Why'd you marry her, then?" the other one says. And he says, "Only for the maggots."'

Bennet cut short any chance for laughter, shouting at Goldwin, 'He's tapping your woman's tush, and you're giving him a fucking short back and sides.'

'What can I do about it?' Goldwin shouted. Disturbed, Mina staggered to her feet and let out a whimpering bark.

'You do what a man does: make sure it's you and not him. You staked your claim; you damn well fight for it.'

'So a man's in bed with this Polack woman,' Otto cut in loudly. 'She says to him, "I wish you'd take your ring off when you do that." "That's not my ring," he says, "that's my wristwatch."'

'Ay,' Sal shouted. 'Why that's got to be a Polack woman? That don't have to be no kind of woman.'

'I was inspired.'

'You shuddup you. *Sono stanca della tua bocca di merda.*'

'You say another word.' Though Bennet pointed at Otto, who immediately raised his hands in a gesture of submission, he didn't take his eyes off Goldwin, who stood helpless, bent forward as if his stomach hurt. Mina looked on with pricked ears.

'That damn Irishman's the only one of you with more than a rat's fart in his balls,' Bennet said – and then directly to Goldwin: 'He leave you a tip?'

'What the fuck am I going to do?' Both agitated and despairing, Goldwin staggered a few paces away to listen to the hounds. 'That's Rusty. He's on to something. Bench-kneed little sucker, but he's got a good nose on him.'

Mina dragged herself after him, her back legs beginning to give out.

'You're a fuck-up, Goldy,' Bennet shouted. He had him by the throat now and wouldn't let him go. 'Only two pleasures in this world: when a man's on his knees; and when a woman's on her knees. Look at you, listening for your fucking dogs. That Englishman's with your woman right now and you're tripping over your own guts, you panty-waist.' Bennet passed his rifle to Siggy, nodding toward Goldwin. Siggy carried the rifle to him.

Goldwin took it, swaying and confused.

'Look at that poor gyp. Can't walk; can't barely stand. Go on, you peckerwood. She's on her knees. You look her right in the eyes and finish it.'

Goldwin examined the rifle as if he had never seen anything like it before.

'You think those dogs are howling?' Bennet said. 'You want to be in Ruth's bedroom right now. Bet she's a screamer. Bet she lets loose like a goddamn banshee. Can't you picture it, Goldy? You've seen dogs do it. They learned that from the English.'

Goldwin was staring at Bennet, his expression like that of an infant trying to decide whether or not to cry.

Bennet's voice went briefly high-pitched: '"Oh Goldy, I'm just not sure I can be with anyone right now." Ain't that what she said to you, sucker? Ain't it? Weren't more than three days on she gives that limey bastard a place to bury his fucking bone. Then he comes to you for a fucking shit, shave and a shampoo. You've always been the same. Look at you. Can't even put that fucking old gyp out of its misery. That's why that Johnny-come-lately's ploughing your field right now. You were always soft, even when we were kids. Man, if I didn't know you I might start wondering which way your pecker points. Might start thinking you're one of them ho-mo-sexuals. That it, Goldy? You playing for the pink team?'

Goldwin levelled the rifle at Mina's head and pulled the trigger. The bolt snapped forward. The chamber was empty. Goldwin staggered back, as if it had gone off.

'Jasus.' Finn pulled a dollar out of his pocket and handed it to Bennet. All the other men but Magnus did the same.

'I said he would,' Sal said.

'You said shit,' Otto said.

Goldwin dropped the rifle on the ground and lurched off into the woods toward the baying of his dogs. Mina, like a living wound, dragged herself after him.

Dear Ruth

    Will you let me no why I am so bad? A friend told me he thought this young man was kin of yours but it is clear now that what is going on between you and this young man is of a man– woman kind. You think I have no place to speak. But many people in this town new we were dating so it is bad for me. We spent much time together of a man–woman kind and I thought we would be together in a man–woman way I do not get why for four months you said yes to me taking you out. You even let me buy you a stake at a very fancy place that you did not even eat. What did you think I wanted. You are a single woman and I am the same, did you think I just wanted to feed you up. Not that I mean you had to be my girl or nothing but why did you keep saying yes. That diner cost me near fifteen dollars. I am torchered to think maybe I should have been more bold. I saw a movie with a man taking hold of a woman even though she hit him and wandered maybe if this is what you wanted. You did not seem to like my place and now your with this young man. Did he buy you a more high price stake in New York City. And he is much younger and not from this country even.

    Goldwin

PISGAH, 1956

Frank lay under Mr Florsham's Dodge Dart working on the front axle. It had been a week since his stomach had been pumped out and it still felt painful to swallow. The only thing he remembered from that night was the desire to save Annie. From what, he didn't know.

'Frankie?' His mom appeared at the back door in her dressing gown. 'A sandwich you want, honey?'

'I'll get it in a minute.' After pulling himself out, he leaned back against the car's grille, but eased off as the two jacks holding up the front end creaked ominously.

'I don't mind, honey. I get it for you.'

'Why don't you get dressed?' he said. 'Least give that thing you're wearing a wash.'

'What's wrong with you?' She came into the yard.

Anger flared in him, made him feel rigid and brittle.

She stood close now. 'In one week you haven't looked me in my face.'

He kept his eyes on her feet in their pink furry mules: bunions and painted toenails.

'Look at me, Frankie.'

He glanced up. Her hand clutched modestly the collar of her robe. The cut was still visible on her lip. She told him he hadn't meant to do it, thrusting his hand out blindly in his drunkenness. He tried to meet her eyes. All at once he saw her on the bed in that miserable room, thrusting a thick wad of tissues between her legs. Wasteful. As she always was. When she spilled something on the linoleum in the kitchen, she would just drop a clean tea towel on the floor, push it around with her foot, then throw it away.

'What's wrong with you? Why don't you look at me?'

'Why don't you put on some real clothes, tie up your hair, and damn well do something with yourself? Then there'd be something to look at.'

The feet remained in front of him for a moment. Finally they swivelled around and she returned to the house. Easing back under the Dart, he felt as if something massive were being slowly lowered on to his chest, crushing the life out of him. He imagined the car slipping off its supports: real weight, not this phantom weight. Placing his hand against a jack, he gradually increased the pressure. All at once there was a creak and shift, like ice about to give. With frantic haste he caterpillared himself out.

His heart pounded, pollywog lights swimming in his eyes. A moment later a knock came at the back gate and he went to answer it.

Miss Kelly peered up at him through her thick glasses. 'I had a bit of a spill.' She looked down at her bike. Her knuckles were grazed and bleeding. 'The handlebars have gone funny and I can't get the chain out.'

'Let me have a look at it.' He was still struggling to get his breath from the fright as he carried the bike into the yard, leaned it against the fence, and knelt down to check the chain.

'It's pretty well jammed in there,' he said, meeting the anxious enquiry of this woman who had been his teacher for years: so thin and nervous, with that exploded frizz of hair, those thick glasses. He was still not quite in the world, his heart about to jar loose inside him. How easily he might have died. It came to him then: in the graze on her hand; in the funny way she walked, almost as if her knees were hinged side to side, rather than back to front. It came to him like the decision to drink, to get to that place where nothing mattered and something might just be revealed. *Reveal*: the fleshy, vulnerable or obscene hinge between one thing and another, between touching and not touching, desiring and feeling numb, bringing to life and destroying. The hinge: his mother's open legs, a hung pig's cut throat, Miss

Kelly's cleavage all those years ago when she bent down to his school desk. As he stood up, he felt as if he were Bennet, felt that man's hulking gravity and dogged focus, even the slight list of his body, as if Bennet's weighty and impenetrable hide had been placed upon him. And what a relief it was to feel that combination of numbness and singular will.

'I have to get this Dart done by five. I'll drop you off home. I can bring the bike round later.'

'Oh, I can walk,' she said. 'And I'll collect the bike. I'll come round after school tomorrow. How much do you think?'

He made a dismissive gesture.

'No, I must pay you.' She squinted anxiously at him through those big glasses.

'Do you want some iodine for your hand?'

'Oh no, I'll do that at home. All right then. Thank you.'

A sudden, agonized creak was followed by a heavy crash.

'Oh, good heavens,' Miss Kelly said, cringing as she stared behind him. Her expressions were always ridiculously exaggerated. He had heard somewhere that this was because her parents had both been deaf from birth. The shifted jack had failed. The Dart had fallen off. Frank didn't even turn around. He felt exhilarated.

Frank rode the bike to her house at almost nine thirty that evening. He had been tempted to drink, but didn't want to confuse that with this. All afternoon he had thought about her: not unattractive, this strange woman, with her puppet-like movements, who released herself with such abandon to her singing in church. She threw herself into every town event – the Wednesday pot luck socials, the bake sales, the high school teams – but she didn't have any close friends. Perhaps because she would never speak in any personal way, refused to gossip, and talked about nothing but school. And what of men? As far as he knew, she had never dated anyone. He remembered Jude's crude joke about why she rode her bicycle so much.

Propping the bike against the porch, he climbed the steps and knocked on the door of her old cottage, which was almost completely swallowed by a snake jaw of bougainvillea. The gutter was coming away, paint peeling from the siding, the porch listing.

The inner door cracked and she peered through the screen door. 'Frank?'

'I've got your bike, Miss Kelly.'

Still chewing, she wiped her mouth with a napkin. 'Thank you. You can just leave it out there.'

He waited, looking at her through the screen.

'Oh,' she said abruptly, 'let me fetch my purse.'

'No, no,' he said. 'I'd like to talk to you about something.'

'Yes?'

'Can I come in?'

She glanced back into her house with such concern that he wondered if someone were there. 'It's a mess.'

'Don't worry. I won't tell anyone.'

She hesitated a moment longer and finally opened the screen door. Following her in, he was struck by the smell of grease and mildew. They passed the tiny kitchen, which was filthy, the dishes piled in the sink. Damp patches covered the ceiling, the wallpaper peeling everywhere. She had hurried ahead of him into her sitting room and was snatching her washing off a little line set up near the kerosene heater. With the clothes piled in her arms, she ran out. The sofa was covered in junk and the only place to sit was a single armchair with a blanket on it. Open and face down on one arm lay a romance novel titled *A Man to Tame Her*. On the front, a wild-looking woman in a dress that had all but fallen off her body stared with furious defiance into the face of a muscular man who had taken hold of her wrist. On the little table beside the armchair were a plate of vegetables and an open jar of peanut butter. It felt almost too intimate to imagine her sitting here, wrapped in that blanket, dipping vegetables and reading this book.

She hurried back in carrying a folding chair, which he took from her. She seemed a little distraught, as if she had realized what a mistake it had been to let him in. She snatched up the book, but then clearly felt foolish and put it back down.

'Would you like some iced tea?'

He shook his head.

'Look, Frank, I don't know what the problem is, but you'd best see Reverend Hewitt. He could counsel you better.'

'You were my favourite teacher.'

He unfolded the chair as she sat, and set it down right in front of her.

'You've got a lot of damp. I could fix your gutters for you.'

Her body was closed up, clenched, rocking a little, and he felt his resolve flagging as he sat so close their knees were almost touching.

'I've been so busy,' she said.

'I miss your class.' Steeling himself, re-imagining Bennet's body as his own, he leaned in a little.

She stared at him like a nocturnal creature, her eyes huge behind those thick glasses.

'When you came today with your bike – for my help – it's funny, I realized I wasn't in school any more. I realized I didn't really know you at all and . . . and that I liked you.'

'I have lots of students who keep in touch with me,' she said almost curtly. 'So what did you want to talk about?'

'Well, that.'

'What?'

'That I like you.'

She made a bizarre grimace, clearly unconscious, flowing through her from her deaf parents, and scratched her scalp with both hands through that wild, frizzy hair. When she set one of them back down on the arm of the chair, he put his own gently upon it. She froze. He brought his other hand to rest on her shoulder. Her body was trembling. As he leaned in toward her, she made a strange, helpless sound, deep in her throat. He could smell the peanut butter and beneath that her stale breath. She didn't respond in any way as he pressed his mouth to hers. Her eyes continued staring; her lips remained unyielding. All at once some distilled tincture of the rank smell of the house, of her breath, of the insipid cloy of her loneliness, seemed to find its way into the back of his throat and cling there. He felt sick, overwhelmed. He ran into her bathroom and leaned himself over her sink. The bathroom was filthy: the little bucket she used as a garbage pail overflowed with pieces of tissue; the toilet was spattered and choked with brown limescale; a slick black mould surrounded the drain of the sink. He dry-heaved a few times and spat. What was he doing here? Why had he done this?

When he returned, she was still sitting in the armchair in exactly the same position, her posture bent and stiff, like a propped doll. Endless pain. She didn't look up at him.

'I'm sorry, Miss Kelly.'

She didn't move or respond in any way.

'I didn't know what I was doing. I'm sorry.'

When Frank got back to his house, he went straight to Annie's room. She was asleep and he gently prodded her arm. Pushing his hand off, she turned away, mumbling, 'Papa, I want to sleep.'

'It's Frank,' he whispered.

Rolling back, she half opened her eyes. 'Are you all right, Frankie?'

'Shift over.' Kicking off his shoes, he got into her bed and pulled her up into his arms. He just wanted to smell her, her hair and her neck.

'Have you been drinking?'

'No.'

'What's wrong?'

'Nothing's wrong. I'm sorry for messing up your room.'

'You've said sorry.'

She tried to look at him, but he couldn't bear the thought of being looked at and gently pressed her cheek against his chest. She was almost asleep again when the door opened and his mom walked in, switching on the light.

'Jesus, Frank, what you doing here? Are you drunk?'

'I'm talking to Annie.'

'What you doing in her bed?'

'What do you mean?'

'Mom,' Annie cut in, hooking her arm around Frank's head as if he were a big dog, 'we're just talking.'

'You too old to be like this.'

'That's rich from you,' Frank said.

'What?'

Annie got out of bed like a sleepwalker, took her mom's hand and led her out into the hall. Then she came back in, closed her bedroom door, and returned to bed, laying her head back against his chest.

Frank wanted desperately to get it out of him, to try to describe to Annie what he had felt at the heart of Miss Kelly, that fibrous knot. Nothing would ever unravel it. It was death. Always there as she sang her songs, flew around town on her bicycle, that terrible, snarled, morbid knot in which every fibre of her life was wound and caught.

PISGAH, 1959

They flutter like dreaming eyes, delicate parts removed from the machine of sleep. They fall from the sparrow tree, soft fruit of their bones. Sparrows mating, fine clocks mating, begetting time, which scatters at angles, always at angles.

Lewis's head begins to hurt, his thoughts splintering like the sun in the branches of this tree, along a limb of which he now lies. He wants this place to have no voice; or to speak to him as light speaks to water, as it once spoke to his brother. Sparrows mating, female waiting, bent, her wings winnowing, soft gills of the wind, the softest register of the voice of Wa-Kon-Te, flutter of reeds, grasses, leaves, flutter of the sparrows. Male flutters, mounts and remounts. Begetting time and breath. All of this, life after life, the exhale of God, growing thinner as the great lungs empty until you find yourself in the place between. Neither breathed out nor drawn in. Both breathed out and drawn in. Agony.

She.

Annie.

Always Annie to make him *him* again. A scar in God's eye, projected upon the sky. No matter what God sees, Annie is always there, floating in the vitreous. She has the power to make him want his life.

She. Also he, now approaching through the trees. Raj, his brother, made from all that has fallen out of time. Smiling liar, who in dreams will strip off your skin and leave you shivering, clinging to the yolk of the sun. Through him I become both the bird with the broken wing and the cat that licks the frantic beat of my heart: this dark boy climbing the tree to me.

There is a mark on his face.

'Hey, Lew.'

'Annie not coming?'

'She's with Evy and Nora. Told me to come get you. They want to make us up like girlies. I said no way.' Raj settled against a branch. 'Annie tried to put lipstick on me.'

'You still got it on you.' He touched his own face to show where, and Raj wiped it off.

'Just a couple months now.' Raj let out a long, tired breath. 'No more high school. What are you going to do?'

'Don't know. Thought I might like to be a park ranger or something.'

He climbed down from the tree and Raj followed. They meandered toward the river, idly plucking up the long grasses.

'Would you leave the state?' Raj said.

He shook his head. 'Wouldn't want to be too far from my pop. What about you?'

'I've applied to some places to study physics – Stanford or MIT.'

'Annie told me Barrington's scared to have you in class because you know more than he does.'

'A lobotomized bullfrog knows more than he does. I'm hoping to turn him into an alcoholic with this slightly troubled frown I've perfected.' Raj demonstrated.

'What are me and Annie going to do without you?'

'Come with me.'

Lewis looked around at the brown, green, wet, spongy world. Earth isn't mother but child of the sun; light runs in its veins. Sun begat Earth to make peace with what must come. Here Sun is learning how to go cold, to die, laying a mind to rest in the shade. Light's rendering of the dark is life: silt, blood, scat. Sun fills the mouths of caves with its hoard of darkness, the minds of men with annihilation.

'Hello-ow-ow-ow.' Raj had made a bullhorn of his hands, and was calling with a feigned echo into Lewis's ear. 'Is anyone-un-un-un in there-er-er-er?'

'I couldn't imagine leaving.'

'That's why you should leave,' Raj said. 'I always feel like I've done everything wrong, messed everything up.'

'What have you messed up?'

He shrugged. 'I guess I just like the idea of coming back; being different. New and improved.'

'Don't seem to me there's anything wrong with you.'

Pressing his hand coyly to his cheek, Raj became a Southern belle: 'Why that's so sweet of you to say, sir. Fact is, I'm *so* wrong, sir, I'm right.'

A gusty wind flung Lewis's hair into his face as they got to the bluffs above the Missouri, eighty feet below. Brown, broad river, its surface as grained and knotted as bark. A vast, gnarled, liquid tree set in the earth. Dead wood, holocaust, naked, agony of limbs piled against the banks. His brother had been found caught in the branches of a dead tree, dead fruit of the dead in the dead river. Lewis walked out to the jagged edge of the promontory.

'Lew,' Raj called. 'You've got to watch out. Those edges aren't solid.'

He turned back to his friend. His heels at the precipice, he closed his eyes, could hear the river below, and felt as if he were suspended above the earth.

'Lew,' Raj called gently. 'The edge could give.'

He opened his eyes. 'Raj, do you think about your mom and dad?'

Hunkered down, his friend was holding one hand out and staring at him strangely. After a moment, Raj's hand withdrew and he said, 'I think it's odd they're still alive somewhere. And my dad even knows where I am.'

'Why doesn't he come for you?'

'Multiple choice, Lew. Is it because A: I'm too beautiful? B: too brilliant? C: a lanky, dusky, illegitimate child begat from a shameful union?'

'Or D: he's a bonehead, peckerwood, half-ass pile of horse shit.'

Raj looked into the ground.

'You're lucky in a way,' Lewis said. 'My dad doesn't even understand what I say half the time. Spends his life fixing broken things.

He's never going to die; Wa-Kon-Te doesn't know how to kill him because he made him out of dead things. Everything around him has died instead. Life begins with a mistake. What's living is alive because it's *wrong* in some way, Raj. And I'm left to teach myself the language of death-in-life, so I can say what I did to my brother, so I can say I did it, and if I can say it in *that* language then my brother will not have died. He will return from the waters.'

Raj was just staring at him, crouching, almost cringing.

'Does this sound crazy?'

'Come back from there.'

'Does it sound crazy?'

'No. Lew, I swear it doesn't sound crazy. I've never heard you say a thing that sounds crazy. Never. Not once. Not once. *Please* come over here.'

'I'm not crazy.'

'You're saner than I am, Lew. I'm just slightly more athletic and attractive. Come away from the edge there.'

Lewis kept his eyes on his friend, who was hunched low and looked as if he wanted something desperately, but was afraid of being beaten. He could feel the birds, suspended in the wind behind him, as if they had unfurled from his back, were his own freed wings. Soon they would return, dig in, nest, mate, quarrel, preen. He felt something at his nape. With a shock, he realized what it was, could feel that tentacle inching into his throat. He reached both hands back to get it off, but felt nothing and saw then that Raj was afraid for him.

Dropping his hands, he returned to his friend, who stood up, exhaling, puffing out his cheeks with relief. All at once he realized why Raj had been so afraid. 'You thought I was going to do something?'

'No.'

'You should never worry about me like that. I'd never do nothing like that to you and Annie. Or my dad.'

Though Raj nodded, Lewis felt his friend's arm slide firmly around him.

'Come on, Kemosabe. I promised Annie fresh blood.' He slipped into his black mammy voice: 'Why, lordamercy, massa, she gon be madder than a wet hen.'

Annie wondered where the boys were. Card games always made her impatient, though Nora and Evy seemed engrossed. This irritated Annie, who was in a slightly peevish mood. Nora sat in her prim manner, her legs tight together and tucked out to the side. Annie and Evy had just braided her hair and had wound it up into a Dutch twist. Now Nora looked like a woman in a Dutch painting, Annie thought, a solid, red-faced woman washing things in a pail. Full-figured, fertile, and fresh, she was bread and pears and large dull green grapes on a pewter plate. She had a man's strength and a woman's stamina in that hairless, buxom body (peevish, peevish), with her thick ankles and large hands. Annie turned to Evy, with her mousy brown hair, curled away from her face and sprayed stiff. Evy had a girlish floppiness about her, double-jointed, sitting with her legs angled out either side like a frog. She looked closer to thirteen than eighteen, a freckled girl with a sweet gap between her front teeth, pretty greenish eyes, a shapeless little knob of a nose, and that underbite her dad had inflicted on all his girls. Somehow she hadn't become gormless, though, like her sisters: her particular combination of features and petite proportions made her cute in the way a baby monkey or ogre is cute, because everything is so small and appealing (peevish, peevish, peevish), because the baby ogre giggles and flicks her hair, and has a couple of disarming gestures.

She glanced back at Nora, who had just told Evy to 'go fish': not dignified exactly, just careful and blank and determined. Nora had made the astonishing decision that she wanted Raj. People would be horrified. Her dad would kill her — or kill him. But Nora had clearly put things in the balance and decided that being with him would outweigh even the fury and despair of her family. She had selected Raj despite the huge disadvantage of his skin, which, even for Annie, who adored him, was a qualm. Annie was always aware that he was dark; not a Negro, but blacker than some Negroes. She often caught herself focusing on what made him different from a Negro – his hair, the features of his face, his hands – and she would find herself thinking, He's white, only with dark skin. Nora was winning him by playing, as women did with men, upon his weaknesses – his innocence, ready guilt, and, of course, desire. Around him she glowed and looked beautiful. She was preparing him as the little factory of her womb prepared itself for production. (Peevish, peevish, *peevish*.) Annie couldn't imagine making such a decision about a man at this age, the inverted pyramid of your whole life balanced over this one opportunity.

Nora laid down her last card triumphantly. 'Go Fish.' She had won again.

'Aw rats.' Evy pettishly flung down her hand.

Nora gathered and shuffled the cards. She would win again. Would always win. Annie felt so confused: full of love and desire for Lew, but pity also. Not the slightly revolted pity one reserves for the weak and helpless, but that shriving pity one feels for something beautiful, powerful, which has been trapped and is to be broken. She loved to be with Raj, who was funny, silly, elusive and so brilliant. She hated herself for thinking in practical ways, but Lew was never going to graduate high school, while Raj was being courted by the Ivy Leagues, would live in an exciting place. Unlike Nora, though, she couldn't marshal her resources to one end. She wasn't even sure what her resources were or how to refine them. They felt vast and useless, great forests and tracts of prairie, which she faced without skills or tools, envying those with a house and garden. Besides, to decide felt like death. She wanted everything. She wanted them both, and she wanted more.

Trying to clear her head, she glanced back at Evy, whose only interest was boys. She looked as if her limbs had melted beneath her. She was the youngest daughter, the most spoiled and loved. Her brutish sisters sat around gnawing on human bones, while little Evy just chewed delicately upon a sugared earlobe or pickled pinkie.

Evy caught her staring. 'What are you smiling at?'

'I think if someone you love dies, you should eat them,' Annie said.

'What made you think of that?' Evy screwed up her face. 'That's disgusting. Eewwwww.' She always seemed as if she were slightly over-acting.

'Don't you think so, Nor?' Annie asked.

'I hope my dad doesn't die, then,' Nora said. 'I'm on a diet.'

Annie persisted. 'Seriously, Nor, could you eat someone?'

Nora shrugged, still focused on the game. 'If I had to.'

'Eeewww, stop it.' Evy flapped her hands.

'If we were in a desperate situation,' Annie said, 'I'd be the first one to die, Evy would be next, and Nora would survive.'

Nora glanced up at Annie from her cards, smiling, and singsonged like radio chimes: 'I don't think so.'

'You think I'd eat you and Evy?'

'Stop talking about eating people. You guys are so weird.'

'Sebastiana Regina Celli,' Nora intoned calmly, 'you wouldn't even wait until we were dead. You'd slit our throats in the night and you'd feel bad for just a little while.' Nora made a pinch of her fingers to show how little that while would be, before attending to her cards again.

Both shocked and impressed, Annie's peevishness instantly evaporated as Nora's poise and tenacity, which Annie had been holding at a contemptuous remove, struck – indeed penetrated – her with its full force. All at once she felt vastly – and gratefully – inferior, and was almost overwhelmed by a desire at once to possess and to *be* Nora. Yes, to eat her, that's what she wanted, to bite into the soft flesh, tear out the sinews, lick through her vertebrae, suck the marrow from her bones. Catching Nora's eyes again, she made a little nod toward Evy, baring her teeth and biting them together. Nora smiled and put down her cards. They both stared at Evy, who now looked up at them.

'What?' she said.

Annie took hold of Evy's right wrist, Nora the left.

'What are you doing?' Evy protested, as the two girls forced her over on to the carpet. 'What are you doing?'

Holding her down, they arched over her, panting and licking their lips.

'Stop,' Evy said. 'That's not funny. Don't even joke about it.' Now she screamed as the two girls, with bared teeth, descended.

The door swung open to reveal Annie's mom, with Raj and Lew behind her.

'What you girls doing in here?'

'They wanted to eat me, Mrs Celli,' Evy squealed.

The boys entered. Raj put on his upper-class English voice. 'Oh, I'm most partial to the pancreas, if that's not already taken. That, steamed adenoids, lashings of lumpy plasma, and I'm happy as a little sand boy.'

'Shut up,' Evy screamed.

Now he became an Indian, with an exaggerated accent, his head rocking from side to side, 'Oh, it reminds me of our last famine. The priest told us not to eat the cow so we ate the priest. It was a lovely family time.'

Lew sat on the bed. Annie got up and went to the door, her mom just outside in the hall, staring at Raj with a troubled, curious look. At five in the afternoon she was still in her filthy robe, her hair unwashed and scraggly. She had one arm hooked under her breasts and was a little bent. Annie was filled with a welter of feelings – pity, anger, shame. Big blonde, but not like Nora, her feet not planted in the earth. Her centre of gravity was somewhere far beyond her, in another time and place. Out of her element, she was slowly dying.

'Thanks, Mom.' Annie put her hand on the door.

'Please you leave the door open, Annie.'

Annie didn't say anything. As her mom turned to walk down the hall, she shut the door. She almost wanted her mom to storm back in, scream, but knew she wouldn't. She might think about it for a second, but her resolve would subside. She would go down to the kitchen, light a cigarette, and stare out of the window.

Annie felt almost sick, as she turned back to her friends, to have belittled her mom in front of them. Nora's face was slightly flushed and the boys had averted their eyes. Only Evy seemed oblivious.

'We've got them now.' Annie spoke quickly and enthusiastically to clear the air. 'We're going to make them look *super*-delish.'

'Not again,' Raj keened as Nora took hold of his wrists to stop him escaping. The boys were forced to sit on the bed and the make-up box was pulled out.

'Evy, you help me with Raj,' Nora said. 'He's still struggling.'

He wasn't, but Nora clearly wanted to take the opportunity to keep holding both his hands behind his back with her body pushed up against his.

'You can't even see the make-up on him,' Evy protested. 'I'm going to do Lew.'

Evy tried to make this seem a lighthearted refusal, giggling and girlish, but Annie knew it was because she didn't want to touch Raj. She never joined in any conversation about Raj, and when he was around never looked at him or called him by his name. She acted as if he were an imaginary person in whose existence she wasn't will-ing to participate. Crowding Annie out of the way, she began to work on Lew's eyes. Nora applied herself to Raj, apparently becoming so short-sighted her face had to be practically pressed against his. Annie just sat back on the bed. Still feeling horrible about treating her mom so rudely, she had slipped out of the mood for all this. Once more everything was grating: Nora's single-minded pursuit of Raj, Evy's girlish flirtations with Lew.

When they were done, Raj resembled a clown. Lew, though, looked profoundly beautiful and strange, his thick male neck in vivid contrast to those lovely feminine features. All of them were stunned into silent awe, unable even to laugh.

There was a thumping of feet up the stairs and her brother came in. His gaze was drawn immediately to Lew. 'Jeez Louise, what are you guys doing?'

Like all of them, Annie could see that he was both captivated and disturbed.

'We're making them beautiful,' Annie said.

Jumping off the bed, Evy snatched up Frank's hand. 'Now we're going to do you.' Pushing him into Annie's vanity chair, she threw herself into his lap and began to apply lipstick. Though Evy was being silly and almost manically flirtatious, the playful mood had vanished from the room: a process begun with the way Annie had treated her mom, exacerbated by this annihilating beauty that Lew bore with a kind of hopeless clairvoyance, and finished off by the stench of beer coming from her brother. He was clearly half drunk, sleepy and soggy, and his hand had fallen across Evy's thighs.

'I thought you were going to drive Evy home?' Annie said.

'S'what I'm here for.'

'Have you been drinking?'

'It's five thirty.'

'I can smell it.'

'I was helping Jude clean up after his party last night. Got beer on me.'

'Yeah, the beer that missed your mouth.'

'Frankie's going to look *priceless*,' Evy sang, pretending oblivious-ness to the tension.

Annie glanced down at her brother's hand and he removed it.

Nora had begun to clean the make-up from Raj's face. Annie hated herself for feeling like this: desire and jealousy. Nora was right: she would kill them in their sleep. Raj was hers; Lew, with his disturb-ing, unreal face, was hers. Nora too. She felt almost sick, wanting, wanting, wanting. And she was furious at her innocent brother, who might do something stupid with this silly little girl, throwing herself at him. Evy's high-pitched squeal grated like a draw-saw across the bone of her chest.

Annie started to wipe the make-up off Lew's face.

'You'd better clean Frank off,' she said to Evy. 'You've got to go back now. I'm going to come with you.'

'You can't,' her brother said.

'Why not?'

'I'm meeting Jude and Linus in KC, so I'm just going to head right on from Evy's. Don't have time to drop you back here.'

'You were at an all-night party last night.'

'We've got tickets to see Marley's Hep Cats.'

'All righty, Frankie,' Evy cut in, having just put on the finishing touches and acting as if she hadn't heard anything that had been said. 'Now you look *super*-delish.'

This was the same phrase Annie had used a little earlier, and uttered in as fake a fashion. As Frank left to wash his face, Evy hurried around to gather up her things.

'All right, guys.' Her voice was high and wheedling. Her eyes fluttered, and she seemed unable to look directly at any of them. 'This was such a blast! You guys are crazy! *Aloha!*' and she almost skipped out of the door.

Frank wished Evy would just sit quiet. She chattered nervously, and every now and then some flirtatious gesture would geyser out: she would heft her hair with both hands on to her head; or rest her foot on the dash, seemingly intent on examining her own little painted toes; or she would become suddenly infantile, balling up her body and speaking with a lisp. It was a confused and embarrassing display. Frank, who had known her all her life, and who thought of her still as a little girl, met it with silence and a few weary smiles.

He lit a cigarette and opened his window.

'Can I have one?' she asked.

'You smoke?'

'Who doesn't?' She rolled her eyes as she took a cigarette from the pack he had thrown on to the dash and cupped her hand around the lighter he held out for her as if they were in a high wind.

'You need to suck in for it to stay alight.'

She sucked in a little, blew the smoke out, and then held the cigarette above her head.

'Does my sister smoke?'

'Annie does a lot of things you don't know about,' she said, drawing what power she could from the cigarette, which she clearly had no intention of putting to her lips again.

'Like what?'

Clutching her knees into her chest, she rested her chin on them and smiled up at him with sly innocence. He knew she was just fishing for something to get his attention, but with this she had touched off all that confused anger in him. What was more, with her chin pushed out and her eyes shadowed, he became more acutely aware than he had ever been of her father's face in hers.

'Like what?' he said again.

Examining her cigarette as if such things bored her, she said, 'Like we're not kids.'

He looked at her again: Bennet's face, Bennet's daughter, her slender legs. He turned back to the road. What was wrong with him? He thought of what happened last night at Linus and Hattie's engagement party. Esta and Rudy were there. God, that hurt. Hattie was showing everyone her ring. Drunk, he danced suggestively with her. People were smiling, but he could tell it was getting uncomfortable. He was killing the party, but he couldn't stop himself, couldn't stop thinking about that day he had driven Hattie home. She was as two-faced as the rest of them. A terrible convulsion of shame now moved through Frank. In the middle of the dance he had asked Hattie to go outside with him. In front of Linus; in front of everyone. Hattie pretended she didn't understand, smiling. Everyone was smiling, a whole room full of stiff smiles, no one knowing how to react. And smiling Linus said, 'Quit messing, Frankie.' And smiling Jude saved him by taking hold of him like King Kong, bellowing and carrying him outside. Frank's fingers now tightened around the steering wheel as he again endured a spasm of intense shame and sadness, the feeling like a flame, though cold, spreading just beneath the surface of his skin. Jude had tried to talk to him, but he had just pushed him away and had driven off, his mind infested with all those images: Esta in that bastard's arms; Hattie in his truck; Miss Kelly, her filthy home, peanut-butter breath, and that knot at the heart of her life; his mom, in sluttish, senseless rut; Annie when he went to her room the other day and she was doing her homework, wearing only her favourite Steamboat Mickey T-shirt, a T-shirt so old it was almost transparent. Through it he could see that her body wasn't a girl's any more. God, she wasn't far from eighteen now. It made him so afraid and angry that she didn't seem to know, was just sitting there doing her sums.

'Frankie, Frankie,' Evy crooned coyly.

Snatching the cigarette from her hand, he flung it out of his window. 'Take your feet off the seat.'

She did. Smoothing her skirt and blushing, she became once more the little girl he had driven home hundreds of times. He put his hand on top of her head and squeezed it affectionately.

As he turned into the driveway of her house, he saw Mrs B. sitting on the porch, smoking.

Just before he pulled up, Evy said, 'I'm sorry, Frankie. I didn't mean nothing. I didn't mean Annie was doing nothing.' She looked as if she were about to cry.

'I know, honey.' He playfully pinched her cheek. 'I know you didn't mean anything.'

When Evy had got out, her mom came round to his side of the truck and leaned in.

'Thanks for driving her.'

'No problem, Mrs B.'

She was a handsome woman whose hair was always curled and set. She had a broad, smooth forehead, which softened her somewhat hawkish look. Whenever he thought of her, he thought of her nostrils, for some reason, perhaps because she tended to speak with her head tipped back, and had the charmingly unfeminine habit of blowing smoke out through her nose.

'Where's Mr B.?'

'Hounding around with the boys somewhere, I guess.'

Mistress: the word came to him. He had heard rumours of others, one in Jenison, another – half Osage some said – in Marriotville.

'What fun there is in chasing little critters through the woods all night, I can't imagine,' she said, leaning into the open window but looking off toward the cherry orchard. He wondered if she were lonely out here, spending most nights flicking through magazines, playing cards with her daughters, ordering her maid around.

'I'm heading in to KC.'

'Paint it red, uh?' She let her gaze slide lazily down the little barrels of her nose to him.

'Something like that, I guess. Thought I'd check out some of the joints on Fifth with Jude and Linus.' He didn't know why he was lying – why he had lied to Annie. He wasn't going to the city.

'You all will be in hog heaven.'

'Hop on in, Mrs B.'

She rolled her eyes. 'No place to bring an old lady.'

'You look young as your daughters, Mrs B.'

She smiled. 'Funny you said that. Had a feller in here the other day to build some cabinets ask me which of my sisters was the eldest. Said I must have sold my soul.'

There was something both sweet and sad about this vanity, which she was trying to undercut with a wry smile.

'Come on. Hop in. Let's paint the town.'

She didn't seem to hear him. 'The Cadillac's making a kind of knocking sound when it turns corners. Mr B. says he can't hear it, but can you take a look? I'd bring it to the dealers, but I'd rather give you the business if you want it, Frank.'

'Sure. Have someone bring it down. I'll give them a ride back.'

'I'll bring it Thursday. Got to drop Evy at vacation bible school.'

She stepped away from the truck. 'Give my best to your ma and pa.'

Frank swung round the circular driveway. He could see Mrs B. in his rearview mirror. He hoped she would go in, so he could take a right turn back to town. All at once he wanted desperately to see Annie, show her he wasn't drunk, just to talk to her. But Mrs B. remained smoking on the porch. He had no choice but to follow his lie: turn left and head away.

*

Nora was frantic. The guests would begin to arrive in under an hour for her eighteenth birthday party and she still hadn't washed her hair.

Her dad was firing up the barbecue, her brother seeing to the polka band, and her mom, who had been preparing the food and decorations for what seemed like months, was only now getting dressed. As Nora came out of her room and hurried across to the bathroom, her mom called for her in a thin, wavering voice, which Nora felt tempted to ignore. When she put her head around the door to her parents' room, her mom looked both surprised and guilty, like a child who had called simply to call.

'What?' Nora said shortly.

'Oh.' Her mom, standing in her underclothes, gestured vaguely toward a purple satin dress, which she had spread out on the bed. 'This is that dress my sister sent me at Christmas.'

'Uh huh, looks nice. I told you it looked nice when you got it.'

The dress was low cut at the back, crossed over at the bust, and had one side of the neck hem frilled with violet silk. Her aunt worked as a saleswoman in Saks Fifth Avenue in New York and often sent slightly damaged or out-of-season clothes.

Picking the dress up very carefully, her mom held it against her own body. 'Do you really think I could wear this?'

'Why not?'

'Well, I'm just . . . It might be all right for New York, but it's . . . a little much, don't you think?'

'It's pretty. You'll look beautiful in it.'

'It's very . . . revealing at the bust.' She laid it back down on the bed and began to wring her hands.

'Don't do that, Mom.' Nora walked over and gently pulled her mom's hands apart. 'Look, it's not any lower cut than the dress Miriam wore to Donald's party.'

'Oh yes, but Miriam has such a lovely figure.'

'*You* have a lovely figure.' Nora rubbed her mom's shoulders encouragingly. Her head was beginning to ache: this could go on for ever.

'Look, Mom, I've really got to go wash my hair. You haven't got the washing machine on, have you?'

'No, but the faucet's on in the kitchen. Your dad's trying to defrost the last of that chicken.' She threw on her robe as if relieved to get away from that dress. 'I'll turn it off and knock on the bathroom door on the way back.'

Nora went to the bathroom and waited. They had a shower-bath unit with glass panels. If anyone used water anywhere else in the house, you would find yourself trapped in the back corner behind a torrent of freezing or boiling water. When her mom knocked, she turned on the faucet for the shower and slipped off her robe. Just as she was about to get in, she noticed a shadow flickering on the wall opposite the frosted glass slats just above the shower. A bird perhaps. Glancing up, she was horrified to see a hand reaching in to push the slats at a downward angle. A loud crack came from outside, as of something breaking, a shout, and then she could distinctly hear her brother laughing. Throwing on her robe, she ran out of the bathroom, through the kitchen and into the yard. Jude and her dad were trotting hastily back toward the barbecue. Her dad was carrying a chair with a busted leg.

She ran up to them. 'What were you doing?'

Her brother's smile quickly vanished. Her dad, trying to look like a naughty kid, was hiding something behind his back. After a few infuriating seconds of cat-and-mouse with him, she saw what it was: a camera.

'Birthday girl in her birthday suit,' her dad sang. 'Come on, Cupcake, we're just fooling.'

'Just fooling?'

'There's no film in it,' Jude added hastily, looking increasingly sorry. 'Just a joke.'

'It's *not* a joke,' she shouted. 'I'm not a child.'

Her brother, now bright red, glanced behind her. Nora turned to see Annie, Raj and Lew standing at the gate. They looked embarrassed. She forgot they were coming over early to help. She ran back into the house and went straight to her mom's room to tell her, to cry. When she entered, her mom was holding that dress draped across her arms, an expression close to anguish in her face. It reminded Nora abruptly and bizarrely of the picture Annie's mom had up in their sitting room, of Mother Mary holding the dead Christ. It was shocking, repulsive somehow. Apologizing, she left and ran to her own room.

Sitting at her dresser, she felt dizzy with humiliation and outrage. Annie came in a second later. 'What happened?'

'My dad's being a jerk.'

'Being a jerk how?'

'Just being a jerk, just . . .' Choked with frustration, she stared at her face in the mirror, a new spot just above her lip, her nose already shiny with grease. 'God, I wish I could tear my skin off.'

Annie settled two reassuring hands on her shoulders. 'Nora, you look great.'

Nora was feeling something for herself she had never experienced before. Not loathing exactly, but as if that loathing had gathered about her and was making its little siege. She could feel the pressure of it, an intimation in her joints, her glands, like the signs of an impending sickness.

She glanced at her friend's reflection. 'Annie, if you were a boy, would you go out with me?'

Hunkering down, Annie rested her elbows on Nora's thighs and stared directly into her face. 'No. I'd go out with me because I know how to make me put out.'

Nora smiled. She loved the way Annie's mind worked. She had never had that kind of quickness. Like Raj. All at once her feelings for Raj surfaced. She was determined that something definite would happen between them today. And just like that, the little siege was broken. She felt whole and desirable again. She couldn't wait to put on her polished yellow cotton dress, with its beautiful gored skirt. She was a woman now. She was eighteen.

After she had showered and dressed, she went to the kitchen window to see who had arrived. The band — the same one her dad used in his dealership promotions – was playing, and the yard was full. The usual gang had gathered around Mr B. at the barbecue. Siggy and her dad had pulled their shirts up and seemed to be comparing bellies.

Most of the women had settled at the picnic tables in the shade of the candy-stripe canopy. Ruth was chatting with Maud. Judy sat just behind Ruth. Nora had noticed on a number of occasions how intensely Judy would stare at Ruth, as if angry or obsessed. Reverend Hewitt moved through the women like a little bantam cock among larger chickens. He was talking to – or rather *at* – Annie's mom, who seemed, with every forced smile, to wish that someone would just come and take her big, dreamy, voluptuous body away. A little distance from the tables, on a chair she had pulled into the sun, sat Shannon, eating a small pile of sandwiches. She wore a threadbare green dress, and had piled and pinned her lovely red hair elaborately on to her head. She never spoke to anyone. She could look astonishingly beautiful, and then she would grin in that silly way, revealing a couple of missing teeth. Some claimed she was simple-minded but Annie said she just put that on so people would leave her be. What would it be like, Nora wondered, to know that people never looked at you without thinking about you being raped? She knew she would never have told anyone if her cousin . . . But that wouldn't be rape. Anyway, the worst thing would be if anyone knew. It hurt her so much that her dad had seen her like that. All at once she felt confused, sorry for him, sudden guilt clinging to her shoulders and back like a deep winter chill.

She shook it off and saw Annie, joining the women, wrapping her arms around Maud and saying something to make them all laugh. She was so lively and pretty, with that long, curly black hair. Raj would call her 'the diplomat' to tease her, imitating her in her party mode as if she were a slimy politician until Annie would chase him down. The biggest surprise was to see that Mrs B. had turned up, sitting at a separate table with her three older daughters, whom Annie once said were men dressed as women, like Tony Curtis and Jack Lemmon in *Some Like It Hot*. It was just a joke, but Nora couldn't get it out of her head. Evy was hounding Frank. She was clearly trying to break him away from his little group, made up of Nora's brother, Linus and Hattie, and looked like a persistent beggar, trotting out every trick she could to get a dime out of someone.

At last she spotted Raj, who was with Lew, Alv and her other school friends down at the far end of the yard near the band, and left the house.

Just as she crossed the driveway, she noticed Olenka and Pela, at the buffet table her mom had taken all day to arrange. Olenka was holding a large tote bag, which Pela was filling with food, putting in, one after another, whole plates of appetizers. Nora hurried over.

'I'm glad you both could come,' she said, out of breath.

'Happy anniversary,' Pela said.

Olenka smiled dreamily, her face clownish with make-up. 'We has a big white one like you. They chop tail. Papa he say he can't stand its behind to look at him all day. Mama she not speak to him for weeks because he say it in front of us children.'

'Our gift is with others,' Pela said, as if she could think of no other reason for Nora to have come over.

'Bulbs,' Olenka said. 'Crocus. We find them. Or wild onions. Has you seen our horse?'

'Yes, it's very nice,' Nora said. 'Now—'

'When I come eighteen,' Pela declared proudly, 'Papa he makes me a party on an island in our lake.'

'Our servants they even puts on our shoes for us,' Olenka said. 'Lovely shoes, he makes them, a man in the village.'

'My papa own this man,' Pela said. 'All people in village belong my papa.'

'His hands is like leather,' Olenka said. 'Once I say to him, You make shoes out of your own hands. Good joke I make. But Katerina she says she make it.' Abruptly Olenka looked on the verge of tears.

Nora examined the ravaged table. Her mom had worked all week to prepare this food. Gently she prised the bag from Olenka's hands. Pela looked away. As Nora replaced the plates, she told them the food was for everyone, that they were welcome to all they cared to eat now, and when the party was over they could take home as much as they wanted.

When she was done, she headed off toward the back of the yard, being complimented, hugged and congratulated as she went. Finally she joined Raj and Lew, who were leaning against the fence, and Alvin, who was sitting cross-legged on the grass at their feet. They were all eating hot dogs.

'Nice dress,' Alvin said. 'All it needs is whipped cream and a cherry.'

'Shut up, you.'

'You're a woman now,' Raj declared dramatically, raising his opened arms. 'I feel an overwhelming desire to ask you for an allowance.'

Smiling, she tried to think of a comeback. All she could manage was, 'And you're a man.'

'Is that what that smell is?' Lew said.

Alvin laughed at this, spraying bits of hotdog.

'You're disgusting,' Nora said.

In response he opened his mouth, poking out his tongue to show her all the chewed-up food. Why was he always like this?

'Lew, when's your birthday?' she asked, leaning against the fence beside Raj.

'Late winter. Haven't done nothing for it since my mom died.'

'Mine's November sixteenth,' Alvin shouted.

'When's yours, Raj?' she asked. 'I can't believe we've never done anything for it.'

'Couple days ago,' Raj said.

'Why didn't you tell us?' She squeezed his arm.

'Didn't want a fuss. Actually, birthdays make me a bit sad. They just remind me of the birthdays I used to have in my village in India.'

'You can remember them?'

He nodded. 'In the evening there was this ritual where they'd give me a drink made from crushed tamarind roots mixed with just a little goat urine.'

'Goat urine?'

'It dissolves the root and increases its narcotic effect. Then my mom and her four sisters would do a ritual dance called the cobra dance in front of me. Watching them under the influence of the drug on my birthday, I was meant to be able to see my future.'

'Did it work?' Nora was amazed by this glimpse into another world.

He nodded, frowning. 'On my last birthday in India, as my mum and her sisters danced, a face appeared in front of me.' He looked almost fearfully now into Nora's eyes. 'And I was speaking to this face, and this face seemed to be believing everything I was saying even though it was just a whole bunch of baloney.'

Raj began to smile now, which confused her, and she noticed that Lew was also smiling. Suddenly Alvin let out a nasty guffaw.

Her whole body tingled. 'That's no fair.' She hit Raj's arm, and he started to laugh. 'How am I meant to know what they do in India?'

Alvin now leapt up and began to perform what was clearly the cobra dance. Lew and Raj joined him, all of them singing nonsense, their arms writhing above their heads.

'That's no fair.' Now she pushed Raj against the fence, laughing.

A second later her dad's voice came from just behind her. 'Having fun?'

She turned around. He was out of breath, as if he had run, and was still holding a big fork and spatula. He glanced at Raj, who quickly moved away. The other men, gathered around the barbecue, were staring over.

'Where's your mom, hon?'

'Don't know.'

'I need some help out here. Go fetch her.'

'Why can't Jude—'

'Go on now.'

Nora hurried back into the house and found her mom in the bedroom, still holding the dress in her arms.

'Mom, what are you doing?'

Her mom didn't answer, just looked up anxiously.

'Mom?'

'I'd wear my grey dress,' her mom explained, 'but it's got a grape juice stain on it from Nedra's christening. It's not really noticeable, though.'

'Don't be so silly.' Nora took charge, helped her mom off the bed, out of her robe and into the purple dress. Then she marched her into the yard, as if she were a child resisting her first day of school, released her into the big group of women under the canopy, and returned to Raj and the boys.

Quite a few couples were now dancing to a lively polka. She wished Esta and Rudy weren't holding each other so close. Annie had told her how upset even the mention of them made Frank, who was still cornered by Evy. Tall, fragile, dignified Magnus danced with stocky, red-faced Maud. Finn, wearing his sweet, silly grin, danced with Ruth. When Nora asked Raj to dance, he began to do the cobra dance again, but she snatched up his hand.

He pulled back. 'I don't know how to dance to this. I dance by raw animal instinct. This music was invented by the little people who live in Swiss clocks.'

'Come on.'

'Let me at least wait for the glockenspiel solo.'

He kept resisting, being silly, but she finally dragged him into the group, and put her arm around him. 'It's easy. Just look at what everyone else is doing.'

He yielded somewhat, counting the beats: 'Einz, vei, drie, sveinhunt, fair, phumph, dumkopf, shnell.'

'You've got to lead,' she said.

'Into Poland then, *mein liebchen*.' Pointing, he began to goosestep toward the fence.

'Raj, shut up,' she hissed, jerking him back. 'Half the people here are German. I'm half German.'

'I'm sorry.' Genuinely mortified, he made an effort to dance.

Nora noticed Annie dancing with Siggy. She had to stick her butt out because of his belly. It was as if they were dancing with a small child between them. Why wasn't she dancing with Lew? At social gatherings she hardly ever spent time with the people she cared for most.

As Nora drew Raj a little closer, she felt a hand in the crook of her arm and was abruptly spun around. It was her dad again, wearing an almost ghoulish grin. He began to dance clownishly with her.

'Dad,' she protested, trying to pull away.

'Don't I get to dance with the birthday girl?'

'Let go of me.' Wrenching free, she called to Raj, who was walking back toward Lew. He lifted his hand to say no, but she beckoned him over insistently. Just as he got back to her, her dad snatched up his arms and began to dance with him in the same clownish way he had been dancing with her. It was clear that Raj couldn't get out of her dad's grip as he spun Raj toward the fence, almost crashing him into it. Hurrying over, she could see that her dad, still trapping Raj's wrists, was saying something to him. Just as she got there, her dad let him go and walked away, doing a funny little jig and curtsy for the benefit of the barbecue crowd, as if it had all been a tremendous joke.

'I don't know what's wrong with him. What did he say to you?'

Raj was rubbing his wrists. 'He said I was captivating and danced like an angel.'

'What a jerk. Let's finish this dance.' She held her hand out to him.

'Look, I really don't want to dance any more.'

'What did he say?'

'He said I should give you a chance to mix with some of your other guests.'

'That's not what he said. What did he say?'

Raj sighed. 'Please, Nor, I don't want to cause trouble. Just leave me alone for a while. Please.'

She was so mad at her dad. She looked over at him, playing the fool at the barbecue, being too loud. When had this unpleasant stranger come to live in her house?

Turning back to Raj, she snatched up his hands and said, 'Raj, what are we?'

'Don't.' Raj pulled his hands away, glancing over at her father.

'Do you like me?'

'Sure.'

He wouldn't meet her eyes.

'Let's do something Wednesday after school,' she said. 'Just you and me.'

He didn't respond.

'Okay?'

'Your dad said that monkeys should stay in trees and that if I ever touched you again he'd do something to me with a meat hook that I won't repeat.' He still wouldn't look at her.

Annie joined them, out of breath. 'God that was so weird. What was your dad doing?'

'Just being a jerk again.'

Nora felt a tap on her shoulder. It was Maud, who beckoned her aside.

'Nora, I think I've upset your mom. I don't know how. I just told her I liked her dress and she took off into the house.'

Nora quickly made her way back across the yard. She saw that the two sisters had managed to get hold of another bag and were again filling it with plates of food.

Her mom was prostrate on her bed in her underclothes. The dress lay crumpled on the floor.

'What happened?' Nora said.

'I *knew* I shouldn't have worn it.' Crying, her mom was barely able to get the words out as she turned to her. 'Maralyn said, "Oh, you don't usually wear dresses like that."'

'Well, you don't. What's wrong with that?'

'I know what she meant.' Her mom's voice became shrill. 'They all said something. Maud said, "Oh, that's a nice dress."'

'It *is* a nice dress.'

'It's the *way* they said it, like "Why are *you* wearing that dress?" You should have seen how Diane looked at me.'

Nora sat beside her mom, letting her cry and taking up her hands.

Rubbing them, she saw how red and raw they were from all the preparations of this past week, from making everything perfect for this day.

Maud had already banged on the door to Magnus's cabin twice, her red face further flushed with exertion, anger and anxiety. There was so much to do today; six new customers would arrive this afternoon. She cleaned the cabins with furious energy, her anger at Magnus, his laziness, periodically breaking out of her in little ejaculations. *If we both sat on our damn derrieres all day*. Finally she stormed into his cabin. He was lying in bed, but awake, the sheets pulled up to his neck with both hands. His eyes clung to her feebly as she entered.

'For God's sake,' she shouted. 'Are you going to do anything today?'

'My dear,' Magnus replied with struggled-for dignity, 'my body appears not to be responding too well.'

'What is it, a hangover?'

Grimacing, he pulled the sheets aside and tried to stand up.

'What's wrong with you?'

'My legs, they feel numb.' He stumbled sideways, putting his hand out to support himself against the wall.

'Maybe you need to walk,' she said.

'I know we have a lot to do. And I will endeavour to do it, my love.'

He seemed to be having trouble catching his breath, his body trembling.

Her fierceness waned. 'Well, maybe you should rest for a little while. I'll call Dr Menchen.' She helped him back into bed. 'I'll call him now.'

'Thank you, my dear.'

As she was about to leave, he called and she turned back. 'Could I trouble you for a spot of breakfast, just some coffee and a roll? That might be all I need.'

She remained at the door looking at him for a moment. Clutching

the sheets like an invalid, he was staring out of the tiny window in
his cabin, gaunt and helpless, but also somehow utterly self-absorbed,
less a person than a portrait of a tragedy.

Nora was leading Raj to the sinkhole. He would kiss her on the rocks
at the pool's edge: that's how she imagined it, with their feet in the
cool water.

'My dad was so mad at my mom for telling me about this letter
they got from some sicko. Said awful things about them.'

'Like what?'

'She didn't give me details, just said it wasn't signed and said awful
things.'

Raj nodded and didn't ask any more, which wasn't like him. He
had been unusually quiet.

'So you're definitely going to MIT?'

'They accepted me. It's nice to be wanted.'

'You're wanted here.'

'But there's evil out there, my child, which I must face alone.'

'How long are you going to be gone?'

'At least until my voice breaks. It's quite embarrassing. I'm wondering if something's not connected. What are you going to do?'

'Got a place at nursing school in Jackson. Maybe I could transfer
to a school in Boston.'

'Annie said she'd like to live in Boston. Maybe we could all live in
Boston. You and Annie could share a place.'

'Why would I share a place with Annie?' She was getting exasper-
ated.

He shrugged.

A loud Tarzan yodelling came from somewhere close in the woods.
Nora looked in the direction of the noise, but couldn't see him.

'God, he's so annoying. Must have followed us from school.' She
shouted, 'Alvin. Go home.'

They walked on. Raj hadn't looked her once directly in the eyes.
Funny how he could be so theatrical and so shy at the same time. Just

as they came to the steep, rocky path down to the sinkhole, she slipped her hand into his.

'Oh, no!' He looked horrified.

'Oh, no?'

He stared down at their hands. 'God, you turn your back for one second and they're at it like knives.'

'At what?'

Lifting their joined hands gingerly between them he whispered, 'Now they have to be together like this for close to an hour. The male of the species, which is actually the small pale one, has to prevent the large, dark female from devouring it during the mating process.' Arching two of his fingers like mandibles, he began making strange guttural sounds.

Taking a firmer grip, she pulled his hand into her belly. 'Look, Raj, I like you.'

He nodded. 'I'm very likeable. It makes me think I might be slightly retarded.'

'I don't understand what you're saying.' She kept her gaze intently on his fluttering, elusive eyes. She wasn't going to let him joke his way out of things.

Glancing around, he said more seriously, 'Do you think Alv's still following us?'

'Who cares.' Her heart was thumping. She adored Raj. She couldn't imagine not being with him. She knew he liked Annie, but who didn't like Annie, and Annie had Lew. She wasn't clever like him, but she would be a good wife, and he, she knew, would be a good husband, was a good man. She found everyone else just gross. He was refined and intelligent, and he was from somewhere else – from two places else – and he was going somewhere else. He wasn't a Negro, he was English, and he would be a doctor or something. His life telescoped both ways: a mysterious past, an exciting future. She wanted desperately to be a part of that; to get on here. Today could be the most important day of her life. If they kissed, they would marry, she was sure of that.

'Okay, I'll go first,' he said, and the two of them, unbalanced by their joined hands, carefully descended.

Annie sat with Lew on the rocks at the edge of the sinkhole. 'My dad went ape,' she said. 'Took off to see a lawyer in KC this morning.'

Lew was tapping the thumb of his left hand against the tip of each of his fingers, as if counting or playing some kind of tune. 'What about your mom?' he said.

'She cried for hours.'

'Frank?'

'Dad wouldn't show me or Frank the actual letter. I guess it said stuff about us too. Thought it was Otto at first, but he can hardly write his own name. Had big words in it. Dad got the dictionary and had me look up words and tell me what they meant. One was like a phosphorescent light over a marsh or something. He said it wasn't even English.'

Annie took hold of his hands to stop him doing the counting thing. 'What are you doing?'

'Nothing.'

'Lew, you seem very far away.'

'I'm sorry.'

Their first kiss had happened here, his brother lost in the worming light on the other side. She loved Lew, loved even, in a way, the absorbing complexities of his mind, and was glad she was still a part of whatever strange world he saw about him. The distance created by his mind made her feel much of the time as if she were observing him, as one might a portrait. He came to life between her careful engagement and the exacting craft with which he had been fashioned. Genius had made him: something so exquisite at its surface, so wrong at its heart. She thought of *The Picture of Dorian Gray*, the last book they had read in Miss Kelly's class, and dimly understood something about art, the beautiful and redemptive bound to the mouldering and corrupt. At times it felt as if she were dreaming him, that he was utterly familiar but unknown. It wouldn't surprise her if he now lifted his T-shirt to serenely reveal some awful wound. Perhaps this was, in part, because her desire for him felt incestuous. They had lived the lifetime of childhood together before they had become lovers. But she knew he was dying, dying to the world of time and change, and knew that to stay with him was to die too.

'I'm going in,' he said. He took off his clothes. It still thrilled her to see him naked. He waded across the shallow rock shelf that stretched out a few feet before the deep water. The bright sun angled in through the trees, its reflected light snaking over the fleshy lime-stone that rose high on the far side. She watched his muscular buttocks flex as he dived and disappeared.

If she left him, he would have no one, would be lost in his madness. She and Raj kept him in the world. He was their responsibility because he loved them. Which was the surrogate of their own love, made from pity and desire. She and Raj could not love in any pure way. There was something wrong with them. Feeling was like resonance in empty chambers, chambers eaten out with increasing precision by restless-ness, despair, longing. A love song sung beautifully by someone heart-less and vain. If one has imagination, one doesn't love, one imagines love, one makes the chambers for the song with such tools as those lovely buttocks, tensing before the dive. They were too much alike, perhaps, she and Raj. Whenever they were alone together they found themselves in a kind of no-man's-land. They starved each other, raven-ous for intimacy. She thought about Raj all the time. It frustrated her. Why not both? Why couldn't they both love her and she them, completely? But the fat boy bellows in the woods, the monster, the monster. This world wasn't fair. Lew's head broke up from the water.

'Annie!' He waved her in.

'Too cold,' she shouted.

He pulled himself up on the shallow ledge and then flung himself backwards, arcing, splashing thunderously.

As a child he had sat beside her here, hating his brother. A day later Roh was dead and he was mad. Now he called her into the water, almost a man. She didn't want this. Again he pulled himself up on to the shelf and stood, sunlit water sluicing from his body. So beautiful. He was tall, broad, muscular as a man, but pale, hairless as a young boy, his penis shrunken from the cold. Lew reached out to her.

She shook her head. She didn't want this. He waded up to her, came to a stop with his toes overlapping hers beneath a foot of water.

'Come on,' he said.

'No, no, no, no, no.' She put her hands flat out against his thighs to stop him. Thick as molasses, desire pooled at her crotch, sticky tendrils leaking down her legs. She didn't want this.

Squatting, he brushed aside her arms and began to undo the buttons of her blouse.

'You're getting me all wet.' She tried to sound irritated. 'Someone's going to see us.'

'No one's going to come all the way out here. The kids go to the quarry.'

He pulled her blouse over her shoulders and undid her bra. She said nothing else. Why had they become physical? They had just been curious, like children; it was lovely, but she wanted this to stop. And she wanted him to know that she wanted this to stop. But she was naked now. He lifted her in his arms, gently at first, as if she were a sleeping child. Abruptly, then, he flung her over his shoulder and carried her to the edge of the ledge.

'Don't you dare,' she shouted. 'Don't you dare. I mean it. Don't you dare.'

Swinging her back down into his arms, he gave her a look of faintly mocking sympathy. She loved him more than anything in the world. All at once, with that inhuman strength of his, he flung her far out into the pool. The shock of the cold sealed her skin, and she could taste immediately the limestone, earthbone, and let herself sink for a moment into the veining light, as into the memory of sight in a blind eye.

So it began. She surfaced, breathing hard, and each time she tried to get out, before she could pull herself completely up on to the rock shelf, he would lift her with his stone strength, and fling her back into the deepest part of the water. It was heartless: a lover's game. He would kill her. At last she had no choice: clinging to his leg, she begged him. Lifting her into his arms again, he carried her back to the bank, sat with her body, which he had reclaimed, across his knees. She couldn't take her eyes off his powerful neck and shoulders, the veins in his arms. How effortlessly he could kill her.

'I love you,' she said.

He smiled, absorbed in arranging the thick wet band of her hair between her breasts.

After a little while, very softly, he said, 'Sad.'

'What?'

'You might go away. I mean . . .' He frowned. 'I think you should.'

'Should what?'

'I don't know. Go away or something.'

All at once it collapsed her. He wasn't reclaiming her, but was offering her exactly what she wanted. He was letting her go.

'Lew, what are you going to be doing next year – in five years? Where are you going to be?'

He took a moment, running his hand from her cheek down the full length of her body. This was the Lew she had forgotten, with his quiet understanding, the cool and complex shades of his mind. She thought all had been lost into his madness and wondered now just how much he was aware of. Compared to him, she and Raj were children: neither could have survived what he had experienced, what he was living through.

'Can't see that far,' he said. 'Can't think about much right now. I'm so close.'

'Close to what?'

He seemed to take a moment to gauge her. 'Remember that thunderstorm last week?'

She nodded.

'I came out here.' He spoke softly, almost whispered. 'I'd heard my brother call from the river. Wa-Kon-Te was fierce. But in my dreams my mom was teaching me the names of things. She said Wa-Kon-Te wasn't my dad like I thought. He was another brother. She told me she had saved Roh by turning him into light. I spoke in the storm. You don't know that feeling, Annie: to bring back the dead with one word.'

Annie put her hand against his face. She felt as if he had just told her he was going to die. 'So what am I, Lew? What am I in all this?'

He frowned. A second later he reached to the back of his neck and she realized she shouldn't have asked him this.

'Who do you think sent that letter?' She wanted him to focus on something else.

'What?'

'The letter. To my mom and dad. Who would send it? My dad thought it was you or your dad. But I told him your dad couldn't write and I knew it wasn't you.'

'I wouldn't write nothing like that.'

'Lew, do you say these things to anyone else?'

'What things?'

'What you said to me about your brother and mom and things.'

He shook his head. 'Only Raj. But Raj understands.'

'No he doesn't. And no one else will. And if you say these things to anyone but Raj or me, they'll put you back in that place. Lew, you're eighteen. You can't spend your life here wandering around the forest trying to forgive yourself for what happened to Roh. Your dad is Clyde. Your mom died. Your brother died. They're dead. They died like people die. They're not coming back. I don't know what happened to Roh. I don't know if you did it or who did it and I don't care. You're good and I love you and I want you to be normal. I want you to stop this. I want you to live a normal life. With me. I'll help you. Raj and I will help you.'

A pine cone, flung from the woods somewhere behind them, flew over their heads and splashed into the water.

Rolling off Lew's legs, Annie reached over the rocks for her clothes. They were gone. Lew's were gone too.

'Christ,' she said.

She and Lew sank their bodies into the cold, shallow water and looked around. Stones clattered down from the loose shale path that descended from the ridge and a moment later Raj emerged, Nora just behind him.

Seeing them, Raj waved and called, 'Hey, guys.'

Annie put her hand out. 'Raj, don't come any closer. Can you see our clothes over there?'

'Your clothes?' Raj looked around.

A shout came from behind them. 'I can see your lily-white asses!' Alvin was looking down from the top of the high limestone ridge that formed one side of the sinkhole, grinning.

'You damn goober,' Annie shouted. 'What you do with our clothes?'

'What clothes?' He disappeared, emerging out of the path just behind Raj and Nora a few seconds later.

'You little jerk, go and get them,' Annie shouted.

'Go and get their clothes,' Nora said.

'How should I know where they are?' Alvin shrugged, pouting out his lower lip.

'I could get you some leaves,' Raj suggested, 'but there's only maple round here and that's *so* last season.'

'You've got your underwear on, haven't you?' Nora said.

Annie didn't answer.

Nora was shocked. 'Why aren't you wearing anything?'

'They're nekkid, nekkid, nekkid!' Alvin was doing a reprise of the cobra dance.

'Raj, will you search for our clothes?' Annie said.

Raj began to look around.

'Alvin, where d'you put them?' Annie shouted again.

'I didn't put them anywhere.' Though trying to look innocent, Alvin could hardly stop himself laughing.

Annie felt so furious at him. She was freezing. 'Are you going to get our clothes or not?'

'I don't know where—'

She pulled herself out of the water.

'Annie,' Nora screamed.

Raj glanced over and then immediately turned away. Alvin, toward whom she now walked, stood frozen, staring at her.

'I'll get them,' he said. He sprinted off into the woods and returned a moment later with the clothes. Annie was squatting down, her knees tight together, covering her breasts with her hands. As soon as he put the clothes down in front of her, Alvin ran off. Annie dressed quickly and then brought Lew's things to him. She was soaked, her clothes sticking to her body. Standing in front of Lew to hide him as he dressed, she wrung her hair out. Raj seemed to have found something to investigate a little distance away.

'Why did you do that?' Nora said, still standing at the entrance to the path.

'I was freezing. I had to get my clothes. I *hate* Alvin.'

'Why didn't you have any clothes on?'

'We were just swimming.'

Nora seemed both angry and upset. She went to say something else, but clearly would have started crying. Abruptly, she turned and ran back up the path. Annie chased after her, catching up at the top.

'What's wrong?'

Nora wouldn't look at her and didn't say anything, just kept walking as quickly as she could.

Annie took hold of her arm, but Nora snatched it away.

'What's wrong? Nor, what's wrong?'

'You *ruined* it. I was on a date. Why would you do that?'

'What else could I do?'

'You didn't have to do that in front of Raj.'

'Nora, please.' Annie took hold of her arm more firmly and pulled her around.

'How could you stand naked like that in front of a boy?'

'Nora, I was so cold. I wasn't thinking.'

'You know Raj likes you.'

'He doesn't—'

'I'm not stupid, Annie. You think I'm stupid.'

'No, I don't.'

'Raj won't be serious with me.'

'He will.'

Just then they heard Raj screaming, 'Ge-ron-i-mo,' followed by a thunderous splash.

They both laughed just for a second. Then Nora began to cry. She squatted down with her back against a tree.

Too wet to take hold of her, Annie hunkered close and rubbed her friend's knees. 'I'm sorry,' she said. 'I'm really sorry.'

After a moment Nora said, 'My dad's being such a jerk. He tried to take a photo of me in the shower on my birthday.'

'Haven't you said something to him?'

'He just acts like it's some big joke.'

'What about your mom?'

Nora let out a despairing little snort. They remained quiet for a while.

Finally Nora said, 'Annie, are you going to marry Lew?'

'I guess,' she said.

'You guess?'

'Ge-ron-i-mo.'

Lewis watched Raj plunge into the water. He sat at the edge of the stone shelf, the cool water up to his chest. *What am I?* Annie had said. He was trying not to think about it. He felt, though, as if he could rip his skull bone off like rotted bark, his thoughts a pale roil of termites.

Raj clambered back up the rock face to dive in again. He knew Raj was the key. Raj, the self-begotten, created of dust, wind and the snatch of a strange, familiar song.

Raj plunged in again, holding one leg under him for maximum splash. A second later, he swam up beside Lew.

'Can you believe Annie did that?' he said, out of breath. 'I think Alv and Nora are scarred for life.'

'It was my fault. I made her come into the water.'

'You should be ashamed,' Raj scolded. 'I mean if I'm forced to look at another beautiful naked woman there's going to be some heads rolling around here, buddy.'

'What's going on between you and Nora?'

'We were just coming down here for our usual naked romp in the woods.'

'Have you kissed her yet?'

'How dare you, sir.'

'That means you haven't. Why haven't you?'

'Well, when her tongue shot out of her mouth and caught a dragon-fly, it kind of put me off.' Raj suddenly seemed a little ashamed of himself, and after a moment answered seriously. 'Don't know why. I like Nora.'

'So why don't you kiss her?'

'You mean apart from the fact that her dad would feed my tally-whacker into the nearest corn-shucker?'

'Is that it?'

He shrugged. 'I don't want to lose her.'

'Why would you lose her?'

'Can't be on my own like you, Lew. Couldn't stand it if she wasn't my friend any more. Or you. Or Annie.'

'Have you ever kissed anyone?'

'I've kissed Suzybelle. That heifer's got a tongue that won't quit.' They laughed.

'What were you doing here with Annie?' Raj said.

'Just swimming.'

'Could you be with someone else, d'you think?'

Lewis shook his head.

'*Please.*'

'What?'

'I'm only kidding.' Raj swam out to the centre of the sinkhole and turned back to Lew, treading water. 'When you kitch her, massa, alls I wants her lips. I wants her lips with gravy and chitlins, massa.'

'Guess what I realized today, Raj? I'm a Jew.' As he said this, Lew felt the tentacles at his neck and put his hand back there to protect himself.

'Can I be a Jew too?' Raj said. 'We could do that funny dance together. The one they do at weddings.' He flung his arms up and began to chant, 'Hey ya, he he he hey ya, he he he hey ya.'

'Do you think the girls are coming back?' Lew said.

But Raj had sunk, only his raised arms above the water, which churned with bubbles as he continued to sing.

The Reverend Hewitt seemed to have finished his sermon, which had been tedious, Annie thought, even by his own standards. He had performed none of his usual gestures and flourishes, which distracted the eye at least, like an elaborate garnish around a dish of pickled hog's brains and kidney-flavoured ice cream. In the pews, people were rubbing their necks, the young children asleep or crying. Like everyone, Annie turned her eyes to Earl Shlockenburger, who was holding a list of the sick and shut-ins and other local announcements. Earl was a little deaf and never really understood any of the Reverend's sermons anyway. Many times over the years he had stood up, declared that God's word had been rightly divided, and had started towards the altar only to have the Reverend continue after what had merely been a dramatic pause.

Earl's wife, Brenda, nudged him. He glanced around at the congregation. All eyes were upon him. They wanted to see his bent old body shuffling up the aisle, that little piece of paper, their reprieve, in his hand. Earl had become so associated with the end of Hewitt's sermons it had become common in town for people to say, 'It's time for Earl' whenever anything unpleasant or excessively extended had to end.

Like a tremulous dissenter, Earl rose, clutching his rag of paper.

'We have heard the word of God rightly divided,' he announced and began to make his way to the front.

Annie noticed now that the Reverend was watching Earl with a dark, brooding expression, and as the Elder turned toward the congregation and opened out his sheet, Hewitt declared with more passion than he had mustered during the whole sermon, 'Of God, certainly. But not of the devil.'

Abruptly Hewitt lifted a sheet of paper over his head and addressed the congregation in a tremulous voice. 'I received this . . . *thing* three days ago. It contains the most vile and vicious calumny against me and my wife.' His voice had risen to a shout.

A murmur ran through the church as he took a moment to compose himself, gently patting and stroking his immaculate hair as if it were a high-strung pet he had unintentionally startled.

Earl stood frozen and bewildered for a moment, which made him look uncannily like an aged version of the wooden Christ behind him, and finally made his way back to his seat.

'Most insidious of all,' Hewitt went on, 'this *thing* was written by someone among us, someone here today. A person who seems to feel that here in God's own house, the Almighty cannot see into his heart.' He paused, panning his head slowly over the congregation. 'I do not call this a letter because it invites no correspondence. It is an act of vicious cowardice intended to poison me at the very root of my life. Its insidious aim is clear: that I should look out every Sunday at this, my congregation' – he held his arms out wide – 'in the knowledge that one of you holds me in contempt. It is the serpent in the garden.'

Pausing again, he drew himself up. It looked to Annie as if he had added a few more inches to the box he stood on behind the dais. She could hardly believe what was happening.

'I prayed for God's wisdom in this matter, and He guided me to do what I shall do now.' Here he glanced down at his wife in the front pew, who was as surprised and confused as everyone else. 'I'm going to throw this coward's lies back into his face. I'm going to say to Satan, I'm not afraid. I will not keep it in darkness to fester. I am going to read every word.'

He was still holding the piece of paper away from him in his pinched fingers. He shook it for a moment, as if he were throttling a rat, then placed it on the dais. After putting on his glasses, he read.

Dear Reverend Hewitt,

This Sunday you gave yet another one of your interminable sermons. Small, gleaming man, you are the evolution of some medieval instrument of inquisitional torture. You wield yourself against us, your poor heretics.

Can't you see us writhing in the pews? Of course you can't. Your ego is impenetrable, a shell of vanity around what was once your life. Your now putrefied life: if nothing can break in, nothing can break out. You are a dead chick in the hollow of the inviolable egg of your ego. Not a gesture made, not a glance given, not a word spoken that is not preconceived. And yet, like all those without imagination, you are completely sincere. You make me shudder, the manly firmness of your handshake, the cupping of my elbow, utterly rehearsed, constraining me as you try to suck me into the null vacuum of your eyes. In that moment I know you would preach hatred as mindlessly as you preach love, would shoot a man in the head as readily as deliver him a homily. Like so many priests and conservatives, you are the voice of the void. I keep expecting your face to fall away. All at once to see through the little proscenium of that hair you so love into space, without stars, an utter darkness that speaks not just of individual death, but of the annihilation of us all. The horror. The horror. The horror is the void with a bad haircut, with a ridiculous little moustache. *Heil* the horror. You are the horror, which is the profundity of all space and time trapped in a little vain man, whose every feeling, if he can be said to have feelings – tenderness, regret, piety, love – is an inflected reflex of hatred and anger.

I find myself morbidly fascinated by how you and Judy got together. No doubt she was one of your parishioners somewhere, staring at you implacably from the front pew. You were drawn to her severe attention in the great sea swell of yawns and eye-rubbing. Rigid in her posture, unadorned and un-made-up, she seemed unsexual, which also drew you, since you had always felt something of a qualm at the thought of having such demands placed upon you. She never spoke about herself, which suited you, since you have no interest in other lives. You saw in her an acolyte, an echo chamber for your vanity.

I like to imagine that on your wedding night she took you by surprise, meeting your dry kiss with liquid passion, filling you with a visceral horror. You had missed it, that yearning deeply buried in her basilisk eyes. To your surprise, she wasn't quite dead. A necrophiliac's nightmare: the corpse has opened her eyes, her livid skin takes colour, a lewd grin distorts the rictus of her mouth. Quickly you thrust the stake through her heart: as she went to kiss you again, you flinched and told her that her breath was bad, that her body had an unpleasant odour, that her breasts were strangely stretched and slack for one so young. Whenever she spoke, you stifled yawns, checked your watch. Under such tutelage, Judy became the irredeemably loathsome woman she is today, vile, hateful, baulked, everything in her curdled and corrupted. I prefer you. She is a wound, merely, whose suppuration has crusted into the semblance of a woman. Gall, canker and no more. While you, with such limitations of mind and sensibility one is astonished you have brain enough to take your next breath, are among the best of what you were born to be, she is the worst of what she was born to be. She is unbearable because she might truly have been other than she is. She makes me never cease to be amazed by what any human being can allow herself to become.

Yours faithfully,

A Friend

Taking off his glasses, he looked up at the congregation.

Abruptly, Annie's dad, who was right beside her, stood up. 'I get one,' he shouted. 'I get one of these. I gone to a lawyer.'

Then Miss Kelly's thin body curled up as meekly as a sprout. 'I got one too,' she said. 'It was dreadful. I . . .' Overcome, she sat down.

Reverend Hewitt clearly hadn't expected this. 'Who else got one of these?'

Slowly hands were raised, one coaxing another until almost a dozen were up. Annie put her hand inside her father's elbow and eased him back down.

'One among us,' the Reverend declared. 'One here has betrayed our fellowship. I speak now to that one: if your heart is not completely black, here, in the house of your Lord, you will now stand up.'

Annie hunched a little lower, as did everyone, as if they feared that against their wishes, as in a dream, they would find themselves standing. They all glanced around, the usually sleepy air of that church utterly evaporated. With blood in the air, guilt in all their hearts, evil among them, this place had become, for once, a real church. The air electric, every one of them waited for the snake, the kiss, for the hanged man to show his face.

As they drove home from church, Alvin felt as if his face were scalded, his heart knocking and shuddering like an old two-stroke. He wasn't sure if he was terrified or exhilarated. His dad actually seemed energized, muttering to himself at the wheel as if composing another sermon. His mom, though, looked like someone who had lost a lot of blood: hunched over, staring into the dashboard, breathing shallowly as if about to vomit. He couldn't believe his dad had read the letter out in front of the whole town. He had only sent it as a safeguard, to put his family above suspicion in case an enquiry ever got started. But he had been sure people would keep the letters – so cruel, but so true – secret. Exploding out from him, he imagined those letters lodging like shrapnel near the heart.

'Mom,' he called softly. 'Mom.'

She didn't respond. His dad was now tapping his wedding ring against the steering wheel and humming. Alvin knew he hadn't delivered the letter just as a safeguard. It was the first one he had typed out on Hoffmeyer's Gourland, and he had felt almost sick with excitement at every word, switching 'he' to 'you', that voice filling him. He loved his dad, but wanted, somehow, to see him unsure, not always thinking he was God's gift to other people, spending all his time with strangers. He had handed his dad the letter himself, mixing it in with the other letters in the mailbox. But his dad hadn't mentioned it. In the following days, rather than seeming upset, he had seemed excited, almost manic.

All at once, then, it struck him and he looked over at his mom again: surely his dad had shown her the letter and had discussed what he was planning to do today? Surely this wasn't the first time she had heard it, sitting there in front of the whole town? But even as he tried to deny it, he knew, just looking at her, that it was true. He went hot and cold suddenly. Aiming for his dad, he had hit his mom. No. He had aimed for them both. Why? He had no idea. All he knew was that he had never felt so excited or, in some way, so close to them as when he had typed out and brought that letter into their house.

'Mom.'

She didn't respond. Thank God this stuff about his parents had been in one of the older journals, written when Miss Winters used to attend church. She hadn't gone now for many years; otherwise she would be the most likely suspect. And if she had heard what his dad had read today, she would have known it was him doing it, since he had left out the part about himself — that 'little toad of a boy'. Things were hard enough for him as it was.

'Mom.'

Still she ignored him.

His dad pulled into the driveway. When they got in, his dad went straight to his armchair in the parlour and put on his favourite record, a medley of stirring classical hits. The *William Tell* overture thundered through the house.

His mom still hadn't said anything or even looked into his face. Like a robot, she pulled the quiche she had made this morning out of the fridge and put together a salad. After cutting a big slice of the quiche for Alvin, she carried the rest into the parlour. Alvin wondered why she was doing this, since his dad was waiting to be called to the table.

There was a thud and the music abruptly stopped.

'Damn it, Judy,' his dad shouted as his mom re-entered the kitchen with the empty plate.

Alvin got up and ran into the parlour, almost colliding with his dad coming out. She had dumped the quiche on to the record player.

'Are you *insane?*' his dad shouted at his mom, who took a seat at the table.

'Oh, I am sorry,' she said. 'I'm such a goof. Did I forget the salad?' With a sweep of her arm, she shoved the earthenware bowl full of salad on to the floor, where it shattered. 'Lemonade?' The big glass pitcher went the way of the salad bowl, exploding at his feet. 'We have banana pudding for dessert. Just let me know when you're ready.'

'Is this about me exposing those foul lies?'

'Is it about that? How could it possibly be about that? It was just wonderful to have everyone in this town hear me described as a sapperating wound.'

'Suppurating,' he corrected.

'To be described as a loathsome, *loathsome*, desperate, disgusting woman; a corpse; to have our intimate life described like that in front of everyone. *Everyone.*' She was shouting now.

'But it's just lies.'

'Without saying one word to me,' his mother screamed. 'Not one damn word, you vicious, *vicious* man.'

'But it's just lies.'

'Reeking canker, the worst, *the worst* of what I could have been.'

'Alvin, go to your room,' his dad said.

Alvin quickly ran through the kitchen, sending a piece of the glass pitcher skittering against the refrigerator, and down the hall. He listened at his bedroom door, his mom's voice getting shriller and shriller, his dad trying to reason with her, until every time his dad went to speak, she would let out a hysterical scream. Alvin felt as if everything inside him had gone soft and was starting to rot. The strangest thing was that his dad seemed genuinely surprised, as if he had been untroubled by the content of the letter. Was it possible that he had not seen anything of himself or his life in those words? Was it possible it just hadn't occurred to him to show the letter to his mom before he read it out to the whole town? It seemed to Alvin that he could better imagine and understand what was going on inside Hoffmeyer's head than his dad's.

The screaming stopped and he heard his dad go into his room. He listened to his mom sweeping up the pieces of shattered crockery and glass. Half an hour later there was a knock at his door and his mom put her head in.

'It's all right now, honey,' she said. 'It's over. Come out and have your lunch.'

She sat with him at the kitchen table as he picked at his quiche.

After a while she said, 'I've been wanting to talk to you about something. Listen, you said you were helping Nora paint her bedroom the other day. I met her in Sal's and she said she hadn't seen you.'

'I *was* helping her.'

'The week before that you said you and Raj had cycled up to Booneville to see the parade. Well, I went to see Ruth that day. Raj was at home, said he hadn't seen you for weeks.'

'I got other friends.'

'So why did you lie to me about where you were? What on earth do you do all day?'

'Lots of things.'

'Like what?'

'I go fishing and stuff.'

'Why are you lying to me?'

'I'm not lying.'

His mom was now staring at the fridge, which was spattered with lemonade. After a moment she said, 'Can you believe he read that out in front of everyone?'

Late that night, Alvin lay in the hallway, watching his dad through the gap under his door. His mom had gone to bed early. His dad was reading a comic, which was on a music stand, since both his hands were resting, as if in blessing, on the metal dome of his Van Graff generator. According to Dr Feldman, from whose catalogue his dad had bought the generator, static electricity prevented baldness by stimulating the scalp. His dad's hair was becoming ghostly, exploded out from his head. This was his dad's usual routine. He seemed happily absorbed in his comic, while his mom lay now in bed like someone wounded. Alvin wondered how it was that he could understand completely a man who had pressed a rifle to his heart and ended his own life, but couldn't feel any connection at this moment to a man who was his own father.

A few weeks before Nora's birthday, he had asked Eileen Metzler if she would go to the prom with him. She said she would rather go with Raj, which, for her, was the worst insult she could give. Later on that day, feeling miserable, he had been thumbing through Ruth's journals in the basement and had glanced up at Hoffmeyer's type-writer. Just like that, the idea for the letters had struck him, flood-ing him with euphoria. He had never felt so happy or focused.

He could hear his mom crying again. Utter revulsion for himself rolled through him and back, through him and back, like a heavy pan too full of water, the struggle to stop it overflowing only causing it to get worse. Again, vividly, he saw Annie come out of the sinkhole and walk toward him, naked. So painful. It showed how little she cared that she felt no shame, as if he were no more than a child. He had felt like a child, an irritating child, had seen himself in the eyes of his friends as he saw himself in the mirror every day, with his big head and squat body. All of it meaningless, sneaking around with that rifle, loading it carefully, taking beads on people, imagining them heartshot, the grief and the horror, all that feeling with him at the root of it. Pathetic. But he couldn't seem to *be* anyone else. He had tried, but always fell into his old patterns. He thought about that strange dream of a couple of nights ago, where he snuck up not just on Lew and Annie, but Raj as well, all three of them at the sinkhole – naked, writhing and intertwined like snakes.

He wondered if the dream had come from reading *Othello*. Miss Kelly met with a group of them after school to talk about the play.

She had intended to do it in class, but Eileen Metzler told her uncle, who was on the school board, and they banned it. He only went because Raj and Annie did, but was amazed at some of it – *the beast with two backs, his black ram is tupping your white ewe*. He realized this meant sex, though Miss Kelly called it 'congress'. The phrases kept running through his head. More than that, their speaker, Iago, had excited him, doing all that harm more or less just because he could. He was like the devil. It made him think of that opening speech from *Richard III*, which he had had to memorize last year as his perform-ance for the summer pageant: *since I cannot prove a lover, I am deter-mined to prove a villain*. He had been mad at first to have drawn that speech. Like everyone he wanted 'To be or not to be' or 'They are honourable men.' But after Miss Kelly went through it with him, explaining what everything meant, talking in that excited way of hers about Richard's character, he began to get strange little chills running through him whenever he looked up at himself in the mirror, a throw-pillow making a hump in his back, beginning, 'Now is the winter of our discontent.' It was a kind of faith: not for good, not holy sacri-fice, which was for those whom God had blessed anyway or for fools, but for nothing, for meanness, taking advantage of faith, trust and vanity. It wasn't about winning; it was just about knowing what you were going to do next. In the end, though, it seemed more about loneliness: Iago, King Richard. What really drew him to them was that they seemed alone. They did what they did because it put them at the heart of extreme human feeling. When he typed up those letters, and sent them out, it had made him feel both deeply alone and profoundly a part of things. It didn't make him feel any less isolated, but it did, somehow, give a shape or purpose or power or something to the feeling of being alone. After Hoffmeyer killed himself, he heard his dad telling Jason Adams that a sign that someone who is depressed is going to kill himself is that he suddenly becomes active and happy. It was like that in some way. There was also the thought of doing something that was against your nature, which you could never undo, so it would change you for ever. Pulling the trigger; Ruth collapsing into the cabbage bed. Senseless.

His dad's hair was now completely wild. His mom was still crying in bed. He was lying on the floor looking at a person who was as far away from him as any stranger. He wasn't Richard or Iago. Richard was a king, could destroy a whole nation. Iago was subtle and clever, powerful in his language. He himself couldn't manipulate anyone, had no presence, command, no gift with words. Lying on the cold floor, he felt melted, confused and bereft: he would have taken any life in the world other than his own right now. Any life at all.

The second she got home, Nurse Gordiano ran to her vanity mirror. The woman Nurse Fontaine had recommended to cut her hair had deliberately ruined it. She looked as if she had been sheared by a mob after fraternizing with the enemy – dear Günter, who was just showing her how to unload his Luger. She should have realized something was up when the woman had told her she had broken the only mirror she owned, which meant that Nurse Gordiano hadn't been able to see what she was doing. Nurse Fontaine was behind this, she was sure. Now she had no choice but to shave the rest of it off and wear a wig to work.

She did what she could to avoid Dr Weaver the next day, but in the afternoon she was called into an emergency appendectomy. The little girl was in a critical condition. Dr Weaver was barking orders to a number of nurses, including Nurse Fontaine. Joining the mêlée, Nurse Gordiano sopped blood, wiped sweat, handed around instruments, and gifted the child's family, who had forced their way heedlessly into the operating theatre, with the brooding solace of her brown and liquid eyes. Within moments, her chest was heaving this way and that like a Roman galleon of sweaty slaves under the ramming-speed drum of her heart. All at once, Nurse Fontaine, feigning to reach for something, pulled off Nurse Gordiano's hat and wig. An astonished gasp arose from all those in the operating theatre. Even the little girl's convulsing body seemed quieted for a moment.

'Your hair, Nurse Gordiano,' Dr Weaver said. 'Where is it?'

'Perhaps, sir,' came her curt response, 'that might be best answered by Nurse Fontaine.'

Dr Weaver turned to Fontaine, the bloody scalpel in his hand. She met his eyes defiantly. In response he shook the great mane of his own dark hair, hair that bespoke not one day of dandruff, lifelessness or chemical build-up, innocent of split ends, frizz and dullness, immune to pillow- or hat-head. It was a gesture at once subtle and overmastering. But Fontaine, as if struck by a mischievous wind, suddenly lost her cap, releasing a deluge of red curls about her face and shoulders. In making a pretty show of trying to get it all back under her hat, she drew in the assistance of two other nurses, the anaesthesiologist and a couple of the child's family members.

'The patient!' Nurse Gordiano screamed. 'We're losing her.' Getting back to work, she bent over the wound as Dr Weaver continued with the operation. She was unaware that her head, beneath the bright operating lamp, flashed and glinted magnificently, showing every part of her well-shaped cranium. She looked like an albino Nubian chieftainess, like the ball joint into the love socket, like the very cudgel of desire. At last the offending organ was removed.

Dr Weaver followed her out of the operating theatre.

'Nurse Gordiano,' he called with his usual imperiousness, which she ignored. Then more softly: 'Angela.'

She turned around.

'Fontaine's hair could have cost that child her life. Hair or no hair, you were pretty good in there.'

'Pretty good?' she said, cocking one eye at him.

He smiled: 'Damn good.'

'Just doing my job.' She turned back quickly, so he wouldn't see her happiness, and the heaving slaves of her breasts rowed her with long, sweeping, prideful strokes down the corridor.

Ruth wondered why she had bothered trying to get back to this damn book, pulling out its dusty manuscript this morning. It had just vaguely amused her. Strange: she realized she was treading water, waiting for Raj to get home. In a couple of months he would leave for Boston; the house already seemed empty. Raj, she knew, would be good at keeping in touch: he was a very loving boy. Often she felt as if she were taking advantage of him. He would massage her shoulders or her slightly arthritic hands, and never let her wash so much as a dish. But she wondered now if his feelings went much beyond a sense of indebtedness. And what of her feelings? When he had told her this morning of his impending date with Nora, she had been gripped by a sudden and cruelly unfair animosity toward that girl. She hadn't been able to think of her as anything other than a plodding, earnest creature who, in the next couple of years, would transform from comely and buxom to stolid and heavy. And Raj was vulnerable because he had such a need to be loved. Before this morning Ruth had managed to convince herself that her relationship to him was that of a friend, made possible because he was so mature. He had all the playfulness of a child with none of the egotism. But she had felt this morning as she suspected a mother might feel: possessive and protective.

The screen door at the back squealed and banged shut. She heard the fridge opening: he always went straight to the fridge. Sometimes he would take something, but often he just seemed to need to check it. She went out to him.

Still staring into the fridge, he exclaimed in the execrable Southern accent that had recently replaced his favourite hillbilly voice, 'Why, madam, I could have sworn there was a piece of pie on that there bottom shelf.'

'The pie didn't make it, Raj.'

'Well that surely is a crying shame. Did it suffer?'

'But briefly; and dear sir I vouchsafe there will be other pies, other fillings – possibly even this very evening.'

At this he gave her a greedy, wide-eyed smile and pulled out a carton of milk.

'Use a glass.'

Getting one, he joined her at the kitchen table.

'So how did your date go?' she asked.

'Well, something kind of happened and I ended up hanging out with Lew at the sinkhole for most of the afternoon.'

'What happened?'

'I'm not sure I should tell you.'

She took up his hands, trapping them in hers. 'Imagine a world without pie.'

'You mustn't tell anyone.'

'Who would I tell?'

'Well, we went down to the sinkhole. And Lew and Annie were there already. And they didn't have any clothes on.'

'None?'

He nodded. 'Anyway, Nora just bugged out for some reason. Ran off. Annie chased after her, and I decided that the most responsible and caring course of action was to spend the afternoon swimming with Lew.'

'Gosh, that Annie is quite something.'

Raj made a wry little shrug.

'So what do you think of Nora?' she asked.

'What do *you* think of Nora?'

He often did this, turning the question back on her. She answered carefully, trying to keep her tone reasonable and even. 'I think that when you go to Boston, you're going to meet lots of people – attractive, accomplished, clever people. Now is not the time to get tied up with someone.'

He nodded gently and took a deep breath, not looking at her. 'Do you think Annie and Lew will get married?'

'Well they've been inseparable for ever and if you were going to match the two best-looking people in the town, it would be them.'

'Is he handsome, then?' Raj attempted a genuinely curious frown. Strange what a ham he could be, she thought, but how bad he was at lying.

'He's beautiful,' she said, 'and very appealing because there's something so . . . helpless about him.'

'He's not helpless.' Raj was clearly trying to find a way to disagree with her.

'You know him better than I do.'

'What about Annie?' he said.

'Are you really asking me if she's beautiful?'

'No, I mean . . .' Obviously frustrated, he began to chew at his lip, and all at once she realized what he meant.

She took a moment before speaking. 'There's a lot going on in Annie. It seems to me she'd be a bad choice for anyone right now.'

'I don't think that's true.'

Gently she squeezed his hands, which she still held. 'This is very clever, Raj. You're getting me to say what you don't want to hear, so you can disagree.'

Though his face had gone utterly still and serious, a faint smile flickered at his lips. It was a combination that made him look cruel. Without his usual goofy animation, he became a man rather than a child, his large eyes both seductive and chillingly devoid. It was as if his face had turned transparent only to reveal nothing, the window in a lit room at night in which you fear that a face, an awful face, might appear. All at once she became profoundly aware of the darkness of his skin as something absolute and impenetrable, and of how little she knew him. Just momentarily he seemed like a figure in a bad dream, as if his smile might broaden to reveal a rodent's teeth, and she felt as she did sometimes when shocked out of sleep by that recurring nightmare in which someone whose face she couldn't quite see was playfully, caressingly, trying to suffocate her.

All of this was just for an instant, like a moment of vertigo, before her silly boy returned, his playful and loving self re-animating his expression. 'You're the smartest person I ever met, Ruth.'

She laughed. 'That's what my boyfriends used to say just before they dumped me.'

'They must have been crazy.'

'Do you like Annie?'

Making a dismissive moue, he said, 'Doesn't matter what I think of either of them. Lew's my best friend and Nora's dad would kill me if he even knew we were on a date.'

All that terrible mystery in his face had vanished, leaving a matt, almost dumb innocence about him. With real pain she sensed he was entering a difficult time, which all his humour and sweetness couldn't save him from. She thought of herself at his age, knowing nothing, falling for difficult, brilliant, heartless men. Utterly vulnerable, she had no self-confidence and was armed with just a few whacky adolescent ideals. She had known only the isolating love of a mother who adored her but hated everyone else. The heartache she felt now for this boy was profound. And yet, holding his hands, she also felt what she hadn't in so long: that something with all the complex wonder of life had rooted in her. Before him she had tried to live with a ghost, a man eternally approaching. She had tried to perceive the distance, the waiting, as love, hoping that the increasing vacuum inside her would be, at the last, insupportable, would break her open and let everything flood inside. But this was it, holding the dark hand of this odd boy, feeling sick with worry, fear and hope, feeling as if she would gladly take into herself every moment of pain he might ever suffer. Gladly.

Frank had just finished replacing the fuel pump on Mansard's Buick when Mrs B. entered the yard from the house.

'I wondered where you did your work,' she said. 'I've got the Caddy out front.'

As she handed him the key, he told her he would take her back as soon as he washed up. When he came down from the bathroom, Mrs B. was drinking iced tea in the kitchen with his mom. The first thing that occurred to him, strangely, was how much more appealing his mom was than Bennet's wife, who wasn't unattractive, but had a certain severe matter-of-factness about her.

As soon as they got into his truck, Mrs B. lit up a cigarette. 'Your mom's such a sweet woman.'

'What about you?' he said.

'Me?'

'Would you say you're a sweet woman?'

She pouted indifferently. 'Sweet enough, I guess.'

'You seem sweet to me.' Stupid, a stupid thing to say.

She stared at him, frowning and smiling at once, then laughed, a harsh, almost manly laugh. He was ready to give it up, but there was that dead place inside him which fascinated him, as it used to amaze him as a child when he slept on his arm and it went numb and limp. He wanted feeling gone, to act on what he had learned about women: faithless, they were made to be seduced. To feel for a woman was to be a fool. He wanted to do what the coyotes had learned to do: take the bait and leave the trap unsprung.

'Reckon you're happy, Mrs B.?'

'What's it to you?'

He shrugged. 'I just wonder what makes people happy.'

After another drag on her cigarette, she turned to look out of the passenger-side window and said, 'You have a sweetheart, Frank?'

'I don't believe in sweethearts.'

'Well, you're young.'

'You're young too. What that guy said about you, that's true, Mrs B., you look younger than your daughters.'

She turned around to him now, leaning back against her door. Holding the cigarette close to her face, as if she wanted the smoke between them, she examined him with an expression that wasn't quite wry.

'I'm very lucky with my skin,' she said. 'That's from the Irish side. My sister was always the pretty one, but she had hands like a little old woman even when she was in high school.'

His heart had begun to throb unpleasantly, that numb limb returning to life. Reaching over, he took up her left hand. It didn't look particularly well preserved. The diamonds and rubies in her engagement ring were so big they looked fake. 'You have nice hands.'

He lost track of the road and the front tyre got caught in the depression of the unfinished shoulder. It took a bumpy second for him to return them to the blacktop.

'Sorry,' he said.

'Jesus, Frank,' she exclaimed, her hand flat against her chest, 'you've got to keep your eyes on the road.'

After a second he glanced toward her and forced himself to say it: 'Rather keep my eyes on you, Mrs B.'

She laughed, that harsh, manly laugh, ending with a phlegmy smoker's cough. He could feel his face burning.

'What in sweet heaven's got into you, Frank Celli?'

'I don't know. I like you, I guess.'

She didn't laugh at this, just narrowed her eyes, her expression speculative and slightly suspicious.

As they turned into her driveway, he took hold of her hand again and pulled up a little way from the house.

'What are you doing, Frank?' She was looking at him very seriously, her back against the door.

'Why do you think it's so strange that I like you?'

'You're a silly boy, Frank. This is ridiculous.'

He leaned over to kiss her.

'Frank, stop it.' Snatching her hand free of his, she pushed him back. 'I'm a married woman.'

'Your husband's married too.'

'What's that meant to mean?'

'I know how faithful he is to you.'

She didn't say anything for a moment, the nostrils in that sharp little nose of hers flaring.

'You know, do you? You and everyone else in this piss-ant little town. I don't give a goddamn if he has ten whores, including your filthy slut of a mother. I'm his wife and the mother of his children, and if you think I'd be the least bit interested in a drop-out spick grease monkey who I've seen shitting in his diapers, you're dumber than people say you are.'

She opened the car door and got out. Without looking back, she strode down the driveway and into her home.

*

Alvin was scared. Siggy had figured out, because of the distinctive 'e' the old Gourland made, its loop filled with ink, that the typewriter used for the malicious letters was the one stolen from Hoffmeyer's garage. He had come round this morning to talk to his dad. Siggy now believed that Hoffmeyer might have been murdered for some reason and was determined to track down the missing evidence. After he left, Alvin decided to get rid of the journals and the typewriter, figuring it safest to dump them into the river up by Hunter's Point.

He wanted to use the big backpack he had in his cupboard, but was worried his mom or dad might ask him what he was doing with it. He opened his bedroom window as quietly as he could and dumped it outside in the iris bed. His dad, reading the paper, didn't even look up as he walked by and out the back door.

After retrieving the backpack, he made his way across the fallow field behind their house, around a copse of maples, then along the shoulder of the blacktop to the abandoned house. Getting his flashlight from where he had hidden it beneath a piece of corrugated iron, he opened the cellar doors and descended. As he put the typewriter and journals into the backpack, it struck him that he should get rid of everything he had collected over the years. Of course, the one thing he needed to get rid of more than anything was Hoffmeyer's rifle.

He slid the rifle out from where he had hidden it, behind a shelf of dusty old mason jars. He loved this rifle, the heft and history of it. The typewriter too. In the past couple of weeks, getting used to the stiff mechanical action of the Gourland, he had thought so much about Hoffmeyer, who had used it to turn out page after page. He had looked through the box-file he had taken from Hoffmeyer many times now. There were lots of anatomically perfect drawings, mostly of insects, particularly bees, wasps, and hornets. Hoffmeyer would often scribble out plans for longer works with titles like, *To End All Wars; Escaping Time; What The Truth Is*. There were lines of dialogue, poems, letters to politicians, passionate speeches about injustice and inhumanity. Breaking through all this, every now and then, would be a note addressed to his sister, which was like his real voice, sad and clear, reaching from beyond death. Everyone called him Crazy John, but all these things, though in pieces and scattered like those clocks, didn't seem crazy. Reading through it made Alvin realize that no adult had ever spoken to him as if he were anything other than a child. It all felt very precious to him, needful. But John Hoffmeyer had killed himself. This terrified Alvin, since it revealed that sadness, loneliness, even if you were sane and good, might never end. In the notes Hoffmeyer would often quote his sister, always in German, and Alvin wanted desperately to know what these sentences meant. They seemed like a key somehow, the secret of feeling, the reason for a man to put a rifle to his own heart and pull the trigger. He had tried so hard to imagine what Hoffmeyer had been thinking about while he sat on that running board. Alvin had gone through all the motions a few times: reading the journal, typing the note, loading the rifle, and stepping out into the sun. He wouldn't take the loaded rifle with him, though: it scared him too much. Each time he tried to imagine ending his life he would just feel dizzy. He wanted desperately to keep the rifle, to hold it and whisper that last entry – especially the German. It made him feel as if he were someone, even if it wasn't himself exactly. Just as learning those lines from Shakespeare had, if briefly, filled him with real meaning and feeling.

He knew he had to get rid of everything, though, and strangely, despite his regrets, he was actually excited at the thought of throwing it all away – these things that had meant so much to him. If he could do it, he had the sense that he would somehow be changed.

He filled the backpack, put it on, took up the rifle, and climbed out of the cellar. Closing the cellar doors behind him, he felt a kind of relief that he would never need to go down there again. But as he turned around, the sight of his mom, standing at the corner of the house, caused him to stumble backwards. Unbalanced by the pack, he fell.

She approached, smiling strangely. 'I was in the garden having a cigarette when you threw that pack out the window. I knew you'd been lying to me. I just didn't know what you were up to.'

'Mom, I found this stuff in here.'

'Is that the rifle they're looking for?'

'I found it. It was all in here.'

She took it out of his hand and leaned it up against the wall. She tried then to get the pack off his back, but he hunched his shoulders, resisting her. 'I found these things, I swear on my life. I found them.'

Forcefully pulling it off him and on to the ground, she opened it. She took out the tobacco tin which contained Mr Didka's kidney stones; then came Mrs Lemister's prosthetic wooden foot. The typewriter was next, and then the journals. Opening one of them, she flicked through, quickly at first, pausing here and there. Then she read something that caused her to sit back heavily on to the ground. She read more intently, looking through one journal and then another, her face going pale.

'Where did you get these?' she said.

'I found—'

She shouted: 'Where did you get them?'

'They're Miss Winters'. She wrote them. I took them from her house.'

She was staring at him as if she had never seen anything like him before.

'You sent out those letters.'

'No—'

'You little *shit*,' she screamed.

'No, Mom, I didn't. I swear I didn't.'

She took out Vincent Pollock's Purple Heart, then a pair of stained panties. 'Jesus.' She covered the lower half of her face with both hands.

'Mom . . .' He didn't know what to say.

After a moment, with a furious energy that terrified him, she shoved everything back into the pack and zipped it up.

'Bring it,' she said, snatching up the rifle.

'Where are we going?'

'Home.'

'Please, Mom, you're not going to tell Dad. Please, Mom. Please.'

'Your dad just headed out to check in on Mrs Katz. He won't be back for a little while. You and I are going to decide what we're going to do about this.'

She walked quickly, taking the most direct route along the road. He stumbled after her. A car passed them, the sound of its approach flooding Alvin with terror, since his mom wasn't even trying to hide the rifle.

When they got in the house, she told him to put the bag on the dining table.

Breathing hard, she said, 'We're not going to tell people about the journals or the letters.' It was clear she had figured out what she was going to do on their walk. 'Or the rifle, I guess. Or they'll know you took the typewriter.' She opened the bag. 'Take the type-writer, the journals and the rifle, and put them under the bed in the guest room for now. Make sure you can't see them under the dust ruffle.'

He did what she said. When he returned, she was arranging every-thing else on the dining table.

'Oh, Mom, please, you can't show him this stuff. Please. I'll take it all back secretly. I'll mail it back to them. Please, Mom, please. You can't tell him.' He tried to take hold of her arm, but she snatched it away furiously.

'Mom' – he took hold of her arm again – '*please.*'

Turning to him, she allowed herself some time to examine every part of his face as if it were grotesquely fascinating. 'Did you enjoy typing those things about me?'

'I never thought he'd read it out, I swear. I swear.'

'You know what I thought?' She started to laugh, which horrified him. 'I thought you were queer. That's why I thought you were lying and hiding. God, that would be punishment enough, but *this*? This is worse. You're disgusting.'

She didn't really even seem angry with him any more, just pity-ing and revolted, like everyone else.

His dad's car crackled on the gravel. He was sure for a moment that he was going to throw up. Pressing his hands to his ears, he squatted down.

'Get up.' She tugged at his arm. 'Stop acting like a baby.'

His dad walked in with a quart of milk and stopped. Still squatting, Alvin looked at him, then at his mom. He couldn't recognize her. She was standing up straight and tall, her face severely attractive and triumphant. She couldn't stop herself smiling.

'Your son,' she said, 'has something to tell you.'

Annie hadn't really admitted to herself where she was going until Ruth's house was in sight. Raj would be heading off to Boston at the end of the summer and she had not been able to stop thinking about him. Her own life felt hopeless: Frank was coming home drunk – if he came home at all; her dad was waking her every few nights with his nightmares; her mom, though physically present, was otherwise gone. Annie had taken over most of the cooking and cleaning, since her mom had become so careless her food was often inedible and everything she washed seemed dirtier after she had finished with it. Annie also tried as best she could to hide all the endless packages of useless things her mom ordered from catalogues.

She felt trapped by her family and by Lew. It didn't seem fair that Raj could just leave.

Ruth answered the front door. 'Hey, Annie. He's out back. Come on through.'

'I don't just come here to see him, you know.'

'Oh,' Ruth said smiling.

'Were you writing?'

'Writing?' Ruth rolled her eyes as if this were a ridiculous notion. 'The amorous adventures of Nurse Gordiano are not going very well, I'm afraid. How are your mom and dad?'

'My dad's obsessed with this letter thing.'

'What letter thing?'

'You didn't get one? Lots of people got one. Didn't you hear about

Reverend Hewitt reading his out in front of the whole town at church? I felt sick for Mrs Hewitt. If our one's like that I know why Dad wouldn't show it to me.'

'A letter? What do you mean?'

'They're vicious. Reverend Hewitt's described him as a dead chick in an egg and as a void with a bad haircut. What it said about Mrs Hewitt was worse, though. She was just sitting there at the front, white as a sheet. Can't imagine why she let him read it.'

Ruth's face became strangely expressionless. 'Sounds awful,' she said finally. Without another word, she stepped into her room and shut the door.

Annie, left alone in the dark entranceway, was shocked by the rude abruptness of this, and wondered if Ruth had perhaps received one of the letters.

She made her way through the house. Peeking out of the open back door, she saw Raj on the porch steps reading. Fifty-Three lay asleep beside him. Sneaking up, she put her hands over his eyes.

'Whoever this is,' he said, 'I want to make it clear that what you are smelling at this moment is canine. I vehemently deny all association with a recent flurry of noxious emissions provoked by a particularly lively dream.'

Reaching back, he felt her face like a blind man. 'Oh, mercy.' He sounded horrified. 'Thank you for covering my eyes.'

She slapped his head and sat down beside him.

'What are you doing here?' he said.

She put on an English accent. 'I just wanted a chat.'

'Well, splendid. I'll arrange for tiffin to be served in the conservatory.'

'Tish tosh, let's take a stroll,' she said, getting up. 'Stretch our trousers.'

'Lead on, Macduff.'

When they were a little way from the house she said, 'So how are things going with Nora?'

'Haven't seen her since the infamous day at the sinkhole.'

'We were just swimming. Lew . . .' She stopped. Explanations were quicksand.

After a moment she said, 'I don't know what Lew's going to do without you.'

This was unfair of her, she knew, but some part of her wanted to be cruel, to force the issue.

'He has you,' Raj said.

'It's not fair you're going.'

'I've asked you guys to come to Boston.'

'That's just dumb. We're not kids any more, and you don't really want us to come there anyway. What's Lew going to do? I don't know how he's ever going to keep a job, talking about those things he talks about. They'll lock him up again.'

Raj looked serious and deeply troubled. He couldn't meet her eyes. This was too easy. Annie wanted to have a fight with him, wanted him to look at her directly, even to hate her a little, perhaps.

'What do you want me to do?' he said.

'Stay here. Just for a year. Help me with him.'

'He doesn't think there's anything wrong with him.'

'That's the problem. Every time I see him it's harder to get him to come out of his head. The more he's on his own, the more he disappears into all those things he makes up.'

Raj looked as if he were in physical pain. 'I don't understand.'

'Understand what?'

'I don't understand . . . You're talking as if he's sick and we have to help him and make him better, but you were . . . you were naked with him. He thinks of you as his girlfriend and you . . . I mean sometimes you act as if he's your boyfriend and sometimes you talk about him like he's just sick.'

'He took *my* clothes off——' Annie stopped, abruptly flooded with loathing for her mean, shallow, spineless self, betraying Lew, who had already half vanished into the woods and the waters. Who loved her. Whom she loved.

'All right,' Raj said.

'All right?'

'I'll stay. Maybe they can postpone my scholarship. I could work up at The Lodge. Ruth says Magnus is sick or something.'

There it was. With barely a struggle. Her heart broke for him. How pathetic and diminished everything she felt and wanted was compared to what he felt and was willing to give up for Lew's sake, and for hers.

They were at the crest of Meadow Hill now, the sun a reddish yolk, the dry grasses simmering in the breeze. Her rush of feeling for him was almost overwhelming, and as he moved in front of her at a narrowing of the path, she pushed her arms under his and around his chest, forcing him to a stop.

He spoke in a pompous, nasal voice, as if to an audience. 'There is only one way to escape the deadly embrace of the full-grown female Sebastianus Cellius, indigenous to the Missouri tundra.' Annie clutched him harder. 'You have to make contact with the vulnerable neck area, which it protects with its prodigious, mane-like hair.' Reaching back, Raj was trying to tickle Annie beneath her chin. She tripped him forward on to the grassy path. They wrestled for a moment, but Raj was only playing around, while she, using all her strength, finally pinned him on his back beneath her knees.

'You're going to have to kill me, see,' he said, imitating Cagney in *Angels with Dirty Faces.* 'I ain't afraid of you, copper.'

He wouldn't meet her eyes. The sun's yolk had broken into the trees, the cicadas in endless friction churned out the late summer heat. She couldn't believe he would so soon be gone, felt bereft and desperate. She bent her face down to his.

'You'll have to beat it out of me, see,' he said.

Her hair formed a dark tunnel between their faces. 'I didn't really mean it about you staying,' she said. 'Maybe we can come to Boston, Lew and me, sometime.'

Gently biting his own lip, he still wouldn't meet her eyes. He would stay if she asked him to, but he wanted to go. It was unbearable. She wanted him to want to stay. To want her.

Getting up, she helped him to his feet and asked if he would like to listen to some records she had just bought. He said sure and they walked into town.

In her room she put on 'Que Sera Sera' and joined Raj on the carpet, leaning back against her bed. As she sat, she noticed a large tick on her calf.

'Jeezle-peezle.' After prising it off, she crushed it between her fingernails.

'God, you'd never be able to see one on me,' Raj said.

'I hate ticks. My dad had to shave all my hair off once when I was a kid because I fell into a whole bunch of them.'

Raj was examining his legs. He would return, she knew, on visits, but things would never be like this. Quickly, she undid her skirt and pulled it down. 'You've got to check me.'

'What?' Raj was clearly shocked.

She got up and threw herself face down on the bed. 'For ticks.'

'Oh.' He sat on the bed beside her legs, glancing shyly down at them.

'You have to look close,' she said. 'They can be real, real small.' She raised her pinched fingers. 'Like a little speck.'

'Okay.' Shifting further down, he bent low over her ankles, his hands clasped in a matronly way at his chest. He frowned and looked very serious as he moved his examination up her calves.

Hesitating, he pointed at the back of her knee. 'Do you have a mole?'

'Check it.'

He dabbed at her skin. 'A-o-kay-o, Capitan.'

As he moved up her thighs, she reached under herself, undoing the buttons of her blouse, and pulled it off, dropping it on the floor. Bunching the pillow beneath her cheek, she looked back at him.

'All clear.' He had finished examining her legs and gave her the thumbs-up.

'Keep looking.' She indicated toward her back. 'And check under the elastic.'

'The elastic?'

She tugged the elastic of her underwear.

He rubbed his chin and cleared his throat, looking down at her panties as if they were a particularly complex maths problem he had been asked to solve. She would have laughed if she hadn't felt so nervous herself. He checked under the elastic. Then he scrutinized her lower back.

'Raj.' She showed him her pinched-together fingers again, and he ducked closer.

As he got further up, she reached around and undid her bra strap. 'Check under it.'

Gingerly unpeeling the strap, he dabbed at another mole. Then he lifted her hair aside to check her shoulders. When he touched the downy hairs just above her nape, she shivered.

'I'm sorry,' he said.

'That's okay.'

'You are officially tick-free,' he declared.

She tried to meet his eyes, but he was still too shy, glancing off into her room.

'Been a while since I hunted ticks in the wild,' he said.

Hooking her arm around her unclasped bra so it wouldn't fall off, she turned herself around to lie on her back.

'You have to do this side now.'

'Yes'm,' he said, tugging his forelock. Shifting down the bed again, he checked her feet and ankles, moving up her legs.

'The elastic,' she reminded him again as he got to her panties.

Scrupulously, he folded the elastic down rather than lifting it. He rubbed his thumb gently in the hollow of her elbow. His gaze skipped right over her bra, lying loose across her breasts. Right at her shoulders now, he moved her hair aside. Then he got her to turn her head by touching each cheek and examined her neck.

'They get on your face,' she said. 'You have to look close.'

He bent down again so his face was just inches from hers. Gently and forgetfully, he pushed his fingers through her hair as he inspected her chin, her lips, her cheeks, her ears. He examined her nose and then told her to close her eyes. She could feel his breath, shallow and erratic, against her eyelids. He shifted up to her brow and she opened her eyes to look at his lips. His whole body was trembling. Reaching up, she put her hand against the side of his face. She felt as if the air she was breathing were condensing to cool water in her throat. She felt clear as glass, a window with rain upon it, droplets swelling in places, abruptly sliding down through the maze of other drops. She didn't want him to move, wanted to watch his lips a while longer, and the swallowing of his throat, to feel the trembling of his body, his hand combing through her hair. Precarious, arousing, but also clean, somehow, this feeling, tasting of light and chalk. It was so different from what she felt when Lew touched her, which was more purely sexual, viscous, a molten slide down defined channels, from her lips, her neck, her breasts, to pool heavily between her hips, its taste a little duller and more bitter, of blood and soil.

Raj abruptly sat up as they heard her mom at the bottom of the stairs. 'He call for you,' she shouted. 'He say you didn't get his Roadster done.' She began to ascend.

'Oh, cripes.' Annie pulled herself up, briefly losing hold of her loose bra before getting it back on and hooking up the strap. Raj helped her with her blouse.

Luckily, at the top of the stairs, Frank shouted something and her mom stopped to call back down. 'What you want me to say? My son, who knows where he is, drunk somewhere, with some girl somewhere. What you want me to say? Uh?'

Annie pulled on her skirt as Raj tackled the rest of the buttons on her blouse, snatching his hands away just as her bedroom door opened.

Her mom pulled up at the door. 'What's going on?'

The record player, scratchily circling, had long since stopped playing. Annie could feel how flushed she was and Raj looked like he had just murdered a baby and was hiding the body behind his back. 'Nothing, Mom,' she said.

'You' – her mom pointed at Raj as she took a few more steps into the room – 'you go home.'

As he passed her, she said angrily, 'You shouldn't be in a room alone with a girl.'

'I'm sorry,' he mumbled.

'We're just listening to records,' Annie protested as Raj disappeared down the stairs. 'You can't just come into my room like that.'

Her mom sat down on the bed beside Annie. She looked horrified. 'What you doing with this black boy?'

'Nothing. And he's not black. He's not a Negro.'

'What you doing?' She had reached up toward Annie's shoulder as if she were going to shake her. As ever, though, it was a helpless, self-thwarted gesture, and her hand quickly fell away. She sought the window, stared out at the sky, and Annie felt that old yearning in her mother to escape.

'Annie—'

'I know,' Annie cut her off, putting her arms around her mom. 'I wouldn't do anything. I wouldn't get pregnant or anything.'

'Annie, why any one of them? You is so pretty. There so many . . .' She faltered. 'At least Lewis he's . . . I like this boy' – she gestured toward the open door – 'but he's black. His skin is almost black. For my family even your daddy was too dark.'

'Is that why you don't speak to your family?' Annie said softly.

Her mom didn't respond.

'It's like you came from nowhere, Mom.'

Her mom was lost in the window again. After a moment she went to get up, but Annie refused to let her go.

'Mom, why did you marry Papa? I don't mean why, I mean . . . how did you meet him?'

Her mom seemed to think about this. After a little while, she stared down at her hands and said softly, 'My uncle and auntie they owned a boarding house in Chicago. And he was one of the boarders, your dad. I help them with the business. I clean the rooms. So on the stairs a few times I meet him, and in the hallway, and he is very handsome

and charming and he smell nice – cologne. The other men, they was
. . . crude, gave me the eye, you know, sometimes say things. He
never did. Always polite. And his room was next to the bathroom.
And when I clean the bathroom, I hear him singing sometimes. I don't
know what it was. Italian. Lovely voice. Ach, how neat his room was,
and he do things not like the other men. Flowers, in his room, he
picked them himself. This seems incredible to me. A man to put flowers in his room. My uncle and auntie they was very strict, of course,
and they would have been crazy if they caught me talking to any of
these men, which I never do. One time, when I was about fourteen,
I was cleaning the bathtub and one of the boarders, an Irish, don't
remember his name, he walk into the bathroom. Horrible man he
was. And I say, I'll be done in a second. And he doesn't say nothing.
He close the door, and he starts, you know, to make water into the
toilet.'

'While you're still there?'

'I still there. And I try to go out, but the toilet it was near the
door and he put his hand out' – she put her palm out to demonstrate
– 'against the door. And there's this banging, and the door is pushed
open, and is my uncle. He drag this Irishman out; gone the same day.
And he never been too . . . kind, you know, my uncle, but he never
hurt me or nothing. But on this day, with my auntie watching and
with some strange man he's watching also, he beat me with a belt so
hard I still remember it. I thought it would never stop.'

'Who was the man?'

'Never seen him. My uncle he say to him, "You tell him." And the
man he nods. Maybe someone he's going see my dad. They want him
to know, you know, they was bringing me up right.'

'Your dad? So where—'

'But anyway, this was earlier. I was sixteen and I'm cleaning the
bathroom all the time, trying to hear Sal, and if I'm upstairs and hear
him leaving his room, I jump out into hallway, you know, like I'm
just finished, and "Oh, what a surprise," you know. Just to see him
and smell his cologne. He must have known. It was so obvious. And

one day, he ask me in his room. And my uncle he was at the race-track, and my auntie she was cooking downstairs, so I say yes. About the size of this bedroom, his room, smaller, with one window, looks out over roofs, fire escapes, you know. The first time he show me some pictures of his village. A few times we did this. And it was so silly, he would know I was up there. When my uncle he's gone, I would go past Sal's door, making to cough, and then clean the hall-way floor or something, you know, banging around. And out he come with his coat on and hat on, like he's leaving. Aha! so surprised to see me, and he would ask me in. And neither of us we spoke hardly any English, so we just sort of stare at each other, you know, smiling. Sometimes a few words we teach each other. He teach me Italian, I teach him Polish. And we might share, you know, a piece of fruit. I was such a naïve girl. I know it doesn't sound naïve going to a man's room like that, but really I didn't know anything about anything, and he . . . he could have done anything to me, but he didn't. Oh and I was so in love. When he was at work and I was cleaning his room, I would even smell the insides of his slippers.'

'Mom!'

'Yes, everything, his bed and his clothes and everything. Like a dog, I was.

'And then one day my uncle and my auntie they tell me they find-ing me a nice Polish boy, very handsome, butcher, he own his own store. Few times we went out, chaperoned by my auntie or my grand-mother. He love it when is my grandmother because she has very bad stomach – cancer, but we didn't know – but she keep going to the bathroom, stay there *long* time. And he's not like Sal. God, his hands go everywhere. He makes sure he knows what he's getting. Every time my grandmother she went to the bathroom – and sometimes she have to run, you know, God bless her, holding her backside – for the big wrestling match I have to make ready. And always he smell of old meat, you know.

'And so he gets me engagement ring, this butcher, and the marriage is set. But all I can think about is Sal, you know. And I avoid him for a few weeks. Then one Saturday afternoon I just can't stand it no more and I go right up and knock on his door. Very happy to see me, he is, and I came in. He wants me to sit, but I don't. I just stare at him, you know, and I was so . . .' Annie's mom fluttered her hand over her heart with her eyes closed and made a deep sigh. 'And I show him my engagement ring. In my hand I'm holding because I never weared it when I was cleaning. And I keep pointing at myself and all I can think is to say what I think is the Italian for I'm married, "mi spose, mi spose." Over and over, I'm saying, trying to explain I'm getting married. But he's looking at me like he doesn't understand. I said "arriverderci", and he's really confused, and I embrace him. And the two of us holding each other very hard. I was holding him so hard he could not breathe, I think. I was frightened we might, you know, kiss or something like this. So we're like this for who knows how long. Then I run out. And later this night I go up to the bathroom again. Just one more time I want to hear him. And he's crying. I can hear him. Crying like a baby and saying things to himself in Italian. This was it. My heart it just broke. And he and I we got married.'

'But how? What did you—'

'Another time I'll tell you, maybe. Not so nice a story. Not so . . . romantic. Anyway, almost one year later, I was really pregnant with Frank. In St Louis then we were living, the two of us. We had to escape from Chicago.'

'Is that why you don't talk to any of your family?'

She nodded. 'And we have a little store there. And I had come home from shopping, and I am in the back, and I can hear him telling some story to a bunch of guys he knows there, showing off, you know what he's like. Talking about some girl he said he once knew. And he says how this girl she was crazy over him, you know, and every time he opens his door there she is. Then one day, he says this girl she knocks on his door. He's making it a funny story, like I was a crazy girl. He doesn't say is me, but I'm so hurt – oh, it was like my heart is just torn out of my body. And he says to them he open his door one day and this girl she pushes him into his room, and she has hold of a ring from somewhere and she is demanding he marry me – her. Marry her. Pointing to this ring, saying, "marry me, marry me". And he says he never forget the day because he has a crazy girl asking him to marry her in the morning and his baseball team – I don't remember which – loses World Series in the evening. Said he cried like a baby. God, I was so pregnant, and I feel as if I died, and I wondered how the baby inside me could live when I was dead.'

'Do you think he really thought those things?'

'I don't know.'

'Didn't you say anything to him?'

'I don't want to know,' she said. 'I shouldn't have told you that.'

Annie hugged her harder, but her mom felt like a husk.

'I don't know why I tell you this. I'm sorry, baby.' Pulling away, sighing, she got up.

She looked down at Annie, her hands clasped at her belly, her face suddenly so old and lifeless. 'You don't want to have dark children,' she said. 'It's hard enough.' And she left.

After Raj headed out with Annie, Ruth went straight up to the attic. For close to an hour she sat on the edge of an old sewing table in the dormer's little tooth of light staring at the place where the journals had been. She had not penned a single hateful word in more than two years, having lost the need for that particular relief and connection to her mother. But she could remember clearly what she had written – every vicious phrase and trope – about Annie's mom and dad, Reverend Hewitt and Judy, all of them. Her true and grotesque art, that voice was at once connection and isolation, love and loathing. It was her mother: the waste of a brilliant mind. Crone becomes witch, with her witch's brew, this art of hopelessness. Ruth sat in a wash of horror and shame, alternately scalded and frozen, imagining everyone in Pisgah reading what she had written. Every memory she had of Raj, from the first time she had seen him at the morgue in Jackson till now, played over and over, her mind convulsing with his image as if she had taken some kind of hallucinogen as she tried to work out what she had missed that might possibly have suggested he was capable of this. To think of him sneaking up here, finding the journals, typing the entries – probably on her own typewriter while she was away in Boston or New York – and then sending them to people. Had every act of kindness and affection on his part been a lie? Was he nothing short of evil? Or was this an act of revenge? Timed perfectly, just as he leaves and no longer needs her. Had he, perhaps, planned this for years? To devastate not just her but the whole town by disseminating what she had generated here in her moments of rage, loneliness and grief. Exposing them, exposing her and walking away. She remembered showing him the attic key all those years ago: an act of faith on her part, which she felt he deserved. To think of all she had felt, was *feeling*, for this boy, this *semblance*, who felt nothing but hatred for her. She had spent her life loving men who weren't there, deflections, humour: horribly right then that this should be the child of her life. Little black boy, black nigger, nigger child. Her hatred felt distilled, burning her throat and veins. That creature, that animal, that black nigger. And all at once she began to sob, her whole body shaking. He had violated her, violated all of them. Damn him. And she could not destroy him. Only herself.

Once she had calmed a little, she left the attic, went down to her room and lay on her bed. An hour or so later she heard the screen door screeching, that sound filling her with fury and fear. The fridge opened and shut. The creature called her name. Down the creaking boards of the hallway he approached. She felt something close to a seizure of loathing and horror as he came closer. Did he truly hate her? Or was this just the perverse pleasure of someone with no feeling? She didn't know which was worse. Her bedroom door opened. Violation. Her name called softly, 'Ruth?' The loathsome dark head emerged. Monster, semblance, devil, mocker, thief, liar, betrayer.

Smiling. Now a show of concern. 'Are you all right, Ruth?'

'Get out of my room. Get out.'

'Ruth?'

'Get out of here,' she screamed. 'Get out. Get out. Get out.'

He left. The lining of her throat felt torn; specks of light floated before her eyes. She lay there, then, listening to him creeping around her house, the creaking of the floorboards both pathetic and pitiless, like the pain of someone you have ceased to love.

Alvin couldn't stop crying. Standing at the entrance to the dining room, he was watching his dad trying to reason with his mom.

'Judy, now—'

'He stole these things while he was with you.'

'I could just return them myself and say that someone—'

'Lie? *You?* The man who read that disgusting letter out in front of the whole town? What do you say to Satan? "I'm not afraid." Isn't that what you told them?'

'Listen, Judy—'

'Well, now you're going to take our son house to house, and with equal . . . *integrity* face this. He needs to repent and ask these people for their forgiveness.'

Alvin wasn't even aware he was crying. It took him out of his body even trying to imagine it: having to return underwear, love letters, pictures of the dead, wedding rings. Everyone in town would know, including Annie, Nora, Raj and Lew. He would lose his friends.

'I'm not going,' Alvin shouted. He felt as if he were six years old.

'Judy,' his father appealed, 'look at the boy. He's—'

'Your son stole these intimate and precious things from people who invited you into their homes for spiritual guidance or because they were sick. They *trusted* you. If you don't tell them, I will. You're going to have to face them, then, and let me tell you, if you get kicked out under these circumstances, you will *never* get another congregation as long as you live.'

'Judy, you wouldn't—'

'Yes, I damn well would.'

His dad examined his mom as if she were some large, obstinate animal he couldn't shift. He stood with his arms akimbo and chest thrust out, trying to draw himself up, but with his shoes off, his head barely came level with her chest. 'This is about me reading out that letter, isn't it?'

His mom laughed, as if the laughter were something caught in her throat, and cocked her head a little to get another perspective on him. 'Why on earth would I be mad about that?'

'You're upset. I can tell.'

'Upset? Didn't God His Almighty Self tell you to read that damn thing out in front of the whole town without saying so much as one word to me?'

'But the letter was a lie. Evil gathers strength in darkness. I brought it into the light.'

All at once his mom looked despairing, almost pitying, her eyes narrowing upon his dad. 'A lie? Did nothing in that letter . . . Didn't *anything* . . . Oh, Jesus.'

Rubbing her eyes, she took some deep breaths. For the first time, with tremulous hope, Alvin felt she might be on the verge of giving this up. She looked utterly bewildered and exhausted. But all at once her fingers slid down from her eyes to pinch together the wings of her nose and her face went hard again as she looked back up at his dad. 'God told you to expose that liar. The same God would never let you cover up what your son did. Look at him, God help us, crying like a baby.'

'I'm not going to do it,' Alvin shouted. He was just going to take off, head into the wild, never see his mom or dad or anyone in this town ever again. He would kill what he needed to eat and live unseen in the world.

Marching over, his mom snatched up his wrist and dragged him into the sitting room, slamming the door behind her.

'You listen good,' she said. 'I have no idea who you are any more, what disgusting things you do when you sneak off every day. I don't know who would steal these things and who would type out that cruel filth and send them to people. Send them to *me* – to your own mother – to *me, me*.' At each 'me' she dug her finger into her own chest so hard he could see crescent marks left by her fingernail. 'Now you listen, I'm not telling anyone about those letters you wrote.'

'They'll know.'

'They'll know there's no way you could write those letters. But what you're doing is going to stop here. You're going to go with your dad and give back—'

'No, no, no.'

'Give back every one of these things. Every one. And if you don't do this, I swear to God I'm going to get up on that pulpit next Sunday, and I'm going to bring your bag of goodies, and I'm going to tell everyone what you did, and I'm going to tell them who wrote those letters.'

'You wouldn't—'

'Yes I would. You look in my face, young man. You look in my face. Yes I would.'

Spittle had gathered in the corners of her livid lips, her chin trembling. It was as if the anger of years had finally found something to take hold of: him. Still clutching his wrist painfully tight, she bathed him with pure hatred. Alvin felt dizzy, overwhelmed: he had done this, made this. He had emptied the one person who loved him of all feeling for him.

'Mom, please,' he said softly, and as if he were speaking to himself. 'Everyone's going to hate me.'

'They're not going to hate you; they're going to pity you like they pity me. And I want you to know just how that feels.'

Approaching Lew's farm, Annie felt both leaden and hollow as she rehearsed what she was about to say. She was so glad nothing physical had happened with Raj. She wouldn't have wanted to do that to Lew – to either of them. But what was going on between her and Lew had to end.

His dad was in the lower ten acres, rattling up and down in that ancient tractor, which kept cutting out. A clockwork figure, coarsely hewn. Everything in his home was jerry-rigged, the door handles made out of lengths of bent pipe, the roof a crazy patchwork, whole rooms abandoned to damp and decay. Knocking, she entered the kitchen and called for Lew, remaining for a few moments in that desolate place.

Coming out again, she caught sight of a flash of bright blue through the open door of the barn. Approaching, she could hear Evy's high, fake voice and laughter. She entered. Evy was doing an Irish dance for Lew, who was clearly trying to fix one of the cattle stalls, a hammer in his hand, a couple of nails in his mouth.

'Annie!' Evy squealed. 'I'm showing Lew the dance I'm doing with Nora and Kathy at the county fair.'

Continuing with the dance, she stuck her tongue out of the side of her mouth in playful concentration. She acted and looked so young, substituting noise and gesture for some more solid self. She was desperate for a boyfriend, desperate not to end up playing euchre with her mom and three sisters for the rest of her life. She had dated Liam Mann for a little while, clinging to his neck like a curse, staring at everyone as if to say, 'I've got one!' It lasted just a couple of weeks. A silly girl, and yet Annie couldn't help but feel a tinge of jealousy. Evy, who had all the money she wanted, was wearing a beautiful new dress, her breasts, which seemed to have grown overnight, thrust out, her chestnut hair whipping around her flushed, cute-little-ogre face.

Annie glanced at Lew, who smiled thinly around the nails. He had clearly been trying to get on with his work for a while.

At last Evy finished and made a little bow.

'Looks great,' Annie said.

'I tend to go too fast.' Evy was out of breath, tossing back her damp hair.

Lew removed the nails from his mouth. 'Evy's collecting for the sponsored stay-awake at church.'

'Sixty dollars and fifty cents so far,' she declared, adding, as she cupped her hand to her mouth in feigned secrecy, 'Of course, sixty of that's from my daddy.' Abruptly, she took hold of her hair in both

hands and covered her face with it in mock shame. It was a ridiculously exaggerated gesture, even for her, and she seemed to become
aware of it. Letting go of her hair, she calmed down a little.

Annie knew she couldn't possibly be here for money. No one would
be thoughtless enough to embarrass Lew and his dad by asking. She
remembered then, with a little surge of shame, how ambiguously she
had responded to Evy's enquiries about her feelings for Lew.

'I'm going to leave you two love birds.' Evy revved the little engine
of her animation again. 'You're looking radiant, Annie.' Flouncing over,
she took hold of Annie's hands and glanced back at Lew. 'When you
two get married, we should have the service at the bluffs; and I've
got this idea that the bridesmaids – me included, of course,' she added
coyly, '—will wear different shades of cream and we'll line up beside
you from darkest to lightest. Isn't that a great idea?'

Annie could feel how thin and tight her smile was as she nodded.
Evy was still clutching her hands. It was as if this were a scene in a
play for which she was auditioning.

'You two will have the most beautiful children in the world.'

This was agony.

'Annie, darling, can I come see you tonight?'

Annie, darling? 'Sure.'

Evy squeezed her hands, said goodbye to Lew, and left.

'How long's she been here?' Annie asked.

'Few hours.'

'Few *hours*.' She knew Lew wouldn't say anything mean about her.
'Did you manage to get any work done?'

'Doesn't matter,' he said. 'I'm repairing these pens and we don't
have any animals left 'cept that old cow and a few pigs. My dad's been
out there trying to repair that piece of junk for four days. This is the
first day he's got it going for more than ten minutes at a time. Without
that tractor we're just dirt farmers. He knows it.'

He sat on an upturned pail. She approached, but cautiously, perch-
ing on the edge of the feed bins a little way from him. The late sunlight
pooled in the barn, mealy, stagnant, making the space between them

more dead, unbreachable, than it already seemed to her. She had murder in her heart, and Lew didn't know yet that he knew it. He would, though, the instant it happened, as in dreams. Of everything fear and desire might have conceived, only one dream was exactly right. Perhaps it was she, in this morbid light, sitting on the feed bin in which Lew knew his brother was suffocating. But when he tried to push her away, she would wrap her body around his like a python. Wetly, then, she would feed from a hole in the back of his neck.

But Evy had saved them from this, her gaudy little carnival still echoing in the barn, making the two of them, by contrast, sure and real. Still, she had to end it and went to speak, but he spoke first.

'I've got a job.'

'What?'

'Saul Hirsch.'

'Insurance?'

'Said he'd train me.'

She couldn't believe it.

'He's a Jew. Got talking to him one day outside Snyder's. He knew a little something about my mom, asked me about her. I told him a few of the words she taught me. Says he wants to teach me some stuff. It was nice, Annie. Showed me some things in his house – Jewish things. Said he'd try to help me find out where my mom came from, if she had any people. Treated me like I was family or something. Couldn't promise too much to start in the way of wages, but thinks the two of us could do well.'

Annie felt the pressure of tears, deeply confused: happy for him, with this unexpected hope, but still thinking about what she had come to do. 'That's so great!'

He seemed a little suspicious of her emotion. 'Just a job.'

'When we were kids you told me once you wanted to sell insurance, do you remember?'

He shook his head.

The physical distance between them was getting awkward now.

She needed to be closer to him to say what she had to, to be able to touch him, and she asked if they could go to his room.

They sat on his bed, which was against the window. Roh's was across from them, that small bed left unmade since his death. Birds that had nested in the eaves squabbled above them. She was so glad he hadn't said anything strange yet. Nor had he tried to touch or kiss her, clearly sensing that she didn't want him to.

'You look nice, Annie.'

She found it so hard to look at him directly, those blue and crystalline eyes, which could bear and brook no lie. Every time she went to say what she had to say, her throat clotted. She took hold of his hand.

'Are you all right?' he said.

A few tears had escaped now. She kissed his hand. It was the pity she felt that revolted her, though it wasn't for him, exactly, but for the waste of him in this world. It was as if she were to lose him completely, all these years. She thought of that day in the institution when he had seemed so insane, but had struggled back to her through the briars of his mind. She pressed his hand, which smelled of sun and hay and manure, to her face, the hand of this uninflected, beautiful man, afflicted but without bitterness. What she had to do now went against every impulse and need in her. She longed for intimacy, deeper and deeper. Then she remembered the fat boy in the woods: hated herself.

'Annie, what's wrong?'

He put his other hand against her cheek, trying to get her to look at him, clearly worried that something terrible had happened. At last he lifted her into his lap. She kissed him. It was lovely to kiss him, even more so, somehow, to kiss him while she was crying. They kissed for a long time, sliding down on to the bed. She undid the buttons of his shirt, and he of her blouse. He kissed her breasts. She could hear the birds, and that tractor cutting out and moments later roaring to life, rattling across the field, squealing as it turned to a new furrow. Futile, futile, it fed her grief. Frantic, they pulled at each other's clothes. She was using her feet to tug down his pants, finally jerking them free. He broke the buttons of her skirt as he pulled it off, his body bearing down on hers, fiercely, and she was fierce too, clawed him and bit his shoulder until he trapped her arms, pressing her hard into the corner of the bed and wall. Finally freeing one arm, she reached down and guided him in. For a second it was very painful, but it was just a moment before he made a soft, ragged grunt and pulled out, reaching down to stop the mess from getting on to his bed. Breathing hard, he kissed her in the hollow of her neck, damp with sweat now, and looked up. He seemed a little bewildered. She felt numb, headachy, trying to understand why she had done this, why she was like this. She had come here to break up with him and had, instead, lost her virginity.

'I love you, Annie,' he said.

She smiled.

'God, I've made a mess.' Glancing down, he frowned. 'You're bleeding a little bit.'

'It's all right,' she said. 'We'll clean it up.'

Annie heard Evy's high-pitched and wildly inflected voice downstairs: her brother must have answered the door. She had forgotten that Evy was coming round. Since dinner, she had been sitting on her bed, steeped in and somehow salved by her own despair and disgust. Only in the most perverse mind would what she had just done with Lew mean what she had meant it to mean – the end. Desperate to talk to someone about it, she had even contemplated telling her mom. That story her mom had told, as painful as it was, had changed Annie like nothing else, allowing her to really believe, for the first time, that her mom had once been as young as she. To hear it had made something harden inside her, in a good way, as if it were something solid on which the rest of her could build. But she couldn't tell her mom about losing her virginity. Perhaps she would talk to Nora. Even Ruth. And yet despite everything – and she hated herself even move for this – she was afraid it would get back to Raj.

As she began to wonder why Evy hadn't come straight to her room, she became aware of a rhythmic thumping sound. Evy was doing her dance for Frank. In a little while she heard her running up the stairs. After knocking, Evy peeked her head around the door. Annie felt a rush of loathing for that flushed, fake, baby ogre face, but Evy seemed to notice something, and became serious – or at least recalibrated her act – entering the room like a little supplicant. Rather than joining her on the bed, she sat on the floor in front of Annie in her floppy frog way, looking up at her with shy, slightly guilty awe. It made Annie feel almost regal, which somehow sealed her around the overwhelming emotions and changes washing through her.

'I didn't mean anything by going to Lew's,' Evy said.

'Oh.' This candidness surprised her. 'Did you think I was mad at you?'

Evy nodded.

After a moment Annie said, 'You should cut your hair. It looks better short; you have such a pretty face.'

'You think so? You and Nor have such lovely hair. I hate my hair.'

'Are you kidding?'

'It's just mousy and it's so thin.'

'No it isn't.' It was a relief for Annie to talk about this, about nothing.

'You know I did see a cut.' Evy pulled a little scrap of paper out of her purse.

'You brought it with you?'

'I wanted to ask you. Can I put on a record?'

Annie nodded and Evy, hopping over to the record player like a rabbit, becoming again a little girl – but naturally this time – put on 'All I Have To Do Is Dream'. Then she jumped on to the bed, pushing herself up against Annie. Annie's dark thoughts about her instantly dispersed. Evy was as she used to be: girlish and physically close, which Annie had always liked. Nora wasn't any good at touching. Evy showed her the head shot of a model she had torn out of *Tempo*. Annie made some suggestions and the two of them talked for a long while about the other girls in school and actresses and hairstyles. Then Evy told her about Liam.

'I think he broke up with me because they weren't big enough.' Cupping her hands under her breasts, she looked ruefully down at them.

'Why do you think that?'

'He said if he was going to marry me he wanted to see them.'

'And you let him?'

Evy made a goofy face. 'Well, I thought if we was going to get married.'

Annie gently squeezed Evy's earlobes. 'You silly goose.'

'Anyway, he looked so disappointed, and the next day he tells me – get this – he doesn't want to marry a girl who'll show a boy her naked body before they're married. Said he was testing me.' Evy sighed, looking down at her hands, which were picking at each other. 'I bet he's saying horrible things.'

Annie put her arm around her, pulling Evy's head against her shoulder. She felt close to her now, as she had when they were younger. It was such a relief to have the old Evy back. Feeling so much better, Annie wanted to seal this moment, to give Evy something. 'I lost my virginity today.' She felt silly saying it.

Evy looked up at her. 'What? With Lew? Today?'

She nodded. Evy frowned slightly, as if she were trying to remember something. Finally she said, 'What was it like?'

Annie shrugged. 'Okay, I guess.'

'Okay?'

'I wish I hadn't done it.'

'Do you feel different?'

She laughed. 'Not really. No.'

'Did he ask you to marry him?'

'I'm sure we could get married if we wanted to.'

'You don't want to?'

'I don't know. You won't tell anyone?'

Evy shook her head. 'I swear.' She glanced pensively out into the room. 'I bet Liam's going to tell everyone what I did.'

'He won't. And your breasts are perfectly normal.'

Evy gave Annie a searching look. Suddenly she reached inside the collar of her blouse, rummaged around, and pulled out two thick, satin-covered foam pads, which she threw into Annie's lap. Then she caved in the empty cups of her bra with both hands. 'I don't have any breasts. I'm never going to get married. My babies are going to starve.'

Evy looked abject in a way that was both comic and serious, on the verge of either laughter or tears. Annie, examining the pads, couldn't stop herself laughing, and that clearly decided it for Evy. The two of them laughed uncontrollably for a while. Finally Evy shoved the pads back into her bra, which set off another round of laughter as she poked and squeezed them with a look of mock lasciviousness.

'Listen,' Annie said after she had caught her breath, 'Liam's just a goober. Last girl that dumped him was called Esmeralda. When he was born they slapped his face and tried to feed his butt. If he bends over, dogs try to sniff his face.'

Evy smiled. 'Did you think of those?'

'Raj did the other day,' she said. 'We were making up insults.'

'He's funny, isn't he?'

Annie nodded.

'Do you understand it, though?'

'Understand what?'

'I mean, I guess he's cute an' all, but . . .'

'But what?'

'He's black.' She whispered this as if she might be the only person who had noticed. 'I mean he's blacker than some of them Negroes I seen up in Jackson. I don't mean to say he's a Negro. I mean he's so clever an' all, but . . . My dad would kill me before he'd let me marry someone like that.'

Evy was looking searchingly at her now.

'He's not that dark,' Annie said – a stupid thing to say, she realized. 'Well, he's going away anyway now.'

'But he's dating Nora. She might go with him.'

'They're just friends.'

'He kissed her yesterday. Didn't Nora tell you?'

Annie felt a pressure, like something swelling in her lungs.

Shivering her body, Evy made a little snort of disgust. 'I couldn't imagine kissing him; could you *imagine*? I mean he's so nice and all, I know you're real friends with him, Annie, but . . .' She shivered again with exaggerated revulsion. 'I didn't know what to say when Nora told me, and she seemed so happy.'

All at once Annie realized she had made a terrible mistake. Evy hadn't come here to cry about Liam: she had come here to tell her this and to see her reaction. Evy wasn't a fool. She must have noticed the change in Annie's mood whenever Raj was around. Nestled in Annie's arm, she looked for all the world like a sweet little monkey, but there was an intense and calculating curiosity in her gaze. Though Evy wasn't consciously vicious or conniving, Annie knew, with a flush to the very roots of her scalp, that she should never have told her what had happened today with Lew.

There was a knock at the door. It opened and Frank entered. He seemed ten years older, unshaven, his hair unkempt, his eyes bruised with tiredness.

'All right, kiddo, I'd better get you home.'

'Frank, have you been drinking?' Annie said.

'Annie girl, you've got to stop worrying; it's putting lines on your face.'

'I'll be down in a minute, Frankie,' Evy said.

The instant he left, Evy jumped off the bed, adjusting the pads in her bra and smoothing her dress. After checking herself thoroughly in the vanity, she went to leave Annie's room as if she had completely forgotten her. Abruptly she seemed to become aware of this and skittered back to the bed. Snatching up Annie's hands, just as she had in the barn, she took on the vapid hysteria of the ingénue. 'You're a peach, Annie. And that's great, with you and Lew and all. I mean I don't mean it's *great*, I mean . . . I mean I'm glad we can talk about things.' Smiling, she turned to blow Annie a kiss on her way out of the room, and after doing so actually hesitated a moment, as if expecting applause.

'Hey, Frankie,' Evy called, thundering down the stairs.

He noticed she had grown her hair long, like Annie's, but it looked funny on her, like a wet towel, perhaps because her head was so small.

Before she got into his truck, she used the wing mirror to apply lipstick.

'Whyja wear that stuff?' he said.

'I like it.' She looked at him with a kind of challenging self-satisfaction, hooking one side of her hair ineffectually over her ear.

As he pulled on to the highway, she said, 'You haven't shaved.'

'Nothing gets by little Evy, does it?'

'Can I touch your beard?'

'It's not a beard.'

'Can I touch it?'

He felt the back of her fingers rubbing gently across his cheek.

'Annie and I were having girl-talk today.'

'No kidding.'

'Can you believe Nora's dating Raj?'

'Not if her dad has anything to say about it. Anyway, he's taking off, isn't he?'

She went quiet and he glanced at her. She was leaning back against the door, looking at him through the mess of her hair, biting coyly at the skin around her nails. It was a ridiculous pose.

'Don't lean on the door.'

She turned herself in the seat. 'I think he likes Annie.'

'Annie's a smart girl. Anyway, he's all right.'

'I don't know,' Evy demurred. 'About Annie, I mean. I worry about her sometimes.'

'You worry about Annie?' He let out a snort of a laugh, which sounded more derisive than he had intended.

'Lots of things you don't know about Annie,' she said, clearly annoyed.

'I know she's not going to cross the line with Raj. Anyway, what's all this to you? You're just a kid.'

'I'm not too a kid. Liam and I were that close to getting married.'

'Yeah, sure you were. Now he's that close to marrying Marca, and two months ago he was that close to marrying Valerie, and in another month he'll be that close to marrying some other dummy.' He pulled her hand out of her mouth.

She was agitating him. She had been such a sweet kid. Now she was always acting dumb, flirting. Mixed in with this, he knew, was her resemblance to Bennet: the slightly prominent brow, the under bite, so brutal on Bennet but cute on her, somehow, with her dimples and big eyes. He could still feel the touch of her hand against his face, could see the painted toenails of her pretty little feet, which were propped up on the dash. All this felt like a slope of scree in his chest, which he was trying carefully to ascend. One slip and he would clatter to the bottom in an avalanche of stones and dust. Almost wanting this, he wished he had drunk a little more. The buzz he had now was like flies around a porch light.

'Annie's not even a virgin any more.' There was a firm and satisfied retaliation in her tone.

It took him a moment to take in what she had said.

'She told me today.'

He wanted to keep calm. 'With Raj?'

She made a disgusted sound. 'No.'

He glanced at her. She looked sheepish now.

'I only told you because I'm worried about her like I said.'

He didn't respond.

'You're not mad at me, are you?'

It was amazing: that your heart could break as if it had never been broken. After Esta and his mom he didn't think he could ever feel

anything like this again. Now Annie, and it was new. On the other
side of the road a semi thundered toward them. Turn this steering
wheel one inch to the left and it would all be over.

'You're not mad at me, are you, Frankie?'

'Who was it?' His hands tightened on the wheel as the semi got
closer.

'I shouldn't tell you.'

The semi was on them now and he turned sharply, pulling up in
a cloud of dust on the shoulder as the semi shuddered by.

'Who was it, Evy?'

Shocked by the sudden stop, it took her a moment to say, 'Lew.'

Her window was open and cicadas screamed in the humid night.
He saw that the handle on the passenger door hadn't been pulled
completely up, and realized that she really could have fallen into the
road. He reached over her to shut it.

'Oh Frankie!' Evy almost sobbed out, and before he knew what
was happening her forehead had collided with his mouth.

'Jesus.' He dabbed at his lip, which had split on his teeth. She was
rubbing her head.

'I'm sorry, Frankie.' She giggled.

Clearly having thought that he had leaned in to kiss her, she recovered quickly, and craned up to kiss him gently and frantically around
his mouth. He neither responded nor moved away, his eyes upon her
little close face with its clamped-shut eyes. Bennet's daughter.

'I love you, Frankie.' She kissed his mouth more firmly and directly
now, getting his blood on her own lips.

A car sped by and the two of them instinctively ducked. He pulled
back on to the blacktop. Just a few miles ahead there was a turn-off
that led to the flood plain. If he stayed on this road, they would be at
Evy's in ten minutes. She nuzzled close to him and switched on the
radio, as if the loud music were a part of how she had imagined this.

'Annie's going to be mad at me. Will you tell her?'

'What?' He was still thinking about the turn-off and could hardly
hear her over the music.

'Will you tell her we're seeing each other? I don't want to tell her.'

He made something he realized was a nod, and knew then that it was decided. He took the flood plain road and after a mile pulled up near the river.

'I wonder if my mom called your house and knows when we left?' Evy said.

Without responding, he turned to her. Looks like a child, he thought, but she's not a child. Annie. Annie had lost her virginity today. With the boy who had tried to kill their father. If not me, someone else. All of them the same. Evy was looking at him nervously. He felt no attraction to her. Bennet's face. The images: his mom and Bennet in rut; the flayed body of an animal, sinuous and sticky, raw as a hound's pizzle; his mom cleaning herself. He could feel Bennet's hulking frame around his own, his own aspiring to it: hanged man to the scaffold. This was what he wanted, a single coarse will, his body no more than meat. He would never be like his dad. They were all the same. He had seen other women do it, giving you the come-on even as they were petting with their boyfriends. Annie. Why would she sell herself so cheap? To the mad boy with the fugitive father, the boy who killed his own brother? With his tongue he rooted at the swelling in his lip.

'Is your mouth all right?'

'Sure, honey,' he said. After adjusting the bench seat as far back as it could go, he lifted her into his lap. He kissed her, gingerly because of his cut, and she returned his kiss, her eyes closing. Her breath smelled like candy.

'I love you, Frankie.' She seemed to believe it, her body trembling. Tomorrow, with another boy, she would believe it just as intensely. The day after that with another. He began to undo her blouse.

'Frankie.' She gently touched his hand. 'My mom must know we're on our way back. It's going to take us a while to get on the road again.'

Her blouse was open. Reaching quickly around, he unhooked her bra. Two shiny pads tumbled out. She snatched for them, but they fell on to the floor. Rather than swelling into Bennet's form, into the lust and the meat and the blind rutting will, he was shrinking, turning to ash in that shell.

'Frank,' she said more firmly, 'I want to go home. You're being strange. Why aren't you talking?' Abruptly she screamed as something banged heavily against the driver's side window. Light beamed into their faces. She flung herself off Frank, frantically doing up her blouse. The knock came again and Frank rolled down the window.

Siggy peered in. Evy was crying now, her lips marked with his dried blood

Reaching across Frank, Siggy switched off the radio. 'I'll take you on home, Evy,' he said.

Frank just stared through the windshield at the bugs in his headlights and the slow, black river as Evy got out. Siggy lit her way to his patrol car.

When she was in, Siggy leaned into Frank's truck. 'What happened to your lip there, Frank?'

He didn't say anything.

Siggy stared at him for a while. 'You'd better get on home.'

Frank remained after the patrol car had pulled out. The night descended, heavy with the scent of ragweed and river mud, the cicadas screaming in the trees. Bennet would know, but Frank didn't care. Let him think what he wanted. He didn't care. No traction in his mind, images sliding by: Esta, his mom, Annie, Miss Kelly, Mrs B. As he shifted his foot, he felt something on the floor and picked up one of the little bra pads. It smelled of her, like soap, lavender, like a little girl. Little Evy; silly Evy. All at once he felt as if he were going to throw up. Opening the car door, he took in some deep breaths. He wanted to sob, he knew it, but didn't let himself. He felt as heavy, saturated, rank and as full of that senseless insect screaming as this night. Finally, he pulled himself into the truck. As he headed back to the highway, he flung the bra pads out of the window.

*

Evy lay curled on the couch, her face raw with tears. Her sisters sat around her, but not too close, as if she were evidence that mustn't be touched. In the doorway stood her mother, smoking a cigarette. Headlights swept over the room as a car came up the driveway. Moments later Bennet entered and approached his daughter. Glancing up at him miserably, she began to cry again. He indicated for everyone to leave and they did.

When she had stopped crying he said, 'What happened?'

'I thought he was taking me home.'

Bennet waited.

'He kissed me.'

'You didn't want him to?'

'No . . . no.'

'Siggy said his mouth was bleeding.'

'I tried to get him off me.'

He nodded. 'All right. You go on to bed now.'

Evy got up and went to the door.

'Siggy's in the hall. Tell him to come in here.'

She turned around. 'Frank wouldn't have . . . He was drunk. He wouldn't have hurt me. He—'

'All right now. You go on to bed.'

'He wouldn't—'

'Go to bed.'

She left and Siggy came in.

Staring hard at his cousin, Bennet picked up the phone and dialled. 'Annie, honey, it's Mr B. Could you get your dad for me?'

The deep blue end-of-summer sky was visible through the collapsed roof of the derelict warehouse. Bennet, Siggy, Goldwin, Otto and Finn formed a closed group some distance from the entrance. Bennet had brought along a case of Jim Beam, and they were all drinking, deliberately and without pleasure. Their faces were serious, the atmosphere strained. In discord with this, Siggy played his belly like a tom-tom, farting out his lips in vague accompaniment. At the entrance were three other men, also drinking. One, with the face of a back-room pugilist, sat on the remains of a buggy, examining his ruined hands as if he weren't happy with a recent manicure. Behind him, digging at the ground with the point of his cowboy boot, was a Mexican, squat but powerful-looking, his long dark hair in a pony-tail. The third was a much older man who looked as if he had been made from chewed gristle.

'So what's wrong with Maggy?' Bennet asked.

Finn shrugged. 'Can't get out of bed. Says he feels weak in his bones. Seems cheerful enough, though.'

'Wouldn't get out of bed neither if I was married to Maud,' Otto muttered. 'Man alive, think of waking up to *that*.'

'He's lucky to have her,' Bennet said.

Leaning in, Goldwin whispered, 'Do you think he's . . . thinking about things?'

'Didn't say nothing,' Finn said. 'Could be. Become a bit of a holy old Joe. Wooden cross you could nail yourself to above his bed now.'

Goldwin clearly wanted to be a little more specific. 'I mean . . .' His eyes met Bennet's and he faltered.

They all remained quiet for a while, taking bitter slugs from their fifths, glancing toward the door. Indignantly, then, as if he had convinced himself of his right to speak, Goldwin addressed Bennet: 'I want to know something. How come Clyde didn't do nothing?'

All their heads turned at the sound of a car on the road by the factory and the three men at the door became alert. The car didn't stop.

Bennet looked as though he wasn't going to speak, but after a while, with a glance at Siggy, he said, 'I'll tell you a story. It's about someone you'all never knew. And if one word of this is ever repeated there's going to be a reckoning. That clear?'

The men nodded.

Bennet and Siggy mixed a smile between them. 'They going to believe this crazy story, cousin?'

'Not 'less they're cre'ins,' Siggy said.

'They're going to get here in a minute,' Otto complained, looking toward the road.

Bennet turned his gaze on Otto; only after he had swallowed back the whole mess of his impatience did he begin. 'Forty years ago, give or take, a kid, let's call him Nate, was born somewhere in West Virginia. One of a big litter of kids. But this one had a bit more to him than the rest and headed off to make his fortune.'

Finn rubbed his hands together with delight. 'Sure, it sounds like a fairy tale.'

Siggy grinned. 'In this one the grandma eats the wolf.'

'So he hobos around,' Bennet went on, 'getting work where he can, ends up in Texas, hand on a big cattle farm, working for a woman, let's call her Patrice Leroy.'

Bennet stopped because one of the men at the door – the pugilist – clearly curious about the attentive clot of men, had moved in closer. Bennet drove him back with a fierce look.

'Now this Patrice she's in her late fifties when Nate starts working for her. From a wealthy old New Orleans family. At fifteen she was married to a Texas cattleman – let's call him Cunningham. Part of a business deal, more or less, between her daddy and the cattleman. Cunningham thought he got the best of the deal: she came with enough cash to buy another ranch he was eyeing in Mexico. She had two sons by him. But the first died at a year old. Second got the scarlet fever when he was six. Rumour had it the fever made him an idiot. Patrice denied this, said she'd sent him to a boarding school in France, and when he was too old for school, said he was living in Europe. Most believed he was quietly suffocated and buried. She was an empty-headed woman, living a fantasy life. Some said losing her boys had made her crazy; others said she was always like it, not enough between her ears to feed a tick. From the beginning she tried to live in Texas like she'd lived in New Orleans, with fancy servants, dresses costing as much as most hands made in a year. Cunningham came to hate the sight of her and ended up living full time at his new ranch over the border.

'Then one day handsome Nate catches her eye. She gets him work-ing round the house, just to talk to him. He doesn't know what to make of her, done up like a Virginia ham, speaking French and flut-tering that fan of hers, laughing all the time like he's being funny. Here's a man you'd be lucky he says one word in two days. Sometimes out of the blue she acts like she's mad at him, makes a big scene, orders him out of the house. Then she chases after him, makes up and calls him a silly boy. Thing is, he needs the job – though he ain't sure any more what his job is – and who knows, maybe he smells an opportunity. She buys him fancy clothes. He sits around the house drinking iced tea. Or he takes a stroll with her round the garden, embarrassed if any of the other hands see him. Then one evening she has a big party, invites all the ranchers and other important people. Insists he's there, and much to his surprise introduces him as André, her son, back from his travels.

'Within weeks everyone's calling him Master Cunningham. Sleeps in his own room in the house. Soon he's running the ranch while also keeping up this strange role he has – somewhere between her kid and her sweetheart. Not that anything happened in the bedroom, but she'd kiss and pet him. At parties she'd cause a scene if a woman paid him any attention. Which would happen. Far as anyone knew, he was heir to a fortune.

'Then her husband returns. Rumours had gotten back to him about this son of his. When he confronts her, she tells him jealous people have been lying, and Nate's just the foreman. It's clear she can turn this fantasy on or off whenever she wants. Cunningham doesn't trust her, though, and stays. Not only this, but he's brought with him a Mexican woman and an infant he tells her is his son. Says it's his right since she didn't have any living children. He moves this woman into the house and tells Patrice she can put up with it or go back to New Orleans.

'Few days after Cunningham's return, Nate's playing poker with some of the hands when she comes storming over the dirt, raising dust with her skirts like a wild turkey in heat. She tells the other hands to leave. Then she rages for a while about her pig of a husband, his Mexican whore and his bastard. She shows Nate papers, which have his picture on them and which she says identify him as her son, as well as a will, as yet unsigned, that makes him her sole heir. Course he can't read, but it all looked legal enough. She tells him her husband's going to send him back to the gutter, send her packing to her family. Then she makes it clear what she wants him to do. But for Nate, pretending he's someone's son is one thing, murdering a man, woman and child is something else. He won't do it.

'Couple weeks later, he gets called up to the house. She tells him he's no longer the foreman, just a common hand, and she wants him to go right now to the lower field to fix a broken fence. He goes, and there, near the fence he's meant to fix, he finds Cunningham's body, beaten to a pulp with a fence stave. Some other hands turn up just minutes later, told by Patrice to hurry out and fix the same broken fence. Nate tells them he just found the body and they fetch the sheriff. That same day the Mexican woman and her baby disappear.

'Not wanting anything to do with this, Nate tells Patrice he's leaving. She tells him if he does she'll tell the sheriff he murdered her husband. Facts were against him. He was found at the scene. She'd deny she told him to go out there. She also has a *witness* who's willing to testify Nate was under the delusion he was going to get the farm, that he cursed the cattleman, picked up a fence stave, and stormed out that night. She'd also show he wasn't her missing son, claim he was a confidence man, playing on a mother's grief. She'd worked everything out. And she tells him if anything unnatural was to happen to her, everything's in a sealed box with her lawyers.

'So he's trapped. Has to become her son again, and she returns without missing a beat to her fantasy. He has to accompany her to his "father's" funeral, with all those eyes looking sideways at them, has to watch Patrice throw herself on the coffin, wailing and then fainting in his arms, forcing him to carry her through the crowd and back to the house. I'm sure Nate felt the cattleman deserved to die as much as any man of that kind, but he also knows that buried deep somewhere on those ten thousand acres were the bodies of that Mexican woman and her baby.

'About a week or so after the funeral, Patrice's maid comes running, hysterical, into his room. Patrice lay dead in her bedroom, beaten and strangled. Remembering what she said and sure he'll be blamed for this murder as well, he runs. He buys the identity of one of the thousands who died in the flu epidemic from a hospital orderly in Tuscaloosa.'

'Clyde.' Goldwin couldn't stop himself. 'Clyde!'

'With this new identity, he settles himself in another state.' Bennet went quiet.

'Jasus H.' Finn said. 'Jasus H., Mary and Joseph.'

'Maybe he did do it,' Otto said. 'Maybe he killed all of them.'

Glancing at Siggy, who was relishing the men's astonishment, Bennet leaned in again. 'What Nate didn't know was that the day after Patrice's murder they arrested two hobos trying to sell some of her jewellery. One gives evidence against the other, and admits she hired them not to kill her husband but to tie him up and bring him to that field: she did the killing herself. Same with the Mexican woman and her kid, whose bodies they took the sheriff to. They said they tried to get more money off her, claimed they didn't intend to kill her but she resisted and things had gone south. What Nate, AKA Mr John Doe Alabama, don't know was that there was a search out for dear André, notices in all the papers down there with his picture. Maybe he saw the picture – it was on the front pages for a while – but because he can't read, figures it's a wanted notice. What he don't know is that she has no secret file on him with her lawyers. Her last will and testament still names him her sole heir, with a notarized photograph, fingerprints and identification papers. What he's running away from is two cattle ranches bigger than some states, property in France, Spain and New Orleans, and her entire fortune. Not only that, but six years ago, oil was found all over that Texas farm, and that land's now worth ballpark fifty million dollars. Up until three years ago – *three* years ago – he could still have claimed it all.'

Bennet was done. The men were quiet, aghast.

Siggy, glancing from man to man, pinching his smiling lips and shaking his head, repeated, 'Fifty million dollars.'

Otto was staring at his boss as if Bennet had just grown another head; Finn, hunkering down as if he didn't have the strength to stand, mumbled, 'Jasus H., Jasus H., Jasus H.'; and Goldwin looked as if he wasn't sure if he were going to say something or throw up.

'Fifty million fucking dollars,' Siggy shouted triumphantly. Now his big belly began to shake.

With a broadening smile, Bennet repeated it, 'Fifty million fucking dollars.' Finn also began laughing, scratching his scalp as if it were infested, then Otto, his phlegmy laughter torn like an old chain out of his throat. Goldwin was the last to go and looked very much as if he were crying at first.

At the door, those three men peered over, curious and perplexed, as that little clan at the heart of this desolate place erupted into screaming, howling laughter, every now and then one of them crying out, 'Fifty million fucking dollars!'

The sound of another car instantly quieted them. This time it turned toward the warehouse and pulled up outside. The men followed Bennet as he walked toward the entrance, on either side of which those other three men stealthily positioned themselves. Frank entered, followed by Sal, who was speaking loudly and patting him on the back. Sal stepped away as the three men moved in around Frank, who looked confused and then angry as the Mexican and the pugilist took hold of him. He glanced toward his father, who looked back as if over a crevice that had just opened up in the earth between them.

'You bastard,' he shouted, struggling. 'You goddamn bastard. He's fucking your wife. You know it, every goddamn week, you fucking coward. He's—'

He was cut off as the older man, who had taken a moment to wrap something around his knuckles, struck him with dispassionate expertise right on the side of his nose, causing it to crack and shear, sending a stream of blood over his lips and chin. Sal cried out, tensing up his body as if he had been struck himself, and turned toward Bennet with an expression of helpless pleading. The beating continued. None of the men but Bennet and Otto could watch. Goldwin flinched at the sound of each blow; Finn had walked off a little distance and was speaking softly to himself, as if he had gone a little mad. Frank continued to struggle and kick out until the two men either side of him thrust their knees into his thighs, collapsing him to the ground. Then all three hailed blows down on him. Curling up, Frank tried to cover his already ruined face. Sal circled like a helpless tern watching its chicks being torn apart by a gang of seagulls. The stocky Mexican was carefully aiming blows from his cowboy boots between Frank's legs. Frank started to become a carcass, limp, ceasing to cry out, the pugilist brushing his hands from his face like cobwebs before hitting him.

'It's got to stop,' Siggy said. 'Mr B.'

Bennet did nothing. Frank's eyes began to roll back in their sockets.

'Ja-sus!' Finn screamed from way across the factory. Suddenly Sal pushed through the men as through a fire, and threw himself on his son's body. The three men stopped instantly and walked away. This was what they had been waiting for: their instructions from Bennet had been to stop only if Sal intervened – risked himself. Sal was the only one not aware that he might have stopped this at the first blow, Frank walking away with no more than a broken nose. Now he lay unconscious, almost unrecognizable. The men helped Sal get Frank back into his car.

After he had driven off, the five men stood outside the warehouse in a yard full of rusted machinery overgrown with ailanthus and lilac. None of them spoke for a while. Bennet stared off at the ruined factory, his usually implacable expression wavering, his brow wrought with confusion.

Finally he looked at his cousin, who was working a cud of chaw, then around at the other men, bewildered. 'Goddamn,' he said softly, and as if out of breath. 'His own fucking son.'

'It's bad enough he brings him,' Siggy said, 'but to damn near let him die.'

'You know—' Otto began.

'You shut your goddamn face,' Bennet shouted so fiercely that Otto backed up and ducked his head, staring at the ground like a cowed dog.

Bennet, trembling now, still seemed to be having difficulty catching his breath. All at once, under that buckling pressure of confusion, his face collapsed into senility. 'His own fucking son. He just had to say one word. One fucking word. Goddamn it. God*damn* that fucking pantywaist, yellow, hog-humping, pussy, shit-for-brains . . .' He spat out one obscenity after another, getting louder and louder, trying to re-bolster himself with ferocity, while the other men waited patiently for their own miserable portion of this.

Annie was cleaning the living-room windows when she heard a knock at the door.

Evy stood sheepishly outside.

'Hey, Evy.' She didn't want to let her in. She had too much to do.

'Is Frankie around?'

'No. He went somewhere with Dad.'

'Did he tell you?' She was biting at the skin around her nails.

'Tell me what?'

'We're dating now.'

'Don't be silly.'

'We are.'

'Don't be silly, Evy.' Anger seethed in her stomach.

'We kissed last night.'

'Why?'

'What do you mean why?'

'What are you doing? Why are you doing this?'

'What am I doing?'

'Why are you acting like this?'

'I'm not acting like anything. I thought you'd be happy.'

Annie just stared at her. She couldn't stand it and finally shut the door. What was her brother doing? She was so sick of it all. Now her mom came into the hall, still in her robe, a filthy rag in one hand, a cigarette in the other.

'Who was it?'

'No one.'

'You sounded upset.'

'Mom, you're dropping ash.'

Her mom quickly cupped the hand with the rag in it under the cigarette, but the ash had already fallen. 'God, I wish we hadn't started this.'

'The house is filthy, Mom.'

There was a hammering at the door. Annie opened it.

It was Evy again, but she looked out of breath and stricken. 'Frank,' she said. 'He's in your dad's car.'

Her dad appeared on the porch.

'What's going on?' Annie said.

Evy had started crying. 'He's dead.'

'What?'

'He's okay,' Sal said. 'Evy, shuddap. He's okay. He's okay. We just need to get him in the house.'

Pushing past him, Annie ran to the car. Frank, almost unrecognizable, lay in the back seat. She felt dizzy and had to support herself against the car. When her mom saw him, she screamed, 'Frankie!' Behind her, Evy was squealing and crying. Annie was aware of all this, but still felt numb and on the verge of fainting. Frank shifted, his head falling back as if he couldn't lift it. A bubble of mucus and blood swelled out at his lips and burst.

Her dad's hand was on her shoulder. Shifting her gently aside, he opened the back door. 'We get him in now. It looks more bad than it is. He's okay. We'll be okay.'

'What happened to him?' Annie wanted to regain control of herself, to feel her legs again and shake this fog out of her head.

Her dad didn't say anything.

She said, 'We've got to get him to the hospital.'

'No, no,' her dad said. 'No. We get him in.'

Annie pushed the back door shut, almost catching her dad's hands, got into the driver's seat and turned the ignition key. The car made a horrible sound. It was still on. She knew something had to happen with the gears.

'No, Annie.' Her dad reached into the driver's side window and put his arm across her. 'We take him inside.'

Annie thrust her open hand at him, hitting his face and knocking him back. She was trying to figure out what to do. The gears were making a horrible sound.

Her mom opened the door. 'Move over.'

As Annie did so, her mom got in and put the car into gear. It jerked forward, hitting a pile of empty crates. She slammed it into reverse, backing into the old pump and breaking one of the rear lights.

'I'll drive it.' Shouting, her dad was holding on to the driver's side door, trying to get it open, but they were already moving. He kept holding on, running beside the car, hitting the door. As they veered sharply into the alley, he fell, rolling over into the dirt. Annie glanced back as they turned on to Main. He had pulled himself up, raising his arms in despair. His hat crushed, his clothes filthy, he looked, for all the world, like a scarecrow.

They had been walking around the city for much of the night. For all his arrogance, Dr Weaver had not presumed to kiss her. But time and again their eyes would collide, grappling like love-wrestlers, he in the piercing blue, she in the deep and liquid brown corner. And Nurse Gordiano was getting the better of him, his eyes having stumbled against the sinuous ropes of her neck, and tumbled more than once to the soft canvas of her breasts.

It had become chilly. Mindful that 73 per cent of body heat is lost through the head, Dr Weaver lifted one side of his long, thick hair and laid it gently over her naked scalp. Thus they walked, sharing hair. Heedlessly they entered the bad part of town, whence one of its dusky inhabitants emerged from an alley with a pistol. When Dr Weaver stepped forward to protect her, the bald nub of her noggin was exposed once more. The robber immediately broke down, telling them it made him remember his old mom in her last weeks on chemotherapy. Gravely, Nurse Gordiano knelt before this little man, let him caress the top of her head, sobbing, 'Mama! Mama!' This gave Dr Weaver a chance to garrotte him into near unconsciousness with his stethoscope. They then beat this creature senseless, which thrilled Nurse Gordiano, for she had never struck a man. Whipped into forbidden passions, they then ran into a nearby nightclub, firing that man's pistol into the air, setting off a stampede of screaming humanity. Nurse Gordiano had always wanted to do this, and with Dr Weaver felt she could do anything.

As dawn broke, he took her to the zoo. There, an old school friend of his let them into a cage full of baby animals. He kissed her at last, laying her into the hay, softly whispering, 'Excuse the scat.' They made love as baby ocelots, giraffes and baboons gambolled about them. Afterwards they discovered that Dr Weaver's friend, who was a bit of a joker, had stolen their clothes and locked the doors. But when the crowds gathered about the cage, no one laughed, so taken were they by these magnificent human animals, Adam and Eve in this arc of new life. So Nurse Gordiano and Dr Weaver decided to stay there, to raise their young with the young of all the species of the earth, fed by the kindness of strangers and admission fees.

Ruth pushed herself away from her desk, disgusted, and went into the living room, where she threw herself on the couch. Why was it she couldn't gain enough traction even to imagine desire and love in something as inane as a ten-cent romance? All her life she had felt a little superior to those around her, conceiving the source of this pride as a kind of sacred seed. Seed sown, she realized now, into ground that had been for too long made up of contrarian, adolescent ideals: love is an exquisite form of isolation; what doesn't kill you makes you stronger; the perfected life is sustained by nothing but beauty and truth.

She thought of Goldwin's grief over her, his clumsy letter. Would any man be better than no man? How many times, writing her romances, had she imagined the clutch and kiss? For all the cliché of it, she had succumbed to Chuck Wainwright, Aaron Blacksmith, Gunther Peterson, all those muscular names. Better them, perhaps, than the awful men to whom she had yielded in her youth, who recognized her vulnerability, knew she would be a zealot for their self-love. And when she was sure it could no longer happen, she had fallen in love again. With Raj. What he had done tortured her: that her love, once more, could have been so mistaken and misplaced. Had he used her journals in this way because of what she had written about him all those years ago? Could he possibly have feigned affection and schemed revenge for so long?

There was a knock at the front door. Both insistent and tentative, it could only be Judy. Ruth wanted to be alone. To avoid being seen through the window, she gently lowered herself on to the floor and began to crawl out of the room. The front door opened, sunlight flooding over her.

'Ruth?'

Ruth rolled over and sat up to face Judy, who stared at her severely.

'What are you doing?'

'I fell asleep.'

'On the floor?'

'My back was hurting.'

'In all your clothes?'

'Suddenly I got real tired.' Ruth got up as Judy came in and sat down on the armchair.

'Would you like some iced tea?'

Judy looked as if this question were a fly she was trying to swat from her face. 'I suppose,' she said finally.

As Ruth headed to the kitchen, Judy called out, 'I believe I might like something to eat also.'

The rudely imperious tone of this caused Ruth to look back at Judy, who wore the kind of frozen, grinning snarl one might see on the face of a stuffed critter.

'I'll see what I have,' she said, suppressing a churn of irritation and revulsion.

She brought out the iced tea and some cookies, and sat on the couch to face Judy, whose body, as ever, was so clenched and guarded it looked as if she were bound hand and foot. But there was something different in her expression, and Ruth even wondered if she were a little drunk.

As ever, Judy kept quiet. Ruth reciprocated, determined not to fling herself, babbling, into the silences this woman created.

'Do you know what I discovered?' Judy said at last.

Ruth shook her head.

Judy looked down into her iced tea, tapping the glass with her fingernails. 'I discovered that my son is a thief.'

She went quiet again. Ruth kept silent also.

'My husband's going to take him a little later today to personally return all the things he stole.'

Again she rapped against her glass, absorbing herself in it. Finally she looked up at Ruth. 'He also took something from you.'

'From me?'

'Said he found them in your attic.'

'My journals?' For a second all she could think about was how she had been treating Raj, how deeply hurt and confused he must be. Flooded with a desperate energy, she stood up. But hard upon this the creaturely face of that woman broke through, its expression at once victorious and pathetic.

'Did you hear what my husband did?'

Ruth sat. 'Oh . . . yes.'

'A sapperating wound. In front of the whole town. I had to look up sapperating.'

'Suppurating.' Ruth realized it probably wasn't the most tactful thing in the world to correct her pronunciation. 'Judy, I'm sorry that happened, but my journals are private. I don't really feel those things. I write them because it . . . relieves me. It reminds me of someone.'

'Discharging and forming pus. You wouldn't write them if you didn't feel them.'

'I guess I do feel them. At the time. I need to allow myself to feel them. But I also feel other things. Contradictory things. I've written awful things about people I love dearly. I didn't intend for your son to publish them all over town.'

Judy didn't seem to be listening, but displayed a look of proud, slightly wounded triumph. 'Anyway,' she said, 'I'd like us to do something today. There's a big group of Amish just an hour or so north. I've heard they sell wonderful furniture and I—'

'I can't get away today. I have a deadline.'

'I have your journals.'

'Yes, and I'd like them back.'

'Don't you think I should let people know who wrote these vile things?'

'My journals are private.'

'Well, I think your deadline can wait.'

Ruth stood up. 'Judy, I'm not going anywhere with you today or ever. I don't want to see you even near my house again.'

Judy stood also, wielding that taxidermied smile. 'Then you'd probably best leave Pisgah.'

'I'm not going anywhere.'

'There won't be a single person in town won't hate you.'

'Get out of my house.'

'Well, let's do the Amish trip tomorrow then, if you're busy today.'

'Get out of my house.'

Judy seemed perplexed. Ruth walked by her to the front door and opened it. Judy went to leave, but pulled up in the doorway, facing Ruth.

'You promised many times that we'd go to Kansas City together,' she said, clearly trying to generate anger. 'And we never went. That wasn't true what you wrote about me. That wasn't true.' Ruth felt a revolted pity for this woman. 'Why wouldn't you ever do anything with me?' Judy lurched forward in a way that made Ruth flinch and raise a hand to protect herself. 'I *like* you.' Judy looked abject, desperate.

'I'm sorry,' Ruth said. 'I'm sorry for what I wrote. You were never meant to see it. Please, *please* get out of my house.'

Judy walked quickly out, but as Ruth went to shut the door, she saw her purse on the floor by the armchair. Snatching it up, she hurried after her.

'Judy, your purse.'

Turning, Judy took the purse and in that action snatched up Ruth's hand and wrist. It was a hard, almost painful clasp.

'Let go, Judy, please.'

Judy just stared at her.

'I'm sorry, Judy. I'm sorry for you.'

Judy let go, raising her chin and smiling with a kind of theatrical dignity. 'I'll come round later in the week, then.'

'No you won't. You won't ever come round here again.'

Judy's smile broadened and became wry, as if Ruth had just said something intriguing, making some subtle secret available to her. Then she turned around, clutching her purse, and walked away.

Returning to the porch, Ruth saw a large canvas tote bag beside the door. It contained all the stolen journals.

Alvin went into the sitting room where his dad, in his armchair, was listening with his eyes closed to the third track of *Classical Greats* – Holst's 'Mars'. In his lap lay a pencil and a legal pad. When Alvin was much younger, this had been his own favourite track; he would stand in front of his dad pretending to pound that drum. He felt like a child now, helpless and weak from crying.

'Dad,' he shouted through the thundering music.

His dad opened his eyes.

'Please. We can't. I'll send them back. I'll write something to say sorry. Please, Dad. Please.'

His dad watched him expressionlessly as that sinister orchestral build-up was shattered by the pounding drums. Finally, he lifted the needle off the record.

'It's too late for that, son.'

'Talk to Mom. Please. I can't do it.' He began to cry again. 'Please.'

'Yes you can. You can return those things and we shall both ask their forgiveness.'

Alvin couldn't understand. His dad had been on his side and now seemed almost enthusiastic.

'They'll forgive you.' His dad showed Alvin what he had written on the legal pad.

1. *Our Lord had His most precious thing stolen away.*
2. *The meaning of the crucifixion: Shepherd in supplication to His flock is flock in supplication to the Shepherd.*
3. *Ultimate forgiveness is that of Judas.*
4. *Revelation and reconciliation. Return of the Son and of the Kingdom of God.*

'Four sermons,' his dad said. 'It's perfect. It's like a parable. Like the Lord has given us our own parable.' This seemed to strike him suddenly. 'That's right.' He snatched the pad back and began to scribble furiously beneath his list. When he was done, he checked his watch and lowered the needle to the record. 'We'll leave in about ten minutes.' As if sinking into a warm bath, he closed his eyes.

Alvin left the room, which was filling again with that terrible music. Everyone was going to know that he had taken all those precious things, invading their private places. He truly hadn't believed his parents would go through with it, but he could see now that his dad was actually excited. How was it they couldn't see that Sheriff Siggy would figure out immediately that he had to be the one who stole the rifle and the typewriter? Then everyone would know he was the one typing out the letters. Stealing the rifle brought criminal charges, and those letters would make him the most hated person in the world. Where was his mom? She had taken the journals. He guessed she was going to hide or destroy them.

He wasn't going to do it; he wasn't going to do any of this. Fetching the rifle from under the bed in the spare room, he climbed out of his bedroom window into the garden, and sat on the old stump near the hawthorns just a little way from the gate. He wanted his mom to see him. He had to look like he was serious about it. It scared him to point the rifle at his own body, but he forced himself to look into the barrel. Over. Everything over. He began to tremble, sheer misery like a damp, black rot in his limbs. He knew his dad would come out in a moment to look for him, but he wanted it to be his mom. Would they believe him? The rifle wasn't loaded. They would be sure to check. He hadn't brought the bullets with him. Should he get them? Load it? How far could he go? No, the idea would be enough. Of what he might do.

He settled the barrel into the crook of a low, forking branch of the hawthorn. He should load it. For a second he touched the barrel to his lips. Barrel's breath: oil and metal. The blood weighing his saturated heart seemed now to be drawn into his face and chest, as if his whole body were a sponge, his blood pooling in whatever direction he tipped. Liquid weight. Misery. Hoffmeyer. All at once he understood him. Flooding in like a vision: that man's fear and despair. Briefly, completely, he felt for him, for all of them, the injured, lonely, desperate, mad, and the song of this despair was love in another language: *Es ist hier, mein Liebling. Der Hund Bellt, die alte Lokomotive rasselt, dein Schreien ist der Faden, der alles verbindet. Ein weiterer Laut und Gott ist hier. To see my shadow in the sun and descant on mine own deformity.* His flesh tingled at these words, as if the swelling misery had begun to break, like a wave foaming in his skin. *For daws to peck at. I am not what I am. I am not what I am.* Crying now, he set his cheek against the barrel. Could he shoot through his cheek? If he held it in his mouth, the bullet would go right through. It would hardly hurt him. Just the skin there, a small scar. Would it burn his mouth? He knew he couldn't do it. Even unloaded, the rifle frightened him. When he tried to point it, loaded, at people, his whole body would shake. All at once he was filled with the memory of Annie's naked body as she came toward him from the sinkhole. He was nothing to her; an irritating child. He thought of Raj and Lew, always running away from him. Nora said he was disgusting. Now everyone would know. 'Mars' thundered out of the house, the music making him feel even more tragic. Then he saw her, his mom, walking up the road. Damn, he should have loaded it. But he could frighten her like this. It didn't feel fake. He was so miserable he truly felt he could hurt himself. He could, he knew he could, and this would show her he was serious. He wasn't going to let them ruin his life. Panicky now, he wedged the stock hard into that crook. Setting the barrel against his cheek, he cupped his hands around his lips so it looked from the path side as if it were in his mouth. His mom would be at the gate in a moment. She was walking quickly, but looking down, absorbed. Would he have to shout to get her attention? He didn't want to do that. To make himself more visible, he shifted out a little on the stump. As he did so the stock slipped from the crook and hit the ground.

He wasn't sure what had happened at first. Or couldn't believe it, his ears ringing from the percussion. There was blood on his pants, coming down from his mouth. Was his mouth open? There was something gritty on his tongue and he spat out into his hand bloody bits of bone or tooth. He hoped it was tooth. He hoped it wasn't his jaw.

He tried to call out to his mom, but nothing came. He began to panic. Nothing came. What had happened? Loaded. Hadn't he unloaded it? He hadn't unloaded it. He couldn't remember. He felt something go tight in his neck and the side of his face. It wasn't right. It wasn't a right thing. He began to feel warm and strangely relaxed. His mom was running toward him, but something was wrong with his eye. He closed his right eye and couldn't see. Was his left eye closed? He stood up, but he wasn't standing up. With his right eye he could see his hand. It was moving but he wasn't moving it. His mom's hand came down on the grass beside his, taking his, but his kept moving. He couldn't hear anything. He couldn't see the ground. He was rolled over, his head angled up, his mom's face, and then she was gone, just the tangle of the hawthorn. Behind this, the bright sun.

*

Annie sat between Lew and Raj in the hospital waiting room. Linus and Jude stood together by the door. She was leaning back against Lew, his arms around her, and held Raj's hands in her lap. Her mom sat opposite, still in her robe, smoking.

A doctor came in. 'Mrs Celli?'

Her mom stood up.

'Dr Thornsen. Forgive me if I . . . it's my first day.' He looked very young and seemed to want to be congratulated or encouraged. 'Frank is resting now. Do you know who did this to him?'

She shook her head.

'We'll find them,' Jude said.

The young doctor smiled at Jude as if he were a schoolboy who had just volunteered to clean up the classroom. 'Well, I guess he can talk to the police himself when he's up to it.'

'Is he okay?' Annie asked.

'Well, he's okay, but he's pretty busted up.' The doctor examined his clipboard. 'Four fractured ribs. His left cheekbone is shattered, which may lead to complications. His nose is broken. His left fibula – thigh bone – has a very minor hair fracture. His right ear has a ruptured tympanum – eardrum. A number of his fingers have been dislocated.' Pausing, he glanced at her mom a little sheepishly. 'One of his testicles has been crushed. The other is fine. And the rest is just superficial: bruises and abrasions. I think the only permanent damage, apart from the . . . that testicle, will be to the hearing in his right ear.' He had finished and again looked to Annie's mom as if for some encouragement. 'You can see him if you like. He's sedated right now and sleeping.'

As they followed Thornsen into Frank's room, an emergency call came for the doctor over the intercom and he hurried out. At the sight of Frank, covered in bandages, his face blue and swollen beyond recognition, Annie felt a little dizzy again, and angry at herself for being such a baby.

'Goddamn,' Jude whispered. 'Looks like the invisible man.'

They all sat around the bed for a while. Annie couldn't stop thinking about her dad. He must have seen what happened. Why hadn't he brought him straight to the hospital, and why wasn't he here?

Her mom touched her arm, speaking as if out of Annie's own thoughts. 'Your dad, honey, I'd better call.'

Annie nodded.

A little while later her mom returned. 'He's going to stay at the store. Said he come up later.' She shrugged off Annie's questioning look. 'Oh, and Alvin his mom's here. I see her going down the hall. Is she looking for us, you think?'

'How would they know?' Raj cut in.

'Well, forgive me, God' – her mom crossed herself – 'but I hope the Reverend he's not here.' She made a theatrical shudder of revulsion. 'Him I couldn't cope with right now.'

'I couldn't cope with him either,' Annie said, 'but I should see if Mrs Hewitt's here for us.' She needed to go to the bathroom anyway.

When she got out of the bathroom, she checked the main reception and waiting area, but couldn't see Mrs Hewitt and wondered if her mom had mistaken someone else for her. She stood outside in the parking lot for a little while to get some air. When she came back in, it occurred to her to give the receptionist Mrs Hewitt's name. The nurse directed her to the same waiting room they had all just left.

She entered to see Alvin's mom standing in the middle of the room while Reverend Hewitt sat slumped forward on the bench, his hands together as if in prayer. They both looked up fearfully at her as she entered, clearly expecting the doctor.

'Annie?' Judy frowned. 'How did you know about this?'

'About what? I'm here because Frank got hurt.'

Reverend Hewitt spoke. 'Alvin is . . . injured.'

'What happened?' Annie said.

Mrs Hewitt was staring strangely at her. 'Nothing would ever happen to you, would it, Annie?' She seemed angry.

'What?'

'Come on now, Judy,' the Reverend said. 'This hasn't got anything to do with Annie.'

Judy was staring at Annie with what looked like loathing.

'What hasn't?' Annie said.

'You're going to be perfectly happy, aren't you?' Mrs Hewitt said.

The door opened, almost hitting Annie in the back.

'I'm terribly sorry.' It was the same young doctor. He looked very pale.

'Are you related?' he asked Annie.

'I'm a friend of Alvin's.'

Mrs Hewitt's disgusted stare had now fixed upon the doctor. The Reverend stood up. He looked helpless, unrehearsed, his shoulders slumped and his hands not knowing what to do. Annie felt she should leave, but Alvin's mom had moved up next to her and now took hold of her arm.

'It's my first day,' the young doctor said, and there was a hint of self-pity. He checked his clipboard, but seemed then to give up on it, slotting it under his arm as he took off his glasses – both of which seemed the most ominous actions. 'I'm afraid—'

Judy let out a sound like the kind of sounds people release when they're sleeping, a deep-throated whimper, and her body jerked sharply in that same way, as bodies do in sleep.

'The bullet . . .' He began to make an explanatory gesture, raising his hand toward the back of his head, but gave up. 'Well, I'm afraid he didn't make it.'

Annie couldn't believe it. Alvin's mom had now sat on the floor, still clutching Annie's arm. The young doctor was staring at Annie pathetically, as if to say, 'Is any of this my fault?' Inadequate and absurd. She hunkered down beside Mrs Hewitt. Alvin's dad hadn't moved, bent forward, his hands clenched in front of him, as if he were ready to run a race. Annie was unable to feel anything as a sobbing wail began to well up from deep in Alvin's mom. Unreal. Just the doctor's new patent-leather shoes in front of them. He had remarkably big feet. It struck her what strange, grotesque things feet were. Animals, all of them, animals in big buildings with powerful machines; animals in shiny shoes.

*

Maud smoked a cigarette to calm her nerves before going to his cabin. Stubbing it out in the dirt, she steeled herself for his *Good morning, my love*, and entered.

'Good morning, my love.' He looked like a capsized turtle, his head craning up from the edge of the coarse army blanket. He wore a meek smile, his eyes strangely unfocused, as if he had made himself blind by force of will. He even acted as if he were blind sometimes, the way he groped for things. A Bible and a few books of poetry lay scattered over his bed. He had long since had her get rid of every other book, as well as his pillow and quilt, every comfort, even the photographs of his father and *chère maman*.

'Anything in your bedpan?'

He didn't respond. She checked it.

'Just liquid again?'

Frowning, he looked toward the window.

She could feel the heat in her face. 'I know you'd rather you pissed poetry, but I'm the one who has to clean it up.'

At this, he took on a look of pained defiance, like an afflicted actress in a silent movie.

'I just wanted to know,' she said with slightly reluctant contrition. 'Has anything . . . solid come out yet?'

He shook his head almost imperceptibly.

Maud left and returned a little while later with the clean bedpan. As she went to put it on the floor, he tapped the blanket beside his hip and she put it there. He touched it.

'Can't you warm it just a little, my dear?'

'Oh, I haven't got time. I've had to turn over five rooms this morning and Annie's coming round for me in a few minutes.' She checked her watch.

'Will she stay?' Instantly his tragic diffusion was dispelled, becoming transparent enthusiasm.

'We have a funeral. Alvin, the Reverend's son, he died.'

'Will she come back with you afterwards? I have some . . . Couldn't she stay just a little while?'

'It's her friend. You remember Alvin. He died. He shot himself. An accident.'

Magnus sank back again, his face going blank. 'Why do you clean it with cold water?'

'You know Alvin,' she said. 'The Hewitts' boy.'

He didn't respond.

'It'll warm. Do you need to use it now?'

He nodded.

'If you can shift round a little, I'll hold it over the edge here for you. You won't have to touch it.'

With an effort that seemed to exhaust him, he rolled himself so he lay on his side at the edge of the bed. He was like a big infant with that skein of downy hair upon his liver-mottled pate. He struggled for a little while with his underwear until she reached down and helped him. Then she lifted the blanket up over his hip and held the bedpan at his groin. A little shot of urine splattered over the edge, on to the floor.

'Aim it, aim it!' she shouted. He looked at her helplessly. 'You can't be that weak! Come on.'

Finally she shoved his fumbling hand out of the way and aimed it for him. 'Go now,' she said. 'I can't see why you can't hold it. You can hold a damn book.'

He finished and she helped him roll back over. 'The doctor says there's nothing wrong with you.'

A knock came at the door and she went to answer it.

'Who is it?' he called.

'It's Annie.'

Annie put her head in the room.

'Annie!' Magnus cried out, completely animated, pulling himself up, seemingly without effort, into a sitting position.

'Can't stay today,' Annie said. 'We're going to a funeral.'

'A funeral?'

'Alvin. Alvin died.'

'I told you that,' Maud shouted.

As if he had just heard the news, Magnus canted his head back and closed his eyes, grief-stricken, his hand groping up to touch the crucifix. He looked like a suffering saint. Or a ravished Fay Wray.

It was early Sunday morning and Nora hadn't slept well. She was worried about what her dad would do when he found out she was dating Raj. She planned to put her arm through Raj's when people gathered after church today, making their relationship clear to everyone. But should she talk to her dad first? Alvin's death had made her feel grown up, had marked, in the most awful way, an end to childhood for all of them. Dead more than a month now. It gave her a strange feeling to see the turned earth, like an unmade bed. She hoped he forgave her for always being so irritable with him. She would try to visit with Annie today. It had been such a difficult time for her: Frank barely recovered and drinking again.

She had to put that aside for now, though, and focus on today. She wanted a ring on her finger before Raj left for Boston. She checked her face in the vanity. Her acne seemed to be clearing a little, and she wondered if the radiation was working at last. A bride shouldn't have acne.

After locking her bedroom door with a little bolt she had mounted herself, she slipped off her nightdress and put on her robe. She hurried across the hall to the bathroom, making sure to lock that door too, and to close the slatted window.

A few minutes into her shower, she heard a metallic squeaking from somewhere. All at once the water was scalding and she threw herself out of the stream against the back of the stall. She tried to slide open the stall door on this side, but it wouldn't budge.

'The water,' she shouted. 'I'm in the shower.' It had never been this hot. The cold-water pressure was strong enough that if someone turned on a faucet elsewhere, it would just be a little unpleasant. And it was never scalding like this: her dad was too cheap with the thermostat. She tried to reach her hand through to switch it off, but couldn't. It was as hot as water from a kettle; she could barely see for the steam. Her feet were getting burned. She screamed out again, banging against the back of the shower. 'The water. Turn off the water.'

Her dad knocked on the door. 'Are you all right, honey?'

'The water,' she screamed. 'I'm getting burned. I can't get out.'

There was a thundering bang and crack as the bathroom door was pushed in, the little bolt flying off. After slamming back the front panel, her dad turned off the shower.

'Jeez, what happened?' he said, sticking his head in and fanning away the steam.

She covered herself with her arms, crouching over. 'Dad, get out.'

He didn't move, a silly grin on his face. 'What happened?'

'Get out!'

'Well excuse me for breathing. Just trying to help,' he said, now looking hurt. 'Should have let you par-boil in here.'

'Get out,' she screamed.

'Nora?' her mom called timidly from the doorway. 'Nora, are you all right?'

'Tell Dad to get out of here.' She felt so furious and helpless. Her dad just wouldn't move. She reached over and tried to shut the shower panel, but he put his hand up to stop it before it hit him.

'Karl,' her mom wheedled. 'Karl, why don't you leave her to get dressed? Karl?'

He responded indignantly, as if his refusal to move or look away from her body had become a point of honour. 'I'm going to have to fix that goddamn door now. I came in here to help her.'

Her brother's sleepy voice broke in. 'Dad, what are you doing?'

'She was burning. I helped her.'

'Dad, we don't need to be here now,' her brother said. 'Leave her alone.'

'Leave her alone? Should have left her alone five minutes ago when she was getting damn well boiled.' Indignation had become righteous fury.

'All of you get out,' Nora screamed.

'Karl, honey, please let her get dressed.'

With a last lingering, dissatisfied look at her, her dad left.

Only her mom remained. 'Are you all right, Nor?' she called. 'It's really not my fault. I don't have the machine on or anything.'

'Please close the door, Mom.'

Her mom did.

Getting out, she quickly pulled on her robe. She tried the cold water faucet at the sink. It dribbled for a second, spattered, then nothing.

She went back to her room to dry herself off, locking her door. Her feet and shins were badly scalded, a couple of burn blisters forming on her toes. He *had* saved her. Had she been too harsh and rude? But why would he stare at her like that? Did it really not mean anything to him that she wasn't a little girl any more? As she sat there trying to figure out what to feel, she heard that squeaking sound again, and realized it was coming from the basement. Quickly she went back to the bathroom and turned on the cold-water faucet. After a second it coughed and vomited a powerful stream of water. She hurried to the stairs that led down to the basement. Her dad was coming up.

'What were you doing down there?'

'Checking everything out.'

'Did you turn off the cold water while I was in the shower?'

'What?' He looked at her as if she were crazy. 'I was trying to help you. I've got to fix that damn door now.' He almost pushed past her and walked down the hall to his bedroom.

She returned to the bathroom. Standing on the toilet she examined the top of the rail that held in the shower panels. In it was a screw. It was this that had prevented her from opening the rear shower panel. She went back to her room, her spine and neck tingling with fury, though she also felt confused almost to the point of panic. She just couldn't believe her dad would do something so premeditated. She paced beside her bed, going through all the steps he had taken: fixing the panel so she couldn't open it, turning up the thermostat on the boiler, finally turning off the cold water. Surely she was mistaken. Her daddy? Burning her just so he could look at her body?

Was it a joke? 'But who could see this as a joke?' She startled herself as she became aware that she had said this out loud. She glanced down at her scalded shins and blistered feet. Again she saw his face in the steam, that stupid grin. But hard upon this she remembered his face when he had walked in on her and her cousin – it had broken her heart. Why hadn't she called out and tried to defend herself? She was confused, that confusion slowly smothering her fury. He had always loved her, spoiled her. But this, *this* – he had no right to do this. Her fury returned in full, blazing up, and she could barely catch her breath as all her doubts were burned off, leaving an absolute clarity. This was going to stop right now.

After removing her robe, she went over to her closet to get some clothes, but caught sight of her naked body in the vanity. She stared at herself. So this was what it was all about: these breasts, these hips, this scrap of hair between her legs. Abruptly and quickly, fearing she might lose her resolve, she walked out of her room, down the hall and into her parents' bedroom. They were reading the newspaper in bed.

Her mom looked up first, and shrieked. 'Nora!'

Nora walked around the bed to her dad's side and stood not a foot from him.

'Jesus fucking Christ, what are you doing?' he shouted, shifting back against her mom.

Both of them stared up at her as if she were about to bring down an axe.

Her brother ran in. 'Godamighty, Nor, what are you doing?'

She just stared at her dad, who was resolutely looking away.

'Nora, please,' her mom pleaded.

Her brother had gone. The anger throbbed up and down her skin in waves of heat. She took up her dad's hand and tried to press it against her crotch, but he snatched it away as her brother hurried back in with her robe.

'Come on, Nor,' Jude said quietly, putting it around her.

She didn't move for a moment, staring down at her dad, who

looked stricken and confused. Her mom had buried her head in her hands. Nora turned to her brother's anxious, loving face. They had never really been too close, but she felt close to him now, and finally let him lead her out.

Annie woke to the touch of her dad's hand against her cheek.

'Made you hot chocolate,' he said.

She glanced at the clock beside her bed. It was almost one in the morning. She let him lead her downstairs and sat in his lap holding the hot chocolate as he pulled a blanket over them.

'Were you having a bad dream?' she said.

He shook his head. 'Couldn't sleep.'

He smelled a little of sweat and she could feel the throb of his heart.

'On the life of my mama, Annie, I thought they would stop beating him.'

'You said you didn't see them. Papa, what happened? Who beat him?'

He wasn't listening, his eyes wide and frantic, his lips trembling. He raised a fierce finger. 'One by one,' he said, 'I wait for them. Fucking little Mexican; rip his fucking balls off. *Mondo boia!*' The finger was furled now into a fist, which he shook. 'I'm going to beat them. *Nessuno me lo ficca in culo.*'

Annie quickly put the hot chocolate on the little table beside the armchair because he was getting so animated she was afraid it would spill.

'*Bastardo lurido, finocchio.* I'll fucking break all their kids' necks like chickens. I want them—'

'Who?' Annie cut him off. 'Who did it?'

Her dad went quiet, breathing hard, flecks of spittle at the corners of his mouth. All at once his face collapsed in pain and he bent forward, pressing his head into her chest. 'It happen again.' A sound of pure animal suffering came from deep in his throat. 'It happen again.'

'What happened again?'

'What happen to my papa. I didn't know I could stop it. And when it looked so bad, I thought, Better dead than like my papa. Let them finish it.'

'What happened?'

But he had begun to cry now. He sobbed for a long time, soaking one shoulder of her nightdress with his tears. She stroked his hair, kissed his damp, hot forehead until finally he calmed.

When he sat up straight again, she handed him the hot chocolate. He sipped it and the milk scum got caught on his moustache. They laughed as he drew it into his mouth and she wiped the rest off.

'Why didn't you tell Sheriff Judd you'd seen them?'

'What? Oh, they was just punks,' he said. 'Jumped him when he get out the truck to go to the bathroom.'

This was the story in the paper, though it didn't really make sense. Frank wouldn't tell her anything.

They sat quietly for a while. Annie realized this wasn't the best time to tell him, but there would be no best time, and perhaps he would be too emotionally exhausted now to have the energy to blow his top. 'Papa, I have something to tell you.'

He looked at her.

'I'm going to have a baby.'

She could feel his body tensing again and braced herself.

'Who?'

'Lew.'

'That boy? He's mad in the head. He's got nothing.'

He searched the room as if for something to help him. She waited for him to start shouting, but nothing happened. His whole body, which had been tensing and urging forward, suddenly deflated, his head sinking back against the armchair.

'*Mama mia*,' he murmured, letting out a long breath. Staring up into the ceiling, he added softly, '*É la volontà di Dio. La vita che era tolta è restituita. Basta.*'

He kissed Annie's forehead. 'Does the boy know?'

Stunned by this reaction, it took her a second to respond. 'I told him.'

'What he say?'

'Says he loves me.'

'What your mama say?'

'Haven't told her. I'm going to tell her now. Stay here, Papa.'

Annie hurried upstairs and into her parents' bedroom. She could hardly believe how her dad had reacted and felt oddly disappointed. Her mom was snoring lightly. She rubbed her arm.

Waking with a start, her mom looked around and said, 'Where your dad?'

'Downstairs.'

'Is it Frank?'

'No, nothing like that. I got to tell you something.'

Her mom switched on the lamp beside the bed and sat up. 'What is it, honey?'

'I'm going to have a baby.'

Her mom just stared at her.

'It's Lew. I told him. He wants to marry me.'

Frowning fiercely, her mom took hold of Annie's arm. 'Honey, get your shoes on, we go for a walk.'

'What?'

'It works. It works for my friend Myla. Is not unholy, is natural. We just keep walking, tire you out, walk all night, tire you out. Don't eat. It works, get rid of . . . get rid of it. It won't hurt you. Is natural. God forgives. You just get tired and get rid of it. Just a bit of blood, that's all.'

Her mom tried to get out of bed, but Annie took hold of her. 'No.'

'Oh, honey,' her mom said, her body still tense. 'There's more boys in the world than this crazy one and this black boy. You so beautiful. This boy, he's crazy. Got no family, no money. What about college? You go to college, meet handsome man who's going to be rich, look after you and be intelligent and have conversations with educated people. From somewhere nice with a nice family. This boy, he not even finished high school. He not going nowhere.'

'He got a job with Saul Hirsch.'

'That Jew will work him to the bone, won't pay him nothing.'

'Lew's a Jew; his mom was a Jew.'

Her mom snatched up the sleeve of Annie's nightdress, tugging it furiously. 'You know what the Jews did? You know what the Jews are like? They destroy Europe. They destroy everything. Rats. They should have killed them all at the start; they shouldn't have waited. They should have killed every one.'

Annie had never seen her mom like this. She looked crazy, her eyes wide, spit gathering at her lips. While her dad's fury was merely gesture and sound – a gas no sooner ignited than used up – this was deep and real, like fire in a vein of coal, burning underground for generations. For all his posturing, her dad could never hurt anyone. But here was a woman who could kill people, who *wanted* to kill people. Annie had got used to the sad woman looking out of the window, but here was a woman she had never seen, whose face was like something out of a nightmare.

She heard her dad clattering up the stairs.

He ran in. 'Frank's back,' he hissed, out of breath. 'I hear his truck. I think he's with someone. What's he bringing people back here for?'

Scared, he shut the door and joined them on the bed.

As he did so, Annie became aware that she was holding her hands over her belly, protecting what was in it. They all waited and listened, but there was no sound from downstairs, and her dad calmed a little.

'She tell you?' he said, turning to her mom, who nodded.

'*Basta.*' He raised his arms in a gesture of extravagant beneficence. 'Done is done. If is a boy, we call him Eduardo for my papa, a girl after your mama – what's your mama's name?' Her mom didn't answer. 'Anyway, we have the marriage in two weeks, nice reception in church hall. Done.' He made a gesture as of cleaning his hands.

The three of them instantly froze as a tremendous crash came from downstairs. Annie knew immediately what it was. Her mom tended to pile the dishes precariously in the dish rack. Frank had probably knocked into it and everything had slipped to the floor. They heard a woman's laughter.

Her dad, who was now crouched forward, listening, glanced back at them. 'He has a girl here.'

'Is almost two in the morning,' her mom said. 'Sal, you go down there and this girl you tell her she has to go. Tell him he can't be taking people back here.'

Her dad just stared fearfully at the door. Annie could hear Frank shushing the girl, who couldn't stop laughing. Then the sliding hinges of the liquor cabinet. A belated dish hit the kitchen floor and the girl began to laugh again.

'Go tell him,' her mom hissed, poking her finger into Sal's back. He swatted her hand away, not taking his eyes off the door.

Annie couldn't stand it any longer. She jumped off the bed, left the room and went downstairs. Frank sat in his dad's armchair with Mary in his lap, just like she and her dad minutes ago. He still had scars on his face from where they had operated to reconstruct his cheek and nose.

'You guys have got to leave,' she said. 'Mom and Dad are awake.'

'He's over twenty-one,' Mary said.

Annie felt a rush of hatred: ugly girl, ugly clean through. 'Does Cal know you're here?' She had married Cal just three months ago. He was in the navy now.

'Like he's going without,' she said.

'Annie, we're just having a drink,' Frank put in.

'You've drunk enough. That's Dad's liquor. You put that back.'

'We'll stay down here,' he said. 'We'll be quiet. Haven't got nowhere to go. Mary's mom stays up all night.'

Annie ran up to her room, pulled the biscuit tin from under her bed and took out a ten from the little pile of bills she had saved over many years.

She returned to them and put the money on the table. 'You can get a room somewhere now.'

'A room!' Mary put on a show of outrage. 'What do you think I am?'

Frank was just staring at Annie.

'Frank, you get out of this house,' she said. 'You get out of here and you don't ever come back.'

She couldn't stand to look at him any more and ran up to her room. She sat on her bed, her heart beating like crazy. If they didn't leave the house she didn't know what she was going to do. She felt as if she would attack them. But then she heard his truck start up. All at once she felt utterly bereft. She wanted her brother. Wanted to talk to him. She ran downstairs and out into the yard, but the truck had already turned on to Main. When she came back into the house, she saw that the money she had put on the table was gone.

Lewis sct an apple beside the eggs on his dad's plate. There wasn't anything else to eat. The bread he had tried to bake hadn't turned out well in the old stove. His dad examined the apple suspiciously.

'Windfalls,' Lewis explained. 'From Ruth's place. She said I could have them.'

His father put the apple aside.

'They'll just go to waste, Pop.'

Clearly he suspected charity and wouldn't eat it. He was so gaunt his head had become skull-like. His grim face never changed, as if he simply couldn't afford the energy for expression. It occurred to Lew that his dad might live to the end of his days without ever smiling again.

The coffee he had made out of grounds that had already been used a few times tasted like muddy water. He waited until his dad finished his eggs.

'I'm getting married, Pop. Annie and me – next week.'

His dad took hold of his own chin in what looked like a young child's imitation of deep thought.

'I got a job in town with Saul Hirsch. Probably live with her folks for a while before we get our own place.'

'Got nothing to give you.'

'Don't need nothing.'

'Not going to shake his hand.'

'Who? Sal?'

'I won't shake his hand.'

A tentacle scraped and Lewis quickly protected the back of his neck. The window went dark as a cloud moved across the sun.

He and his dad sat in silence for a while. At last his dad said, as if it were all he had left to give: 'You never did nothing. You never did harm Roh.'

It was the first time his dad had spoken about it since the day after it had happened, and he spoke as if it were the most simple and obvious truth. His dad wasn't looking at him. He should have been under glass in the Vatican. Cursed and conscienceless, he was like a weapon once used to murder a saint. The memory Lewis had struggled against all these years returned, as clearly as the night he had seen it: Sal flinging Roh, like a dead rat, into the river. Sal was a part of this. But was Annie? What his dad had just revealed had broken his resistance to what the deepest part of him knew was true, and all at once he understood – the child. The child growing in Annie. He got up, his chair clattering to the floor, and flung open the front door. Dark clouds, black and pink, leached the sky. They were coming. Wa-Kon-Te had never wanted to destroy him – had used him. Wa-Kon-Te was dis-em-body, exiled into immortality, into the air and the earth and the waters, in which all lived and grew and died. Wa-Kon-Te wanted no longer to exist as this field of being, to endure – changeless – all change. No longer to be life and death, but to live and to die, a single being. Lewis's whole body trembled with the clarity of it: the child. He knew it now. But if Wa-Kon-Te found a way into the mortal world through that child then all life would end, for what separated men from gods, that membrane more fragile, more lovely, more sacred than either, would break and vanish. Dreamless, we would all go mad.

Ruth was relaxing on the back porch with Fifty-Three, watching a fleet of clouds drifting across the blue sky. Her latest book was with her editor. Finally she had managed to muster enough discipline to bring Nurse Gordiano and Dr Weaver together without irony. She was, once more, the facile choreographer of all those passionate kisses, lips meeting lips in space. And what are lips, she thought, but a slightly more elaborate sphincter? Our butt lies nestled in our pants like an underdeveloped Siamese half, connected to our face-butt by an umbilical threaded through our lurid guts. As a wildly ambitious young woman, could she ever have conceived she would spend her life imagining all the ways this soft, flanged opening to the grotesque internality of a man and a woman come together? The kiss: faces reverting again to asses, going blind and deaf. *Babies! Babies! Let's make more babies!* More topsy-turvy Siamese twins, more asses searching for asses through the damp gloom of our stupidity and cupidity. Christ! Her heartbeat throbbed spongily in her head. What was wrong with her?

The back door opened and Raj emerged, followed by Nora. The sight of her hand in his sent a fissure of hurt and indignation right through her.

'Hi, Miss Winters.' Nora glanced urgingly at Raj, who was scratching his head and looking thoughtful.

Ruth felt the strain of her own smile.

'Ruth,' Raj said, as if it were an apology, 'Nor and I are getting engaged.'

'Getting married,' Nora corrected, keeping her eyes on Raj.

'Right,' he said.

'Oh,' Ruth said.

None of them spoke for a moment. Ruth knew they wanted a little more from her than 'Oh,' and when she had sufficiently gathered herself said, 'You're not getting married yet, are you? I mean you're both very young.'

'Pretty soon,' Nora said. 'I thought it might even be nice to do it at the same time as Annie and Lew.'

'But that's less than a week away.' Ruth felt suddenly panicked.

Nora stared at Raj. Clearly he was meant to be helping her with this, or at least responding to what she said with enthusiastic agreement. Instead, squatting down, he began to toy with Fifty-Three's ears.

'But Raj is going off to college,' Ruth said.

'I'm going with him.'

'But how's he going to study?'

'I'll be studying too.'

'And you're going to live on his scholarship?'

'I'll get a job if I have to. I'll support him.'

'You're not pregnant, are you?'

'Miss Winters, of course not.'

'Then don't get married. Wait.'

'Raj!' Nora called in despair.

Raj stood up. 'It'll be all right,' he murmured. 'We'll be all right.'

'Raj, what about your studies?' Ruth said. 'You're barely out of high school. Why are you getting married?'

Nora looked as if she were about to cry and Raj put his arm around her. Ruth knew she should accept this and embrace Nora, but it would have been easier for her at this moment to disembowel herself. It was all she could do not to fling this girl off the porch.

'Nor,' Raj said, 'why don't you go on home. I'll come by later.'

Nora didn't move for a moment. She was waiting for Ruth to say something, but Ruth refused even to look at her until she was heading away, and then only to throw an internal rock, stoking her fury with the sight of Nora's clumping, slew-footed walk, that body made for babies and hard work, her erect little ponytail imbuing her with all the oblivious dignity of a shitting plough horse – yes, that was the perfect description of her grace: like the least offensive kind of shitting. Her mother's voice rose shrill in her and right now she couldn't muster the strength or inclination to resist it.

Raj sat in the rocking chair beside her. Ruth felt as if she could breathe in but not out, each inhalation adding more pressure to her chest.

'What on earth are you doing?' she said. He wasn't looking at her, and his anxious profile broke her heart – her sweet, handsome, brilliant boy.

'I don't know.'

'Do you really want to marry her?'

He shook his head.

'Is that why you're getting married next week?'

Reaching down, he again rubbed Fifty-Three's ear, as if it were a talisman. 'Well, I have been meaning to broach the subject.'

'When were you planning to tell her?'

'I've been trying to tell her.'

'Then why does she think you want to marry her?'

He shrugged. 'It's not like I've been enthusiastic. I mean even when I said, "I'll marry you" I did say it almost like it was a question: "I'll marry you?"'

'This is *not* a joke.'

He sighed. 'I was even having fantasies that her dad would maim me so I could get out of it. She's a nice person. And she's brave. I mean I'm hardly the most eligible bachelor, am I.'

Taking hold of Raj's shoulder, Ruth shook him. 'Are you crazy? Are you completely crazy?'

'I don't know,' he said. 'I'm feeling kind of sad.'

'Sad?'

'It doesn't matter. I mean what does it matter who you marry?'

All at once she realized that despite how mature he seemed, he was still a child – deeply, desperately young.

'Why are you saying that?'

He shrugged again.

'Annie.' It suddenly occurred to her. 'Are you sad about Annie?'

After a moment he said, 'I'm the best man. That's ironic, isn't it. I mean that at marriages the best man is the one who *isn't* getting married.'

They were quiet for a moment. 'That's a joke,' he said. 'I don't mean I'm better than Lew.'

'You are better.'

'No I'm not. You don't know Lew. I would never have survived what he's gone through. Even if he went round murdering people, he'd be better than me.'

'That's a stupid thing to say.'

'No it isn't. He's brave—'

'Why do you keep harping on about how brave everyone is?'

'I like brave people. That's why I like Annie so much. I'm afraid of everything. I've always been afraid of everything. I don't *feel* anything properly,' he said. 'Or if I do feel it, I feel it at the wrong time.'

Ruth was still holding on to him. Her hatred for Nora had dissipated. 'You need to go to her today, right now, and you need to tell her you're not going to marry her.' He finally turned to look at her directly. 'You need to do that *right now*. For her sake. Do you understand?'

'She's like my family.'

This hurt Ruth: she felt guilty for how long it had taken her to open up to this boy, this life, for how she had treated him. In part she was responsible for how much he needed the love of others.

'You've just got to be honest. You won't lose her. You need to tell her now.'

'And by "now", you mean . . . ?'

'I mean *now*.'

He got up and ran after Nora.

Ruth waited for him on the porch. He returned more than an hour later and sat down beside her again.

He drew in and released a deep breath. 'Well, that was pleasant.'

'What did she say?'

'She said, "Whoopsy daisy, anyone can make a mistake," and we had a good laugh about it.' His hands were trembling.

'Raj, you can't give everyone what they want from you. You need to decide what *you* want.'

'What if I want to give everyone what they want from me?'

'Then there's no one here.' She poked him gently on his chest. 'There's no you.'

The shadow of a cloud swallowed the barn and eased toward them. 'Sounds perfect,' he said.

*

Annie felt absurd in her wedding gown, like a child playing dress-up, but the whole town was here in the church hall. Between the tables, children unspooled as she once had, dizzy with sly sips of beer, dervishing on the dance floor. Did they feel it as a reprieve? Did they notice Chuck Harris slap his wife's hand away as she tried to stop him refilling his glass? In all the weddings she had been to as a child, Annie wondered how many of those brides had spent their mornings like her, retching.

At the head table, her mom and dad sat to her right, Lew, her husband – *husband* – to her left with his dad, and at the end, Raj, who was engaged to Nora and would leave with her for Boston in a week. Alvin's dad – how strange to be married by him – was doing his rounds of the tables, kneeling down beside the old ladies, patting their frail, liver-spotted hands his while his wife sat grim as a zombie. Judy hadn't spoken one word since she had collapsed to the floor in the hospital. If anyone even approached her she would just stare at them hatefully. Bizarrely, though, she continued to do everything she had done before – going to church and to school-board meetings – though she remained silent and baneful throughout.

Annie just wanted this day over. Lew and his dad seemed antsy. Lew wore a hired suit paid for by Saul as a wedding gift, while his father was in a suit that looked, as her mom had put it, as if it had been stolen off a corpse. Clyde had come late, refusing to acknowledge her parents and ignoring her dad's proffered hand. She thought her dad would be mad, but he wasn't. He was being strange, kept saying it was God's will that she should marry this boy, bear his child.

Olenka and Pela were lurking suspiciously near the stack of wedding gifts. Nora seemed out of sorts, sticking with her family. Evy hadn't come, though her mom and dad were here, as well as her sisters, huddled around the smoking cauldron of their ashtray. Frank, drunk already, sat at a small table toward the back with a frowzy, skinny woman in a low-cut dress. He had met her in a bar in KC. Mary, who was sitting with Cal, on leave from the navy, kept glancing at this girl.

Her dad tapped his glass with his knife, and the room quieted. Grinning, he stood.

'*Bienvenuto!* Annie, she is my daughter – so I'm told – and I'm so glad to get rid of her.' He laughed. 'I say this because – a funny story – I went to a wedding of a cousin many years ago and her old papa who didn't speak English so good meant to say he had joy to give his daughter away into such a good family but kept saying how glad he was to get rid of her to these people. It was very funny and everyone laughed. Annie, as you can see, got her good looks from me' – he smiled at her mom – 'particularly her hair.' He polished his receding hairline. A few people laughed. Childishly encouraged, he added, 'And her breasts.' The room went quiet. He cleared his throat. 'Anyway, today I am glad to give her away into the Tivot family. It was not so long ago, as many of you may remember, that my son-in-law he tried to kill me with a shotgun. But why let such a little thing get in the way?' He clearly meant this as a joke, but no one laughed. Annie couldn't believe he had brought it up. She saw her mom tugging at his belt. Clearing his throat again, he put on a serious face. 'There is much tragedy in Lewis's family. I know tragedy: my own papa, he ended up crippled, in a wheelchair, not able to speak. And I know that over a certain . . . tragic accident with Lewis's brother, blame and accusation was thrown—'

The loud scrape of chair legs over the wooden floor interrupted him as Lew's father got up and walked out.

'Dad, that's enough,' Annie said.

Though he looked anxious and confused, her dad didn't seem able to stop. 'But no, you understand, what I'm saying is . . . is this wedding—'

Bennet stood up. 'Let's raise our glasses to Annie and to Lewis: lifelong happiness,' he announced.

As the crowd murmured the toast, there was a squeal followed by a loud crash from the back. The table at which Frank and his girl were sitting had been tipped over. Frank was circling a bottle of beer above his head in mockery of the toast.

The atmosphere was just poisoned, and for a second Annie felt like telling everyone to go home. But another glass rang with a tapping knife and Raj stood up.

The room settled as he began. 'Annie was the first person I met when I got to Pisgah. She was convinced, I later found out, that I was a young Indian maharaja who'd been kidnapped. Was she going to save me? Well . . . no. She was going to get Frank to save me. This tells you a great deal about Annie: her desire to help, her amazing imagination, and her inclination to delegate the actual hard and dangerous work to others.'

A few people laughed.

'In our first meeting I knew it, as I know it now: *this girl is in charge*. She scolded me for not being able to climb trees as well as she could; convinced me there were certain Australian spiders that wore eyeglasses. She was the only one who ever survived our childhood battles, all of which were conceived and orchestrated by her. If Annie wasn't with us – Nora, Alv, Lew and me – well, we'd be at a complete loss. Even if she were gone for just a day, we'd sit around like nostalgic old people, remembering her. And it didn't escape me that there was one among us who was always treated a little differently. Not that Lew got to survive our childhood games, but I noticed that while I would die face down in a muddy ditch, Lew would always breathe his last in Annie's arms. It soon became clear to Nora, Alv and me that almost all our games culminated in Lew, in one way or another, falling into Annie's arms. In her imagination, while the three of us were treacherous varmints, dispatched with a flick of her blade, Lew was a noble and courageous adversary, who would succumb to her – of course – only after a monumental battle, at the end of which he would . . . fall into her arms, be held tight, praised, and kissed honourably upon his pale cheek.

'So now the game continues and we treacherous varmints – dear Alvin from his place, Nora and me from ours – will continue to watch their struggle. They've fallen into each other's arms for good. As in those childhood games, there is always death in life. We mourn as we celebrate; and today we celebrate as we mourn some other Annie and some other Lewis, who lived among us not an hour ago. In their place, here, *this* Annie and Lewis, whom we shall need to get to know again – as a man and a woman, a husband and a wife, and, if they are so blessed, as a mother and a father.

'Where I was born in India' – he raised his glass – 'there is a toast at weddings, which is given just after we have sacrificed the ugliest person in the village. The full toast is "May the sun-dried dung of the water buffalo burn ever fragrantly in your hearth." But through the centuries it became simply and poignantly: "Fresh dung." So, Lew, Annie, my dear friends, fresh dung!' A murmur went through the hall as everyone repeated this. 'Fresh dung.'

Raj sat down.

The Reverend Hewitt got up. There was an audible deflation in the room.

'I will make this brief,' he said. 'I lost my son, and I wondered why God had afflicted me with this.' His wife sat like the carved embodiment of Reproach beside him. 'And I realized it was so that I could serve you all better, that through Alvin's . . . I hesitate at this, but I'm going to say it, *sacrifice*, I am given to you all, truly, as a father. Our Lord lost a son. I, too, lost a son, and while that loss was man's gain, so this loss is in some small way *our* gain. For I am rendered up to you, through the fires of grief, as His pure instrument. So I stand here proud father to Annie and to Lewis, and I extend the blessing of our Lord upon this union.' He raised his two hands out in this blessing. 'In the name of the Father, the Son, and the Holy Ghost . . .' Half the room murmured with him, 'Amen,' the more drunken half, 'Fresh dung.'

He remained with his arms out for a moment, a strange look of simpering pity playing over his face, and it seemed very much as if he were working himself up to another speech. From somewhere someone shouted, 'The cake. Cut the cake.'

The cake was hurriedly wheeled out.

Strangely enough, it was at this moment, with the two of them clutching a murderous carving knife above that ridiculously innocent cake, that it really struck Annie that she was married to Lew. All the possibilities for her future, which had drawn her like the West, were gone. She was to remain in the Midwest, neither pilgrim nor pioneer, would never see the Pacific into which the sun set. She would have a child and live in this town. Around her some of the women cried, even those in miserable marriages. A bride touched them to something profound, incorruptible, to which Annie could not connect herself. This made her feel unnatural, an impostor.

When the cake was cut, everyone got back to their eating and drinking. Tomorrow, she thought, they will be heaving on their toilets. She saw Maud, flushed and merry, laughing with Ruth, and thought of Magnus, waiting for her in his little cabin, like some horrifically large baby bird a child keeps in a shoe box. Miss Kelly slapped and pistonned her knees in naïve anticipation of the music as the band warmed up, a gob of icing upon her lip. There, barefoot and dreamy, Otto's benighted daughter, Shannon, who would always be the Raped Girl. And right next to Annie, her mom, over whom a lazy, sensual, suggestiveness was draped like a steamed towel, who was a cleavage in a dirty robe, out of which rose the scent of perfume and cigarettes and sweat and sour milk. But at the heart of that soft flesh, hard and bitter as a pit, was the woman who wished the Nazis had finished the job. Perhaps that's why the crying women troubled Annie so much. Weren't those who were capable in the midst of their miserable, married lives to cry with joy at a bride also the ones who leered and grinned with delight beneath the lynched men? They needed only the right sign to release a ready passion. And yet Annie felt insubstantial beside them. They were the weight of water, not the wave. Why was life so hard? She loved her mother, she loved her father, she loved her brother, but they were cowards. *Cowards*, and she wanted to forgive herself enough for not being quite human, for being the hollow bride, to allow herself the emotional right to look at them and think, *cowards*. But this was not what a girl was meant to be thinking about on her wedding day.

The band began. She and Lew had the first dance and the rest then flooded on to the floor. After a little while, Annie noticed that Nora wasn't dancing and looked miserable, so she went over and took the seat beside her.

'Are you all right?' she said.

Nora nodded unconvincingly.

'What's wrong?'

'Me and Raj broke up.'

'What? Why?'

'Said he wasn't ready. Miss Winters hates me. I bet she told him to.'

'I'm so sorry.' Though Annie rubbed Nora's shoulder and said as many encouraging things as she could think of, she couldn't quell a sense of exhilaration: Raj was no longer engaged. A ridiculous and selfish hope returned to life, a venial hope she knew, but couldn't help feeling. All at once she adored Nora, adored everyone.

'I'm going to be an old maid,' Nora declared miserably.

'No you won't.' Shifting her chair closer, Annie put her arms around her friend's neck. 'If I were a boy I'd marry you right now. You're so wonderful and beautiful and scrumptious and delicious and gorgeous.'

Nora squirmed and finally laughed as Annie gently bit her ear. Annie released her and they both looked out at the crowd. Miss Kelly was dancing with Morton's ten-year-old boy, who was mirroring as best he could her strange, jerky movements. Raj was teaching a bunch of the little children a bizarre dance. Squealing with delight, they all flapped their arms, rolled their heads, wiggled their behinds and shook their legs out. Nora's mom danced with her husband in as dignified a manner as she could, though she had to bend almost double to accommodate his considerable belly.

Nora leaned over to Annie. 'You know my dad forgot my mom the other day.'

'What?'

'He's done it a few times now. When he came back from town, I asked him where Mom was and he says, "Oh crap, I left her in Snyder's."'

'Is he still being weird to you?'

'That's all over now.'

'Did you talk to him?'

Nora nodded.

'What did he say?'

She shrugged. 'It's over now. He won't do it again.'

Walter Novus appeared in front of them, a hulking boy with big, sad eyes. Annie had noticed him being pushed in their direction by his two brothers. He asked Nora to dance. As Nora followed him, she turned back, and Annie gave her a wink. Glancing around the hall again, she saw Lew sitting on his own. He had clearly been watching her, and when their eyes met he hooked his finger into his shirt collar and made a funny face, as if it were strangling him. My husband. He is my husband. All at once she was flooded with love, guilt, admiration and pity. Under power of this she went over and led him to the dance floor. In his arms she felt happy, for the first time today, a part of all this: this was her town, these her people, and at this moment she didn't want to be anywhere else in the world but here, dancing with this man, whom she deeply loved, would always love. And yet at some level she understood that this feeling existed only because she also adored the Indian boy, now leading not only children but dozens of adults in his kooky Indian village dance: he was free again, was, for now, hers again. Her mom was dancing with her dad, her brother with his new girl, and the word *coward* had become a mere expedience to give her enough traction to get across a slippery place, from her moment of doubt to faith. Bennet danced with his wife, their three daughters danced in a closed circle, and happiness played over everyone like the sun, the horror gone. She caught sight of Pela and Olenka moving around the abandoned tables like crows, stealing the candles and party favours. The Yosts' youngest boy had been assigned to watch them in case they took off with someone's coat, as they had at Mary and Cal's wedding. The sight of the boy, who was leaning against a wall with a face straight out of Dick Tracy, made her laugh, and in the arms of Lew, whom she loved, she felt as if she would dissolve in happiness.

Then she noticed that Nora had sat down again and was doing all she could to not cry. Her mom was dancing with Bennet, Goldwin was looking over at Ruth with a face like a hurt child, and while Cal had gone to the bathroom, Mary was saying something fiercely to Frank, which he was ignoring. Why did she notice these things? She wanted to be happy, wanted only the dancing and dresses, the surface, Lew's undeniable beauty, the sun in the leaves, the sun on the water, glitter and glamour, mindless light in that place where there is no time, where nothing grows old, nothing changes, nothing dies.

When Ruth and Raj returned home after the wedding, there was a strange truck in the driveway. A man descended from the porch as they got out of Ruth's Model A. Waving, he called her name. He had an English accent.

When she got close enough to make out his face, her heart skipped, and all she could think to say was, 'It's not Haig, is it?'

He shook her hand. 'The anti-Haig in all my diabolical glory. Warren.' He shook Raj's hand.

Part of the shock was because he looked so much like Oliver, but she knew who this was, this tall man with the thick, coppery hair and moustache, his eyes shifty and empty.

'So this is the boy?' He winked at Ruth as if this were all part of some tremendous joke.

'This is Raj,' she said. 'Warren?'

'Gerard,' he admitted. 'I *was* Gerard. Got fed up with it. Everyone called me Gerry. Bad association since the war.'

'Were you in the war, then?' Raj said.

'Was I in the war?' Now he gave Ruth a look of amused reproach, as if she knew everything about him and had simply failed to pass it on. 'You could say that.'

'Do you know who this is?' She turned to Raj, who shrugged with guilty ignorance. 'This is your father.'

'Oh,' Raj said.

'Guilty.' Gerard raised both hands in submission. 'Guilty as charged.' He kept his eyes on her as he said this, only glancing at Raj. Raj was clearly helpless and also looked to her, as if she might be able to save him.

'Well, let's go in,' she said. 'Let's have some tea.'

'Long as it's hot,' Gerard said. 'Bizarre thing' – he slapped Raj on the back as they ascended the stairs and stage-whispered – 'not only do they bring you the tea cold and without milk, they put ice in it. Deuced barbarians.'

Raj laughed, shedding years with each passing minute. Though as tall as his father, he was stooping and gazing up at that man with a helpless, eager, confused expression.

They all sat at the kitchen table. Ruth put on the kettle and gave Gerard a piece of apple pie, which he devoured as if he hadn't eaten in days.

'Got something for you,' he said to Raj. 'There's a suitcase in the truck – go and fetch it for me, there's a good lad.'

As soon as Raj left, Gerard said, 'I'm sorry about Oliver.'

'That was a long time ago,' she said. 'The graveyard's just a couple of miles down the road if you—'

'Oh, sure,' he cut her off, 'I'll get the directions. Listen, Ruth, I was wondering if—'

Raj came back in with a battered leather suitcase. Out of breath, he had clearly run as fast as he could. He looked eight years old.

'Raj has won a scholarship to MIT,' she said as he rejoined them at the table. 'Best scholarship they have.'

'Is that right.' Gerard opened the suitcase. 'I'll tell you, his mother's good looks and my brains.' He laughed and Raj laughed with him.

On the table in front of Raj he put down a large boomerang. 'Had one of the natives – aboriginals, they're called – make it for you. There's a story painted across it – see there. Came to him in a dream. It's about you.'

Raj examined the paintings on the boomerang. 'What's the story?'

'Oh, he told me. Funny-looking chap, I'll tell you. And the whiff off him would poleaxe a donkey, good Lord.' He helped himself to another enormous slice of the pie.

The kettle had boiled. Ruth brought the tea to the table and sat down.

'MIT's one of the best universities in the country,' she said. 'If not the very best for what Raj is doing.'

'Is it now?' He raised his eyebrows. She wanted him to say more, but he didn't and they fell silent.

'How's Haig?' she asked.

'Tell you the truth, I've been out of touch. Been all over the shop. His girl—'

'Cecilia,' Raj said.

'That's her. Wrote to me for a while. Sweet girl. Seemed to think I was a pirate or something. Wanted to know where you were.' He pointed at Raj. 'Guess Haig wouldn't tell her.'

Raj looked stricken. 'Maybe I can write to her.'

'They moved. Moved somewhere. She'll be all grown up now, anyway.'

For a moment Gerard looked tired and serious, and she caught a glimpse of the bitter and dissolute actor behind the scenes.

'I should leave you two to talk,' she said, getting up. 'I'm sure Raj has a lot of questions for you.'

'Oh, look here, Ruth' – he reached over as if prepared to physically pull her back down – 'can't stay long. There's a train coming through here at one. That truck – some chap just lent it to me. Can you believe that? I mean I get off the train, ask where your place is, and this farmer chap says I can take his truck long as I get it back to town by tomorrow morning. But listen, Ruth, I wondered if Oliver . . . if you have his papers, documents?'

'I don't know,' she said. 'I guess they'd all be in the attic somewhere.'

'I could help you look.' He went to stand up, but she put her hand on his shoulder.

'You stay here. I'll go and have a look.'

She went into the attic. All Oliver's papers were in a lap desk in the corner. It amazed her suddenly that she had never really looked through this stuff. There was his passport and birth certificate, and then she came upon a deed for some land in San Francisco, signed jointly by him and Gerard. She returned.

'The crocs are huge,' he was saying to Raj, 'jump right out at you.' He looked up at her eagerly.

'I'm sorry, I couldn't find them.'

'I could have a look,' Raj said.

'Yes . . . the boy can help you. I mean I have a little time.'

It was clear by his hesitation and the way he said *the boy* that he had forgotten his own son's name.

'I have a feeling I sent all that stuff to Haig.'

'I don't think so,' he said. 'I mean . . . we could just go up there now.'

'It's not up there,' she said sharply and sat down.

They were all quiet for a while. Gerard raked his fingers through his hair a few times, staring at her in a way that wasn't exactly pleasant. For just a second she wondered what he was capable of.

He checked his watch. 'Better get going.' He stood. 'You don't even have his passport? Nice for me to have that as a sort of a keepsake.'

'Don't have anything.'

He nodded.

She and Raj walked him out to the truck. Raj was holding the boomerang. Opening the driver's side door, Gerard threw his suitcase over into the passenger seat.

'Well, it was a pleasure, Ruth.'

She nodded.

'We could send you the stuff if we find it,' Raj said. 'Do you have an address?'

'Between things right now,' he said, 'but I'll send you the address soon as I'm settled. Heading west.' He pointed east and patted Raj's shoulder with that same hand.

'You going to take over this farm, then?' he asked, raking his fingers through his hair again.

'I'm heading off to college,' Raj said. 'MIT in Boston.'

'College, eh? Good. You keep that up.' He winked at her, smiling as if Raj were in kindergarten and saying he was going to be a train driver.

'I could come down to the station with you,' Raj said.

'No, no. No need for that.'

He got into the truck, pulled the door shut, saluted with one finger and drove off.

They both stood in the driveway for a little while, Raj holding the boomerang in both hands. Finally she put her arm around his shoulders and guided him back to the house.

'I forgot to ask him about my mom,' he said.

She didn't know how to respond. She was furious at that man and heartbroken for Raj, but felt that the last thing he would want was for her to start crying. Or maybe that was just the last thing she would want if she were in his place.

He raised the boomerang a little. 'Aaron's got one like this.'

'Aaron does?'

'His uncle sent it to him. It's exactly the same. Got the same pictures on it too.' Raj was raking his fingers through his hair just as his father had been doing. 'Didn't work, either.'

Nora was practising CPR on her mom, who was lying on the sitting room carpet. Her dad sat on the couch reading the *St Louis Star*.

'You're not going to push too hard, are you?' Her mom crossed her arms over her chest.

'Lie still,' Nora chided. 'I've got to check your mouth first, see if your throat's clear.'

The doorbell rang. Heaving himself up and going down the hall, her dad answered it, speaking softly to whoever it was.

'Is it a salesman?' her mom asked Nora.

Shrugging, Nora called to her dad, 'Who is it?'

He had already closed the door. 'Mormons,' he said, returning to the couch and taking up the paper again.

Nora had an odd feeling – the way he had held the front door almost shut and how quietly he had spoken. She got up.

'What are you doing?' he said. 'Your mom's dying here.'

She hurried to the front door, her dad following. Opening it, she caught a glimpse of Raj turning on to the road. As she bent down to slip on her flats, her dad's arms slid around her.

'Get off me, Dad.' She struggled, but he was too strong. 'Get off!'

'All he said was goodbye. He just came to say goodbye.'

'Get *off* me.'

As if this were a game, he began to hum, lifting her up and carrying her back into the sitting room.

'Mom,' she shouted, 'get him off me.'

Her mom lay on the floor as if paralysed, looking fearfully up at them. 'Karl,' she appealed softly. 'Karl, please.'

Nora still hadn't touched the ground, her dad waltzing around the room with her, singing, 'Who's me little sack-a-potatoes? Who's me little sack-a-potatoes?'

He had pinned her arms to her chest, but she got a good blow on his shin with her heel. Cursing, he wrestled her face-down on to the couch. She could hardly breathe, his whole weight on her.

'He just said goodbye.' His mouth was pressed to her ear. 'I said I'd pass it on.'

Suddenly her dad's body bore down on hers as if he himself had been pushed and his arms were wrenched free. She struggled out from under him, falling almost on top of her mom, who still lay on the floor helplessly. Her brother had taken hold of her dad, trapping his arms behind his back. Jude looked terrified, her dad cursing and struggling. Nora quickly ran out.

She caught up with Raj a little way down the road.

'Are you all right?' he said, looking concerned as she approached.

She realized there were tears on her face. 'Yeah.'

'Your dad said you were out – among other things.'

'He's just such a jerk,' she said. 'Look I've got to get back. I'm worried about my brother.'

'Your brother?'

'It doesn't matter. When are you leaving?'

'Tomorrow.'

'I'll come to the station.'

'No, I'm leaving really early.' He hesitated. 'My dad came.'

'What?'

'My dad. Turned up after the wedding. Brought me a boomerang.'

'Your real dad?'

'Yeah. Never seen him – not that I can remember. He was waiting at Ruth's house. I think he just came because he wanted some papers he thought Ruth had. Don't think he even remembered my name.'

She didn't know what to say. It was too much for her to take in and respond to right now. 'I have to go.'

'I'll write to you.'

'I'm not very good at writing.'

'Doesn't matter. I'll write to you and you write to me when you can.'

They stared at each other. She wished she could think of the right thing to say, but she was panicked about her brother.

'Remember,' he said, 'I'm not without skills. If you ever want me to perform a Fourier transformation on any ordinary differential equation, I'll fix that right up for you no charge. Don't even think of going anywhere else.' He tapped his chest. 'I'm your man.'

She couldn't really understand what he was saying. She took hold of him, embracing him hard. 'I love you,' she said. 'I'm glad you came here.'

'You're my favourite among all my children,' he whispered, 'but don't tell anyone.'

Releasing him, she began to run back to her house. He called after her, 'When you become a nurse I'll make sure to get really sick.'

In the sitting room, her dad was reading his paper on the couch as if nothing had happened. Her mom hadn't moved and looked like a laid-out corpse.

'Where's Jude?'

Her mom pointed toward the kitchen.

Her brother was rinsing his bloody mouth at the sink. 'Looks worse than it is,' he said.

She didn't know what to say and pushed herself up beside him, sliding an arm around his waist. He put his arm around her shoulders and together they stared out of the window above the sink into the garden.

Annie was scrubbing the wooden floor of the apartment above the insurance office. Saul had told her and Lew that they could use it as long as they wanted. It was just three rooms: the main room, with a Murphy bed and stove; a closet-sized kitchen; and a tiny bathroom.

Lew was working downstairs in the office, and she had been cleaning almost manically for hours, trying to exhaust her despair.

There was a knock against the jamb of the open door and she looked up to see Raj. She stood, wiping her chapped hands on her apron.

'Lew said you were up here. He's looking all smart in his suit down there.'

'I'm sorry,' she said. 'We haven't really got anywhere to sit yet.' She pulled one of the two chairs out from the little table for him and sat on the bed.

'I've just come to say goodbye,' he said.

'We'll come to the station.'

'No, no, it's too early. Four in the morning. Better to say goodbye now.' He sat on the creaking chair.

'How's the baby?'

'It's nothing but a feeling of sickness right now.'

'My dad came to visit.'

'What?'

'My real dad. He was at the house after your wedding. Came and went.'

'Why? What did he come for? What did he say?'

'Didn't say anything, really. Wanted some of his brother's papers, I think. Brought me a boomerang. Couldn't remember my name.'

'Did you ask him about your mom?'

'Didn't get a chance, really. He was in a hurry.'

'What a damn jerk.' She wanted to put her hand on his or something, but she had set the chair too far away. Drumming his fingers absently against his lips, he was glancing around the room. She felt ashamed at how small and bleak it was.

'So tell me about him. What did it feel like to—'

'I'll write you about it,' he said. 'Not sure what I think right now.'

'Write often and write good letters,' she said. 'I'll write you good letters, though there's probably not going to be a lot going on here.'

'And my life studying physics is going to be real exciting.'

'It will be. You'll be in a big city. You'll meet all kinds of new people.'

'Bunch of nerds like me.'

She couldn't stand it any more. 'You're sitting too far away.'

He went to shift his chair closer, but she put her hand on the bed beside her. 'Sit next to me.'

He did so. They were both leaning forward as if they had stomach aches. Annie kept her eyes on Raj. She wanted to remember him as well as she could before he left. He seemed to understand this, submitting himself by looking off into the room. She felt a roiling pressure inside her. She wanted to be unreasonable, to tell him it wasn't fair that he could just get to leave her like this. She wanted him to admit that he wouldn't be happy for one minute without her. God, it felt as if it were happening even now: they were already becoming strangers, would soon have nothing to say to each other. She was just a high-school graduate, married and pregnant at eighteen, and staying here. All at once she felt a little flicker of fury at him. Wouldn't it be easier to cut it off now than to feel that connection slowly die? Foolish, hysterical thoughts, she knew. Bravely, in silence, he offered his vulnerable profile to her like someone yielding to being irrationally beaten. But yielding only because the other person – she – was essentially powerless.

At last he turned to her, but after all she had been feeling she couldn't look at him directly.

'I'll be back at Thanksgiving.'

She didn't respond. If she didn't say anything, he couldn't go, and she wanted to hold on to him for just a little while longer.

'Remember I'm not without skills,' he said. 'If you ever want me to perform—' He stopped.

'Perform what?'

'Nothing.'

'All right.' She stood up, her voice abrupt, almost cold. She couldn't stand this any more. 'You write to me.' She embraced him, but was still unable to meet his eyes.

'I'll write to you pronto pronto,' he said, and she couldn't help but hear the upsurge in his tone, as if he were happy to be released.

She nodded and he was gone.

Lewis was updating Saul's customer list, crossing off the customers who hadn't paid their premiums for more than three months. Raj had gone upstairs to say goodbye to Annie.

The abrupt sound of a chair scraping across the floor above his head gave him a shock, and as he glanced down at the name he had just crossed off – Walter Spetz – he knew this man would die. He flung down the pen. Stupid. He examined all the names he had crossed off. How could he have forgotten who he was, the power he had? Dead. He had killed them all. Dear God. Another sound from upstairs, the creak of the bed. *Lewis. Lewis of the ville. The slugger. Out of the park. Home run!* He knew Kane wasn't really here, but he had been standing there in the corner of the office for a while, picking at his bad teeth. The baby. If he could just hold out until the baby came. He didn't care then what happened to him. He would go to the river, drift free, be eaten by a thousand fish, would enter that new life of scattering and being together at once, like starlings above the fields; to be, at last, the living membrane between the all and the one, the temple ruins and the bone doll, the world-will and the wandering way.

Annie. Annie was unhappy. He clutched his own head. He wished he could tear it open, rip all the knots out of his mind. He didn't want any of this. He wanted to be normal. He heard Raj coming back down the stairs.

'All right, buddy,' Raj said, entering. 'I'll be back at Thanksgiving.'

Lew got up and Raj embraced him. He wanted to say something to his friend but couldn't think what.

'Come visit me,' Raj said. 'It's not far.'

'I can't stop thinking awful things,' he said.

'What awful things?'

He wanted to tell Raj that he couldn't stop killing, that he was the death of life. *You kill me*, Kane shouted from the corner. *You slay me. You made a killing off of me, slugger. Lewis. Lewis of the ville. Out of the park. Home run!*

When he turned back to his friend, Raj was staring with confusion into that corner.

'When I come visit, we can go to a Sox game.'

'What awful things?' Raj said.

'Nothing. I'm just worried, you know. It'll be all right when the baby's born.'

Raj stared at him, searching. Kane kept shouting from the corner and he was trying not to look.

'Listen,' Raj said, 'I know you have a good job here and everything, but couldn't you and Annie come and live in Boston, near me? There are lots of jobs there. Remember you said once when we were kids that we'd all live in the same house.'

'It was Annie said that.'

'Are you feeling all right? If you want me to stay I'll stay.'

'No, no. We're proud of you, Annie and me. Worry is all. It'll be all right. When the baby's here everything will be fine.'

*

Ruth adjusted the collar of Raj's coat as the train came to a stop. It was the middle of the night, and they were the only two on the platform.

'I like the fact that you don't cry, Ruth.'

'I'll cry later,' she said. 'I'll chop onions or something. Now, you have to call me collect when you get in. It doesn't matter how much it costs.'

He nodded.

'I want evidence,' he said.

'Of what?'

'That you cried. I want damp tissues.'

He towered more than a foot above her now, and she remembered the guarded, clever little boy who had come into her life on the day Oliver had left it. She took hold of his chin. 'Look, Raj, you're the best thing that ever happened to me and if you don't keep in touch I'm going to send the Valentine's cards you used to make me in ninth and tenth grades to every girlfriend you ever have.'

His eyes widened with horror and she kissed him on his chin. He got on to the train. As it pulled away, he made his usual funny faces out of the window. She waited in the station until she could no longer see the train or hear its dream-like lament.

1960

Dear Raj,

Just a month now from giving birth. I feel prehistoric. Ruth and I are becoming fast friends. She's going to teach me how to write romances to get a little extra money – things are tight here. We had a good laugh about the two of us writing romances. For me, as soon as the man and woman's eyes lock together passionately, the only thing that opens up is a view into their doom. Relationships seem doomed to me – Oh, I know that sounds awful, but what have I seen? Rev. Hewitt and Judy (she still hasn't spoken a word and haunts this town); Nora's parents (did you know that Nora's engaged to Walter now?); my own mom and dad, who haven't so much as looked at each other with anything resembling passion or even respect in ten years. Strange for me to see so little of myself in either of my parents. Perhaps I just don't want to. I know nothing of their pasts – just fragments, hints – and now fear knowing. I think of my baby all the time, floating inside me, inside her dream of me. She knows me better now than she ever will, my heart and my blood. I wonder if I should tell her everything, *everything*, or tell her nothing. I suppose there is some balance which will keep her in a healthy orbit (excuse me, Mr Physicist) so she won't fall into me or be flung wildly away.

As you can probably tell, I have too much time to think.

Talking of troubled couples, Magnus hasn't got out of that bed in his cabin for more than a year now. He no longer sleeps on a mattress, but on boards, covering himself only in a single coarse blanket. It makes me feel nauseous to enter that close little room, which reeks of his body. Awful to see that skull-like head, with its

swollen, bright eyes fixing so hungrily upon me. He doesn't seem
human, but like a pale snake sometimes, the shadow of an ancient
cunning flickering somewhere deep inside him. He wears nothing
but a kind of loincloth. I think he wants to look like a medieval
saint, his bones all but coming through his flesh, a huge wooden
cross hanging on the wall above him. Oh, but that awful snaky
charm, the way he ducks his head and calls me 'my dearest', pressing his dry lips to my hand – and his own hands, which clasp mine
with shocking strength, are so cold! Each week he recites poems to
me by heart – John Donne and Gerard Manley Hopkins – staring
into my eyes as if they were love poems, his breath so rotten it
makes me go weak at the knees. Just imagine it, Raj: me, hugely
pregnant and trying not to vomit, that wasted man trapping my
hands in his, reciting,

> Take me to You, imprison me, for I,
> Except you enthral me, never shall be free
> Nor ever chaste, except You ravish me.

I know I'm being cruel, but it angers me. I feel used and dirty
when I leave that cabin. I shudder to think what his imagination
does with me from one visit to the next. I spend time with Maud
then, just to feel human again – she's actually a lovely woman, with
such a capacity for joy. But it's killing her to look after Magnus,
whom I can't see as anything but a kind of parasite in her soul.
There are monsters on the earth, and he is a kind of monster, a
helpless monster. I've felt the strength in him, and yet he claims he
can't get out of bed, feed himself, or see to his own toilet. Luckily
Maud and Ruth are getting on famously. Ruth is helping her with
the business, dealing with advertising and such.

It was good to see you at Thanksgiving, though it was so brief.
You did seem different. I felt, in some ways, as I felt when Lew
came out of that awful place. By which I mean that something
essential had changed. You were carrying with you another world,

another hope – or perhaps it was simply something unavailable to me, growing in you. I loved all those wonderful imitations you did of your professors, the way you made it all seem so ridiculous and unreal, like you'd just returned from Patagonia. But this is the unreal place, the place at the heart of things, where there is no fake eccentricity instead of real madness, where, it seems to me, everything is trapped somehow, and has to struggle just not to become grotesque. Blind and blind and blind: people who have blinded themselves to survive. This is madness – which I know too well – the terrible all-seeing of self-inflicted blindness. Alvin's mother. Sometimes Pisgah seems the place where people's souls have been cut out or buried too deep inside them. That's why there is so much water here, so many swift streams to stop the ghosts from crossing. I couldn't help but feel that you probably imitated all of us too, to your new friends, that they are getting the image of some antic town full of goofy characters.

I hate to burden you with this, but I'm worried about Lew and don't know who else to turn to. He often seems to be speaking to someone passionately, angrily. Sometimes when I come down to the store, he will have sweated through his shirt, his whole body trembling, and will look at me momentarily as if he has no idea who I am. At other times he can be fine, but they seem like visits – like your visits from Boston – which deny the truth, the true place in which he has taken hold and is growing. It is the place of his passionate voice and sweating, a place where he is afire. Truer than this place. Truer than I am.

I'm selfish. I hate to be peripheral, my orbit growing ever colder. Especially with my own husband. Especially with you.

I miss you.

Annie

Dear Annie and Lew,

Annie, your visits to Magnus sound like the stuff of nightmares. Ruth has told me a little about this also. Poor Maud.

All is well here. I've made a few friends. My roommate, Craig, is an Iowa farm boy (they put the two rubes together), and my lab partner is a delightful, pixieish woman called Melissa – the only female student in our whole year. She has been engaged for a little while to one of our professors, an arrogant bore on whom I intend to model myself (I'm already growing out my nostril hair).

I am a nerd among nerds, but I do try to get myself a bit of 'kultcha' every now and then. Last week I went to see a famous poet, whose name completely slips my mind, give a lecture on 'virginity' in the nave of a vast and ornate Catholic church downtown. It was one of those entirely artificial situations: the church itself seemed like a kind of elaborate mock-up, and the event was sponsored by a group of extremely wealthy women 'concerned about questions of women's spirituality'. The lecture was a bit thin, though delivered with a flawless pretentiousness – pauses for laughter after jokes made entirely in French or Latin (the poet reminded me of a super-refined version of Alvin's dad); and the pews shone with the hair of dozens of svelte women, hair so smooth and perfectly moulded each seemed like a kind of elaborate baldness, their heads all slightly tipped, their smiles cannily amused. I felt as if I were part of an enormous and exquisitely crafted music box, the kind of thing made in the reign of Louis XIV, derived from a culture at the height of its decadence. It wouldn't have surprised me if the ornate gold-leaf roof had opened up to reveal gigantic rouged faces peering in at us, the poet's voice becoming a soulless mechanical tinkle as our own heads nodded upon their little pivots.

And last night a bunch of us went to see a zeydeco band at the Student Union. This is your basic rock and roll band with the addition of a washboard and an accordion (an accordion, as you know, is the misshapen and sterile offspring of a piano and a bagpipe, a creature with about as much soul as . . . well . . . that famous poet or Alvin's dad). It was actually quite fun, though I felt very sad for the man who played the washboard. Unfortunately a number of drunken students didn't appreciate how difficult an instrument to master a washboard is, and insisted on going onstage, removing the washboard from his neck, and playing it themselves. The numerous times this happened, the washboard player, pathetic as a shucked turtle, stood at the back of the stage looking extremely disgruntled as he listened to those philistines butchering that wonderfully subtle rasping noise that can be coaxed from a piece of corrugated tin.

I have to finish up. I have an exam on Monday and tonight one of my professors and his wife, who have somewhat adopted me, are taking me to see a play called *Zoo Story* or something. I'll tell you guys all about it in my next letter.

Love,

Raj

Dear Raj,

Despite what I thought, it's a boy. Believe it or not we still haven't come up with a name for him. Lew's father says he doesn't want the child named after him or anyone in his family. I know my dad would like him to be called Sal, but while I love my dad, Raj, I am going to admit to you that I don't admire him. My mom is insistent that he doesn't have any of the Polish names of the men in her family. She thinks it best to give him a 'normal' American name – John, Peter, Mark, Simon, Robert, etc.

You said you were thinking of coming back for the break. It would be wonderful to see you and for you to see 'baby', who has a full head of blond hair and the most alert blue eyes (nothing in him of me!). Of course we all suspect he is the most brilliant infant ever born, every frown a sign of intense thought, rather than yet another concerted effort to empty his bowels.

But I miss talking to you. I waited so long for your last letter and I have to admit I was disappointed: nothing of you, really. You were always elusive, but I used to be able to see what you were feeling at times, certainly to know if you were lying to me: few people have a face as delicately responsive as yours. I like to hear about your friends, about the things you are going to see, but it seems to me that your last letter might have been written to anyone. When I went to visit Ruth a few weeks ago, she read me out a funny section of a letter you had written to her – about that lecture in the church – and it was word-for-word what you had written to me. Or rather, to me and to Lew, as you always insist on doing. I wait for your letters with such anticipation. Lew has become as silent as his father. He seems almost afraid of Baby. I've noticed that when he has to touch Baby, he makes a strange little series of motions. He's grown a beard – a scruffy, woodsman kind of beard. There are other things also, but I feel disloyal. I don't want to burden you. I tell you because I don't know who else to tell.

Love,
Annie

Dear Annie and Lew,

I'm sorry about not making it during the break. I really had intended to come back, but have just been overwhelmed by the amount of work I have to do and this break is the only quiet time in the dorms. For some reason I can never say no to anyone and I actually agreed to go to four people's houses for dinner this week. I'm everyone's favourite orphan.

It was fun, though. On Monday it was Professor Corey Thatcher and his wife, Alice. I adore them, but they're like one two-headed creature talking at you without cessation. They finish each other's sentences. My neck gets so sore from looking into one face and then the other. Sometimes, seemingly unconsciously, she feeds him, and he eats unconsciously, as if they don't really differentiate between their digestive systems. It's strange – both enviable and horrifying – to be with people who've been together so long.

Wednesday was dinner at the home of my friend Pierce. Boston blue-bloods. A vast house right in the middle of town with twelve bedrooms. His father, a banker of some kind, just looked as if he wished everyone would go away, while his mom, a professional

socialite, not only remembered my name but also everything that
Pierce had ever told her about me. She even asked after you and
Lew, believe it or not. She is one of those women who have so
perfected their reactions and expressions that with every moment
you spend with her, you feel yourself becoming increasingly handsome, intelligent and witty. She spoke to me with such seeming
intimacy, holding my hand and pulling me into a dark corner of the
room to tell me about the trouble she had with the eggnog as if she
were arranging a tryst. For that brief period she showered upon me
the glamour of the gods, but the instant she was gone, I de-evolved
once more into the lurching swamp-creature I actually am. The
very form of intimacy without anything of the substance. Again,
wonderful and horrifying.

Then to Rachel's house. I can't remember if I've ever told you
about Rachel? I met her in the Student Union. She had been to
India and just came up and started talking to me. Her family's
Jewish, but not very Orthodox. Her father's a lovely man who does
something in textiles. Her mom's job is to be cruel to Rachel –
Rachel warned me. Horribly critical all the time. Her mom seems
obsessed with her. Whenever I glanced at her mom, her mom was
staring hawkishly at Rachel. It's as if she's in love with her and
hates her for it. Rachel told me that her mom lost her family in the
war and spent some years in a concentration camp. I noticed that
she didn't eat any of the cake she gave us, but polished off the
crumbs on our plates. Rachel reminds me a little of you. She has
hair like yours, long and curly and very dark. But she's rather
fierce. Like her mother she can't stand stupid people and makes no
attempt to hide her impatience or contempt. She's very smart, but
I'm not sure how imaginative she is. It's as if she perceives
Imagination as the idle, alluring brother of Intellect, a brother who,
if he ever got hungry, would sell his birthright for a bowl of lentil
stew. Which, of course, he would.

And Sunday I had cocktails with Professor McAlister. It was all
professorial types. Horribly pretentious: people speaking in fake

English accents. His four children had formed a string quartet. They all talked like adults (little prigs), the youngest – six years old – frowning as he spoke to me, and saying, 'Joking aside, Mr Travers . . .' All he needed was a little pipe and a fake moustache.

Anyway, summer I'll definitely be back. Can't wait to see little . . . ?
Love,
Raj

Dear Raj,

Thanks for your concerned note. I'm sorry for not writing back to you for so long. I have to admit I don't know how to respond to your letters, which are general comic set-pieces and not part of a conversation. Your last letter made me angry to the point of despair. How careful you are to make me feel you're not enjoying yourself, that everyone around you is silly and grotesque. And you're doing it because you pity me. You're trying to show me that you are not quite in that world, when I know you are. You are. And to pretend you're not is dishonest and condescending. You even insult the people you like because you think it will make me feel better somehow.

'I can't remember if I've ever told you about Rachel.' How can you not remember? Since you left, apart from this last month, I've written to you every week. You have written to me exactly four times. I have the four letters spread out on the table in front of me. I have looked over them again and again for something personal, meaningful, for something that speaks of you to me. And there is meaning there I suppose – the horror of the couple who have been together for ever, the socialite's empty intimacy, Rachel's hair.

Lew has lost his job. For some reason he destroyed a whole bunch of documents and refused to type out any names because he seemed to believe he was killing them. Saul has been so kind and has let us stay in the apartment. Last Tuesday I couldn't find Baby. Lew was in the kitchen. He had put Baby in a cupboard and was leaning back against the cupboard, crying. He said he didn't know how to protect him and didn't know what to do with a child who was here to destroy us all. I immediately took Baby to my parents' house, where I am staying now. I go to see Lew during the day. Everyone has been trying to convince me to have him committed, but the thought of sending him back to such an awful place, of betraying him, horrifies me. Everyone looks at me with pity here, though I sense that many of the women are pleased in some way, seemed to feel that I needed or deserved to be brought low.

I'm sorry to hear from Ruth that you're probably not coming back in the summer either. She's with you now, I know. She's actually talking about buying a place in Boston. I'd hate to lose her too.

Love,
Annie

Dear Annie,

I'm sorry. I'm so sorry about Lew, so sorry about not coming back. If there was some way I could send you my silence, could express how much I miss you without it seeming – I don't know – inappropriate, I guess. If I could convince you without sounding as insincere as I clearly have been sounding that not five minutes in the day goes by without me thinking about you and Lew. About you. Rachel's hair was the truest thing I spoke of in that letter.

How do I talk to you, Annie? You're married to my friend. You have a child. I've always felt so wrong, always wished I were someone else. Being in Boston is intoxicating. There are so many ambitious and compelling people here and I want to know everything about them. I want each one of them to respect me, love me. That is my flaw, I know it. You and I are very similar in that way.

How do I talk to you, Annie? How can there be any real intimacy when everything I say is a lie. Has to be a lie. Has been – necessarily – for a long while. When you told me you were pregnant and getting married, I couldn't wait to leave. You say you look forward to my letters. I dread yours. I have failed you and Lew, and you – the two of you – are everything to me. And I want to live. I want to have *this* life.

I don't really know what I'm saying. I'm going to send this to you, despite my better judgment, and I will write you a saner letter soon.

Love,

Raj

Dearest Raj,

I wanted to tell you in case Annie hasn't that Lewis has disappeared. He's been gone for more than three weeks now and is officially a Missing Person. Mrs Littleton said she saw a man up in the woods – a 'wild' man – but you know what she's like and now all those rumours about the man of the woods and his white dog have returned. I know you and Annie haven't corresponded for a few months. I don't know why. I've noticed Annie has stopped asking me about you. I asked if she was angry at you. She said she was angry at herself. She said she treated you unfairly, expected too much, and realizes now that she was depressed after the birth of the baby – who still hasn't got a name.

I really enjoyed my last trip to Boston. Rachel seems like a lovely woman and she clearly adores you. But Raj, I have to say it, she looks so much like Annie it's shocking.

I can't stand it that you two, who've spent your lives together, are so estranged. At first I wanted you to get away from everything here. Some of that was petty. I wanted you to be successful. I wanted that damn father of yours, that damn uncle, to see you recognized by the whole world. In the beginning I was afraid, afraid that Annie would trap you here. But she wouldn't do that, I know, and I think that more than anything in the world, right now, she would love to see you. Needs to see you.

All my love,

Ruth

Annie was typing out some letters for Saul. After Lew's disappear-
ance – he had been gone for close to a month now – she had returned
to the apartment and had taken over Lew's job at the insurance agency,
leaving Baby with her mom when she had to work. Her mom and
dad wanted her to remain at home, but it would have killed her to
stay any longer. She tried to go out as little as possible because she
hated the questions and pitying looks. She saw Ruth, mostly, with
whom she was collaborating on a children's book. Nora, now heavily pregnant, came round a few times a week. She had married Walter,
that sweet, near mute man with his sad blue eyes and that hulking
body he hardly seemed to know what to do with.

Every day she expected Lew to reappear, which filled her with
an intense and constant ambivalence: she wanted to know he was
safe, desperately, but his obsession with Baby terrified her. She hated
the rumours that he was naked and wild in the woods, like that
other man with his white dog. How could he survive out there? A
few times, frightened by how numbed she had become with grief
for him, she had gone to the sinkhole. There she had felt him in the
dappled light, the breathing trees, had imagined him emerging out
of the water, sun and shadow giving form to his transparent nakedness. No, not naked but nude, as on the day he had cast her into
the deep water so she would know that nothing lay between loving
and killing, his cold limbs as hard as marble, his heart the stone
heart of youth. To disperse that numb grief, she would stand at the
edge of the pool with her eyes shut, terrifying herself, feeling the
world tip and sway, his breath at her neck, his arms sliding around
her.

Most nights, between sleeping and waking, she half dreamed him
returning to her bed, smelling of the forest. He would come like the
morning at the moment the sun begins to lever the night away, birds
singing out of the day's widening. In that place he was whole and
sane. But some nights, waiting for him, something else would slip
through, from the west, sliding beneath the sheets, rising above her,
a serpent with the face of a lion, ruined wings of bone and skin.

Tearing open her neck, it would draw out the pale sinew of her soul. This, she knew, in that twilit place, was Raj.

She hadn't had any contact with Raj since his last letter, which had made her so mad and upset. At herself. What he had told her was true: she had no right to expect that kind of intimacy from him.

Unable to concentrate on her typing, she had started to stuff envelopes when she heard a knock at the back door. For a moment she remained very still. It was probably Nora, since it was mid-morning. She had begun to dread her visits. Nora spent so much time talking about Raj, reciting from heart whole sections of the funny postcards he sent her, into which Nora read all kinds of hidden meaning. It was a need that resonated too unpleasantly with her own. When the knock came again, she knew it wasn't Nora: she would have tried the door and come in.

She opened it. There, leaning casually against the jamb, stood Raj.

'Oh, there you are,' he said, as if he had just lost track of her for a second.

She could hardly speak, she felt so confused and upset. Getting hold of herself, finally, she said, 'And there *you* are.'

'*There* you are,' he repeated a little more effusively. Suddenly he looked abashed, as if they were acting out a scene and he had forgotten his lines.

She embraced him.

'Gosh, the natives are very friendly,' he said. 'Me here to bring you peace, firewater and sub-standard weaponry. In return I ask only for your land and your women.'

'When did you get back?'

'About an hour ago.'

'How long are you in town?'

Widening his eyes, he puffed out his cheeks. 'Don't know.'

'You don't know?'

'I came to look for Lew. I don't understand why they can't find him. And I wanted to see you and . . . Anonymous.'

'Baby's with Mom,' she said. 'I'll make you some tea.'

He followed her into the cramped kitchen. She put on the kettle and remained at the stove as he leaned against the fridge.

'So there's no news about Lew?'

She shook her head. 'You wouldn't have recognized him. I was so afraid for Baby. Can't imagine where he could go. I don't know how he's looking after himself.'

'How are they searching for him?'

'They just put out a missing persons bulletin, which means his picture's hanging in a few police stations. That's it.'

'Did he have any ID?'

'No. Left his wallet – everything – here.'

Raj went quiet. Clearly lost in thought, he stared absently at a damp patch above the stove. She felt a little ashamed.

'Are you just going to stay here?' he said finally.

'There's nothing wrong with here.'

'No, I didn't mean that.' Frowning as if irritated at himself, toying gently with his lips, he turned to look not so much at as into her. 'Listen, why don't you come to Boston?'

Having grown sensitive to pity, she couldn't help responding sharply. 'I have a job here.'

'Look, Annie, I don't have much, but I could—'

'Don't be ridiculous.' She cut him off. 'We're not kids. We can't live in the trees.'

He went quiet, rubbing his eyes. He looked tired, and all at once it was as if some kind of slippage had taken place, and she found herself in another life, in which she was with this man and they had been having this same argument for too long.

He went to speak, but stopped. After a moment he said, 'I have something to tell you: I met someone.'

'That girl with the hair?'

'Rachel, yes. We've been dating for a little while and about three weeks ago we decided to get married.'

Annie didn't know what to say.

'It's not fair to say that I had to convince myself she's wonderful.

She is. She's incredibly smart, and . . . brave. A good, strong person.'

Annie didn't know why he was talking like this. It was perhaps only the second or third time in all the years she had known him that he had spoken in a serious, direct, considered way.

'But I realized I was feeling sorry for her. Not because she deserves pity, but because there was no,' he searched for the word, '*focus* to my feelings for her. No' – he rubbed the knuckles of his fisted hands together – 'traction. It's hard for me because I never really felt I *deserved* anything. Certainly not to be . . . to have people feel for me. Especially people as nice as Rachel. Or Nora. Anyone. I remember that day Lew and I were playing basketball in the rain and ended up wrestling each other in the mud – I was just getting to know him. I don't think you could ever understand how happy I was. I had never had a friend before then. Ever. I was so happy I could hardly sleep for days.

'Anyway . . .' He looked annoyed, as if he'd messed up what he had intended to say. 'I don't mean we should live in the trees in Boston. I mean we could live together.' He looked utterly miserable now.

She was confused. 'Live with you and Rachel?'

'Oh no, I'm not seeing Rachel any more.'

'I'm married,' she said. Like a silly girl, her legs felt suddenly weak. 'And you're doing this because you feel sorry for me.'

'I'm not.'

'It's impossible. People will know we're not married. They'll know this isn't your baby.'

'We could try to keep him very tanned.'

'Raj, no one would rent us a room. I don't even know why I'm saying that. This is crazy. I wouldn't allow you—'

'I'm *not* doing this because I feel sorry for you. And I know it's impossible right now. And I want to find Lew and I want to make him well. But I need you to know that I'll do . . . anything for you. I'll give up school. I'll come here.'

She felt as if a pulsing current were running up her body, which she didn't quite have the strength to conduct. Why was everything so dream-like with him? She had been thinking about him and suddenly he had walked right in, as if he had never left, to become part of a dream that expressed exactly what she was feeling: he offers her everything she wants, and yet she finds she can do nothing but turn him down. What were her reasons? Lew, of course, but Lew was gone, she knew that. Even if he came back, she couldn't risk Baby with him. And pride, of course: she just couldn't believe that Raj wanted this, at this time in his life, to take on a woman with someone else's child.

'By the way' – Raj leaned in a little closer – 'did you really want me to search for ticks that time?'

She laughed. 'You're such a dumkopf.'

'Look, Annie, though I can't tell you I love you, since it isn't in my nature, I'm hoping you're perceptive enough to see that I do. When I saw you in your dad's store the first day I got here, I knew this Pigs Are Misery place wasn't going to be so bad after all. I should have asked you to marry me then.'

'You weren't talking.'

'Oh, that's right. Anyway, I'm here now. I'm going to spend every day looking for Lew. I'm going to check out skid row and every institution in the state. We're going to find him. And I guess that's all we should think about right now.'

They were quiet for a moment and he began to get embarrassed, biting his lip and taking a sudden interest in the ceiling. She embraced him, looking up into his shy face. It was so troubled and so innocent, somehow, and she was so sick of feeling thwarted, she couldn't stop herself kissing him. He was surprised, and her kiss was so brief he was hardly able to return it. Then he looked as if he were trying to think of some joke to make, but the bell in the store rang.

'I should get that,' she said.

'I've got to go anyway,' he said. 'I want to drop in on Nora.'

She nodded, brushing down her blouse and sweeping back her hair. 'Do I look okay?'

Smiling, he drawled proudly in his most egregious Southern accent, 'Little lady, you done gone look like you been savaged by a wild critter.'

Nora was knitting a jumper for the baby, which was due in less than a week. Beside her on the couch, Walter read the newspaper. Sometimes – her mom told her it was the hormones – she couldn't believe she was married to Walter. This wasn't how she imagined she would feel for her husband. They had started dating after Annie's wedding. He was a gentle, quiet man of German stock, like her, a giant man with a missing pinkie, eyes as blue and hair as blond as hers. On their first date he told her he had decided to marry her on the day he had watched her chase Seamus out of the high-school dining hall after he had punched Annie. She wondered what he thought about her having dated Raj. She noticed that if she ever tried to talk about Raj in front of Walter's family, they would always do the same thing. One would interrupt her to ask the table in general if Raj was that boy from England. Someone else would say, 'Wasn't he the boy who lived with Ruth?' And another: 'Wasn't he the best man at Lew's wedding?' Until, with a round of these vague enquiries, he was both shunted aside and made acceptable. No one ever said, 'Wasn't he the dark-skinned boy Nora wanted to marry?'

She wasn't sure what she felt about Raj any more. He was still on her mind all the time, and she read his postcards over and over. And yet she had never sent him so much as a Christmas card, and hadn't invited him to her wedding, which she now regretted. Whenever she saw Ruth in town, terrified she might say something that would upset her about his life in Boston, she would do whatever she could to avoid her, once squatting down behind the trash cans at the back of Sal's store. She only spoke about him to Annie, though she noticed that Annie wouldn't encourage her and seemed to get impatient. It was a deep injury she felt, as if she didn't really have the strength to love in any concentrated way again. In that sense Walter was perfect. He demanded little and seemed like someone in whom her love could grow slowly. She held a hope that when the child was born, she could somehow use the love her mom had assured her she would feel for it to ignite her feelings for him. He was a gentle presence, perfect for her injury, like a balm, or comfort food, or a quiet, temperate room. If nothing else he would remain this; if nothing else he would not be the cause of her suffering. But she kept having the same awful dream: she was in labour, struggling and screaming, his whole family peering eagerly between her legs, out of which came nothing but air and liquid, an awful mess all over the floor.

Walter roused himself from the couch. 'Honey, can I get you anything?' Since he had given up chaw, he needed to be chewing something constantly.

She shook her head. 'Don't make popcorn. The smell makes me feel sick.'

He hesitated, clearly having intended to do that, and a knock came at the door. He went to answer it. She could tell by his tone down the hallway that it wasn't someone usual. As she hefted herself up from the couch, brushing off her dirty housedress, in walked Raj, smiling. All at once her throat felt as if it had gone solid.

Her husband came in after him. 'Look who's in town.'

Raj tipped an imaginary hat, took hold of his belt buckle as if he were a cowboy, and said, 'Howdy, ma'am.'

She couldn't speak, no traction in her clotted throat, and the silence itself was so airless she could barely breathe.

'Well, park your caboose.' Walter gestured toward the couch. 'You want a beer?'

'No, I'm fine. Can't stay. Ruth's going to be mad if I'm late for supper. Just wanted to say hi. I'm going to be here for the whole summer, so I'll have plenty of time to see you'all.'

'You'll be here for the birth,' Walter said.

'By the looks of it, if I stay another ten minutes I'll be here for the birth.'

'She's that close all right.'

They were both looking at her now as if she were a fine heifer.

Nora couldn't believe what was happening to her. She knew that if she even tried to speak she would break down.

'How are you feeling?' Raj said gently.

She didn't respond. Walter and Raj exchanged a glance, Walter scratching the back of his head.

'You don't want nothing to drink, then?' Walter asked again.

'No, I'm heading back. Good to see you, Walt.'

After shaking Walter's hand, he turned to her. 'Well, next time I see you, you'll probably have subdivided.'

She walked over to him. Since she couldn't speak, she had determined to take hold of his hand, shake it and smile. He looked surprised at her proffered hand, but took it. She felt as if something were cleaving through her cleanly, opening her up from the top of her throat down through her chest. Once she had watched her father gutting live fish with a knife so sharp it made her shiver. It felt like that.

'I'll come back and see you'all in the next couple of days.' Raj gently squeezed her hand as the signal that he was going to pull his own hand free.

But she didn't let go, couldn't stop staring at his face, those big, deeply sensitive eyes, his smooth dark skin. Did he know how much she had given over to him, to those features, how desperately she wished this child inside her were his?

Gently he patted her shoulder, and made another attempt to pull his hand away, but she just couldn't let go. Walter had moved in a little closer, was rubbing her wrist, saying, 'Honey, honey.' But she just stared at Raj, her face burning worse than after the witch hazel.

Raj was trying a little harder to pull free, but she now took hold of his wrist with her other hand.

'Jesus, honey, come on now,' Walter said. 'You're going to put yourself in a state now, come on.'

Both men were trying to pull her hands from his, her husband prising her fingers up one at a time, Raj trying to wiggle free. They struggled in the doorway for what seemed like a long time, the three of them, until she became aware that the hand she now held was

Walter's, as the baby in her was his, and Raj was gone and her throat had softened back to flesh, and she was crying, or doing something between crying and convulsing, and her husband was leading her gently, and with murmurs, back to the couch.

The Four Lakes bass fishing competition was this weekend and Maud was rushed off her feet. Ruth had helped her all morning – even to clean the rooms. Without Ruth, she was sure she would have had a breakdown.

She hurried over to Magnus's cabin with a basin of warm water. As she approached, her heart began to pound and little flecks of light appeared, floating before her eyes. This would happen any time she went near his cabin. As she entered, this incipient panic was quenched by a mixed feeling of revulsion, fury, fear and guilt, a feeling articulated by the awful smell of the room, the sight of the little shot glass from which he drank his warm milk, and that head of his craning up in all its ghoulish need. His thin white hair, which he refused to let her cut, was down to his shoulders, his greyish beard thick, his body skeletal. Now he would produce a pathetic smile and say, 'Good morning, my dear.' Just waiting for this made her feel nauseous.

Laying a playing card between the pages of his book, he smiled and said, 'Good morning, my dear.'

Without responding she checked the pitiful contents of his bedpan: only a little honey-coloured urine. Sometimes he wouldn't defecate for days. When he did, he produced tiny black pellets, often together with blood, since he had developed haemorrhoids. His skin was incredibly dry, his lips cracked, his eyes bloodshot. His gums had gone dark, his breath unbearably rank. And always – *always* – that damn, simpering, sickly smile.

'Would you mind, my dear, propping that door open just for a moment so I can look at the Rose of Sharon outside. Perhaps you could bring me a flower, my love. I had a dream that a woman brought me flowers. White flowers. I think it was Death.'

'Then I'll bring you as many damn flowers as you want.'

'I see souls,' he said. 'And I must tell you, my dear, that your soul is torn.'

'It's damn well sick and tired is what it is. Look, I don't know what's wrong with you and the doctor doesn't know what's wrong with you. And right now I have every cabin full.'

'I pray for you every day.'

'I don't need you to pray,' she said. 'I need you to shit, which means I need you to eat so you can get out of this damn bed.'

'Why hasn't Annie come to see me?'

'She has a baby; her husband's missing; she works; she's *busy*.' She calmed herself. 'Raj is helping her a bit. He's back for the summer.'

'So the Moor returns?'

'The what?'

He didn't continue, just stared into the ceiling, rubbing at his beard.

She went through her Friday routine, rolling his body on to the little gurney, changing his sheets. She gave him a sponge bath, drying him thoroughly, rubbing moisturizer into his skin and antiseptic on his bed sores. Once his body was clean and dry, she rolled him back on to the bed. Finally, she wrung out a face cloth in warm water and handed it to him. The one thing he would still do himself was wipe over his face with the damp cloth. But this time he didn't reach for the cloth. Instead he closed his eyes and craned his face up toward her. She looked down at it with horror, the trembling, translucent eyelids, the grimace of dying, darkening teeth, the cracked lips. Taking a step back, she flung the damp cloth as hard as she could into his face and walked out.

For the rest of the day she dealt with the customers. Ruth came round after lunch to help her, bringing Raj. Maud could see how happy and proud she was. He was such a lovely boy. He cleared out the cabin gutters, and helped her with other heavy work. They all had dinner together and she went to bed. The next day, she didn't go to Magnus's cabin. Nor the next. Annie came round with the baby, but she told her he was sleeping. In the afternoon of the third day, she was working through her accounts on the screened-in porch when some customers she had been expecting pulled up, a young couple. As they approached, she saw Magnus, staggering unsteadily down the steps to his cabin, wearing just that absurd, diaper-like loincloth. The couple looked horrified at this ghost, with his long, wispy hair, who lifted his arms out toward them. As he did this, he collapsed – or, rather, lowered himself carefully to the ground. The couple ran to him.

Maud hurried outside. 'He's fine,' she called. 'He's fine. Don't worry about it.'

'He's collapsed,' the woman said.

'Just leave him be. Come on in,' she said. 'You're both here for a week, are you?'

'But—'

'Don't worry,' she said.

They were young and responded compliantly to her confidence. Besides that, she could tell they weren't married. She had developed an instinct for such things.

'He's gone a bit funny in the head,' she said as she handed them the key to their cabin. 'He does this all the time. But he's harmless.'

When they had gone, she took her knitting out on to the porch. He still lay prostrate on the dirt path. She went in as it began to get dark, and watched him from the window. Before the sun had completely set, he pulled himself to his feet. She watched him labouring up the porch stairs. The front door opened, and there he was, staring at her with disbelief and horror for a moment before lowering himself to the floor, gulping for air.

Picking up the big suitcase she had at the ready, she walked past him out of the door and straight to his cabin. In it she put his few remaining possessions – the books, the old blanket, even the shot glass. The wooden cross wouldn't fit, so she just carried it. She padlocked the cabin as she left.

When she returned, he was slumped in the same place and she put the suitcase and the cross beside him. She took a bundle of cash out of the safe. Then she went to the fridge and pulled out a bottle of milk and the food she had prepared for him earlier, which was in a paper bag. She put the food and money in front of him.

Sitting at the table again, she said, 'I've filled the car with gas.' She pointed at the money. 'That there's two thousand dollars, half my savings. This place is mine. It's in my name and we aren't married. I'm giving you the car. The title's in the glove compartment. Now, listen, I don't care where you go. The only thing I want is not to see you or hear from you ever again. Do you understand?'

Magnus was breathing hard, a crazed grimace on his face.

She went to bed. It began to rain. She couldn't sleep and kept listening for him downstairs. Finally she heard the floor creaking and a little while later the banging of the screen door. Perhaps an hour after that, she heard the car start up and drive off. She couldn't bring herself to go down until morning. He had taken his cross and suitcase, as well as the money and the food. He had also taken all the silver her grandmother had left her and her grandfather's gold pocket watch and Civil War sabre. In fact, he had taken everything of any value. She didn't care. He was gone.

PISGAH, 1952

It was close to midnight and the men, crowded into Goldwin's barber shop, had been drinking for a few hours. Laurel McFarlane, the itinerant so-called man-of-the-woods, accused of raping Otto's daughter, Shannon, had been acquitted that afternoon after a trial that had lasted less than two days.

'Not fucking guilty,' Otto shouted. 'Nigger raped my girl.'

'Nigger?' Siggy said.

Finn shook his head. 'Sure, the gossoon looked like he wouldn't say boo to a goose, all cleaned up like that.'

'Satan shifts his shape,' Magnus announced dramatically, his eye on the fifth of bourbon Otto kept leaving unguarded in his agitation.

Goldwin nodded. 'Would've looked like a Sunday school teacher weren't for those crazy teeth of his.'

'Didn't help any she didn't see who did it,' Siggy said.

'I told her to fucking say it was him,' Otto shouted. 'I saw him from here to there' – he pointed at the door – 'no more 'an ten feet, running from my barn. That fucking dog too. Would've gone after him if I didn't have my gimpy ankle. Jesus, should have seen her, tied to the fucking trough, that sack over her head. Fucking nigger animal.'

'Nigger?' Siggy glanced with a confused frown at Goldwin, who shrugged vaguely.

'Why didn't Erma come down?' Goldwin asked.

'Don't need that goddamn bitch here. She left us; she can damn well stay where she is.'

'Whoa there. Hold on now.' Siggy all but physically tugged back on the reins as he pointed at Otto. 'You haven't told Erma her daughter was raped?'

'Not having that fuckin' woman here causing trouble.'

'Shannon, Shannon,' Magnus lamented, 'our Pocahontas, our Little Wanton, spinning her naked cartwheels around the fort.'

'What the goddamn's he going on about?' Otto said.

Siggy threw out a dismissive gesture. 'He's drunk.'

'Could have been Annie,' Sal put in.

Otto responded furiously. 'What you saying?'

'Not saying nothing.' Sal raised his hands in innocence. 'Just saying could have been my girl; could have been anyone.'

'What you saying about my fucking daughter?'

'Not saying nothing.'

'I could tell you a few fucking things you say anything about my daughter.'

'He's just *saying*.' Goldwin tried to calm things down.

'He's a fucking peckerwood, no-good, eyetie, shit-for-brains, pantywaist sonofabitch.'

'You shuddup, you,' Sal shouted. 'I'm fucking saying for you good things, you fucking. I'm saying coulda happen to all of us, you fucking.'

'Sal's right.' Bennet spoke up at last. He had been very quiet, sitting in the barber chair, staring into Otto with all the brooding intensity of someone staring into a campfire. He pinched together the wings of his nose. 'Could have been any one of our women. Still can be with him out there. So what we going to do?'

Otto didn't seem to think this was addressed specifically at him, but Bennet kicked the side of his shoe. 'He's still out there, numbnuts. What are we going to do?'

Otto didn't have an answer, so Bennet's gaze shifted to the other men. Instantly, the barbershop turned into a classroom full of reprobates, the men looking down at their shoes, scratching their heads. Only Magnus remained as he was, leering blindly, like a mad prophet on the verge of thunderous revelation.

'Is this that damn city-slicking lawyer's town?' Bennet said. 'With his other fucking theory of the case?'

'Bastard,' Otto said. 'I'm going to find out where he lives, fucking cut his pecker off.'

'What about the animal who did it?' Bennet said.

Otto looked a little more troubled now. 'They'll know it's us, Mr B.'

Bennet glanced over at his cousin, smiling. 'Siggy, you going to arrest us?'

'Hell, yes,' he said, grinning.

'We couldn't have done nothing anyway. We were all coon-hunting up at Sharp Top. That's where we are right now, ten miles away.'

'What are we going to do?' Finn said.

'Well, that's up to Otto here.'

'I'm going to use a blowtorch on his balls.' Otto picked up his fifth of Jim Beam, but it was empty. He flung the bottle at Magnus. 'You damn thieving snake.'

'You watch my place, here,' Goldwin shouted.

Bennet pulled himself up out of the barber's chair. 'Sig, where they find him?'

'Had a camp up near Clyde's place, right at the edge of the bluffs. Been there a while, looked like.'

'Why he no run away?' Sal said.

'What you fucking saying?' Otto turned on him again.

'Not saying nothing. If is me, I woulda run away, that's all.'

Otto pushed his face right up into Sal's. 'Woulda run away, would you? You're not the one runs away, you greasy eyetie sonofabitch, you're the one gets hogtied and shafted – every fucking day of your life.'

Bennet wedged his open hand between their faces, and gently eased Otto's head back. 'Are we doing this or what?'

It took the men twenty minutes to get close to Clyde's place, piled into Otto's truck and Siggy's cruiser. They parked a little way into the woods, on a logging trail, out of sight of the road. The moon was close to full, which helped them through the woods toward the bluffs, where the hobo had previously set up camp. In just a few minutes they could make out the glow of a campfire.

'Jasus H., he's still here,' Finn said. 'If I was him I would've hopped the first freight car to Mexico.'

'That's the criminal mind.' Siggy spoke with authority as he thumbed in a cheekful of chaw. 'They have their territory, like to stay near the site of a kill. Tell by his physiog he did it. Rapists have tapering fingers and deep-set eyes. In Europe that's all they need to lock you up.'

'What's "tapering"?' Goldwin was checking his own fingers.

'In their eyes' – Magnus forked his fingers dramatically towards his own eyes – 'you can see the face of their last victim.'

'Or in this case, her ass,' Siggy mumbled through his chaw.

'What we going to do?' Sal asked. 'I mean we just going to tell him to get on his way?'

Otto slapped his shoulder. 'He hogtied and raped my daughter, you yellowbellied peckerwood.'

'He's going to hear us,' Goldwin hissed.

'Listen up.' Bennet gestured for them to gather around. 'North side is a long drop to the river, so he can't go that way. Siggy and Otto, you're the only two who's armed, so you're going to come up from opposite sides, case he tries to run off into the woods. Goldy, you're with Siggy, you two come up on the west side – give a good berth to the bluff so he don't see you. Go on, now.' Siggy and Goldwin headed off.

Bennet gave them a few minutes and continued. 'Finn, you're with Otto; you two come up on this side here. Otto, you better not use that rifle lessen I say, you hear me. We want to know he did it out of his own mouth. Rest of us going to take the deer path, come in on the south side. Clear? No more talking.'

The men split up. A short while later, as Bennet, Sal and Magnus approached the bluffs along the deer path, they heard a shot and began to run. When they got to the small plateau, the hobo was squatting beside his campfire, his arms wrapped over his head. Siggy had his pistol out, Goldwin beside him, his hair flopping loose from his bald crown. At this moment, with a rustling of bushes from the west side, Otto and Finn appeared.

'Goddamn, it's steep that way,' Otto complained, out of breath.

Finn was laughing, as if they had all been playing King of the Hill. 'Almost ended up in the drink, the two of us.'

'What the fuck you shooting at?' Bennet said to Siggy.

Siggy pointed vaguely toward the woods. 'His dog came at us.'

'You get it?' Sal said.

'Almost got me.' Goldwin smoothed his hair. 'Put that thing away, you're drunk.'

'Said the showgirl to the vicar,' Finn put in, winking.

'Clyde's farm's less than half a mile that way,' Bennet warned. 'No more shooting.'

Magnus, who had fallen behind, appeared now, utterly out of breath and grimacing as if he were going to have a heart attack.

The hobo was peering up through his arms, terrified. He was still pretty clean from his court appearance. His shining patent-leather shoes sat on a sheet of newspaper beneath his jacket, which hung from a low branch – the young lawyer had bought him these. McFarlane was a short, scrawny man, his mouth crowded with large yellowish-brown teeth. These he kept trying to cover with his hopelessly inadequate lips, which would instantly slide back away. He wasn't wearing his glasses, also provided by the lawyer. These had made him look like a librarian in court. A librarian doesn't sneak up behind a woman with his own face in a nylon mask, put a knife to her cheek and cover her head with a sack. A librarian doesn't tie her wrists and rape her over a feed bin, holding the sack so tight around her neck she blacks out. Hadley, the prosecuting attorney, on cross-examination had asked McFarlane to take his jacket and glasses off and roll up the sleeves of his shirt. The defence lawyer immediately objected, but Judge Cowper, who played poker with Hadley every Friday and didn't like this twenty-three-year-old straight out of Yale, agreed. Hadley then asked McFarlane if he had ever done hard labour. McFarlane replied that he had done a sight of farm work here and there. 'So you're pretty strong?' Hadley asked, placing himself in the line of sight between McFarlane and his lawyer, whose loud objections were being overruled. Grinning with shy pride, his lips sliding back over his grim teeth, McFarlane answered, 'I reckon so.' Hadley was trying to dispense with the librarian persona and show that this man had the strength to have done what he was accused of doing to a woman six inches taller and forty pounds heavier than he. Instead, McFarlane, without his jacket, looked like a soaked cat. Hadley's plan completely backfired. The jury took ten minutes to acquit him.

The men gathered around McFarlane. Huge trees arched over the little clearing and the roar of the water seemed very close, though it was an eighty-foot drop to the Missouri. Otto, who was behind McFarlane, suddenly kicked him in the back of his head, sending him sprawling in the dirt. At this Magnus let out a strange, almost sensual cry. He was still breathing hard and looked half-crazed.

Siggy, holstering his gun, squatted down to the man. With one hand he pulled the man's arm away from his face, peering into it as if he were looking under a rock. Then he flung his fist against the side of McFarlane's head. It was a glancing blow.

'Shit,' Siggy said, as if he had missed a nail with a hammer.

They all watched as he tried again. This time his fist directly hit McFarlane's temple, knocking his head against the ground. Again, Magnus made that wavering, high-pitched, almost ecstatic sound.

'Jesus, look at him.' Otto pointed at Magnus. 'He's going to cream his shorts.'

Bennet smiled. 'You ever hit a man, Maggy?'

Magnus shook his head.

Siggy had pulled back his fist again, but Bennet slapped his shoulder. 'Sig, let Maggy have a go. Give him some room now, boys.'

Bennet beckoned Magnus in as the others dilated a little. Magnus came to a halt just in front of the curled-up hobo and looked around at the men with a strange, childish glee. Steadying himself as if he were about to dive off a high springboard, he jerked his foot out, like a two-year-old trying to kick a ball, and missed the man's head entirely. McFarlane whimpered with horror, tears streaming down his face, that awful mouth gaping.

'Go on, Maggy,' Bennet encouraged, 'give it another go.'

Magnus, so excited he could hardly catch his breath, lined up his foot again. As he went to kick, the white boxer shot out of the trees, coming to a stuttering stop just a few feet from them, whimpering and circling. Otto pulled up his rifle, and in trying to point it at the dog swept it across all the men, who flung themselves on the ground.

'Put that fucking thing away.' Hurrying over, Bennet snatched the rifle out of Otto's hands, as well as the bottle of bourbon he was holding. He flung the bottle at the dog, which ran off into the woods again.

'Goddamnit,' Otto said, 'you want to throw something there's rocks all over the fucking ground.'

Magnus, with inconceivable agility, scurried over to the bottle, which hadn't broken, and with a face as desperate and guilty as a dog eating its master's dinner, gulped down what hadn't spilled out.

'Goddamn you,' Otto screamed, running up to Magnus and kicking him in the rear.

McFarlane, still covering his head with his arms, was looking up with terrified confusion at all of this.

'Keep your voice down and get back over here,' Bennet hissed at Otto. 'This is your fucking show.'

As Otto returned to McFarlane, all the other men, dusting themselves off, crowded back in. After unloading the rifle, Bennet handed it to Magnus, who was still standing where the bottle had landed.

Sal, looking very disturbed, approached Bennet. 'Mr B., let's get out of here. Somebody gonna get hurt. Already we coulda have people killed. This guy we kick his ass, tell him to get going, uh?'

Bennet, studying McFarlane, didn't respond.

Otto stabbed a finger toward Sal. 'We should send a fucking search party out for your balls, Salvatore. My fucking daughter got herself violated by this nigger.'

'Why do you keep calling him a nigger?' Siggy said. 'He's whiter than your fucking liver.'

Otto was still focused on Sal. 'Problem with you's, you got too used to your women—'

'So what are you going to do?' Bennet cut him off. 'What you going to do about this nigger?'

Otto looked down at the man. 'First things I'm going to knock those fucking teeth out of his mouth.'

'But he says he didn't do it,' Bennet said.

'He did it. I saw him and his fuckin' dog running from that barn.'

'Pity you said it was a big-ass nigger and his white dog before they found him,' Siggy said.

'He was covered in fuckin' shit. Looked like a damn nigger.'

Bennet squatted down and addressed McFarlane. 'You rape that girl?'

McFarlane shook his head. 'No, sir.'

Otto kicked him viciously in the small of his back. McFarlane cried out and Bennet threw his hand over the hobo's mouth to keep him quiet.

'Well I reckon we've got to get it out of him.' Bennet stood up, looking at Otto. 'I think us boys would feel a whole lot better if we're sure he did it.'

Otto nodded, clearly waiting for Bennet to suggest something.

'This is your show, maestro,' Bennet said. 'But we got to keep it quiet.'

Now all the men were looking at Otto. He scratched his head, glancing around the clearing, then up into the trees. All at once he got excited. 'You boys, you build this fire up here.' He ran off through the woods toward the road and returned a little while later with a rope out of the back of his truck, a fishing reel, duct tape and an empty feed sack. The men had built up a good-sized fire now.

'Let's get these fancy clothes off him,' Otto said. Siggy moved forward, but Bennet put a hand to his chest.

'Go on then,' he said to Otto. 'Just keep it quiet.'

Otto pulled out his Bowie knife. The man squealed, covering his face, as Otto cut all the buttons off his shirt. After some rough tugging and tearing, McFarlane lay curled up, naked, whimpering and covering his crotch.

'Mother of God, he's built like a little girl,' Finn said.

'Look how smooth he is.' Goldwin bent down to examine him. 'Like someone's stuck an old man's head on a kid's body.'

All but Magnus, who was still standing out a little way, using the rifle like a crutch to steady himself, gathered around to look at this strange creature, with its weathered, grotesque face upon a child's body, marble-pale and pristine.

McFarlane let out another cry and Bennet hissed, 'Keep him fucking quiet.'

Otto quickly shoved McFarlane's own socks into his mouth and sealed his lips with duct tape. He then forced McFarlane on to his front and used duct tape to bind his wrists behind him. Using the tape again, he fixed a rock to the end of a long strand of fishing wire, and after a few tries managed to throw the rock through the crook of a tree limb high over the fire. Tying the fishing wire to the thick rope, he then threaded the rope up through the tree limb. One end of this rope he tied around McFarlane's ankles. With Siggy's help, he took hold of the other end and hoisted McFarlane up. As he did so, Bennet and Goldwin used a couple of long branches to keep McFarlane out of the fire, so they could get him above it without burning him. There he hung, upside down, some way above the reaching flames, that pale little body wriggling, his face getting redder and redder.

'Jesus, get him up a bit,' Finn said. 'I can smell his hair burning.'

'He can fucking burn,' Otto said.

'Get him up,' Bennet ordered, and Otto reluctantly hoisted him up a couple more feet.

'I thought he had a two-foot-long pecker.' Siggy seemed disappointed. 'That's just a little maggot of a thing. Can't hardly see it.'

'How's he going to confess like that?' Bennet said.

'Jasus, Mary and Joseph,' Finn called out, 'he's going to choke up there.'

Magnus suddenly let out a cry, which might have been extreme pain or pleasure, and raised both his hands as if in supplication, one still clutching the rifle. With a yearning wonder, he stared up at that man suspended in the ghoulishly illuminated canopy of branches

'Keep your hands off the goddamn barrel,' Otto shouted. 'And don't put the butt down in the fucking dirt.'

Obediently Magnus set the rifle across his shoulders, hooking his arms around it. This done, he released himself again to that strange ecstasy focused on McFarlane, who had begun to wiggle wildly like a hooked fish.

'Get him down,' Bennet said.

Bennet and Goldwin used the branches again to keep him out of the fire as Siggy and Otto lowered him.

When he was on the ground, Otto tore the tape off and took the rag out of his mouth. He cradled McFarlane's head. 'Now you tell 'em what you done or you're going back up and I'll bake your goddamn head like a tater.'

McFarlane gulped the air, spit foaming between his teeth.

'He don't understand,' Finn shouted. 'He's just an ijut. Look at him.'

'*Mama mia.*' Sal had put his hands together as in prayer, tapping them against his own lips. He was pacing about like someone desperate to go to the bathroom. '*Basta, basta, basta.* Enough. *É un bambino. É solo un bambino. Guarda!*'

McFarlane lay like a horrific baby in Otto's arms, his eyes bulging, his neck loose, his grim mouth rooting at the air.

Magnus now fell to his knees and began to laugh. With both arms hooked over the rifle, which still lay across his shoulders, he looked like a man in the stocks.

'Maggy's gone loco,' Siggy said.

'Fucking tell 'em,' Otto spat into the hobo's face, taking hold of McFarlane's hair and nodding his head up and down. 'Tell 'em. You fucking did it, didn't you?'

McFarlane seemed to understand that Otto wanted him to nod and continued after Otto had let go of his hair.

'You did it, didn't you?'

McFarlane nodded.

'Look at that,' Otto said triumphantly.

'Damn, he's just an ijut,' Finn said. 'Doesn't know his arse from his elbow.'

'He's fucking admitting it,' Otto insisted.

'Okay, he admit it,' Sal shouted, still fluttering around the periphery like a helpless hen. 'He admit it. Is over now. Over. We take him to the police.'

'All of you, keep your voices down,' Bennet said calmly. 'Bastard can't be tried for the same crime again. So what are we going to do about it? Your call, Otto.'

'Oldentime justice,' Otto said. 'I'm going to fry him.' He shoved the rag back into McFarlane's mouth, securing it with duct tape. He pulled the rope wildly, knocking Siggy back and swinging McFarlane through the fire. Quickly recovering, Siggy tugged on the rope to get the man high above the flames.

'Let go,' Otto shouted at Siggy. 'I'm going to fucking bake his brains.'

But Siggy held the rope firm. He was staring at Bennet. Confused, Otto looked at Bennet also.

'That enough?' Bennet said, turning from his cousin to Goldwin and Finn. Siggy was shaking his head with disbelief as he pulled a dollar from his pocket and handed it to Bennet.

Finn was breathing hard, staring at Otto. 'Jasus, he's a godless animal.'

Goldwin had pressed both hands on to his scalp, as if he feared his thin hairs were too delicate for this. 'Well, I would never have believed it,' he said. 'You are rotten to the bone.' He too got a dollar out and handed it to Bennet.

Sal was sitting on the ground, sobbing, his face sunk into his hands.

'What?' Otto said, looking around, confused.

'You are the goddamn purest thing I ever seen,' Bennet said. 'Everyone in this whole damn town knows you're the one raped Shannon. You're so goddamn stupid, telling everyone you saw a big nigger with his dog, then saying it was this poor bastard.'

'He did it,' Otto shouted. 'Said he did it.'

'And good God,' Finn said, 'if you're not willing to kill this man too.'

'We'd better get him down,' Siggy cut in with sudden urgency. 'He's not moving.'

'Holy Christ,' Finn shouted. He was pointing at a child who had just appeared and was standing a foot or so in front of Magnus, staring into the fire.

'That's Clyde's kid,' Goldwin said. 'The one's soft in the head.'

'Don't look soft in the head to me,' Bennet said.

'Jesus' – Siggy looked around the clearing – 'what if Clyde turns up?'

'Get him down,' Bennet shouted, pointing up at McFarlane. 'Sal, *Sal*, get hold of that kid a minute.'

Sal looked up helplessly from his hands. 'Why does this happen to me?' he shouted, digging his finger into his own chest. 'To *me*.'

'I said get hold of that fuckin' kid,' Bennet ordered.

Sal got up and took hold of Roh gently by the shoulders. But the boy began to scream.

At the same moment Siggy said, 'He's not breathing.'

'Fucking shut that kid up,' Bennet called as he ran over to McFarlane, who was lying on the ground now. The tape and socks had been pulled from his mouth, and he had been cut free of the ropes, which had gouged into his wrists and ankles.

Siggy had his head on McFarlane's chest. 'He's not breathing,' he repeated.

Goldwin, who was standing beside McFarlane's body with Finn, repeated this hollowly: 'He's not breathing.'

McFarlane's face looked as if it had been par-boiled, his eyes grotesquely swollen, his mouth open, those teeth horribly exposed.

Out of breath, Bennet shoved Siggy aside and got down on to his knees. 'He's all right.'

'He's stone dead,' Siggy said.

The child was still screaming.

'Shut that goddamn kid up,' Bennet shouted.

'I can't,' Sal called from the other side of the fire. 'He punching me. He go crazy if I touch him. He crazy.'

Bennet slapped McFarlane's cheeks. Snatching the bottle of bourbon out of Siggy's hand, he splashed it into the hobo's face. 'Damn, damn.' He began to administer mouth-to-mouth, blowing hard between McFarlane's spit-clabbered lips. Then he listened to his heart again. 'Jesus. Jesus.' Straddling McFarlane's chest, he pumped with his joined hands. 'What the fuck is it? On the count of three?' He pumped harder. 'Is it the count of three?' He looked up at Siggy, who shrugged. Finn and Goldwin were like men standing around the opened hood of a truck.

'I think you got to hold his nose or something,' Siggy offered, squatting down.

'It's not a heart attack,' Goldwin put in. 'I think he's suffocated.'

Snapping his fingers, Siggy pointed excitedly at Goldwin. 'Asfisseated. Asfixeated. No air above a fire. Didn't have no air to breathe. Fire uses up the air.'

'Fire uses up the air,' Goldwin parroted blankly. 'No air above a fire.'

'Try turning him on his front,' Finn suggested. 'That's what they do when someone's drowned. Or you could lift his hands above his head.'

'No fucking air above a fire.' Siggy was still clearly impressed with himself for remembering. 'I knew there was something.'

Bennet, his face sheened in sweat, was staring bewildered at Siggy, squatting beside him, when the child let out a piercing and extended scream.

'Keep that fucking kid quiet,' Bennet shouted.

Abruptly the scream stopped. All the men were fixed for a moment. 'Oh, Jesus,' Sal said. 'No, no, no.'

'What the fuck's happened?' Bennet got up from McFarlane's body. He, Siggy, Finn and Goldwin moved around the fire. The boy lay in the dirt, a pool of blood swelling out from his head. Magnus was breathing hard, holding the rifle's barrel with both hands. Sal was still taking slow steps backwards and seemed on the verge of running off into the woods.

'He hit the kid.' Sal pointed at Magnus. 'With the rifle.'

Magnus's eyes were wide. Excited and pleased, almost ecstatic, he made a strange, grimacing smile and let out a triumphant cry.

Bennet rubbed his mouth. He looked like a man who had found himself in a nightmare, a man unaccustomed to nightmares, who wasn't completely engaged or sure of the rules. But here the nightmare was. On one side of the fire lay a naked, dead man, a man with a grotesque old face and the body of a boy. On the other lay a child of no more than six or seven, his skull cleft in. And all around him these drunken men: Siggy, with his fat, baffled, useless face; Finn and Goldwin, who were trying to become bystanders to an accident they had nothing to do with; and Otto, who stood with his back to them, loudly farting as he peed over the edge of the bluff.

'This is not happening,' Goldwin said, shaking his head.

Otto buttoned himself up and turned around to the men. He didn't look in the least troubled. In fact, he looked bored. He surveyed the scene.

'See, it's all fun and games,' he said, 'until someone gets their eye poked out.' He laughed.

Bennet reached down and pulled Siggy's pistol out of its holster. He aimed it at Otto, who howled and threw his arms in front of himself. Bennet pulled the trigger four times, but the hammer fell without firing. He looked at the pistol and then at Siggy.

'Only ever put one bullet in it,' Siggy said. He took the gun out of Bennet's hand and put it to his own temple. 'Only ever need one.'

'You're fucking drunk,' Bennet said.

Otto slowly emerged from behind his arms. Pointing at Bennet, but looking at Goldwin and Finn, since they seemed to have become the witnesses, he said, 'Did he fire on me?'

Neither responded. They were no longer a part of this.

Finally Bennet got a grip on himself, went up to Magnus, snatched the rifle out of his hands and gave it to Siggy. Staring down at McFarlane's body, he took a moment to think.

'All right,' he said. 'Sal, *Sal*, you throw this kid over the side there into the river.'

'No, I—'

He stepped closer to Sal, who cringed. 'Salvatore Celli, you pick him up now and you throw him into that river.'

Tears began again to stream down Sal's face. He looked utterly helpless.

'He's fucking dead,' Bennet said. 'Now you pick him up and throw him in.'

He turned around. 'Goldy, Finn, Otto' – he pointed down at McFarlane's body – 'get him and his clothes into the truck, cover him over.'

'What are we going to do with him?' Finn said.

'We're going to take him to the slaughterhouse and every man here's going to have a part in this. We're going to get rid of him.'

'I couldn't cut anyone up,' Finn said.

'You're going to do what I tell you to. Get him into the truck now.'

Goldwin had already moved, zombie-like, to the body. Finn and Otto joined him.

'You fucking tried to kill me,' Otto shouted.

Bennet ignored him. 'Sal, *goddamn it*.'

Sal was circling the child's body, sobbing. 'How do we know he's dead?' he shouted back at Bennet.

'He's dead. Get him into the river.'

Squatting down, Sal took hold of the boy's ankle and lifted him up. Holding him at arm's length as if he were contagious, he hurried over to the edge of the bluff and flung the body as far out as he could into the black waters of the Missouri.

Bennet and Siggy extinguished the fire, dug out and threw the blood-soaked soil over the bluff, and generally cleared the site as best they could. When this was done, Bennet snatched up Magnus's hand and the rest of the men followed as he tugged Magnus with irritation back through the woods as if he were a naughty child.

PISGAH, 1961

Annie lay beside Raj on the Murphy bed, both of them on their backs, the stuttering old fan playing over them. She had just managed to get Baby to sleep.

'Where would Magnus have gone?' she whispered.

'To the Island of Lonely Women.'

'Can you believe he stole all her silver?'

Raj rolled over to face her, propping his head on his hand. 'Right now he's in his one good suit wooing his next victim.' Raj imitated Magnus's English accent: 'My dear, you see before you one descended from men who took the field of battle, women who held in escrow their hearts. After dear Pater's death, *chère maman* had no choice but to marry a Cursèd Expectorator. By the by, do you own this house outright?'

'Oh stop it,' Annie said. 'Gives me the creeps.'

As he lay on his back again, she shifted to rest her head on his chest. She could feel how nervous it made him whenever she violated the safe space between them. He would go quiet and very still, trembling, like a baby rabbit caught in the open. Fear: she could hear it in his heartbeat. In some ways, perversely, she fed upon it. She had felt so helpless for so long it was wonderful to make him go still and quiet just by touching his hand, looking too intensely into his eyes, or standing too close. How good they had been, not kissing again after that first time. Lew haunted them. For her it was a raw feeling, her nerves like ragged tendrils extending out into the world, into roadside ditches, railway culverts, darkened doorways, beneath bridges where derelict men lay like tree limbs thrown up by the river. Each night as she slipped into sleep, Lew got into her bed, a feeling

so vivid she was sure, in some other life, a parallel life where whatever happened to Roh that night hadn't happened, he was her beloved.
Of course Baby had shifted her centre. There were many who would
say Baby should *be* her centre. He wasn't, though. He was another
person whom she loved, but he wasn't sufficient to her life – no more
the hub of the universe than she was. He was to be cared for, indulged
even. She would be his solace, refuge, but never his husk. Nor would
she allow herself to become a figure for him: a mortified part of his
life's heart. She would not stare out of any windows and sigh; she
would not spend her days planting fields that would be flooded.

With a nervous hand, Raj now combed her hair behind her ear
and neck. How brave – she smiled – to defy her, provoke her. Wielding
this smile, she looked up into his face. She believed and didn't believe
in his love for her with equal fervour. She knew that like her he was
not quite human: a complex semblance. One may as well kiss a mirror.
With this in mind, she did what she had promised herself not to do
again – almost as an empirical act. She stretched up and kissed him.
But the experiment failed. He didn't feel in the least like a mirror.
All at once they became quick, pressing themselves as hard as they
could into each other as they kissed. She could feel his body responding: he was, after all, just a young man. From somewhere a door
banged. She pulled away and sat up, her hand against his chest. He
lay still, as if pinned, breathing hard.

No more sounds came. She looked down at him. There was nothing to be said about what had just happened. After a few moments,
he got up, said he should go, and did.

Annie fell asleep reading in bed. At close to six in the morning, Baby
woke. As she was feeding him, she heard the front door to the store
rattle – the wind, perhaps. Moments later she heard the back door
open and shut. Except for the storefront, she never bothered to lock
any of the doors. Her whole body went numb with fear as someone
began to ascend the creaking stairs to the apartment. With a rush of
panic, she realized she should get up and lock her door, but it was

too late. It opened. It was too dark near the entrance to make out more than a tall figure. She became aware that she had wrapped her arms around Baby, who was still feeding, and then realized she was bare-breasted. She wanted to scream, but nothing would come out of her throat. It was all she could do to pull the sheet up to cover herself.

As the figure approached, her worst fears materialized in the thin lozenge of moonlight from the window: a thickly bearded, filthy and dishevelled man. She could smell him now too – overwhelmingly rank. She still couldn't make a sound or move, her limbs leaden. He sat heavily on the bed.

'They burned me,' he said.

'Lew?' She could see him a little more clearly now. 'Lew.'

With a claw-like hand, his nails long and blackened, he drew the sheet down. Afraid for Baby, she quickly got out of the other side of the bed.

'Where have you been?' she said.

'I thought it was me,' he said. 'But they burned me. They separated my organs.' He made a shape with his hands. 'Hard burned skin – rind – around my heart and my kidneys. My lungs have gone solid and I breathe in my brain now. My brain breathes. I can feel it. They left me for dead, but I put my pieces together. I took my windpipe and I threaded on my organs. I'm a breathing brain, like storm clouds. But it was never me they were after, except that I knew. It was him.' He indicated the child.

Annie put Baby back in the cot, since she felt he was safer out of sight, but he began to cry.

'You have to keep him quiet.' Lew seemed panicked. 'He's calling for them.'

'He's not calling for anything. He's just hungry.'

'You don't understand. They think I'm dead. They don't know I learned to breathe in my brain.'

Annie sat back on the bed and firmly took up his hands. He smelled so revolting she had to struggle to stop herself gagging. 'Lew, do you know who I am?'

This seemed to frighten him. She had asked the question in the wrong way: she mustn't create any space for his diseased imagination to inhabit.

'Lew, I'm Annie. Do you remember? I'm Annie, your wife. This is *our* baby. We've known each other since we were children. I was worried about you.'

'You've got to stop it.' He got up and moved around the bed toward the cot, but she stepped in front of him, pressing her hands firmly to his chest.

'I'll stop him crying.' She lifted Baby out, sat again, and put him to her breast.

Lew kept still and quiet as she fed Baby and Annie talked as normally as she could – about his father, her family, Raj, and other things going on in town. He still seemed agitated though, his eyes frantic and confused. After a while Baby stopped feeding and fell asleep. She laid him in his cot. Then she raised her hand to Lew.

'Lew, come with me. We're going to have a bath.'

To her surprise he took her hand and let her lead him into the little bathroom.

'What is it going to do?' he said, glancing back at Baby.

'He's asleep.'

As she drew the bath, she began, without thinking, to sing to him – just whatever words came to her head in a gentle, calming melody. It seemed to ease his agitation and he let her take off his clothes – a jacket, a filthy pair of tracksuit pants, and mismatched sneakers, none of which she had seen before. Getting him into the bath, she washed him thoroughly, shampooing his matted hair four times. The water turned black. Still singing, she got him out, dried him gently, then clipped and cleaned his nails. He even sat still enough to let her cut his beard, shave him, and trim his hair. Her Lew emerged from this monster. Finally she got him to brush his own teeth, which he seemed to remember how to do, but his gums bled profusely. She sang then to keep herself from crying. Finally she led him to the bed. Getting in with him, she rubbed his back and sang until he fell asleep.

When she was sure of this, she slipped out, got Baby, and made her way as quietly as she could to the landing just outside the front door of the apartment, where there was a telephone. She didn't shut the door, just pulled it to, because she was afraid it would make too much noise.

As she was dialling Ruth's number, the apartment door flew open and Lew, naked, wrenched Baby out of her arms while pushing her back. She just saved herself from falling down the stairs by taking hold of the banister. Before she could regain her balance, he was back in the apartment and had locked the door.

Annie threw her body hard against it, screaming, 'Lew, don't hurt the baby. Don't hurt our baby. Lew, it's your baby. It's your son. Don't hurt him.'

She hammered for a moment longer, then listened, but couldn't hear anything. She sprinted down, out of the store, and up the fire escape. But the back door was wide open, the apartment empty. He must have gone straight out with Baby. She ran into the street and looked around, but couldn't see him anywhere. Running up Main, she screamed for him. Lights came on in the apartments above the shops. She could hear windows opening. A feeling of utter unreality seemed to bore down into her from the suddenly heavy and precarious sky. The bright full moon mocked her, sour in the darkness. Dozens of roads and alleys branched off Main, ending in fields and woods. These paths and fields and woods seemed to multiply around her, Baby, broken into a thousand pieces, absorbed, as air through lungs, into the body of night. From everywhere the cicadas screamed like electric babies.

'Baby,' she shouted. Her child didn't have a name. 'Lew,' she screamed. But that name meant nothing.

She sprinted through the alley between Snyder's and Novus, and up to the edge of the fields. Doors were opening and people were calling to her. She screamed at them to get the sheriff, her baby had been taken. As she went to run into the fields, she felt hands on her shoulders. Mr Talhausen pulled up the fallen straps of her nightdress and a moment later she felt his jacket go around her. Other people were surrounding her now, including her mother.

'Lew took Baby,' she said. 'He's got my baby.'

Annie sat in her parents' kitchen, surrounded by women, the first light of dawn seeping into the room. What she was feeling was like a day of heat-lightning: numbness with abrupt flashes of panic or fury. She had stood up a few times, her body needing to do something, but a soft wave of women would instantly overwhelm her, washing her back into her seat. The fury was at herself for letting Baby be snatched like that. She should have closed the door, gone home to make the phone call, fought harder. She had the bizarre impulse to run up to her apartment and try even now to break through the front door so that she could be sure that it wasn't possible. And all at once these feelings, as if her spine had melted, would dissolve, and she would be sure that Baby was dead. Outside, on Main, she could hear vehicles gathering, men shouting.

Ruth appeared and behind her Raj, who was holding a rifle. Getting up, she took hold of both of them.

'Is it Lew?' Raj asked.

She nodded. 'He came last night. He's naked.'

'Naked?' Ruth said.

'He had a bath. I cleaned him up. He just ran out.'

Again the women softly overwhelmed her and she found herself back in the chair. Of all things, someone had baked muffins and her mom was trying to get her to eat one. She shook her head.

Raj leaned down to her. 'I'm going in the back of Otto's truck with a bunch of the others. We're heading to his dad's place first, case he's gone back there. Then we're going to fan out into the woods.'

As he left, her mom tried to get her to eat some of the muffin again. The warm, new-baked smell of it sickened her. She couldn't just sit around, waiting. She got up, pushing away the women who tried to take hold of her, and joined Raj and half a dozen other men in the truck bed.

'It's my baby,' she declared fiercely, glancing around, even though none of the men had said anything. 'I'm not going to stay here.'

Raj was looking with concern down at her feet, which were still bare. She pulled Mr Talhausen's jacket more tightly around her shoulders.

Finally the little convoy of trucks and cars pulled out. It was already eight – a beautiful clear day. When they arrived at the Tivots', the front door was open. Siggy hammered on the jamb and entered. Bennet waited just a little way outside, his rifle at the ready.

When Siggy came out, his boyish face as bashfully furious as it had ever been, he waved everyone to him.

They gathered around.

'Lewis got hisself a shotgun,' he said. 'He took Clyde's shotgun.' Noticing Annie, he frowned and took a moment before adding, 'Clyde said he didn't see any baby with him.'

In Annie the feeling was like the high-rise she had seen demolished in a newsreel: a dizzying sensation of collapsing whole and upright into her own dust.

'But this just happened ten minutes or so ago and he took out that way into the woods. He can't be far and he's . . . he's still naked. Pair up. We're going to spread out here and move toward the river in twos. He should be considered armed and dangerous. If you see him *don't* confront him. Keep him spotted and call for help.'

As the men began to pair up and move, Clyde appeared in the doorway. He looked stricken. 'You-all did this,' he screamed. 'You-all did this and now you're going to kill him too.'

'Pair up,' Bennet shouted to shift everyone's attention from Clyde, who continued screaming. 'Let's move.'

Annie stayed with Raj and Harry Olsen, who was only fifteen and looked eager to use his new rifle. Less than ten minutes later, a shout came from deeper in the woods, upriver. They ran, joining other clots of men until they arrived at the bluffs. She could hear Baby crying and clambered frantically up to the edge of the little plateau, but Raj hooked his arm around her waist to stop her going any further.

Lew, naked, stood right at the precipice. He held Baby in one arm, the shotgun, pointing to the ground, in the crook of the other. The sun had cast the leaf-shadows of a tall dogwood upon him, so it was hard to see the exact expression on his face as the men spread in a semicircle around the edge of the plateau. Thirty rifles were levelled at Lew. Baby was screaming, his face a mess of tears and snot.

Siggy shouted, 'Lewis, you put that baby down now. That's your baby boy, don't you harm him.'

Baby let out another screaming wail. Annie could feel the front of her nightie soaked with her milk. Raj was still gently holding her, but she surprised him, twisted his arm out of the way as she shoved him back and scrambled up on to the plateau.

'Annie, you get back now,' Bennet called sternly. 'You get back or I'll shoot him right here.'

'Lew.' She tried to be calm, to coax. 'Lew, come here, darling. It's Annie. Come here to me. We'll be all right. You'll be okay.' She didn't really know what she was saying. She wanted to get Baby. She wanted Baby to stop crying. As she went to take another step forward, she felt a hand take hold of her dress at the back and looked around to see Raj, who had also stepped out a little way on to the plateau.

'Lew,' he called, 'it's Raj. You remember me, Lew?'

Annie could see Lew a little more clearly now. He was staring into the ground, quietly speaking to himself as if he were praying.

She took a step closer, though Raj was still restraining her. As she did so, Lew lowered Baby. She thought he was letting him go, but as soon as Baby was on the ground, Lew took hold of his left ankle. Quickly raising him to chest height, Lew turned to suspend Baby upside down and screaming over the edge of the bluff.

'Don't!' Annie screamed, putting her hands out. Hooking his arm around her, Raj pulled her back to the line of men.

'Lew,' she shouted, trying to struggle free, becoming furious. 'It's my baby. Don't you do this. Don't you do this.'

A breeze swarmed the shadows over that figure, that heartless figure, holding a baby suspended over the roaring river eighty feet below. All the men kept very still behind their aimed rifles.

'He hasn't even got a name,' Annie shouted. 'He hasn't even got a name.'

Lew looked up, the sun caught briefly in his blue eyes. Gently he swung Baby back in and lowered him to the ground. She freed herself fiercely from Raj, slapping and tearing at him, and stepped on to the plateau. Baby, crying, began to crawl toward her. Then he stopped, sitting and reaching for her in outrage. He was still within easy reach of Lew. As she took a few steps closer, Lew shifted the shotgun so it was now in both his hands, though still aiming down.

'Lewis,' Siggy called, 'you put that down now. You put it down.'

'Lew, honey,' Annie said. 'Lew, don't do this. Lew.' Baby was just a few yards in front of her. She wanted him to crawl toward her, but he was still just sitting, screaming and reaching for her. She took another step. Lewis raised his shotgun and thirty rifles fired.

SAN FRANCISCO, 1985

Rosa, putting on her coat in the kitchen, heard someone entering the house. No one was expected. Frowning fiercely, she burrowed her burly little body into the hallway, calling, 'Hello? Hello?'

A man's voice sang back, 'Hello, hello, I don't know why you say goodbye, I say hello.'

Delighted, she hurried to the front door, where Raj stood grinning like a guilty schoolboy.

'Mr Travers, you early.'

'One more day in England would have killed me, Rosa. They eat giblets there, you know.'

'Giblets?'

'Out of old newspaper. And blood sausage with lashings of clotted cream.'

She gave him a brief, exaggerated look of sympathy. 'How horrible.'

Rosa's face was either expressionless or at a mask-like extreme. In this she often reminded him of Miss Kelly.

'How the conference?'

'*Symposium*, Rosa. Means you get your own little bottle of Perrier for free – which reminds me.' He opened his suitcase and handed her a silk scarf. 'Woman next to me on the plane fell asleep, so I stole that for you.'

'Thank you, sir.'

'Is my beloved family not here?'

'They think you come tomorrow. They out to eat. They want surprise you.'

'Surprise me?'

419

'Your son, he come yesterday.'

'Clay? From Africa?'

She nodded. 'Is been a year, no?'

'Almost two. Oh, that's great. Did my daughters devour him?'

'They very happy. They want surprise you with him. Go, sir.' She waved her hand toward the door. 'Go. Come back tomorrow.' She laughed – that grimacing, theatrical laugh – as she always did when she presumed to make a joke. And repeated it, as she always did: 'Go. Go, come back tomorrow; come back tomorrow.'

'I'll hide somewhere.'

'Under bed. I feed you like a little mouse.' She had tickled herself so much she could barely speak.

Raj smiled indulgently until she settled. She went to pick up his suitcase.

'No, no, I'll take this.'

She nodded. 'I leaving now, sir. See you next week. We miss you.'

'I missed you too, Rosa.' He put a tender hand on her shoulder as she opened the door, but she shrank away. She didn't like to be touched. Stupid of him to forget.

When the door shut, the house seemed empty – even of him. He had expected to plunge into his loud, happy family. Instead: Rosa recoiling from his touch. She was the same with everyone, but such things took a while to get through his system. He didn't need this. He was already feeling strange – estranged – after what had happened with Melissa. After England itself, which always made him feel both sad and inexplicably nostalgic.

Carrying his suitcase upstairs, he caught sight of his son's backpack as he passed the guest room, and wondered if Clay were here alone. Five years out of college and still a nomad, he would bring home every now and then a girlfriend of the kind that delivers polio vaccines in India. She would touch Clay as if, on some level, she knew he was untenable – in but not *of* this life. Raj understood only too well how little all the suffering in the world can come to mean when you love someone you cannot have.

Untenable: it was how he felt now. As he put the suitcase by his closet, he wished the bedroom wasn't so clean, blank and sterile as a hotel room. He opened the balcony doors. The sea breeze rooted at him, flinging his hair across his face as he watched a massive container ship ease toward the bay.

For almost a month at Oxford he had lectured and chaired debates on alternative energies, the symposium itself producing enough hot air to power the world for a thousand years. At least he had managed to spend some time in London with Cici. When she had put on her barrister's wig, he had looked for his father in her face. Cici had long suspected that they shared the same father. Among Brenna's effects she had found a hastily scrawled postcard from Gerard. It wasn't exactly conclusive, but caused Cici to do some calculations regarding the timing of her conception. They would never know for sure, but if it were true he wondered how many more his father might have fathered. *How many?* What was that story? *How many?*

He went to his office to check his mail and saw the FedEx immediately. After all those last-minute hiccups, Ruth's farm had finally sold. He sat at his desk, surprised by his own rush of feeling. Silly. Nothing in Pisgah now but a few graves. How lucky he was that Ruth had chosen to live out the end of her life in San Francisco, and was buried just a few miles away. Gone nearly two years now, his Ruth, who had first appeared to him in the dim underworld of that hospital waiting room. From his office he had often watched her playing with Lulu and Gayle in the garden, no longer the grieving, irritable, impenetrable woman he had first encountered. He had been too young to understand her particular genius, how she chafed, her extraordinary capacity to feel flaring and guttering around her like the flame around a badly tended wick.

Absently, Raj toyed with his stapler. Well, there it was, he thought, no reason ever to go back, as he had a number of times in these last few years to deal with the farm, evicting the couple he was renting it to after they had switched from soybeans to crystal meth. It was always strange to return, finding himself feeling so little in a place where he had once felt so much. He had arrived in a flood year, by the night train, on tracks raised by men then called Negroes out in the darkness, delivering him into a new, wet world. Its first reality: the dirty feet of a girl in a yellow house dress, sitting on the counter of a general store. Annie—

'Shit!' He dropped the stapler, and with a grimace plucked the staple from his thumb and sucked the little bead of blood. Idiot.

He went downstairs to the kitchen and got himself a Band Aid. He wanted his family here. He was feeling so strange: disconnected and agitated at once. His colleague, Simon, a recovering alcoholic, had once tried to explain to him what it was like, house-sitting for a friend, to discover a single beer in the fridge. Just like that, your whole life can vanish. Raj felt himself struggling against his old unhappiness – that persistent compulsion to go somewhere else, *be* someone else.

He opened the back door. The sun hung just above the Pacific, an orange bleb, heavy, ready to fall. As clearly as Annie in her yellow dress, he could recall his first encounter with Lew, in the spangling light beneath a tree – a girl in the shadows, a boy in the sun. Even from the first he had been moved by the terrible purity of Lew's intimacy – you looked right into the dream of him.

He stepped back into the kitchen. On the fridge was a photo of Nora and Walter surrounded by their six big blond boys. They lived in Jeff City now; a card every Christmas. Her face had changed. Who could ever have imagined that the radiation treatment for her acne would result in a cancer that would require her nose to be removed, reconstructed and covered with skin from her forehead? A perfect little nose now, and not one wrinkle on her brow. He tried to recognize her, but couldn't. And all at once these photographs – his friends and family – were of so many strangers.

Even Alvin – where was this photo taken? Grinning like a little carnivore, he held a hotdog in one hand and was waving the other oddly above his head. Raj looked hard into that face – that happy face into which, not long after this, Alvin would fire a bullet. Why?

Opening the fridge, he stared into it. He felt terrible. How was he going to get Melissa out of his head? Just like that you lose a friend you have known and loved for half your life. Cute, elfin, with womanly hips, a sharp chin and terrible taste in glasses, Melissa had been his co-conspirator against the world since their first semester at MIT. He had been the male maid of honour at her wedding, had seen her through her divorce. At the symposium they had made fun of Oxford, land of the living dead doctorates, laughing like maniacs. And it was just two days ago, walking by the Thames, that she had taken his hand. She often put her arm through his, but this felt different. After a few moments she pulled him to a stop, securing his other hand. Flushed and trembling, she told him that in all these years since MIT, even through her marriage, she had only ever felt truly happy when she was with him. She asked if it might be possible for them to become, as she put it, more intimate.

Rather than saying immediately what he should have said, he remained silent before this, the astonishing fact of feeling – for *him*. It was as if they had been playing some silly game, reckless as children, and he had deliberately goaded her beyond her limits. Now she had fallen, stood before him bleeding. But here also: sex, intimacy, possibility, with a person he admired, was attracted to, and cared deeply for. He remained quiet for too long, she began to cry, and he embraced her gingerly, as if they were acquaintances at a funeral. He had left England early because he didn't want to see her again: he did not trust himself. If he had been a good man, he would have said immediately that it was impossible: he loved his wife and family.

He *loved* his wife and family. And yet, on the flight home he struggled with that part of him that wanted change, wanted to *enact*, not imagine, a new story, wanted perhaps to be ruined. He allowed it no voice, but its pressure had rendered him silent when he should have been a good man, when he should have said, *I am married; I love my wife*. How pathetic a claim to courage: that he had remained silent *just* long enough. This was why it so troubled him that his family wasn't here. He needed their reality to overwhelm the part of him that even now was appropriating his imagination and using it against him, casting up images, both graphic and tender, of him making love at this very moment to Melissa in an Oxford hotel room.

He finally closed the fridge. Had he really not changed in all these years? He thought of Nora's eighteenth: *Raj, what are we?* It had moved him so deeply. No one had ever unequivocally wanted him. When Nora said his name, it seemed truly that someone with that name must, at the very least, exist; might even be desired. He had never rid himself of his sense of wrongness. Wrongness at his heart. As a child he would spend hours imagining himself ruggedly handsome, laconic and dangerously impulsive as the men of Ruth's romances. Brutally powerful, morbidly sensitive, he was the perfect man. Would it ever leave him, that desire to shed himself like a skin, to abandon whatever life he was in, to become, again, a stranger, fraught with mystery and potential? To be anything but *this*, this skinny, silly, nattering fool, who mugs, teases, touches and laughs like a little girl.

And dark. Yes, dark. Wrongness at his heart. He remembered when his children were born, that flush of nerves, that feeling, the articulation of which he did not allow himself, but could not deny: he was glad – so glad – they were not as dark as he. This sense of wrongness had always made him deeply impressed by any glimmer of real integrity. He often thought of that day he was sure Lew was about to throw himself over the edge of the bluff: *I wouldn't do it to you and Annie*. It was the kind of egoism that reveals a proper humanity: it is never sufficient to love; you must also have faith in the love of others for you.

Annie and he could never quite believe they had substance enough to be loved. That was why they sinned. They had no faith. They had to know.

At times it astonished him he had managed to salvage *any* integrity from a childhood so infested by furtive and treacherous longings. On the day he and Nora came upon Lew and Annie naked together at the sinkhole, the sensation in him was like a bomb-blast being rewound, collapsing him into a feeling of condensed and incendiary self-revulsion. Thief and fetishist, he had nothing of Annie but his secret hoard – lips, clavicle, ankle – her body in constellation, her rumour in his bones. Certainly nothing real or whole, nothing that penetrated or overwhelmed, except in dreams.

Wrongness. He never felt in the right way even with his daughters. Gayle, nearly fourteen now, called him Daddy, addressing him sometimes as if they were strangers. She didn't like his sense of humour, hated lies. Brittle, anxious, idealistic, she would be deeply hurt, and in anticipation of this he suffered endlessly for her. Lulu, on the other hand, filled him with her childish joy. She ran around brazenly naked, quaffed Kool-Aid, her mouth lurid with it, and laughed like a pirate. She called him Boobie, and whenever he tried to quietly read the newspaper would throw herself across his lap, looking up at him as if she were all the news he would ever need.

Mrs Barnacle – that was it! He remembered. Galloping after that young lad on her roan pony. *How many? How many?*

Returning to his office, he opened the FedEx and signed the documents. Would he ever go back to Pisgah? The younger people had left for bigger cities, the older – those who could afford it – for Florida or Arizona. On his last trip he had run into Miss Kelly. Overjoyed, she had performed a spontaneous little dance, like that of a mechanical ballerina in a music box. Pela and Olenka were now buried under cheap wooden crosses in the graveyard. Sheriff Siggy had found them one winter huddled together beneath a blanket on the floor of their kitchen, dead from hypothermia. Their Cincinnati bank account contained nearly two million dollars. Frank had only ever been back once, for Jude's wedding, where he got so drunk he fell over and cut his head open. Last anyone heard he was in Alaska, a world of men. Bennet and his cronies replaced the old guys on the porch of the Franklin and spent their last years in penny-ante purgatory. All dead now, except Finn, waiting on that porch like a child whose parents have forgotten to pick him up from kindergarten. Clyde was still alive too, living in a miserable state-run nursing home in Booneville.

Raj returned to the bedroom to close the balcony doors. Gone.

Such a beautiful place. He thought of the blue chicory along the dusty country roads, lightning bugs over fields of white daisies, humming-birds in the honeysuckle vines. He often felt nostalgic, but had become enough a part of that place for it to be tempered. He knew that when the crows took the fields, raucous, and winter returned, so too would the old injuries, passions, resentments, which were not buried, but gestated in the silence. In his time it had been the Depression, the influenza, the wars, the dead children, the homesteading husbands who never came back, the relentless mothers-in-law, the sister lobot-omized to cure her promiscuity. And the midwife whose strong hands suffocated all the ones that came out wrong, covering their mouths, holding their noses, and hushing them. *Hush now. Hush now.* Lew. Lew. Lew. Would he ever stop seeing it? Or waking in the night with the feel of that rifle stock at his shoulder?

As he went to shut the balcony doors, he hesitated, let the breeze play over him as the sun melted into the Pacific. What had happened on the bluffs above the Missouri on that day seemed the source of his life, more real than he, as if that pale, naked body at the precipice were dreaming him, dreaming all the people of Pisgah, dreaming this world. He could never deny it: he had once stood with a phalanx of armed men, discovering he was one of them.

But what choice had they?

Again, and as vividly as the sun upon the ocean, that glittering path to the edge of the world, he saw Lew's body, could almost smell the acrid discharge of the rifles, their reports ringing in his ears. In span-gles of sunlight between leaf shadows, Lew was as Raj had first seen him. In the end as in the beginning: Lewis of the light.

Amazing: of the thirty men who fired, only twelve hit him. Of those, only one – *one* – was a fatal shot, clean through the heart. It was his, Raj was sure. He often suspected this was the reason he had wanted a home with a view of the ocean. Which absolves. Gentle or furious, illuminated or in darkness, like anything helplessly powerful, like God, it can't help but absolve.

He and Annie had thought so long about names for Baby, thought even for a while that they might call him Lewis. In the end, though, like so many immigrants from another world, they decided to give him a name that set him as free — as any child can be — from the past. Clayborne, Old English, meaning a dweller in a place with clay soil by a brook. More important, it meant nothing to them. There for this boy to fill. They should have known he would have no choice but to fill it with a manifestation of their silence — about his father, about the past.

Raj closed the doors. Turning back he caught sight of something under the bed and picked it up. It was one of Annie's little paper-clip sculptures, wrought from nervous energy whenever she was concentrating hard on another instalment in her astonishingly popular series of children's stories. Deep into a book, she could go through dozens of paper clips, unconsciously unravelling and retwisting, dropping them all over the house like some exotic scat. If he disturbed her while her fingers worked one of these, she would turn an empty, annihilating gaze upon him, as Ruth used to do.

There it lay, in the palm of his hand, evidence, like the new Band Aid around his finger, and this house started to feel like his home again as he began to fill, at last, with a longing for this, his present life, Annie, his two daughters and Clay. He would surprise them — yes, he would jump out at them from behind the coat rack in the hall. He could see it already: Annie and his daughters screaming, mobbing him, while Clay, in Lew's body, with Lew's face, just smiled at them all from far, far away.

Tonight he would share a bath with Annie. He would sponge her back, peruse lightly the braille of her spine, heft her breasts judiciously in his palms. Closing his eyes he could almost feel her soap-slick skin. And yet it was difficult to evoke her distinctly. As invariably happened when he was away for a while, she had become a spectrum, her face and figure that of every Annie, from the girl he had once so earnestly examined for ticks, through the new mother grimacing in labour, to the woman she was now, her hair a little shorter, straighter, her face and its ardency, like her voice, of a deeper tone, more subtle and richly tempered. All at once he was seized by such an intense love and desire for her he felt physically weak. Closing his hand around the destroyed paper clip, he generated just enough pain to return him to a world, at this moment, without her.

But in which she was both immanent and imminent. In the bath tonight she will ask him about Melissa, whom she adores. As if out of the place of his wrongness, pain and shame will leak into him, as into his blood, like sepsis from that congenital wound. Annie will notice the lacuna in his response, the sensitivity of his eyes to hers, but will say nothing because sometimes, as they have both come to understand, there must be silence.

They will sit in the bath struggling with that silence, suddenly awkward, like the two twelve-year-olds they have never ceased to be, unchanged from their first encounter; and utterly changed, heading toward that kind of rough and difficult perfection of whatever they are, the two of them, together. They will become aware of the sound of Gayle and Lulu through the walls, squabbling over gentle Clay – *Clay look, Clay listen* – of his silence joining theirs, familial, since it reaches back just as far, to that first thing that cannot be spoken, containing it as we all contain, ravelled in us, the first man and woman.

Raj closes the balcony doors. Tonight, sharing a bath with Annie, exalting in her nakedness and his, in their still vigilant love, he will listen to his daughters' voices and Clay's silence. In this he has faith, and so begins to be. Headlights sweep across the house behind him. The sun is gone. It is dark. The old driveway gate squeaks open. Hurrying downstairs he hides himself behind the coats on the rack. Car doors slam, releasing Gayle and Lulu's voices in happy strife. Raj raises his arms; his hands become claws. As the key rasps rudely into the lock, his lips draw back to reveal a row of salivating fangs.

The door opens.

Acknowledgements

I would like to gratefully acknowledge, for their invaluable help and encouragement, the following people:
Averill Curdy, Christian Wiman, Akhil Sharma, Peter Murr, Eileen Murr, Alan Cross, Susan Sandon, Justine Taylor, Caroline Knight, Richard Cable, Ellen Levine, Tony Deaton, Penelope Pelizzon, Nancy West, Craig Kluever, Sherod Santos, Lynne McMahon, Stuart Dybek, Arnie Johnston, Fred Leebron, and Peter Stitt.

429